MISS PERFECT

BERNARD HALL

Matador
9 Priory Business Park,
Wistow Road, Kibworth Beauchamp,
Leicestershire. LE8 0RX
Tel: 0116 279 2299
Email: books@troubador.co.uk
Web: www.troubador.co.uk/matador
Twitter: @matadorbooks

ISBN 978 1785899 300

British Library Cataloguing in Publication Data.
A catalogue record for this book is available from the British Library.

Printed and bound by CPI Group (UK) Ltd, Croydon, CR0 4YY
Typeset in 11pt Minion Pro by Troubador Publishing Ltd, Leicester, UK

Matador is an imprint of Troubador Publishing Ltd

Thanks to Becky, Jakob, Jane, Janet, Marilyn, Teresa, Tom as well as Marian, Geraldine, Graham and all the others who were there at the time.

There was an old woman who lived in a shoe.
She had so many children, she didn't know what to do;
She gave them some broth without any bread;
Then whipped them all soundly and put them to bed.

Anon, 1794

EASTER TERM
1983

Chapter 1

Unlike the old woman who lived in a shoe the middle-aged Miss Madge Perfect, declared age fifty-three, actual age fifty-seven, lived in a cottage not a shoe.

Having started work after training as a child care officer she was now a social work manager with so many children on her team's caseload that there were times when she didn't know what to do but, if they were hungry or cruelly whipped, she went to the court and applied to the magistrates for a care order. More often than not she succeeded. Once in her care she placed them with foster parents, or in a family group home, where they were well fed, neatly clothed and sure of a clean, warm bed. That at least was the theory; that moreover was county council policy. However, theory being one thing, practice another, county council practice lay somewhere betwixt the two.

When she looked back on it all from Ireland what did she see? Only when it was all over, and she remembered her years in the north-east of England, could she pinpoint the day when the first urgent memo arrived from County Hall and changed everything.

It was one of those mornings when nothing went according to plan and as a result she was not in the best of humour. As Controller, Area 13, Rudham Social Services, based at Moortown, she now found fewer days going according to plan. She sometimes wondered if this was due to the world around her changing or her disinclination to change in step with the world. But then, why should she? It was beyond doubt that things were different now, the world rushing in all directions, helter-skelter, but for whose benefit, she wondered. Then she remembered how older people sang the same old tune when she was young.

The social services were certainly changing with the gobbledegook of highfalutin management jargon, the pressure to drive down costs, always to do more with fewer resources; these were the things eating into the satisfaction she had always found in her work.

Brenda from Typing was standing at her door giving her earache like a bossy pithead gaffer. 'Urgent,' she said, 'a memo from Mr Puttock, Head of Staffing.'

'Urgent?' Madge said snatching the memo from Brenda and dumping it dismissively in her bulging 'pending' basket.

'Sorry, I'm sure,' Brenda said, 'but remember he's County Hall.'

'I know, I know,' Madge said, 'but it's I who should apologise for my irritation. We just seem to get too much thrown at us by County Hall these days.'

'I knaa, Miss Perfect, I knaa.'

Madge was cross she had snapped at Brenda who only ever wanted to be helpful. She noticed that the memo from the blessed Puttock was indeed labelled 'Urgent'. To Puttock everything was urgent. Perhaps that was how he had progressed swiftly from starting as a mere administrative officer to his present lofty position somewhere in the tier of senior men below the Director. The Director was next down from God himself. Although it was rumoured that the Director harboured further career ambitions no one in the department seemed to know where these might lie, for it was beyond belief that in the whole county of Rudham there was anything greater than the Director of Social Services.

As Brenda scuttled out of the room Madge reached down the Puttock memo. It begged to advise that a Professor Mitchell from Rudham University would be visiting Area 13 in the near future and should be 'accordioned maximum co-operation'. As a consultant to the county council and partly funded by a central government 'grunt' his purpose was to investigate the 'efficishency' of Area 13 which had been selected for his case study.

She was becoming convinced that the frequency of errors in memos in the otherwise healthy northern air indicated genetic decay resulting from inbreeding in the south. Few new arrivals on her desk showed signs of healthy tissue, either in their grammar or spelling. Did some deadly virus escape from London, the national centre of physical, moral and spiritual decay, gather strength under cover of darkness and then, borne on the wind head north towards the purity of the lands in the lee of the Pennines where it fatally infected the memos that reached her from County Hall? Perhaps, just in case, she should wash her hands after reading all memos.

Spluttering at the mistakes she painstakingly inserted corrections till her biro ran out of ink and she focused instead on the content. Apparently Professor Mitchell's project was largely funded by some government department in London, something called the Home Office, an odd name for what appeared to be a place of work. The project had the full backing of both senior management and the social services committee. Any clients interviewed by him were to sign in triplicate at paragraph 31.3.17 to confirm they had agreed to be interviewed. Copies of these signed agreements would be included in the subsequent report and findings. The appropriate forms would follow from headquarters and must be 'countersinged' by the Area Controller before all copies were returned marked 'Confidentshull' to County Hall.

Well, Madge thought, I will 'countersinge' them with pleasure, but to think that this level of literary incompetence was presided over by the Director, that smug man who loudly proclaimed his insistence on high standards.

Nevertheless she must put these distracting thoughts out of her mind and set about arranging a visit by this nosy parker busybody who had nothing better to do than go around poking his nose into other people's affairs.

She lifted the phone and dialled the university number given on the memo. A woman with a clipped, upper-

6

class voice answered, 'Sociology Department, Professor Mitchell's secretary speaking. How can I help you?'

'Well,' Madge said, 'I think it is I who can help you. I've been asked to make an appointment for your Professor Mitchell to visit my social services area office. I'm Perfect by the way. Might I have a word with him please?'

There was a pause before the answer then, 'Not possible I'm afraid, he's away down a mine taking photographs for his research project on colliery accidents.'

'If this talk of a miners' strike comes to anything it should cut down on colliery accidents,' Madge said. She laughed at her own joke but the remark landed like a rock fall in an underground tunnel, not even a chuckle from the other end.

'Indeed,' replied the same polished accent, 'I have his diary beside me so I can arrange a day and time convenient for you both. He will probably be accompanied by his research assistant.' No chit-chat here then, just brisk and business-like efficiency from the seat of learning.

In the pause that followed Madge tried to picture this world of which she knew nothing. She saw a vision of this secretary person: long-limbed and slim, probably aged about thirty with manicured nails and flaxen hair falling loosely on to her shoulders after a recent and regular hour or two reading magazines at the posh hairdresser in the Market Place in Rudham City. Her make-up was tasteful and perfectly applied. She wore perfume not scent. Jewellery? Yes jewellery but she could not picture that. Pearls perhaps? Pearl stud earrings in her perfectly formed ears? Certainly discreet. At home there would be a husband

and no doubt children, well-mannered and not at all like the young people Madge dealt with in her daily grind.

The voice at the other end regained speech. 'His diary is in the most frightful mess, there's something scribbled down about a darkroom meeting, don't know what that's about,' it said, followed by further silence.

Madge pondered the likely attributes of the research assistant who would of course be younger, even more attractive than the secretary person. As for the professor there could be no doubt that a glamorous wife would be waiting with his meal on the dining table when he arrived back at their comfortable home each evening. He would read to the children at bedtime. How different from her work, her empty home life. How was it that she had allowed her life to run its course with so little other than her work to show for it?

The plummy voice of the snooty secretary at the other end returned. 'Professor's diary drives me mad and I know it's very short notice given today is Wednesday but would Monday morning at ten be all right? He likes to start early and I know he regards it as urgent on account of the tranche of Home Office funding.'

Early indeed. If her staff arrived in after eight-thirty they were, under council policy, liable to a reprimand.

Madge glanced at her diary which was also in the most frightful mess. At least they would have something in common. 'I can just about fit them in but they'll have to be brief.'

'The professor is rarely brief,' his secretary said, then added, 'May I just ask, you said you are Perfect, is it Mrs, Miss or Ms?'

'Miss!' she snapped, irritated at the increasing emphasis on what was coming to be known as 'political correctness'. At moments like this she thought how much less irritating it would be just to answer 'Mrs', not that matrimony was a price she had ever been prepared to pay. Then she reminded herself that her willingness to pay the price had never been put to the test, now surely never would.

Stuck-up tart, no doubt a Tory voter, Madge thought, this secretary, a younger woman, her looks undimmed by age or real work pressures, sitting cosily with a two-bar electric fire beside her desk in an office in the university where nobody ever need get their hands dirty sorting out the lives of less privileged people; a world where people could go home at five every day of the working week, probably early on Fridays, and never a social work client in sight. Only a few miles up the road was this different place where some workers, for that was all they were, even those dubbed 'professor', enjoyed the privilege of a secretary to make their phone calls.

She entered the meeting in her diary. The review of the waiting list for admissions to the Brownlow Aged Persons' Home would have to be postponed. Somehow she must fit the professor into her crowded schedule. Neither Puttock, nor the Director, nor the cushy councillors on the social services committee would expect less.

But why had Area 13 been chosen rather than any one of the Areas 1 to 12? Men were the answer. All the other area controllers were men. Puttock was obviously shielding his mates and their work from prying eyes. It might even be a ploy to undermine her position. She had no doubt that some in the higher ranks would prefer all thirteen areas to be ruled by men.

When she came to look back it was this memo that rang the bell signalling the unexpected changes that would eventually sweep away the life she had known and loved.

***

Thursday. 8.30 am. A distant telephone broke into the silence, ringing insistently. The sound came from somewhere down the long corridor that housed the welfare in the leaky prefabricated huts that smelled of mould, summer and winter. The duty social worker and the telephonist should be in by now. Clearly they were not. Brenda, queen bee in the admin office, was always early. Not today. Young people could no longer be relied upon. But she must stop repeating, 'young people nowadays', must remember she too had once been young. The phone continued to ring, drang-drang, drang-drang, drang-drang...

She hauled herself up and moved quickly towards the door, carefully dodging the desk corners that in careless moments left purple bruises unseen on her thighs. Not that she was obese, she comforted herself, just a teensy bit overweight. There had been times when she laughingly described herself as having 'a touch of middle-age spread'. No longer, things had moved on, bits had moved out, there was evidence of sagging, and traces of creases were starting to vein her face.

When she reached the phone it was young Simon, one of her social workers, on the other end. 'I've a right crop from last night, Miss Perfect. Moortown and Brownlow went mad, not least the Farrants.' The Farrants came high on the list of 'problem families' or, as she preferred to think, families with problems.

The fact that Simon still called her 'Miss Perfect' was one of the things she liked about him. He had joined the staff not long before Lorraine, another newly qualified social worker. Lorraine was from Cape Town, said 'ach sus' all the time, oozed brash informality, and was inclined to be far too touchy-feely with the younger men. Regrettably, some amongst the younger men visibly enjoyed such attentions whereas Alan, and most of the mature men, bristled at such inappropriate behaviour.

'Sounds like a tough night, Simon,' she said. Out-of-hours duty through the night or at weekends could sometimes be uneventful, making the welcome overtime money something of a steal. At other times the number of calls and the complexity of problems demanded stamina, sympathy and brain power beyond all reason. She remembered all that from her early days, remembered not knowing what this night or that weekend might bring. No wonder Simon was tired.

'Can I give you the details?' he said. Simon was one of the few who volunteered for the out-of-hours team. As long as people of his calibre were willing to train and come in to the profession as basic grade workers the future of social work as she knew it was assured. Not like Dan, a little older than Simon and on the make from day one until, in what seemed no time at all, the Director had promoted him to be her deputy. Simon was nice; Dan was not nice. She tried hard not to be judgmental. 'Take folk as you find them,' her father used to say or, 'If you can't say something nice don't say anything at all', not that her father ever practised what he preached. She had taken Dan as she found him and so far, albeit with difficulty, had somehow managed to say nothing at all. Her thoughts she kept to herself. Thanks be to her father who, for all his many faults, bequeathed to her a few useful pointers for coping in a hostile world.

'Nothing too serious I hope, Simon?' She felt she knew him well enough by now to feel comfortable calling him by his first name.

'Mainly the Farrants over in Brownlow I'm afraid. The police were involved in one of their fracas. A disagreement between mum and dad. The police reported bruising on little Gary aged eight. Mum got a poke on the nose as well.'

'One of your cases isn't it? What did you find when you visited?' she asked. She was writing down the details as he spoke, hoping all the while her pencil lead did not break.

'Yes, was mine but now transferred to Lorraine. Sorry, but I had no time to visit, there was too much else going on I'm afraid.'

'We'll talk about that when you come in later today. It should have been your priority to make a home visit, examine Gary, try to establish the facts, who alleged what.'

'I'm sorry. I seemed to spend most of my time trying to get a mental welfare officer to turn out for Mr Timms who was being Napoleon again.'

'The silly hat and the hand stuffed into his waistcoat as usual?'

'Afraid so, plus the promise to create a world empire with Moortown as its capital.'

'You arranged for him to be packed off to St Helena?'

'Yes, an ambulance and police escort landed him in the secure ward at St Clement's Psychiatric Hospital. He is now safe on his isolated island.'

She had always liked Simon: lacking experience but an essentially decent man, someone she could trust, her kind of person. She had watched him slowly rebuilding his life after arriving in the office leaving behind a lectureship at the university when his wife went walkabout with a woman. Had she gone off with another man that would have been tough but something he could have lived with. That sort of thing happened all the time. It was the fact that she had taken off with a woman that seemed to hurt most. The office tittle-tattlers gnawed hard on that bone. Surely if Simon had been man enough with rock-hard lead in his pencil it would never have happened. Perhaps he was too clever-clever; people like that were just not up to it; all brain and no manhood.

She headed towards the sounds of life now emerging from the social workers' office: a kettle boiling, mugs clinking, chit-chat.

Most of her staff had drifted in by the time she entered the open-plan room where tides bearing the flotsam of conversation drifted around the islands of desks. The topics never changed: last night's television programmes, Thatcher, the possibility of the miners going on strike, or the end-of-season travails of the rival local football teams. It mattered not at all to her that Newcastle United were doing well in the Second Division while Sunderland were languishing in the First Division but to most of the men it mattered a great deal. No sign of Dan. Absolutely typical.

It was Lorraine's case now. She was expecting Lorraine to be late as usual. For once she was wrong, a rare misjudgement she liked to think. She paused as Lorraine announced, 'Sus, I've started my monthly, make me a cup of tea, someone.'

Old Alan twisted his face in disapproval. Alan disapproved of a lot of things with youth followed by women high on the list. Young women were in fact top of the list, number one. He had begun his working life down the pits, joined the merchant navy in the war, seen many of his mates drown on the north Atlantic convoys, become a social worker. Now he stared blankly at Lorraine in her short yellow skirt sitting with her legs spread-eagled at the adjacent desk. They shared a telephone, a cause of endless battles. Miss Perfect guessed he was thinking Lorraine did not behave as young women were meant to behave. She could not help but agree. Times had changed and certainly not for the better.

'Lorraine.' The name came out louder and more imperiously than she had intended. The slim young South African looked up and nodded.

'Ja Madge?'

She ignored the unwelcome use of 'Madge' and said, 'I've just had Simon on the phone. He was out-of-hours last night. One of yours has blown up. It's the Farrants over at Brownlow. It's little Gary, bruising on his face. We must ensure that he is medically examined, we may need a hospital admission.'

They moved into the office labelled 'Miss Perfect' where Lorraine sat facing her looking ready for a fight.

'Madge, you know I've just taken over the Farrants. I've not made an introductory visit yet. And I've got a lot on today. Simon should have followed through on it.'

Miss Perfect's resentment was accentuated by the guttural South African accent. How she hated that South African accent. It was an irritant which, unlike grit in an oyster, produced no auditory pearls. And it was Lorraine who had opened the mineshaft into which standards of conduct were rapidly falling. Over-familiarity was but one example. Now more and more of the staff called her Madge rather than Miss Perfect. If only she had been more alert, seen what was happening, stamped on it when it started. She never minded 'Miss P' or even 'Miss' but would have much preferred to draw the line short of 'Madge'.

'Ah, yes. A lot on.' From the rumours sweeping the office she knew that Lorraine frequently had a lot on, or in some senses a lot off. Or perhaps not with her 'monthly' and Simon working out of hours. The office gossips had the two of them on the way to becoming an item.

Nowadays girls like Lorraine seemed to think nothing of having sex as casually as they might say 'yes' to a cup of tea. She remembered times in her own brief youth when she would have preferred a cup of tea. But then her thoughts strayed back to the love of her life, the young man who had spoiled it all by going away and shattering her dreams. That had been different. She had been loyal to him. It was about loving a man, feelings for a man, not just animal lust. Clearly Lorraine, a 'daughter of the veld' as she liked to call herself, fell into the lust camp.

She did so hope young Simon was not taking a wrong turning in befriending Lorraine. He had explained at interview how he had come into social work 'to make the world a better place', perhaps his first mistake. High ideals had been attainable goals when she started out as a child care officer but that was in a different age — then was then, now was now. Hopefully Lorraine was not his next mistake. She was fond of Simon.

She looked at her notes and said, 'Please bear with me while I try to decipher my writing...'

Lorraine sat looking as though it was all too much for her. Surely she must know by now that it was in the nature of the job that these crises never arrived to suit the convenience of the workers? Miss Perfect remembered from her training course that in his book on asylums Goffman pointed out how workers often meet their own needs rather than the needs of those they care for. It was one of a very few ideas learned from a book that lodged an insight in her brain that remained there down the years.

Her immediate task was to placate Lorraine. 'Simon was snowed under with difficult calls.'

Lorraine looked unimpressed. 'That's all very well, Madge, but Simon would have been on big bucks with overtime rates and, anyway, Dan's my line manager and he says with all the work we have on here we don't have time to take on out-of-hours work as well.'

'No, no, only our own work of course. Perhaps Simon should have done as you say but that is not for now. Besides, there are some of us, myself included, who think these things are best done by the family's regular social worker when that's at all possible.'

'Ach sus man,' Lorraine said.

Miss Perfect struggled to conceal her irritation and find a soothing tone. 'Sometimes night and day overlap as you may discover quite quickly if you get around to joining the rota.'

Lorraine scowled at this. Looking at Lorraine Miss Perfect wondered what it was about her she did not much like. There must be more to it than her accent. As her manager, she was aware that she ought to be objective and as a social worker she knew she ought to be non-judgmental. It was unreasonable to think badly of a young woman who, coming to the north-east corner of England from Cape Town, had in all probability never heard of Goffman. Young, pretty and vivacious she certainly was but – was there something cold and grasping in those restless green eyes? Time would tell. Or not. 'You never can tell' was after all a well-known fact – even if known only to her father, mercifully long deceased.

She went on, 'I will ask one of the senior practitioners to go with you. We need to investigate thoroughly and, if necessary, case conference it early next week.'

'Do we really need to do all that, Madge? I mean it's Thursday, tomorrow's Friday, ach sus it's almost the weekend…'

'It's county policy. Which of the senior practitioners is in today?'

Lorraine grinned. 'None. Dan let them all take a day's leave.'

'Oh dear, then I'll have to ask Dan to go with you. He won't be pleased.'

Lorraine laughed. 'He's not coming in today. He's at a management training session with the Director at County Hall.'

Dan should have consulted her before allowing all the senior practitioners to take leave on the same day and, at the very least, told her he would be up at the Hall on a training day. Now there was no alternative but for her, as the senior member of staff present, to accompany Lorraine on a home visit to the Farrants. That after all was county policy where non-accidental injuries were suspected. Besides — whisper, who dares — though now 'middle management' there were remnants of Madge that secretly enjoyed going hands-on once in a while.

'In that case it will have to be me,' she said, knowing that all the while Dan would be ingratiating himself with the Director.

Lorraine smiled so sweetly that it felt as if she was silently saying 'Up yours, Madge'.

'We'll set off in ten minutes,' Miss Perfect said, shepherding Lorraine back into the social workers' room. At the sight of the re-entry of the boss the chatter dried, magazines were shuffled out of sight, heads went down, telephones scrambled for, notepads scribbled on, and files minutely examined. Ah yes, how busy they all were, a suddenly silent monument to the commitment of the modern slave labourers of the people industry. That was after all what social work was becoming: a branch of industry.

Chapter 2

County policy dictated that they must travel to the Farrants in Lorraine's car; mileage rates were lower for junior officers than for area controllers. It was an economy measure. 'Save the pennies and the pounds take care of themselves,' the old Director used to say. With the new Director it was more a case of saving the pennies to inflate the pounds in his salary. There were few men whose work she could respect or admire. Neither the Director nor his underling Puttock found their way on to her long list of such men. Neither did the absent Dan. In fact where men were concerned the long list was rather a short list.

Lorraine unlocked the car doors and they climbed in. A nervous passenger at best, Miss Perfect could only hope that Lorraine's driving might prove more sensible, more sedate, than some other aspects of her behaviour.

A pretty little thing, she thought, looking at Lorraine. If only she would cover more of her body with work-day clothes, if only she used less make-up, more subdued colours. As it was she might be better employed behind the cheap cosmetics counter at Woolworths in the High Street. Yes, definitely more suited to shop work even if she was a qualified social worker with a degree from some university or other in Cape Town. 'A typical shop girl,' her father would have snorted. She redoubled her determination never to eat South African oranges.

On these rare occasions when she went out of the office she much preferred to be driven by one of the men, preferably one of the more mature men. Alan was very reliable even if his car always smelled of cigarettes. Now she would have to be brave and make sure Lorraine kept her eyes on the road.

As the car juddered into motion she gripped hard on something close to her right hand till Lorraine said, 'Madge, can you take your hand the fuck off the handbrake asseblief?'

'So sorry, I thought it was a… oh, I don't know what I thought, didn't think I suppose.'

When she released the handbrake Lorraine said, 'buy a donkey.'

'Why would I buy a donkey?'

'Ach sus Madge, I'm sorry man, I just slupped into Afrikaans, baie dankie is thanks.'

She closed her eyes. To take her mind off Lorraine's use of the four-letter word and her driving she gave thinking time to one of the great issues currently plaguing her: she had known for a while that the usage 'Miss Perfect' would have to go – at first she had held firm against change but now she must give in and accept the social workers calling her 'Madge'. Lorraine had fired the first shots in the battle but so far it was only the bolder staff following her into the breach. Surely it would be better if everyone called her by the same name. Why fight a battle she had no hope of winning? She might as well surrender, lay down her arms, show the white flag. There would be applause, men and women in tears, children dancing in the streets of Moortown as the cry went out: 'Miss Perfect has moved with the times, all hail our modern Madge'.

Ha! Ha! To hell with moving with the times. Bow to the inevitable more likely. But the office staff, the admin girls, the typists, that would be different, they must continue to show respect.

Lorraine drove erratically, jabbering away while steering with one hand and all the while gesticulating with the other hand as they breasted the hill out of Moortown and followed the road that threaded through the genteel villages on the way to Brownlow. All the way cloud shadows lay floating like restless blankets on the surrounding hills.

'Have you been out on a possible non-accidental injury investigation before?' Madge asked.

'Nee, nicks man. But you know what, Madge, I was sorry to hear about you leaving soon.'

'Who told you that?'

'I can't remember, nobody, nicks, it's just going around.'

Madge laughed. 'Well you can put it around that it is not true, a mistake, I'm not intending to go anywhere. The notion is quite ridiculous, I can't possibly afford to retire before I am sixty. Now let's concentrate on this visit.'

Somebody must have started this tittle-tattle. Dan? She certainly wouldn't put it past him.

'I've put my finger on the Farrants' problem,' Lorraine said. 'I see from the file that Mrs Farrant has a problem with masturbatory guilt. Perhaps I could do some hands-on work with her on that?'

'Hands-on?' Madge queried.

'Ja.'

'Perhaps you could.' Madge preferred not to contemplate what form this 'work' might take.

Madge remembered only too well the beginning student who, while undergoing part of his training in a placement in the office, had so diagnosed Mrs Farrant's 'problem'. The young man in question seldom strayed from talking loudly about the current success or otherwise of his beloved Manchester United and this foray into an aspect of masturbation represented a rare diversion. Almost everything sat oddly with his frequent proclamations that he was a Marxist; he seemed not to have read *Das Kapital* or fully understood any of the theoretical evils alleged against the capitalist mode of production beyond the rhetoric of the well-worn slogans. Garbled insights into Marx were like scrambled eggs in his head, sitting uneasily on toast made from the leftovers of the psychosocial theories of social work academics from America. Half of the lecturers on his course seemed to have favoured the psychosocial approach while the other half followed the red flag of radical theories of social work. Poor lad; little wonder that he was confused; hardly surprising that he failed to choose between or even marry the psychosocial and the radical into one coherent understanding of the trade he was about to enter. He was on safer ground with Manchester United.

Just as well that he had moved on from his placement in Moortown before testing his ideas against the intimate realities of Farrant family life. Writing down such a confused and foolish belief about Mrs Farrant in the privacy and security of the office to impress a visiting tutor was one thing, drawing the hypothesis to Mrs Farrant's attention would be quite another. On the other hand the poor boy was not to know that the next but one person to pick up the file would be Lorraine, on her own admission one of Cape Town's finest. Simon, trained in down-to-earth Newcastle, had shown good sense in ignoring the diagnosis while the Farrants were on his caseload.

Lorraine went on, 'As the file note points out, in the particular sub-culture this family inhabits the father has very little interaction with his son, so we must also do something to modify the father's behaviour in that area.'

'You mean encourage him to take his lad to the football?'

'That as well, but more importantly we need to get to the crutch of the matter.'

'You mean crux?'

'Ach sus, ja man, crutch, like I said. It may be that mum's masturbatory guilt indicates sexual dysfunction in the marriage. I'll have to involve Mr Farrant of course. He may suffer from erectile dysfunction – not uncommon in men who drink too much, even at his youngish age. We may even have to look into his prostate.'

'Would that be wise?'

'Yis, vital. I think I'm going to find that erectile dysfunction is a factor. And counselling them on their lovemaking techniques may help. I could try that. I covered it in my degree. There is considerable statistical evidence that working-class men are incompetent at lovemaking. Especially in the north of England. Man, they never allow enough time for foreplay. I even read about it in a magazine when I was still in Cape Town. Ach man, don't you just know it, sex must be a big problem in the north of England.'

When Madge was young and in love she had somehow managed without 'foreplay' which sounded like a warm-up for a game of tennis. Things had been different then. Thinking of the number of children on the office's caseload Madge was not as sure as Lorraine about impotence in the northern male.

'You think that?' she said.

'Ja, I've found that already with the men around here.'

So that settled it, personal observation blanketing in its judgement of the men of the north.

'Perhaps the climate explains the difference,' Madge said. 'It being so hot in Africa must be a factor.'

'Ja,' said Lorraine, 'those boys in Cape Town sure are hot as hell, ja man, hot like an Indian Curry Madras in Durban.'

Worrying about Mr Farrant's reaction to the planned course of action, Madge started to say something but only got as far as, 'But...'

'No but about it, Madge, we must confront Mr Farrant with his inadequacy, in a constructive way of course. They only have one child. That is significant. Why aren't there more kids? What have they been doing all these years? Mr Farrant needs to know what his impotence means for Mrs Farrant. We must tackle the problem at that level if we are to have any hope of ending young Gary's sense of alienation, his feeling of falling through the cosmos and landing all alone on the veld outside Brownlow. We have to help him connect, get his fingers hooked in the safety nets of society, thus ensuring he is treated kindly by loving parents.'

Madge was rapidly losing the will to live, wondering again about the merits of euthanasia. If only Lorraine would say 'I' rather than 'we'. For 'we' were not going to do anything of the sort.

Hidden in a haze of smoke the rambling council estate at Brownlow awaited their arrival.

Slumped silently in her seat, a nervous passenger now anxious about what awaited them at their journey's end, Madge let the conversation lapse. The rolling countryside slid past lit by pale spring sunshine. The leaves on trees were at this moment greener than they would be all summer; heat and dust would soon dull their freshness. Examining her dislike of Lorraine she wondered if it could be envy that caused her to so resent this pretty young woman with every prospect of marriage and children. She so hoped it was not envy, a fault she despised.

They flashed past a roadside sign announcing 'You are entering Brownlow'. Almost immediately another sign proclaimed a thirty speed limit quickly followed by a notice warning that 'Speed Kills'. She glanced at the dashboard; Lorraine had slowed to fifty. Could she ever feel safe with Lorraine at the wheel?

How would Lorraine get on with Mrs Farrant? And Mr Farrant? The mischievous imp buried deep in Madge almost looked forward to Lorraine's first meeting with the Farrants, Lorraine tackling Mrs Farrant's little guilt problem. Then there was Mr Farrant and his little problem. There hadn't been a murder in Brownlow for a year or two.

The car swerved off the main road clipping the pavement on their way into the dreary post-war Coronation Gardens council estate on the outskirts of town. More often than not streets were named after favoured councillors; in this case it was a reminder of a Labour stalwart as they reached Keir Hardie Close, the Farrants' cul de sac. She wondered how the morning would end.

The tired curtains of the row of uncared-for council houses lining the street, the overgrown privet hedges, and the refuse-strewn front gardens offered little cheer. How would Lorraine approach Mr Farrant? 'Nice to meet you. Do you suffer from brewer's droop, Mr Farrant?' Madge had met the man but once, enough to remember a stocky man with a body like the trunk of a mature oak tree and murder in his eyes. A gentle giant? No, his police record spoke for itself.

As it happened, their visit took a while to begin as Lorraine was forced to brake, suddenly finding the road inexplicably blocked by an old carriage pram tipped on its side next to a derelict mattress that had long outlived its nocturnal usefulness, its rusted springs bursting through remnants of stained fabric. Beyond that lay two shredded car tyres.

Realising further progress was impossible without reorganising the impromptu street furniture, they abandoned the car where it had jerked to a stop. Hooking up their briefcases, differentiated in size and colour in line with their relative status, they advanced towards number 9. Council

27

policy dictated a standard plastic issue of briefcases for junior officers and a fake leather issue for more senior officers. Though unconfirmed it was rumoured that the Director carried a genuine leather briefcase for his sandwiches which he brought from home prepared and wrapped tightly in greaseproof paper by his wife. Council policies like those that differentiated briefcases, office furniture including carpets, and car allowances, were all aimed at reducing waste and minimising error. Stuff and nonsense, thought Madge, considering the waste that went on up at County Hall. Clearly it all came down to class distinctions.

Reaching the cracked concrete path leading to the house, their final approach was temporarily halted by an old car seat reclining on the pavement barring normal access to the front door. Lorraine leapt over it, her long, slender legs scissoring through the air while Madge clambered awkwardly over the obstacle. More ladylike my way, she thought. No need for me to show off like that.

'Ello Miss Pisspot!' It was young Gary Farrant, loud as usual, who had tumbled laughing and farting in his torn and ill-fitting clothes down the path to meet them. Gary Sebastian Farrant in full. Mrs Farrant had wanted to add Valium to the list of names, remembering the relief the tablets had brought to her pregnancy, but the vicar had demurred and, after some resistance, had managed to deflect her from such a secular act. Yet Mrs Farrant confided later that she still thought of him as Valium. Boys, she said, needed names more than girls and Valium sounded foreign. It had been a difficult choice between Gary and Elvis. She hoped he would grow up to be a rock star on TV called

Gary Valium. Valium, she believed, sounded better than Farrant. Gary's ambitions lay in other directions, however, for Simon had reported back that he had already decided he would become a pilot with the Red Arrows.

'Hello Gary,' said Madge cautiously, pleased at the apparent warmth of the welcome.

'Fuck off,' shouted Gary. There was a sudden menace in the way he snarled, his face folding like plasticine sausages of loose skin from an innocent smile to a blank, expressionless stare. Perhaps he saw the unexpected visitors as a threat. 'Hoo's she?' he demanded, pointing a fist suspiciously at Lorraine.

'She's Miss Burgher. She's your nice new social worker from South Africa.'

Lorraine smiled broadly. 'Hello Gary, I've heard so much about you and it is lekker to meet you. Ach sus you are a big boy for seven!'

'Ah'm eight. Fuck off.' Gary laughed hysterically but without mirth.

Mrs Farrant emerged from the front door looking dismayed. 'What gans on? Ye knaa, Gary, yer not te talk to the people from the effing welfare like that. Ah ken the lass taalks funny but… the lass is foreign… eeh Miss Porfect, ah'm sorry, but ah divven knaa where he larns that effing aaful language. Ah've complained to the school ye knaa. And his father's cracked him. Kids got no respect these days. By – but ah would never have dared taalk te me social worker or me probation officer like that when ah was a bairn. Ah'd have got a good hiding off me daa, bastard God rest his soul.'

Sounds just like mine, Madge thought. Men.

'It's all right, Melanie. This is Miss Burgher, your new social worker.'

'Oo, that's nice, ah'd rather have a woman, that Mr Aubrey, Simon they caall him, did ees best yer understand, nee offence yer understand, but a woman can taalk aboot things that wouldn't be right with a man… well yer knaa what ah mean.'

Yes, thought Madge, a monthly conversation no doubt, certainly nothing to do with masturbatory guilt.

'Please call me Lorraine, or Lorrie if you prefer.' Madge cringed as Lorraine applied her professional smile and warmth.

'Oo, that's a nice name. Ah'm Melanie, Mel if you like.' Mrs Farrant simpered and smiled awkwardly through the lank hair that framed her face. 'Ah can see we will get along champion. Do you have any bairns, Lorrie?'

'No, I'm not married.'

'Whyaye man, ah wasn't married when ah had our Gary.' Madge thought Mrs Farrant's puzzled expression indicated surprise that marriage might in some circumstances be seen as a natural precursor to parenthood.

'I agree we are going to get along fine, Mel,' said Lorraine, 'and I've some ideas about ways in which I might be able to help you change things for the better – if that is what you want?'

Madge cringed. Please God, she thought, cross my heart and hope to die, not the 'M' word.

'Whyaye, it would be aalreet if yer could get us some more money from the benefits people. Mean bastards them. Mr Aubrey, well he tried, ah have to say that, but he didn't get nowhere. Perhaps they'll listen better to it coming from a woman, a young woman.' At this Melanie glanced awkwardly at Madge. 'Sorry, Miss Porfect, ah didn't mean, like about yer being old and that…'

'That's all right, Mrs Farrant, age has its virtues too,' said Madge, who just at that moment could not think of a single advantage other than wisdom which no one seemed to value nowadays.

Undeterred, Lorraine marched on across her chosen battlefield. 'Sus man, well actually, I was thinking more of, well not material things in that sense so much as…' but she got no further before Madge interrupted.

'Oh, by the way, Lorraine, I think young Gary is about to hit you on the backside with a piece of old fencepost.'

'Fuck, leave her bum alone, yebuggermar Gary, ee Gary, for fuck's sake leave her bum alone,' shouted Melanie. 'Can yer not see it's got a rusty nail in it?'

Then, as if in response to all this excitement, her nose began to bleed and they all went inside.

When her nose bleed stopped Melanie laughed and said, 'Me husband sometimes gives it me up the bum – but not with an old fence post!' Madge raised her eyes heavenwards. So much for his erectile dysfunction, she thought. Melanie laughed so that her remaining teeth, all nicotine-stained like the fingers on her right hand, seemed in danger of tumbling from her broad mouth.

Lorraine only managed to say, 'Your husband…' before Gary made to mimic his mother, 'Me husband gis…', but Melanie saw it coming and swung her fist at his head. He ducked and laughing at her ran outside.

'Jesus,' Melanie shouted, 'me husband will crack him when he comes home. Yer have to crack em don't you, boys specially?' Then she shouted, 'Do you hear what ah say, Gary? Yer father's going to crack yer for is.'

Knowing it would be difficult to examine Gary's body in any detail, Madge stepped outside and after taking one look at the bruising on his face said to Melanie, 'We must go down to the hospital, you and Gary, for a check-up. With any luck Gary won't have to be admitted but we shall see.'

'I'm sure Gary won't have to be admitted,' Lorraine said, causing Madge to silently curse her for a fool. What if the paediatrician decided he must be admitted? Where would that leave Lorraine?

Melanie was suddenly angry, her cheeks flushing. 'Yer divven't think us would harm our Gary does yer, Miss Porfect? Yer knaa we never would do that.'

'I'm sure you wouldn't,' Lorraine chipped in.

'We'll have to see,' Madge said. 'That is what we have to find out when the doctor sees Gary undressed and examines his body. If he decides Gary's injuries are accidental then all will be well.' The case files more often than not told a different story, a slow trickle of relatively minor injuries that had led to Gary being placed on the at-risk register.

'Well yer see, Miss Porfect, he slipped and fell on the hearth and that's why he's got some bruising round his eyes. Yer knaa he marks easy. Some kids dee. We never injure him. Never lay a finger on him.'

Madge looked steely-eyed at her. 'I'm sorry, Mrs Farrant, you know by now we have to pop you and Gary down to the hospital for a check-up.'

At that moment the fight seemed to go out of Melanie. 'Aye, aalreet, I should knaa by now. Well, ah suppose they always give yer a good cup of tea there – and a biscuit, ah'l say that for them. Ah like it in the canteen, aall bright and cheerful and warm amongst aall those doctors and nurses in their nice clean uniforms. Like judges them, they treat yer like yer really matter. Mebbes Lorrie might pay for us to have our lunches? Mr Aubrey used to dee that at least. But ah divven't knaa what me husband will say when he gets hyem from the pub the neet.'

Madge doubted he would say very much; it was more likely that Melanie herself would have one if not two black eyes in the morning.

Now quite suddenly Madge decided that enough was enough. 'I must get back to the office, Lorraine, pressure of work I'm afraid. You go with the Farrants to the hospital. Dr Wainwright will look after you,' she said.

'But I'm finding it difficult following what they say. How will I tell it to the doctor?'

'Don't worry, Lorraine, Dr Wainwright is used to northern voices.'

Lorraine looked far from convinced but surely there was no need to do any more hand-holding with her. Madge knew she could rely on Dr Wainwright and his staff on the paediatric ward. They would ensure that any necessary actions would fall into line with county policy. It would not matter what Lorraine might think; Dr Wainwright would translate if necessary, see things right. It was safe to leave it to him. On the other hand Dr Wainwright was unlikely to be familiar with the South African accent

Madge so detested. Funny that, because over the years she had come to cherish the local accents: warm, rich in grain and belonging to the area in which they were spoken.

She walked out of the council estate and past the large and tidy houses and gardens of the more affluent people of Brownlow till she reached the High Street. A bank of high clouds now hid the sun, leaving a canopy of gloomy sky with a watercolour wash of iron grey to match her mood.

Opposite the war memorial she waited a long while till a bus came and rattled her safely back to Moortown. There had been time enough to read down all the names on the memorial including two Farrants in the war of 1914-1918. Perhaps by the war of 1939-1945 the Farrants had learned to keep their heads down. Who could blame them? Brownlow was little more than a smudge on the landscape and yet the list of the local dead in two world wars stretched over the four faces of the stone pillar. As far as she knew there had been no casualties of local men in Thatcher's recent Falklands War.

Then once on the bus her thoughts turned to wondering how Lorraine had come to hear that she was leaving when she wasn't. She didn't need to think for long. Dan was the obvious suspect.

***

No sooner had she settled at her desk the following day than Dan breezed into her office and, with a smile on his face said, 'Sorry to hear you're leaving us.' She noticed he was observing her reaction carefully as he spoke.

She laughed. 'Funnily enough Lorraine mentioned it yesterday. Absolute nonsense, just a silly rumour. Might you know how it originated?'

'What, me? Not me, not sure where I heard it.'

She did not believe him. Why was Dan still smiling, looking down at his feet? It was in that moment that the first grains of doubt crept in to her mind. The rumour must be the result of a mistake, surely there could be no other explanation. As Dan's manager she must suspend value judgements and hide her doubts behind a calm, professional manner.

So, in her best attempt at a business-like approach she said, 'Be assured that short of sudden death I am not leaving until I retire in about three years so do not let any tittle-tattle to the contrary reach other ears in the office.'

'Not a word will escape me, your secret is safe with me,' Dan said, transparent in his insincerity. She even thought he was half smiling hearing the words 'sudden death'.

'It's not a secret,' Madge said, 'I am not leaving. I have not even applied for early retirement. But now to get down to work-related matters. We must meet today with Lorraine and Simon to discuss the Farrants. In your absence I visited with Lorraine yesterday. Bruising on Gary and a dodgy explanation from mum.'

'Any meeting will have to be later, I'm at a session with the Director most of the day. Will four-thirty do?'

'Sounds like it will have to.'

Here she was, his manager, and there he was her deputy, her staff member, but somehow he held all the power.

***

The well-worn refrain 'something must be done' echoed frequently around the patch and now came out of its lair and bit her when the phone rang.

Picking it up she felt like saying, 'Bung-Ho Social Services, Crackpot Area Office, Perfection speaking', or even 'Perfect Area Office, Nurse Crackpot speaking', but her impulses and her feelings, like her greying hair, were always kept firmly in place. So instead she stated her name and rank in a calm, measured, 'professional' voice.

'Moortown Area Office, Miss Perfect, Area Controller speaking.'

This time it was PC Pyott from the cop shop. She liked Jim Pyott, a man about her age, vastly experienced, knew the patch, cared about people.

'Miss P, ah need ye te send one of yer nutter people te Garbutt Close where a man armed with a yard broom is gannin up an doon the street beating aall the cars while screamin that he's clearing pink giraffes off the windscreens. Several windscreens have aalready been shattered. Aall the local residents are afraid and some very angry.'

'Oh my goodness,' Madge said.

Jim Pyott continued, 'Accordin te the man with the broom the giraffes are breaking the windscreens. Accordin to me lads, the car owners and various bystanders, it's the man with the flailing broom who's shatterin the windscreens.'

'I'll send someone down, Jim,' Madge said.

Clearly there were two sides to the story, a simple difference of perception.

The next time the phone rang it was a helpful member of the public who repeated over and again that as he once shared his crops with the pigs in Africa he was in a position to inform her that the man with the broom must be wrong about it being giraffes to blame because giraffes were never pink. Perhaps, he suggested, the man was mad.

So something was being done but it was never enough, for at that moment Simon came into her room with another 'urgent' referral. Old Mrs McVeigh from the sheltered housing had gone walkabout. The warden was concerned as Mrs McVeigh was becoming forgetful.

Priorities, priorities. So much of her time was spent choosing between situations involving risk. Some risks were in your face, some stretched into an unseen future where they lurked to catch you out. She listened, decided the warden should put on her shoes and search for her missing resident. If that failed social services would see if they could help. As always it came down to judgements about urgency and just at this moment Simon would have to look after giraffe man.

***

When four-thirty came and went with no sign of Dan she found Lorraine and Simon talking in the corridor.

'It's the local dialect,' Simon said, 'you'll get used to it.'

'You call it dialect,' Lorraine said, 'yuk, ach siss, there's nothing like that in Cape Town.'

Madge smiled at this announcement coming from the woman with the enhanced South African twang. She summoned Lorraine and Simon to her office to discuss the home visit and the final handover of the Farrant family from Simon to Lorraine.

'We were just discussing the Farrants,' Simon said.

'Last night too,' Lorraine added. She looked momentarily embarrassed as she caught Madge's eye. 'Down at the pub, of course, we met for a drink.'

Madge was not altogether surprised. She would have to keep an eye on Simon. Next the two of them would just be 'popping out for a pub lunch' and going over the allotted hour. Besides, Simon was still vulnerable after his divorce and all that unpleasantness without any need for fresh entanglements just yet.

Dan chose this moment to swagger into her office to join them. As usual he looked more than pleased to be sharing his own company as he announced, 'Lorraine and I can sort out the Farrants. Should be a piece of stotty cake.'

'I'd like to be kept in the frame,' Madge said, 'it might become high profile.'

'Of course, Madge, of course, I'll certainly keep you in the loop.'

'Hold on,' said Madge, 'Lorraine, what was the outcome when you took Gary to the hospital?'

'All clear,' said Lorraine. 'Dr Wainwright was on leave but we saw a black doctor. I wasn't too happy about that, a black doctor examining a white kid. Dr Khumalo or something like that he called himself. Melanie wasn't happy about it either. She couldn't understand what he was saying. He didn't understand what she was saying any more than I did. Even the nurses couldn't understand what he was saying. Anyway he had a quick look and said Gary seemed to be OK. Said it could easily have been an accident like Melanie said. I don't think he was keen to have Gary on the ward at all.'

'Lorraine, a doctor is a doctor, black or white, you're not in South Africa now.'

Lorraine snapped back, her cheeks reddening, 'You people who think you can change the world by not eating South African oranges make me sick. It costs black people good jobs. It harms black people more than us whites when you won't play us at cricket and rugby. Black is black and white is white. God made the world like that. It's all in the Bible. You don't understand. Because you have not seen for yourselves how it is in South Africa. Man, you cannot understand because you never lived there.'

Dan smirked but said nothing. Simon leant against the filing cabinet, looking awkward.

'Enough,' Madge said, 'we must concentrate on Gary for now. I'm not at all happy with what we've heard so far. Dan, what about you?'

Dan looked shifty; body language had been covered on Madge's training course. She knew all the signs to look for. Shifty.

Dan said, 'We've got a medical opinion so I think we should run with it.'

'But what about the bruises?' Madge asked. 'County policy is such that we are bound to investigate abuse and take the necessary action. It's a policy I agree with.'

Ever since her own childhood she had hated physical violence to children and this was one area where she agreed whole-heartedly with council policy.

Dan was not to be deterred. 'At our most recent session up at County Hall the Director stressed the need to be cost-conscious. He wants us always to consider the costs as against the possible benefits of any intervention. I think money spent on the Farrants may as well go down a mineshaft for all the good it ever does. It's money that could be better spent in other ways. Paying their train fares to leave the area would be money well spent.'

'I'm going to pretend I didn't hear that,' Madge said. 'Tell me more about what the doctor said about Mrs Farrant's explanation, Lorraine.'

'He thought Mrs Farrant's explanation of Gary falling against the lamp post in the street was credible.'

'But that wasn't the explanation mum gave us yesterday was it, Lorraine? Melanie said he slipped and fell on the hearth.'

'No Madge, not quite the same.'

Madge looked at Dan as she struggled for the right words. 'From what you are saying it sounds as if we, on behalf of the county, indeed the Director, are not much interested in the welfare of the child or the actions of the parents. But our primary concern must be the child. I want a report for the Director by first thing on Monday morning and it must include details of the bruising, its likely cause, and what you intend to do about it – including your justification for not involving a further medical opinion at this stage.'

'But,' said Lorraine, 'the bruising is superficial; surely it is the emotional lesions that are our prime concern. We have to begin with the sexual problems of the parents. I explained to you all about that. If we can modify their functioning along the lines I said then we can modify the environment this kid is growing up in.'

'But me no buts. Simon, you know what is needed, you will assist Lorraine until you complete the paperwork in the handover. You have the advantage of knowing the family.'

'That's all a bit over the top, two workers to one family,' Dan said.

'Just do it,' Madge said.

As the trio shambled out, Simon looking chastened, Dan and Lorraine looking furious, she remembered something she must mention to Dan.

'A quick word before you go, Dan.'

He paused, scowled. 'About?'

'Just to keep you in the picture. A Professor Mitchell from Rudham University is visiting our office on Monday.'

'What's he coming here for?'

'It seems he's researching the work of our area office.'

Dan said, 'Pity I can't be here to get him up to speed on current developments in service delivery. These academic types just don't have a clue when it comes to the real world.'

'Can't be here?'

'No, County Hall calls, well, the Director actually.'

Then he was gone, leaving behind a whiff of something remembered from long, long ago, a waft of – what was it – carbolic? Lifebuoy soap? Or was it Harpic down the toilet? 'Kills all known Germans,' her father used to joke. Humour was never his strength.

The void left by the departing Dan was quickly filled by Brenda who came in brandishing a referral form: an old boy whose wife had recently died was complaining that his neighbour who hated him was forcing a gas pipe through their common wall so he could pump gas through into his house to poison him.

There were simply more demands than her staff could satisfy. Occasionally, as now, life events affecting other people jarred a nerve in feelings buried deep in her own past. Social work sometimes meant having to share the angry or depressed feelings of clients. She was always vulnerable when referrals spoke of death or child cruelty.

Sleep rarely came easily to her and that night she lay thinking alternately of the old boy being gassed by his neighbour and the rumour going around that she was about to retire. Fiddlesticks! Then she wondered about the professor. What would he be like? Being a professor he must be very clever. When speaking to him she would have to choose her words carefully just in case any wrong impressions were communicated back to County Hall in his report. Clients could be difficult but professors were an unknown quantity.

Chapter 3

She woke early the next day with a gust of cold air brushing her face and the sound of the wind rattling the loose-fitting bedroom window. Must arrange for a man to fix it. Picturesque old cottages in pretty villages swallowed money in maintenance costs but at least it was out of sight of Moortown and the sort of areas that housed clients. Perhaps she should live among clients in a modern council flat on the Stephenson Estate but no one else in the office apart from Simon did that so why should she? In the meantime a few minutes more in bed could do no harm, legitimate time for coming to life on a new working day.

Little Gary? Lorraine was sorting all that out. What was it she said? Something about hooking his fingers in the cosmos... already forgotten the rest. What TOSH!

Dan in the office today? A mixed blessing when he is in, resentment when he is away at County Hall. Why doesn't he check with me before going off on his training jaunts with the Director? Must introduce a diary system in the typists' office and require all staff to note down authorised leave, training days, or when out on home visits. Need to speak to Brenda about a diary, take money for this from petty cash to avoid more form filling. Hate bureaucracy. In the old days things seemed to run smoothly with goodwill on all sides. It had always been hard work but then it had been fun.

No more time for thoughts tumbling around in her head. Get ready for work. The new shower over the bath had been ridiculously expensive, an indulgence, money that should have gone into her savings account at the building society even if it meant queuing on a Saturday, adding to the nest egg for her eventual retirement.

Then she came fully awake and remembered it was Saturday, no work till Monday, a chance to relax. Silly me.

Luxuriating under the shower, the hot water tingled her skin and turned it from alabaster to mottled pink and red. Over the years she had written endless social enquiry reports on her clients. Now, demanding objectivity as always, she silently composed an updating report on herself:

STRICTLY CONFIDENTIAL

Subject: Miss Perfect, a middle-aged lady, well presented and mild mannered, somewhat overweight and with greying hair, takes little exercise and eats frugally if not particularly healthily. She is careful of her appearance though her fashion sense is dated and she frequently complains that the shops no longer sell the clothes she likes or indeed any that fit her. She lives alone. With the exception of her rare visits to the local doctor it is over three decades since anyone has seen her undressed.

Current employment? States she has worked for Rudham Social Services 'forever', first as a child care officer, then social worker, before rising through the ranks to her present position as Area Controller. Further career progression she believes to be 'impossible' as she is not a man and is no longer young.

Immediate concerns? Mostly around work, increasing demands to provide services, budget cuts year by year. Recently received a memo about a visit to her office by a professor from the nearby university. What did he want? What might he report back to County Hall?

Nervous tics? None observed.

Elimination? Bowel movements regular. No reports of nocturnal enuresis.

Attitudes? Deplores cruelty to children. States that there is a reason for this yet fights shy of discussing her own childhood experiences. Dislikes the 'modern world'. Expresses concern that she may become 'bitter and twisted' as she ages.

Family background? Mother died when client was very young. Father? Deceased. Beyond that, least said the better apparently, unwilling to discuss in interview. No known siblings or other living relatives. Two aunts, long deceased.

Sex? Apparently no need to enter anything under this heading. Asked if she would like to be in a sexual relationship she replied, 'Almost forgotten what it was like, a messy business'. Mutters something about a young man in the long ago but declines to elaborate further except to say that she was very young and foolish at the time. At length described her distaste for the way young people make such a fuss about sex nowadays. Blames the pill. Getting enough sex is everything to them. When asked,

'What is enough?' all she would say in reply was, 'Well, let them get on with it.'

Lonely? Yes, at times.

Regrets? Only a fool or a liar has no regrets. Referred interviewer to someone called Piaf. Said Sinatra was a fool for doing it his way regardless of what it was he did. Musical taste somewhat dated.

Leisure interests? A cause for concern. Regrettably few nowadays. Why? Pressure of work. No cinema nearby, can no longer be bothered to drive to Rudham City to watch one of those 'new-fangled films, all sex and violence', once could but now can't sing a note so Moortown Ladies Choir ruled out, can't stand the thought of the Women's Institute (not her scene apparently); her list seems endless. Once had a cat she named Sophie-puss. Said cat arrived unannounced and invited herself to stay. Seemed homeless so subject took her in and enjoyed sixteen and a half years of feline company. The death of Sophie-puss brought great sadness, apparently reviving earlier episodes of unresolved grieving. Occasional thoughts of another cat came to nothing. Miss Perfect is clearly risk-averse and not proactive in her private life.

When the job comes to an end? Leaving party, a card with good wishes and a present – no doubt something ghastly she would be expected to put on a shelf or hang on the wall – followed by retirement.

Upon retirement? Her job is everything and when retirement does come it will inevitably be solitary. Fat chance of anything else. Perhaps make friends if she still can, meet people beyond the world of work, find leisure interests. Sees little prospect of achieving anything much along these lines.

Conclusion? Presenting problem: the subject anticipates a solitary old age followed by what she describes as 'planting by the Grim Reaper'. In spite of these negative attitudes there is no evidence of clinical depression although she does demonstrate a number of risk factors. Social work intervention not indicated at the present time. Might come a time when she would benefit from attendance at the 'Over 50s Club' in Moortown or the monthly talks by visiting speakers at the town's Thursday Club.

***

Mustn't waste water. She turned off the shower and stepped on to the mat, still sniffing in the pungent aroma of the soap-scented steam. Chilly bathroom. Still only April. Lots of people had installed central heating but that seemed a luxury too far. Come next winter she might think differently. She decided this was not the moment to step on to the bathroom scales. Any old maid in waiting – but waiting for what? – can face only so much reality. She reached for a towel from the heated rail – an extravagance she had permitted herself – and gently dried her body. Somebody had to love it, goose pimples and all. Go on, Madge dear, I dare you, stand naked in front of the full-length mirror. Truth or dare? She dared and gazing on the view before her saw only a coating of steam on the glass. She knew without looking that she was as plump a little dumpling as ever was.

Over the weekend she pottered aimlessly in her garden, raking the fallen leaves that had lain neglected since autumn. Safe from her neglect a hotchpotch of bulbs — daffodils, tulips, narcissi and lily of the valley — had emerged from the soil. The summer bedding areas were empty except for a carpet of weeds. The herbaceous border had run wild. Once upon a time her garden had mattered so much to her. Why did she have so little time and energy for all the things that once gave her such pleasure and satisfaction? Over by the fence the stems of Albertine, her favourite rose, were running wild and spiralling straggling stems in all directions like a head of hair in need of a hairdresser. Unkempt it might be but every year she looked forward to its large flush of pink flowers in bloom in the summer.

Thoughts of the visit by the professor on Monday were unsettling her. He would wear a suit and be quite out of place in the office. Even Dan never wore a suit. What would the clients make of a man in a suit? She must prepare, be ready to make a good impression, for what he found out was bound to get back to County Hall. Yet it was like preparing for an exam on a subject she had never studied. What might he ask? Would she know any of the answers? Probably not. Walking slowly around the garden she was not looking down till she felt something soft underfoot. Squelch. It was a dead robin, perhaps the very bird that often waited on the fence outside her kitchen door to take porridge oats from her outstretched hand. Feeling a wave of sadness sweep over her, she forgot the professor and remembered her mother.

***

When Madge was six Aunt Enid arrived for a surprise visit and a few days later came into Madge's bedroom and said, 'Your mother died in the night, she's dead.' Just like that. The exactness of the moment lodged in her brain forever. She remembered that her mother had been coughing a lot and then all of a sudden the coughing stopped. So that was it; if you stopped coughing you were dead. But what was 'dead'? Up till then she thought that when people stopped coughing they were better.

'Dead?' she said, anxious and knowing something was wrong.

'Yes, died, went to sleep in the night.'

'But…' Just then her father put his head round the door. He had on his cross face. 'But me no buts, young lady.'

'You mustn't trouble your father at this time,' Aunt Enid said.

She remembered the strong smell seeping from under her parents' locked bedroom door when she passed down the passage, how it caught in her nose. Quite nasty it was and much later she thought it must have been disinfectant, perhaps Dettol? Why did her dead mother need Dettol in her sleep?

What was 'dead'? Aunt Enid explained again that her mother had gone to sleep in heaven. Heaven was a long way away, too far to go and visit. It would be a very long sleep. For days Madge silently stalked the house trying to find her sleeping mother but Aunt Enid was right: heaven must be even further than the front door.

A week later 'a friend of the family' came to look after her 'for a few hours'.

'Don't let Madge catch sight of things.' It was her father's voice.

From her bedroom she heard subdued men's voices, voices she did not recognise — 'Careful there... mind the turn in the stairs' — the sound of something heavy bumping into the wall followed by the slam of the front door, then silence. The family friend, someone never seen before or since, kept her away from the window when all she wanted to do was to look out to see what was happening in the street below.

The next day Aunt Enid sorted through her mother's clothes while Madge played on the carpet in her parents' bedroom. 'Your father wants her things out of the house before he gets home tonight,' Aunt Enid said. But Madge noticed how she left her mother's dressing table untouched, saying, 'Your father wanted that left as is.' Later Madge remembered the polished, wood-grained dressing table backing into the window, its round mirror blocking out the light. On the surface was the big wooden hairbrush her mother used to tease out Madge's hair in moments of long-remembered pleasure, and alongside that was the little china ornament decorated with rose buds and holding hairpins, tubes of she knew not what, a jar of powder, the fluffy powder puff just showing out from under the lid of the container.

Come the next morning Aunt Enid packed Madge's clothes and toys in a suitcase while her father was away at work and then they set off by train from Staines to London and London to Eastbourne where Aunt Enid lived in a house she shared with Aunt Christabel. That night, and for many nights to come, Madge cried herself to sleep. No one came to ask if she was all right. Her father had not even said 'goodbye'.

***

On Monday morning she drove through heavy rain on her way in to work with her car making the most disgusting noises. Clearly it now came into the 'something must be done' category.

At ten o'clock her visitors from the university were shepherded into her office by Brenda. The professor came first, windblown and wet, dripping water off his ill-fitting raincoat, a camera in a leather case slung on a strap around his neck.

As he advanced towards her desk he reached out awkwardly to shake her hand, an action he volunteered so forcefully that she would not have been surprised had he wrestled her to the floor, for in that moment he was like an uncoordinated, deranged client wanting to settle a grudge. But no, he shook her hand as she rose to greet him just as his camera swung around and hit her left breast.

'Ouch,' she said, gently stroking her hurting breast.

'I am most frightfully sorry,' he said. 'So nice to meet you.' It was a nondescript southern accent. 'I'm Sociology, Mitchell's the name, Professor Mitchell, so looking forward to working together.' She saw a tall man, slightly built and with thinning hair. In retreating from her desk he somehow managed to knock a pile of reports, files and miscellaneous pieces of paper off her desk and on to the floor.

'So sorry,' he said, bending down to make good the damage.

'You look rather wet, the rain cannot have eased,' she said. 'Your camera undamaged by the blow I hope?'

'Yes, yes, camera undamaged and dry in this excellent genuine leather case. Sorry it knocked into your chest. Good thing I didn't have the telephoto lens on, sticks out further.' He tapped the leather case, looking embarrassed.

This was a man who called a breast a chest, a man in a protected occupation that did not involve real work. He smiled at her, then dried his glasses with a shirt tail dragged up past his belt from below the waist.

'Let me take your coat, I'm sure we can hang it somewhere.' It smelt musty.

'Thanks awfully,' he said, struggling to take it off. No suit, corduroy trousers, well worn, a rust-coloured shirt, collar far from neat and tidy and in need of repair, a scruffy pullover, green and with pulled threads. No tie. Somehow he managed to keep tight hold of the camera as though afraid of losing it.

These first impressions of the professor were not entirely favourable. Here was a shambling man with a nervous disposition, aged fifty plus. He had entered her office with an almost childlike enthusiasm which she immediately diagnosed as an attempt to conceal shyness. Perhaps he had endured an unhappy childhood, unloving parents or been bullied at school? Fortunately her professional expertise enabled her to interpret these signs in other people and, just occasionally, in herself.

Glancing down she noticed the hem of his trousers frayed above his battered brown Hush Puppy shoes which were making squelching noises.

Noticing her looking down at his feet he said, 'They leak a bit I'm afraid, must think about a new pair.'

Nothing about him matched her preconception of what an academic from Rudham University might look like. Almost everything about him deviated from her expectations but then, when she gave it a moment's thought, the people in the world of the university a few miles up the road were as familiar in her experience as men from Mars or, come to that, London.

Then she remembered the glamorous female research assistant she was expecting and looking up noticed that the man called Mitchell was not alone, for behind him lurked a much younger man where she had expected to see a nubile young woman. Mitchell stepped aside and pointing towards his companion introduced him as, 'Marcus, my research assistant on this project.' This was not the glamorous twenty-something young woman she had hoped for, the antidote to Lorraine, but instead an extremely good-looking young man. Scrumptious, Madge thought.

Marcus did not need to say anything or do anything to be a presence. Before he opened his mouth he somehow seemed to hold centre stage. Expensively dressed with perfectly creased trousers, a brushed cotton check shirt perfectly ironed, and a loose-fitting tweed jacket. His hair, dark, bushy and neatly combed seemed moulded on top of his skull. Here was a model of manhood never seen before in Moortown. Was this a Greek hero who had walked free from one of the pictures of friezes she remembered in her school history books? My God, she thought, the women in the office, young or old, will swoon on beholding this creature from another planet. Had she herself been a year or two younger, or perhaps twenty or thirty years younger, this vision might have caused her to faint before returning to consciousness with the aid of smelling salts. Knowing her luck she would have found Dan bending over and reviving her with a pungent whiff of his habitually bad breath.

'Good morning, Miss Perfect, a pleasure to meet you I'm sure,' said Marcus, lowering his eyes as he said the word 'Perfect'. It was the most cultured, class-ridden, insincere voice she had heard since they pensioned off some of the announcers on the Home Service of the BBC of old. Not 'this is Alvar Liddell' but 'this is Marcus'. But Marcus what? That could wait. Although only an inch or two taller than the professor he appeared to tower over him and was soon exchanging effortless pleasantries. Yes, in her school history book she had stared at the fuzzy black and white pictures of the stone statues of the naked gods of old. And here before her was evidence that the breed had survived; it lived on in the flesh not only in marble busts. It was here before her in the stature of this upper-class Englishman, a sight rarely seen in Moortown. Whatever else might be said about him he was certainly not the gorgeous young woman she had looked forward to as competition for Lorraine.

'Indeed,' she said, lost for sensible words, 'please do sit down, both of you, and please do call me Madge, I prefer informality.' Why did she choose this moment to lie? As she waved them towards a chair she realised there was only one spare chair. 'Oh, hmm,' she went on, 'I will ask one of my staff to fetch another chair.'

Poking her head out into the corridor she spied Lorraine heading in her direction. 'A favour please, Lorraine, would you be kind enough to bring in an extra chair for my guests?'

Lorraine scowled but went into the social workers' room and came out with a lightweight plastic chair which she clumped down at the entrance to Madge's office.

'Lorraine,' she said, 'do spare us a moment, I would like you to meet Professor Mitchell and his research assistant Marcus.'

Both men smiled and she noticed Marcus eyeing up Lorraine in one swift appreciative glance. All men were the same.

'Dit is good to meet you both,' said Lorraine, flustered at the sight of the young man but failing to swoon. She ignored the professor. Now what have we here? Madge wondered. Lorraine was certainly looking interested, Marcus merely curious, yet surely it was more than her imagination that saw something in the glances between the two young people? Or was it just what she had learned all those years ago to call 'projection'?

'Lorraine is a graduate of some university or other in Cape Town,' said Madge.

'UCT,' said Mitchell, 'a fine institution.'

'Dankie, I mean thank you, no one here in Moortown has heard of it,' said Lorraine.

Marcus beamed at Lorraine as she turned on her heels and almost tripped over her own feet in her haste to leave the room. Marcus just smiled, his eyes momentarily focusing on her back before scanning down to her departing legs. 'She sees a lot of sun,' he said.

'We must get down to business,' Madge said, clearing her throat. 'I understand you are tasked to study my department here in Area 13 and measure our efficiency?' She was scrambling desperately to remember the memo from Puttock on the subject. So much for the preparation she had intended. 'Of course we will help in any way we can.'

'Area 13?' asked Marcus.

'Yes, Area 13 in the thirteen administrative divisions of the county as determined historically by County Hall.'

'Sounds a bit like communism under Lenin,' said Marcus.

'No, nothing like that, we're staunch Labour in Rudham.'

Marcus smirked. 'Is that any different?' he said. Madge quickly decided that Marcus, like Dan, came into the 'not very nice person' category.

'Don't take my companion too seriously,' said Mitchell, 'he has a mischievous sense of humour. It is most kind of you to offer to help. Our idea is to...'

Before many more words were out she had altogether lost track of what the man and his ideas were about. How on earth could she hope to make any sense of the words and phrases that slid off his tongue with the speed of a cage plummeting down a pit winding shaft? How did they relate to real-world people like the Farrants, people her staff confronted daily? And what did it all mean – correlation coefficients, regression analysis, longitudinal study, and so on, and so on?

'We are but slaves to the scientific method,' the professor announced at one point.

'For what we are about to receive' went slowly through her mind as she gazed silently upon this dishevelled creature from another planet.

She began by trying to explain: 'Could you perhaps put it more simply, or perhaps I should say more concretely? We deal with people who have or cause problems. Children are neglected, abused, commit crimes, fail to attend school. Similarly with elderly people, the mentally ill or handicapped, the disabled… We have limited resources.'

'You mean,' said Marcus, smiling, 'you have elderly people who fail to attend school?'

'Marcus and his sense of humour again I'm afraid,' said the professor, 'but you've said it all.'

'Have I? Said what all?' She felt uncomfortable in the company of the two men, one who talked about things beyond her understanding, the other who seemed to be quietly mocking her.

'Vilfredo Pareto, Italian economist, deceased…' said Mitchell.

'God rest his soul,' said Marcus, crossing himself.

'… saw everything as people competing for goods and services in a world with scarce resources, simple as that,' Mitchell went on.

'Path breaking,' Marcus added.

She did not like to say it but this was a fact of life known to everyone in the office and not a single Italian economist with a fancy name among them. Could the man not give a straight answer to a straight question?

She must try again, even if only one more time. 'What exactly, what precisely is it you need to see or do here? Our files?'

'Yes, your files, your colleagues and real people – we need to talk to your customers. Our ultimate task is to measure your inputs and outputs against your budgetary constraints.'

Marcus nodded agreement as Mitchell paused.

Madge intervened. 'Our "real" people, we call them clients.'

Marcus said, 'Like prostitutes and lawyers.'

'Pardon,' Madge said.

'Prostitutes and lawyers have clients don't you know?'

'Ignore him,' the professor said. 'Clients then. We need to talk to your clients. We need to meet some of your so-called problem families face to face if we are to understand what is going on. Our fresh eyes may even bring new insights that aid you in your work.'

She began to see the light and even to wonder... a break in the clouded thoughts swirling round her brain opened up before her... what if...? Yes, why not?

'Families with problems? An idea is coming to me,' she said. 'For a start I am sure I could ask Lorraine, whom you just met, to take you to meet our Farrant family in Brownlow. I am equally sure that she will be more than willing to discuss her treatment plan for the family with you at the same time. The members of this family are seldom lost for words. Yes, richness of language is one of their strengths.'

'Excellent,' said Mitchell, and both men smiled as Marcus added, 'Spiffing, just the biscuit. I look forward to seeing their pigeons.'

'Pigeons?'

'Yes, pigeons, I know that in the north-east all the natives wear cloth caps and keep racing pigeons.'

'And play football?' Madge said.

'But not very well. Just so,' said Marcus.

Marcus, irritating in the extreme, was clearly a young researcher who had taken the trouble to immerse himself in regional cultural variations as seen from London. If he had not got it quite right then meeting real people in Moortown and Brownlow might round off a few of the rough edges of his understanding. None of us, except perhaps Dan, are immune to change.

But what was she to make of Professor Mitchell? Of course he must be very clever or he would not be a professor. He must have lots of brains compensating for what appeared to be other deficiencies. Hopefully, living in the area and with an interest in the coal mining industry he would be a little in tune with the tenor of local life, the world beyond the university.

'Professor Mitchell' though was too much of a mouthful for routine use. On the other hand he had not given his first name let alone authorised its use. In that moment Madge knew that for as long as he might be around she would drop the title 'Professor' and not strive to find out his first name. There was something about him that tuned perfectly with the name Mitchell. From now on she would simply think of him as 'Mitchell'.

'If you don't mind,' he said, 'I'd like to look at the Farrant files while Marcus heads back to the university to think things over. I will follow by bus as we came in one car.'

Madge said, 'A bus? What bus? I think they run every two hours when there is an "r" in the month. I will ask Lorraine to run you into Rudham when you've had a look through the files, I'm sure she won't mind the mileage.'

As Marcus headed off to the car park she took Mitchell to the admin office and handed him over to Brenda whom she asked to look out the not inconsiderable Farrant files.

When Mitchell finally left the building Madge accompanied him and Lorraine out to the car park. As he climbed into Lorraine's car he said to Madge, 'Your world and mine, they're so different. Those files, the Farrants, I never knew people like that existed, didn't know there were real people like that. Frankly don't know how you stand it.'

'Well, let's just say I've known it all these years, man and boy, I can't imagine another life. I shall work till I drop.'

'Not my ambition,' Mitchell said.

'So just looking at the files came as a bit of a culture shock? I find it strange too knowing nothing of your world.'

'Yes, a shock. But our different worlds... I just wonder if... no, I won't say it now, need to look into it. Meantime Marcus and I will develop a flow diagram showing how we intend to progress our research.'

'Will your diagram have a place for the Farrant family you are going to visit?'

'Most definitely, I look forward to meeting them and will feed back on our visit. I'm sure they will be charming.'

With a wave and a hoot he was gone. Strange, thought Madge, how he often sounds almost like Dan.

Back in the office she had the benefit of the opinions on the visitors as seen from Typing.

'The old guy,' said Brenda, 'by, he's a queer one. Talks funny. And while he was waiting till you were free he just stood next to a filing cabinet dripping water. Fiddled with his camera. Never said a word. The girls in the office stared at him for a while and then they just forgot he was there. It's his wife I feel sorry for.'

'Now, now, Brenda.'

'The young man though was very different, him so young and a real toff. Shook his umbrella over everything. His clothes were as dry as an empty glass of Newcastle Broon. Just stood his umbrella on my desk to dry off. Dripped all over my typewriter. The girls took note of him all right.'

As did Lorraine, Madge remembered. But what about Simon who was still fragile but getting closer to Lorraine?

But all she said to Brenda was, 'To start their research I'm going to ask Lorraine and Dan to take them to visit the Farrants, hence the professor looking at the files. I wonder how they will get on.'

'Oh my God, bloody hell,' said Brenda, 'mebbes you should gan along as well?'

'No, I've thought of that, Dan is the right person and after all he does manage Lorraine's caseload.'

'Oh my God,' Brenda repeated, 'the old guy and the Farrants, and you know what Dan is like.'

'Now, now, Brenda, Dan is my Deputy Area Controller.'

'I knaa, Miss Perfect but…'

Madge did not like to wither people but she chose that moment to silence Brenda with one of her severest withering looks. It was not right for junior staff to criticise her deputy even if it was well deserved.

***

She began the afternoon staring at the new referrals overflowing on her desk. As if the office was not already creaking under the strain there was now this busybody professor ready to interfere, find fault with her admin system, and report his findings back to County Hall. How many last straws did she have to suffer? And the consolation she had anticipated in respect of the glamorous research assistant turned out to be Marcus. Although he was certainly a bit of all right the hope that he would be a she who poured cold water on Lorraine's egotistical fire had proved a mirage.

She had forgotten her demand that Lorraine and Simon prepare a report on the bruising to Gary Farrant, until late in the afternoon Lorraine came into her office brandishing her report, as yet unseen by Madge. 'I need you to sign this,' Lorraine said. 'It has to go now, the Director is expecting it, and Dan has OK'd it.'

'Why hasn't Dan signed it then?'

'He had to go back up to County Hall, something important came up.'

Madge skimmed the report which recommended 'No Further Action'.

'I don't agree with the way this case is going,' she said, 'and most of all I don't agree with your NFA conclusion.'

'There's no time for all that, Madge, it's got to go in the internal post right now. Dan is happy with it. You must agree that sometimes kids need a good hiding. You saw how Gary spoke to his mother.'

'The bruising was on his face,' she pointed out. Madge most certainly did not agree with the report but after a skirmish she signed it with the greatest reluctance and handed it back to Lorraine. Fortunately it contained no mention of masturbatory guilt, a subject she would not want to discuss with the Director after he read the report. The Director was widely regarded as being on the dull side of conventional, something to do with his Scottish Presbyterian origins it was said. But then many things were said about the Director, few that were complimentary and probably even fewer that were true.

With the Farrants behind her for now she had a moment to decide on the next most urgent task. Seeking clinical attention for her failing car could not wait much longer. If her job was her life then her car was vital for her job. Within no more than a week she must seek a diagnosis and possible cure for the ageing rust bucket.

It had been yet another fairly ordinary day in the life of Moortown and Brownlow so why did she feel suddenly unsure, as though something unseen was about to change around her? It was an uncomfortable feeling.

***

Three days later Brenda was jabbering before her with another urgent memo from Puttock in Staffing. She picked it up and was immediately shaken by the contents. Reading down the page she clucked with disbelief for it begged to inform her that her request for early retirement from the post of Area Controller, Area 13, had been accepted. No doubt receipt of this memo would bring unbridled joy to some of her colleagues. Miss Perfect though was shocked at this unexpected news. Startled by the bald announcement affecting her future she slowly absorbed the next step; if she contacted Staffing at the earliest opportunity they would finalise arrangements for her leaving date and pension. As she had chosen to retire early as part of the 'restructuring scheme' her pension would become due to her immediately on retirement thanks to the generosity of the Director, for in normal circumstances she would not have been able to draw her pension until she reached the statutory retirement age of sixty.

There was only one problem: she had NOT applied for early retirement. It could only be an error by one of the army of typists at County Hall. There could be no doubt it was a memo intended for another member of the department which had been sent to her instead.

She lifted the phone to explain the error to Puttock, intending to lay no blame, how she quite understood how easily such mistakes can occur.

A squeaky voice at County Hall answered. 'Personnel speaking, Mr Puttock's phone speaking.' It was no doubt one of Puttock's clerks, young girls who were often quite bright but with little or no hope of career progression in the male bastion that was HQ.

Madge said, 'He must have changed jobs, I have a memo from him in Staffing. Or perhaps I have the wrong extension?'

'He was Staffing yesterday, he's Personnel from today,' the girl said. 'Mr Puttock's been promoted from Head of Staffing to Head of Personnel. It's a new department.'

'Whatever it's now called can I speak to your Puttock please, the man himself not his phone?'

'Sorry, miss, he's senior management, he dizzent speak te people on the phone. Can ah tek a message?'

'I'm Miss Perfect, Area Controller, Moortown, Area 13. I need to speak to him about a memo I have received in error.'

'Sorry, miss, ye have te reply by memo. He dizzent naa speak te people below senior management. It's coonsel policy.'

The phone went dead. Insolent whipper-snapper, Madge thought. How dare she refuse to put me through to Puttock, jumped-up bloody Puttock who only reached a position well beyond his competence thanks to his father being the late County Councillor Puttock? Why can I as a middle manager not speak to a senior manager? How ridiculous!

Nonetheless, reply in writing to Puttock she must; the stakes were far too high for her to put it to one side, simply laugh it off as a silly mistake. Her settled world, the job that was her life, the monthly payments to help fund the education of the daughter of an old college friend near London, her own income in retirement, the overdraft following the repairs to the leaky roof of her cottage, all relied on her working and drawing a salaried income till she was sixty. The girl in question was still at Bristol

University, training to be a doctor, no way could she let her down, not after promising to help her through university.

It must surely be a mistake. Mustn't it? If she couldn't cope without them and what they paid her, the suits in County Hall who hired, paid and fired staff, how could they for their part possibly hope to cope without her commitment and years of experience? No, it was unthinkable. But what if, yes, what if Dan was behind it all? She wouldn't put it past him. In all probability he was one of the network of spies placed by the Director across the county.

The voice of her late, unlamented father echoed round in her brain. He was a man of a thousand real or imagined hurts or insults. 'Up and at 'em,' he used to say. 'Up and at 'em, don't let them get you down, don't give up without a fight.' Even her father had left her something of value.

If Puttock did not speak to people then she would have to reply by memo as the cheeky young girl said. As soon as time permitted she would write to Puttock in no uncertain terms.

Hopefully up and at 'em would not arise.

Chapter 4

Solving the human problems of Moortown and Brownlow would have to wait on one side, for her car was now in need of urgent treatment; further prevarication was out of the question.

After lunch the following day things went quiet, the office drifting into afternoon mode, her social workers out on home visits. There were no known crises on the horizon so she would take advantage of the lull to slip out and attend to her car. What strange grating noises it was making. At first it had been possible to ignore their vulgarity but now they were so loud that when she drove down the High Street pedestrians turned to stare as she passed by. Was that how it felt to be the Queen? The sound effects might be different. Perhaps she should nonetheless wave to the populace, her people, her Moortown. She opened the window and attempted a regal hand flap. Not one of the citizens responded. That's what it's like to be born without royal blood.

Clients often saw their own social status as in some way related to the calibre of their social worker's car: its age, cost to buy and cleanliness inside and out. The newer, the more expensive, the better. Jazzy colours helped as well. And here she was driving around her district in a rusting old tin can which might spray sardines out on the road at any moment. She must not continue to let people down.

She hated the idea of spending money on a car but… how much? That was the question. Just to be sure there was nothing untoward she called on Billy at the local garage. It was not the sort of garage that ran to a telephone.

Billy, the proprietor, a title he insisted on, had been one of her most difficult clients in his childhood, those days when she was still a child care officer. She sometimes thought that in a funny way Billy and she had grown up in parallel even though they had travelled along very different paths.

The now almost respectable Billy was bludgeoning something in the engine of a car with a hammer. Seeing her he stopped bashing things and came over towards her. She explained the problem.

'Ah'll 'ave a quick look now, miss,' Billy said. His work clothes probably served as his leisure clothes as well, oil-stained, well worn.

'I would be so grateful. Would you mind, please?'

She watched with guarded affection as he examined her car. Such memories attached to Billy.

He had always been a tough little bugger but as best she could she polished her juvenile court reports in his favour when he stole from local shops, stressing parental difficulties, hunger, family unemployment, and every other extenuating circumstance she could muster. She spoke up for him at school when he attacked other pupils or the teachers or refused to be caned. She intervened to modify the wrath of his parents when his actions brought the police, the education welfare officer, the probation officer or the social worker unwelcome to their door. Besides all that it was never proved that he burned down a classroom wing of his secondary modern school. He had always insisted that it was another boy though she had her doubts, especially as amnesia prevented him from recalling the name of this other boy. 'Loyalty' he called that. Fear of reprisals more likely.

As his mother had said at the time, 'Ye knaa, Miss Porfect, he's easy led and in with a crowd of wrong 'uns, that's aall there is to it.' All that was before he had gone 'straight', though, as Madge frequently reminded herself, there is straight and straight. At least he had not to her knowledge been violent since those early days and that was one small mercy for which she was truly thankful: now that he was twenty-seven, married with two bairns of his own, and employed, she could take pride in her earlier efforts on his behalf and her qualified optimism about his future.

Besides, she must constantly remind herself, nobody was without fault. Nobody was perfect. She was right to feel a twinge of unease going out of the office during working hours to deal with the repairs to her car, a private matter and hence contrary to council policy.

Billy sighed with exasperation, wiped his oily hands on his jersey, oil on oil, as he worked along the car. She looked at him more closely. What was he wearing today? The jersey all gone at the elbows was far too big as well as far from clean, his jeans torn. Well really, he was letting himself go. He had looked so smart going off to school from the Hills, the foster parents she had arranged for him. Well, at least until the foster placement broke down. But as a car mechanic he could not dress for work like Dan.

And she couldn't take him into care again at his age though she would like to see Mrs Hill, his final foster mother before he was sent down, respond to her arrival on the doorstep with Billy. For things had gone badly wrong at about the time Billy set fire to his school, or not. Madge secured the services of a glib lawyer on his behalf, the evidence was inconclusive and the verdict 'not guilty'. Madge's boss at the time joined the chorus of the education department, the housing department and the police, all of whom said in unison, 'something has to be done'. That 'something' turned out to be the foster placement with Mrs Hill.

He paused over the engine long enough to say, 'Ye knaa, miss, these Morris 1000s are shit.'

'I'm so sorry.'

A vacancy came up with Mrs Hill at just the right moment when all else seemed lost. She was a specialist foster parent. 'Specialists' took on the more difficult cases in return for higher payments. Mrs Hill had a reputation second to none when it came to putting youngsters back on the right path. She had gone all dewy eyed at the first sight of Billy and things began well with Mr Hill encouraging Billy to make model aeroplanes. Regrettably Billy soon found that he was allergic to balsa wood and modelling glue and when he set fire to his own partly finished Spitfire and Mr Hill's entire squadron of World War Two planes the relationship between carers and cared for deteriorated. Mr Hill was patient at first, explaining to Billy that he wouldn't have minded as much if Billy had set fire to the planes of the Luftwaffe, though Billy did point out that there were no such planes in Mr Hill's collection. Then, when Billy started stealing from Mrs Hill's purse, 'borrowing' the sexy magazines from the drawer beside her marital bed, and attempting to have sex with her under-age daughter, it was clear to both foster parents that Billy needed a firm hand, a man's hand.

When Mr Hill had tried to cane Billy for these and other minor misdemeanours it was Mr Hill who ended up badly bruised in hospital. He was a slightly built man and singularly lacking in both physique and judgement. It turned out that Mr Hill's spell in hospital was due to a simple misunderstanding as he failed to realise how much Billy enjoyed being caned by Mrs Hill, or even that Mrs Hill enjoyed caning Billy before they had sex together. 'Foreplay' Mrs Hill called it and how Billy enjoyed his foreplay, took to it with enthusiasm he did. Such subtleties had simply not occurred to Mr Hill. From his responses when interviewed by the police in connection with the assault it was clear that he did not share his wife's or Billy's pleasures in these practices and, on being told that corporal punishment by foster parents was now against county policy, he announced that Mrs Hill would be resigning forthwith.

When the placement with Mrs Hill broke down Billy was sent to a corrective institution up in the dales where he was thrashed into apparent submission in accordance with county policy while at the same time learning more advanced skills in mending and stealing cars.

'Ah can get in any locked car in three minutes flat,' he once announced to her proudly adding, 'Ah'll show yer how.'

'Thank you, Billy, but not necessary,' Madge had said. But then when a day came and she locked her keys in the car she was grateful to be able to call on his skills. Billy had his uses.

Only when he met and married Mrs Billy, a gangly girl with freckles who had grown up in care, did he forego car theft and dodgy deals in favour of car maintenance.

Madge knew the repairs were going to be expensive when Billy's internal examination under the bonnet of her car began with a very loud 'fuck'. The expletive was bad news as whereas a mild, inconsequential fuck could mean as little as £30, on the sliding scale of vehemence a robust fuck could mean as much as £50, perhaps more. And the fucks soon added up. His head still under the bonnet, he emitted two further, though milder, fucks.

When his head emerged from the engine his expression was dour. It was not a good moment to enquire if all was well. Quite plainly, things could not be much worse. When he moved around the car for the external examination her hopes rose at his longest silence so far until, reaching the driver's side front tyre, there was the worst fuck of all. The exhaust, the shock absorbers and an area of rust near the bottom of the passenger door provoked further echoes of that fuck.

'Is it bad?' She knew very well the answer, having counted at least eight expletives, average per expletive based on past experience equaling £50, and total bill therefore eight fucks at £50 a fuck, £400.

'Whyaye, bad,' he said, staring morosely at the car, 'could be worse man. Say four, four-fifty, that's a special rate for yous, miss.'

Fuck, she thought, hating the way her use of private, unspoken language had coarsened over the years. She consoled herself that it was something to do with the job, the company she kept. Besides, thinking of a rude word to herself was one thing, tolerating it in others unavoidable, but such words would never cross her lips when in company.

In spite of knowing Billy as a malnourished-looking babe sucking on the teat of a mucky bottle containing what looked suspiciously like Carlsberg Special lager, and shepherding him through the years of his delinquent teenage court appearances, she had underestimated the quality of these vehemences.

'As bad as that?' she said. 'I suppose it would almost be cheaper to buy a new car.'

'Yebuggermar fuck that,' he said.

'No, no, it's only my little joke; I will have it mended again. What would people say if I was stopped by the police because of the noise and the smoke coming out of the exhaust?'

He looked at her uncomprehendingly. 'Folk roond aboot wouldn't give a fff...'

'Quite, quite,' she interrupted, and then, 'When might it be ready?'

There was a sharp intake of air that whistled through the gaps in his teeth.

'Why man, give us a day or two,' he said, drawing his greasy hands through his long, lank hair. Or three or four, she mused in silence.

Then she noticed he was staring at her as if deciding whether or not to speak out about something that was bothering him. Please God, she thought, no confessions. If he had illegally connected the electricity because the Board disconnected the supply she did not want to know about that or any other criminal activity. But it was not that nor any other malfeasance, for after much shuffling from one foot to the other he skimmed his stone into the conversation.

'Yer knaa the Golden Slipper?'

'Not personally, Billy. I know of it.'

'Yer mebbes knew it as a nightclub. They say Shirley Bassey sang there one time.'

'Heard of it but don't know it personally, not my scene exactly.'

'The nightclub went bust and some old fart bought it up and turned it into a massage parlour. Yer knaa it. One of your lads is a regular.'

'Naa, I mean no, can't be true. Not one of my team.'

'Aye, one of yours. I look in sometimes and I seen him aalreet, smart lad, taalks fancy.'

'Impossible, Billy. What does he look like, this smart lad? Is he young?'

'Naa.'

'Old?'

'Naa.'

Although she did not know much about the Golden Slipper she knew in her bones that Billy must be mistaken about one of her staff. The very words 'massage parlour' made the place sound disreputable even without the benefit of Billy's custom. One of her team? Ridiculous! She shook her head and left with Billy staring after her.

Her annual financial cycle now off to an expensive start, she observed to herself as she walked back to the office that without these unexpected setbacks she would be able to enjoy more of life's creature comforts. But at least her work, and her car, provided income for young Billy; there was thus a social benefit and, after all, was that not what her life and work were all about? If her plans for a water feature in the garden and repairs to the bedroom window did have to remain on hold for another year then how small a sacrifice was that in the wider scheme of things? Meanwhile she would have to manage without a car. That meant begging lifts to appointments and sometimes catching the bus to work. She did so hate being dependent on others.

A shower of cold rain came sheeting across the street and dribbled down her neck as she continued musing as she walked: surely Billy couldn't be right about one of her team visiting the Golden Slipper? But if by chance he was right who could it possibly be? Smart dresser sounded like Dan. Talks fancy could cover Simon as Billy might view him. But surely not Simon. No, Dan was the most likely unless Billy was confused as to who were her 'lads'. Perhaps someone from Housing? But that would not be one of her lads. And if not Dan or Simon then who? Surely not one of the older men. Alan? No, that was laughable. Clearly Billy, never a reliable witness, was mistaken.

Enough of these wild speculations. At least Billy was no longer a prodigal son, a charge on the state, a burden to prudent standard-rate taxpayers like herself; success in her line of work being rare she was willing to settle for that.

And then later, looking back on it all from Cork, how strange seemed the part Billy came to play in the way things turned out.

***

Puttock's memo about early retirement being so clearly in error it was the next day before she finally made time to reply:

> *Dear Mr Puttock, having failed to speak to you on the phone I beg to draw your attention to your recent memo on the subject of early retirement. As I am sure you know I have not applied to go early so must assume that the memo that came to me was in error, no doubt the result of a simple if unfortunate clerical error. But I do understand – these things can so easily happen even in the best-managed bureaucracies. However, I would appreciate it if you would please amend your records accordingly.*
> *Respectfully, Miss Perfect, Area Controller, Area 13.*

She was sorely tempted to add a dash of sarcasm here, a reflection on the performance of Puttock's department there, but no, the man was devoid of humour as is common in people confident in their lack of any failings, a deficiency in many of the senior men in County Hall.

And remembering he was a man who did not speak to people she held back on the P.S. that came to mind: 'I do hope you have got your voice back. I know how painful sore throats can be'. Discretion being the better part of prolonged employment she kept these thoughts to herself. No doubt, and in his own good time, a grovelling, long overdue apology would follow from Puttock.

***

On Monday Simon called at her cottage to give her a lift to work. For a young man he was a sensible driver, his car did not stink of cigarettes and neither did it make loud farting noises attracting attention of the wrong sort as hers had done. Simon's nice new car showed no signs of the mechanical distress to which hers was so prone.

'When do you get your car back?' he asked.

The truth was that with her car in the care of Billy there was no answer to that question so she said, 'Soon, soon.'

'How are things with you, Simon?' She meant, 'Are you getting over the nasty business of the divorce?' and 'How are you finding local authority social work after lecturing at the university?' and, and, something like 'Are you happy in Lorraine's company?' So often the things she wanted to know about colleagues involved questions that could not be asked. It was different with clients, they were there to be grilled: 'How did Gary come by that bruise?' or 'Are the pink giraffes speaking to you, telling you what to do?' or 'Can you manage the stairs?'

All Simon said was, 'So-so.' She left it at that knowing it to mean things could be better. As they drove on silently to work she so hoped Lorraine was not responsible for his downturn.

When they turned into the car park Simon said, 'I'm more than sorry to hear you will soon be leaving us but happy for you if retirement is what you want.'

She was angry; how many times did she have to tell people that it was a silly rumour originating with a memo in error from County Hall. Simon smiled as she explained. 'I'm so pleased you are not leaving,' he said.

***

She had hardly settled at her desk when Dan bounced into her office with the spring in his step that had been apparent ever since his first immersion in the mud bath that was HQ. She almost expected him to open with, 'Hallelujah, sister, I am saved,' but all he said was, 'I'm here,' as though it were not immediately obvious.

As usual he looked excessively washed and scrubbed, his hair slicked down. Did young men still favour Brylcreem? She remembered stroking her fingers through her young man's neatly combed hair all those years ago. Some things change, some not at all. What is better, what is worse, now or then, age or youth?

Then he grinned and pointed to his chest, saying, 'What do you think?'

'About what?'

'My new jacket, bought it at Hepworths in the Market Place in Rudham on Saturday, just under £30.' He held it open to reveal the label and pointed to 'Hardy Amies, dressmaker to the Queen.'

'I see,' said Madge, suspecting no one in the office would give a pint of watered-down Newcastle Brown Ale one way or the other. And for some of the older men, increasingly agitated at the talk of a miners' strike, being clothier to Arthur Scargill would carry more weight. She could not think of anyone in the office who regarded Dan as popular yet he tried so hard to be liked.

To Madge all this spoke of a young man earnestly making every effort to conform to HQ's expectations as he strove to ascend the greasy organisational pole. Yet nothing could be guaranteed; she remembered the men before Dan who had reached the top of the greasy pole in off-the-peg suits from the Co-op, fed their families with help from the Co-op 'divvi' and, come the end of their shift, been buried by the Co-op, the mourning women resplendent in black Co-op weeds and the after-funeral bun fight courtesy of the Co-op grocery department.

Her partial pleasure at his return was entirely selfish. He was organised, his desk the tidiest in the county, his decisions right or wrong taken at lightning speed. These could be admirable traits in the allocation and management of caseloads. Yet she also despised his rational, methodical approach to resources and his ability to put any feelings he might have to one side. Feelings? Who could tell? In the background lurked an unseen wife, two sons and a dog, all proudly on show in a photograph in a silver frame on his desk — Dan, Dan the family man.

'Are all these training days at County Hall useful?' she asked.

'No, not 'training' nowadays, not even old-fashioned 'staff development', that sort of stuff is way in the past, nowadays 'trickle down' is the key concept. Yes, very, very useful. The Director has nominated me to be the change agent for Area 13. He was just back from the annual conference of directors in England and brought lots of new ideas for us to try out in Rudham, all the latest thinking. First off he wants us middle managers to take everything he passes on to us back to our cost centres so that it trickles all the way down the department and eventually reaches the lowest levels, even down to the female care assistants in our aged persons' homes, care staff in day care facilities, that sort of thing.'

'Trickle down?'

'Yes, but he thinks this will soon be superseded by something called 'cascading' but he didn't have time to go into that with us.'

So that was it, 'even' workers at the lowest levels, mostly women doing the hands-on caring, putting food in at one end, wiping it up at the other end, lots of smells, for example. Nowadays there was pressure to reduce the pay of those at the lowest levels while simultaneously inflating the salaries of senior managers. If Dan was the dawn of a new day in the world of caring she did not much care for this glimpse of that prospect. At times she no longer wanted to be part of it though there were many things she would miss. Before the thoughts of early retirement Puttock had floated before her, albeit in error, she seldom looked further ahead than the next day in the office. But after Puttock's memo there were moments now when she was less comfortable in the present, less certain about her future. Needing the money for her eventual retirement she must persevere, she would not be put out on the street with the rubbish bins. When she came to leave it would be on her own terms.

'What does being a 'change agent' involve?' she asked.

'Change. It makes me the axle of a wheel from which the spokes radiate out in all directions from County Hall to the county's boundaries, transforming all our staff, the lives of our clients and the size of the budgets for our caseloads throughout Area 13 and beyond. With thirteen change agents across the county we can transform our sector of the north-east of England.'

'And our staff, how do we transform them?'

'Part of my job as change agent. We no longer think of attitudes and values, skills and knowledge, but efficiency. Those people I can't transform will have to move on, make way for the new way of doing things.'

'I see.' Madge managed not to burst out laughing or even ask him why the Director had not consulted her over the nomination of Dan, her junior, as 'change agent'. No point, Dan had the Director's ear, she never had. Besides, try as she might, she failed to see herself as a change agent.

***

Finding Mitchell bumbling around the admin office getting in the way of the clack-clack-clack of the typists she decided to ask him how the Farrant visit had gone. She asked Lorraine to join them.

Lorraine smiled at the summons but seeing it was just Madge and the professor she looked disappointed and asked, 'Is Marcus not here today?'

Mitchell smiled. 'No, not today, he's number crunching back at base.'

'Professor Mitchell is about to tell me about your visit to the Farrants,' Madge said.

It soon became clear that Mitchell was more than a little excited about the Farrant family. 'Never seen anything like it, and all that going on no more than fifteen miles from Rudham City and the university. A different world. Unbelievable!'

Madge thought she could have told him that but then reminded herself how little she knew about life in the city and the no doubt well-ordered world of the university. How sane, how nice it must be after Moortown and Brownlow. Little wonder the man was in such a febrile state.

'I hardly know where to begin,' he said. 'Poor old Marcus what with his public school and his father in the Cabinet and all that, but somehow he took it in his stride better than me, put them at their ease, or so he said, kept saying "spiffing", asked where they kept their pigeons, said how picturesque it was in their bijou little home.'

'Put them at their ease?' Madge said.

'Yes', Mitchell went on, 'though I did think at one point Mrs Farrant might have thumped him. Anyway, when Lorraine drove us to the house, on the pavement there was a pram, looked like it had survived being shelled in France in World War One, and in the pram was this baby thing, looked human, can't be sure, sucking a filthy teat on a bottle containing what looked like brandy. Can't have been of course. Tea perhaps. There was an empty can of Carlsberg Special in the pram! Never seen anything like it.'

'A bit of a culture shock?'

'You could say that and then some! But in the time I've spent talking to miners and their families, part of my research, I only ever came across decent types in well-ordered families, their kitchens so clean you could eat your dinner off the floor. When we went in to the Farrants all I saw of Mr was a hairy leg fast disappearing up the stairs. Mrs Farrant said we were lucky he was in a good mood or he might have bounced us off the walls. Then she shouted to us to "fuck the bloody off" which she repeated five or six times at least. Her grasp of the variety of words in the English language is severely limited. We left the house rather rapidly.'

'But you got the message?'

'Yes, and then she reappeared in the doorway and was suddenly all smiles as she invited us in to the front room where the litter on the floor shelved like a sloping beach gradually reaching a line a foot or more up the wall. Used condoms, used sanitary towels, empty beer cans and booze bottles, fag packets, crisp packets… I mean, you name it and there it was. She said she always left the housework till the weekend. Of course I offered to take a photograph of Mr and Mrs and young Gary, a family portrait, but that just started her off again, "F" this and "F" that etc.'

'No doubt a lot more household refuse thrown behind what furniture there is if you had got that far,' Madge suggested. 'Happily Lorraine is tasked to improve the physical conditions in the home. I only hope she will succeed where Simon failed.'

Lorraine smiled at the professor. 'I tried to explain, Madge, it's not the physical conditions that matter, more the psychosocial interactions between the parents.'

Mitchell looked puzzled. 'Surely the little boy, Gary, ought to be removed from that environment and taken into your care?'

Madge said, 'I have no doubt that in time he will stop attending school or offend or both. Before that happens a non-accidental injury may force our hand. But we have to operate within the law, produce evidence to a court. A mucky house isn't enough. Besides, having them in our care doesn't always work out either. Foster placements can break down, residential institutions can throw up harrowing stories of abuse of one kind or another.'

Mitchell said, 'Extraordinary! You mean to say you can't lift a finger till it's too late to improve his life chances?'

'Afraid not,' Madge said.

'Extraordinary. I'll have to explore that aspect in my report.'

No doubt, Madge thought, that will not reflect well on me when the Director reads the report. Up at County Hall they were so detached from reality, forever guarding their own backs, ever watchful of scandals that might hit the media fan.

Lorraine looked cross and would have none of this. 'I explained to Professor Mitchell and Marcus how I have studied the situation and diagnosed a need to tackle the psychosocial elements first.' She directed her full attention to Mitchell: 'I'm sure the root causes of all their difficulties arise somewhere in the confused dynamics of their marital relationship, especially in the sexual area. Ego boundaries are very confused in this family. I will of course discuss my treatment plan with Dan in our next supervision session. Marcus knows my views on sex.'

Lorraine discussing sex with Marcus did not bode well. Once again Madge was concerned for Simon. The last thing he needed was another setback in his personal life.

'Absolutely fascinating,' Mitchell said. 'You mean the Farrants have sex? Looking at what I saw of them it seems unbelievable!'

'Mrs Farrant's not your type then?' Madge said.

'Good Lord no, I just can't imagine the bedroom scene between Mr and Mrs Farrant. I did try to outline my research project to Mrs Farrant but I'm not sure she took it all in.' Nor me, Madge thought but said, 'She may have taken in more than you realised.'

Mitchell said, 'She looked pregnant to me, in fact she said all she wanted from me was a letter from me to the benefit people asking for more money because she was pregnant.'

'Pregnant? Unlikely,' Madge said. 'Lorraine tells me that Mr Farrant isn't up to it. Surprising them having sex at all in view of the sexual inadequacy of dad and the masturbatory guilt of mum that Lorraine has identified and no doubt discussed with you.'

'Good Lord no,' said Mitchell, looking embarrassed, 'Lorraine has not mentioned anything like that in any detail. Oh good Lord no.'

Madge smiled before Mitchell went on, 'Poor chap, erectile dysfunction at such a young age, not surprised though having seen Mrs Farrant. Enough to put anyone off. But they have little Gary so something must have taken place. That young man seemed sweet till he aimed a kick at my groin and told me to fuck off. I mean, as I said, I meet a lot of pitmen and find them mostly very polite. Can't believe it, the Farrants I mean, sex, it and them.' Mitchell waved his hands in the air.

'Ah well, early days yet, I look forward to seeing your numbers once you have finished crunching them,' said Madge, glancing at the storm cloud crossing Lorraine's suntanned face.

'And are they typical of the families you deal with?' Mitchell asked.

'Atypical,' said Lorraine. 'In each case the web of ego and super ego is entwined in multi-faceted ways. Mr Farrant's problem is of course very common in men in the north-east. Someone in Cape Town researched this topic and so the results are quite conclusive.'

'I disagree,' snapped Madge. 'Generally speaking families have been recycling problems for generations, material poverty is common to them all. Yet they are all different, there is no such thing as a typical family.'

'Absolutely fascinating hearing the two of you reaching such different conclusions. My only problem is reducing all these elements to numbers I can crunch,' said Mitchell.

Perhaps you can't, Madge thought, but said, 'I'm sure you can.'

Mitchell went on, 'I will of course have to allow for stochastic elements in all of this.'

'Pardon, "stochastic"?' Madge queried. Did he mean 'sarcastic'? But no.

'Stochastic introduces elements of uncertainty. Marcus and I will discuss all that stuff. But first we must look at a wider range of your families and, oh, who will I be dealing with after you leave this job?'

'I am not leaving. Who told you I was leaving?'

She noticed Lorraine staring hard out of the window as though she had just spotted a prime example of big game behind a thorn tree on the African veld.

'Well...' said Mitchell, 'I think it was Mrs Farrant, yes Mrs Farrant who mentioned it.'

'How the hell did she get hold of that silly rumour? It's not true, just sloppy work by a typist up at County Hall. I've fired off a memo to Puttock at County Hall to knock it on the head.'

'I'm sorry,' Mitchell said, 'but I'm glad you're staying, won't disrupt my work getting to know someone different, Dan perhaps?'

Deciding to ignore that, she said, 'By the way, was Dan with you at the Farrants? You don't mention his views.'

'Dan was too busy to go along,' Lorraine said. 'He apologised before heading off to County Hall.'

What was Dan up to with all these visits to County Hall? Surely there must be more to it than endless courses? What if he wasn't going to County Hall? What if he was going to the Golden Slipper in work time? Surely not. But if he was, and if she caught him at it, she would be in a position to see him off. Even his friend, the famously puritanical Director, would not condone that. But no, Dan, this most irritating of men, would not stoop that low. Would he?

When Mitchell got up to go back to the university Lorraine said, 'Let me run you back, Professor. I need to have a word with Marcus about the Farrants.'

Aye-aye, Madge thought, what have we here?

When Mitchell drove off she hurried to the Ladies being in urgent need to trickle down.

***

The next morning she remembered what she had forgotten to say to Dan the previous day. She went in search of him and found him in his office with the door closed and his desk playing host to any number of weighty books. She didn't like to say to Dan that the ideas seducing him were little more than the kind of nonsense that had been circulating around the department for years and years. Only the words changed.

When she pointed an enquiring finger at the books he muttered, 'Ah, yes, from the County Hall library, all recommended by the Director, all analysing the efficient use of scarce resources. Production functions are everything nowadays. I need to be up to speed and ready for an interview when a more senior vacancy comes up.'

If only there was a way she could explain that there were no senior vacancies at the moment, that he was one of her scarce resources, one she needed in action going about the business of Area 13. She never could think of the words that might get through to Dan, drunk as he was with the flattery of the Director's attention and, no doubt, his own thirst for promotion.

'I wasn't happy with the Farrant report and you not signing it although according to Lorraine you approved it.'

'Did I?' Dan said.

'You know I don't agree with its conclusion.'

'Scarce resources,' Dan said. 'It's all down to resource constraints. That's the thing you left out of the equation. Just think "production functions".'

'That's not the point,' Madge said. 'We deal in people not equations.'

Dan pulled a face then smiled. 'By the way, the Director did not think well of your Farrant report.'

'My Farrant report?'

'Yes, afraid so, you signed it, your responsibility.'

Madge was too angry to make any sensible response so she turned out of his office and stomped off down the corridor.

Equations? Dan didn't do people, their feelings, their distress. He lived in a world of facts. But feelings were facts. Caring for people, children especially, was too important to be left in the hands of the unfeeling Dans of this world. How could he hope to become a real social worker, someone like her who cared about damaged children, the vulnerable elderly, illness in others or those struggling to be paid according to their rights? Did he have no memories of unkindness in childhood, cruelty even? Was that the difference between them, her hatred of suffering driven only by what she herself had known?

Back in her own office the phone rang. It was the community psychiatric nurse from the Health Centre. Old Timms, otherwise known as Napoleon, discharged once again from hospital, had the world at his feet again. The CPN wanted to make a joint visit with a social worker. As she organised a response all thoughts of the thrice-blessed Puttock vacated her mind once again.

Her mind empty of Puttock was often the high point in her day.

Chapter 5

Good news was rare. Her car, 'good as new' in Billy's words, arrived in the car park. Less good news was Billy holding out his hand for 'five hundred in notes, miss'. But it was the immediate aftermath of her memo to Puttock that quite spoiled her summer. The phone had rung, the drang-drang-drang drilling into her brain as she tried to ignore it. She thought twice before answering it.

'Miss Perfect speaking.'

'Puttock here,' said the voice at the other end of the line.

'Perfect here,' she replied. 'How can I help you, Mr Puttock?'

Now for the apology. But no: 'Your belated reply to my memorandum... you misunderstand... it was not in error, Miss Perfect. Frankly your reply is out of order and misses the point. Surely you know the Director is planning a complete restructuring of his department.'

'No, how would I know that? I knew nothing of any restructuring. Why were the staff not told? Why were managers like me not told?'

'All managers had an opportunity to attend one of the Director's briefing sessions. You chose not to attend. But young Dan Bagley, your deputy, made himself available in your absence and I know the Director asked him man to man to keep you in the picture.'

Dan! What sort of game was he playing?

'But,' she went on, 'I did not apply – as my memo to you stated – for early retirement.'

'No, of course you did not but the default position in the policy document allowed for that.'

'What default position? What policy document?'

'Dan Bagley took a copy to share with you and your office. In the document it states quite clearly that the Director will assume that staff wish to be considered for early retirement unless they write in stating the opposite. I can find no record of anything in writing from yourself.'

She took a deep breath and said, 'No, there was nothing in writing from me, Mr Puttock.'

'Not good enough, Miss Perfect, not half good enough. Just now you need to get a grip on Area 13.'

***

Not good enough, it was ever thus. At first she did well at school but then when she was thirteen and past the arrival of the curse her father arrived at Eastbourne to reclaim her to do for him in his neat suburban semi in Staines. Suddenly, plucked from the genteel kindliness of the aunts, she was back in the house in which her mother died, her father cold and aloof, going off from the house to catch the six-forty-five train to work in London on weekdays, returning at about seven in the evenings.

Coming in to the empty house from the grammar school where she found it difficult to make new friends she set about the daunting round of homework and housework. In no particular order she cleaned the house, did the washing and ironing, shopped from the list left for her, cooked. Her father said he could not afford 'one of those new-fangled washing machine things' at the moment. She liked Eastbourne, the light on the sea, the band playing to the Sunday trippers, and youngsters frolicking in the waves. These were people her age who laughed and had fun. She wanted to sunbathe and swim like other young people but her father disapproved. She didn't like it when the local paper carried reports of suicides on Beachy Head but her father just said, 'Not to worry, we're better off without them, it's their choice not to go on living.' It made her sad to think of people so desperate they chose to jump from the cliff; she could not imagine ever feeling that sad and it made her cross with her father for being so unkind. Surely something could be done to help such people?

Mrs Dobbs next door sometimes dropped in to chat and often said, 'You're doing champion for a youngster. You're lucky to have such a good father and he's lucky too of course. Perhaps one day he'll find another wife.' He never did remarry and if he found solace with any woman Madge knew nothing of it.

At school the teachers all agreed she had ability, did not work hard enough, and ought to put her back into it, even think of university. Miss Dewar though got the sharp end of her father's tongue at the mention of university at the parents' evening. 'Not my girl', he snapped, 'not good enough, not like her mother, she was very clever.' There was no more mention of a university.

Mrs Dobbs said, 'Not to worry, dearie, a woman's place is in the home. Always has been, always will be.'

Puttock was right about one thing: not good enough, that was what she was.

***

The next phone call she took was from Mitchell who had been flapping around in the office the same morning. 'Our different worlds,' he said. 'I just wonder, the thing I half mentioned the other day, I just wonder if you would be interested enough to attend our faculty meeting in May when my research proposal relating to your office is due to be discussed. It would give you some idea of the world I'm coming from.'

She thought for a moment then said, 'Yes I would.'

'I'll get permission from the Dean,' he said. 'Strictly speaking the invitation has to come from the Dean but I am sure it will be all right.'

'I'll look forward to it.'

Why did he phone from the university with his bright ideas when all he had to do was to speak to her when he was in the district? Surely, him being a professor and all, he could not be lacking in confidence to that extent. An odd man.

***

A week after the phone call from Puttock she was chatting in her office to the gadfly that was Mitchell when Dan looked in to tell her he was on his way up to County Hall or, in the deferential tones in which he preferred to announce it, 'The Hall'.

'Again?' she said.

'Afraid so, another briefing on the restructuring from the Director. The MP may be present.'

'I was going to mention the restructuring,' Madge said. 'I had Puttock on the phone recently. It seems you did not keep me in the picture.'

Mitchell stood up, smiling uneasily. 'I'd better leave you to it,' he said, 'don't want to get in the way.' He laughed and then, in turning around, his camera strap caught on and knocked a foot-high heap of papers resting in her in-tray down on to the carpet.

'Terribly, terribly sorry, Madge, let me pick everything up.'

But Madge was staring at a document left behind in the bottom of her in-tray: a brochure entitled *Restructuring Our Social Services for the 1980s* with a photograph of a smiling Director on the cover dated 7 March 1983.

Picking it up she noticed Dan looking decidedly uneasy. When she opened the document she realised the reason why, for as well as the restructuring proposals there was a letter from Puttock with an attached form asking people to say by the end of March if they did NOT want to be considered for early retirement – and explaining the consequences of not replying. This was the 'default 'position' which Puttock had mentioned on the phone – no reply meant opting FOR early retirement.

She turned towards Dan. 'This is the material Puttock told me about on the phone. He said the Director asked you to bring a copy to Area 13 and draw it to my attention. Now how, I wonder, did it get to the bottom of my in-tray?'

'Don't know how that could have happened, Madge, I'm certain I put it on top so you would be sure to see it.'

Madge knew he was lying but how could she prove it when her desk was always in such a terrible mess?

Mitchell looked at her and smiled, the peacemaker. 'I'm terribly sorry, Madge, all my fault,' he said.

'No Mitchell, my disorganised state is partly to blame.' She looked hard at Dan as she emphasised 'partly'.

Dan smiled and said, 'Well, no harm done, but now I must be off to a meeting with the Director. Today he is briefing the local MP on service developments in the matrix of the restructuring plans.'

'What's going on, Madge,' Mitchell asked as soon as Dan had left.

'I suspect dirty work at the pit head.'

'You mean Dan.'

'Nothing I can prove but, yes, I mean Dan.'

What lay behind all Dan's meetings with the Director at County Hall? Now the MP was involved. One fact she could rely on for certain: Dan didn't do loyalty.

Arriving early at work the following morning she closed the door of her office to deter interruptions and carefully wrote out a response to Puttock. The early retirement memo was not a mistake. Not seeing the brochure and the default position form, time-limit now expired, put her in a very vulnerable position. An appropriate grovel did not come easily. A satisfactory first draft proved elusive until she settled for as much grovel as she could live with.

Dear Mr Puttock, I wish it to be known that I do not have, nor ever did have, any intention of retiring at the present time. My intention is, on the contrary, to work with senior management as, in the light of the government-imposed cutbacks in expenditure, the Director's senior managers issue a clarion call to all staff to contribute to the forthcoming structural reorganisation of the department. The new 'cost centres' will require staff with experience and it is my intention, nay determination, that District 13 shall furnish the department with a shining exemplar of the new way forward. Yours faithfully, (Miss) Perfect

Although she knew it might not carry the day she felt elated walking down the corridor to the typists' office where she handed the scribble to Brenda before taking a deep breath of temporary relief. Let Puttock put that in his pipe and smoke it till he choked on his own smoke and died. She would pray for his death to be painful. If anyone mentioned that Puttock was unwell she would just put on her professional sympathy face and mutter under her breath, 'Nothing trivial I hope.'

With her not inconsiderable weight now behind the Director's plans, she had aligned herself with the forces of change. She had so much more to offer than people like Dan, certainly more than Puttock. How could anyone possibly say 'no' to such an offer? Just to be sure she had all eventualities covered she checked in her handbag to make sure that her Labour Party and trade union membership subscriptions were up to date. Also her Co-op membership. And what, just in case the need should arise, oh what was the name of that solicitor who had been so effective recently in the Willings case? Or was it the Miller case? No, no, the Harris case. Well, someone in the past year. She could always find it should it ever be needed.

Before her celebrations went very much further Brenda, waving the draft and shaking her head, caught up with her in the corridor.

'Do you think this is wise? It doesn't sound right,' Brenda said.

'No, I suppose not. You're our wise owl and at times I am a silly old fool. Give it here and I'll have another go.'

The revised version she took through to Brenda read:

I must apologise for not responding in time to the redundancy proposals so clearly laid out in your restructuring document. Due to pressure of work I regret to say that I did not give it sufficient priority. In the circumstances I hope you will reconsider my situation as I very much hope to continue in office and contribute to the Director's restructuring as contained in the inspiring 'Vision' pages of the document.

Brenda glanced at it quickly and said, 'That's better.'

Madge said, 'Sometimes I think you are wiser than the rest of us put together.'

'It's not reflected in me pay,' said Brenda.

On returning to her office Madge slapped her wrist and said quietly, 'You are a very naughty girl.' A good thing, she thought, that her father was no longer around.

'Not good enough, Miss Perfect,' Puttock had said. How strange that he echoed her father's exact words, the jibe he used to trumpet whenever he perceived imperfections in her all those years ago. Was it in men's nature to be unkind to those they held power over, to always find women not good enough? There were times when painful memories of growing up after the death of her mother, her father ruling the roost, few carrots but no shortage of sticks, ruling with the rod of iron, came to mind suddenly and as if from nowhere.

***

Heading up the corridor towards lunch a few days later Simon fell into step beside her. She had noticed how miserable he looked these days; the spark which he brought with him when he came to the office had flared like a lighted match in his friendship with Lorraine. He now looked defeated.

'You all right, Simon?' she asked.

'Sure, Madge.'

'I don't altogether believe you, Simon.'

'It's nothing, well just… I was getting fond of Lorraine but she gave me the old heave ho when Marcus came on the scene. The dull thud she called it. Lorraine and Marcus are an item now and it hurts a bit. I also worry about Lorraine, he's just not right for her.'

Madge had noticed but all she said was, 'I'm sorry. I know how these things can hurt. For a while anyway.' But she thought, What nonsense I spout at times, I know full well that no matter how far back in the past the shadows may lie there are some wounds that never heal.

Simon pulled a face. Madge said, 'Let's console ourselves with lunch, the canteen's finest.'

'Can I remind you we ought to look into a new family from out of the area and now in the Homeless Unit. Friends or relatives of the Farrants, not sure which. Seems there is a young lad. Should I look into it?'

'Priorities, Simon, priorities, and right now the priority is lunch.'

Back at her desk after lunch she noticed a message in Brenda's neat writing on top of a pile of papers: a Mr Barkle had visited the office the previous day wanting to be assessed for a disabled person's car parking badge. Whilst visiting the office he had been shocked to see revolutionary communist posters in support of the miners' demands on all the council notice boards. Speaking as a retired bank manager he had found it absolutely disgraceful that council workers living off his taxes should behave in this reprehensible manner. He would be making a formal complaint to his friend the Chairman of the County Council.

Bugger, she thought, that's all I need. Then she remembered the blind loyalty to Labour that ran through the council as surely as the name Scarborough ran through sickly seaside rock. Much good would it do Mr Barkle to go to the top. No doubt he would settle in the end for venting his political diarrhoea in an acerbic letter in praise of Mrs T and Mr MacGregor to the *Northern Times*. Then to the Prime Minister, perhaps even the Queen. No doubt there would be no strike, all the talk of a strike around the corner would soon blow over, and Mr Barkle would have to eat humble pie. Except his sort never do.

Then she noticed a second message in Mr Barkle's tiny writing:

Miss Perfect,
I complained about various posters and instructed your staff to take down all their left-wing political claptrap. I phoned later in the day but it seemed no action had been taken. So sorry to miss you personally when I called. Can I count on your usual talk to one of my Thursday Club meetings in the New Year? It's early I know, but I have to get the 1984 programme in the bag soon.
Regards, Barkle.

Chapter 6

'That Mitchell's on fire. He's mad I tell you!'

It was a week later when Brenda, clutching a sheaf of referral forms, entered Madge's office trumpeting this startling announcement. Her first thought was for Mitchell; was he injured?

But what she said was, 'I take it you mean Professor Mitchell?' If Madge chose to call him Mitchell that was one thing; for Brenda in Typing to call him that was quite another matter. Or was it? Times were changing just like it said in that irritating song often on the radio. But changing for the better?

'Yes, sorry.'

Madge recognised Mitchell's shortcomings, but he was not mad, eccentric perhaps. 'On fire?' she asked. 'Was it spontaneous combustion?'

'Yes, on fire like I said. On the road into Moortown. In his car, Lorraine saw it.'

'I assume then it was the car not Mitchell on fire?'

Brenda nodded. Madge had begun to wonder why he was late for their meeting but put it down to the relaxed work ethics in the academic community.

Lorraine came in and announced breathlessly, 'Mitchell's on fire! I passed his burning car on my way to work. He was out of the car and standing on the grass verge. Some men from Housing on their way to a job put out the fire.'

Meanwhile Alan passing in the corridor picked up that Mitchell had been on fire. 'Cremated?' he asked. 'Sad is that'.

Brenda, heading back down the corridor, caught the tail end of this and thinking the conversation had moved on to a deceased client said, 'Surely it was a burial, that's what I put down on the client card in my system.'

'No, cremated,' Alan insisted, 'and I thought they's burned the bugger.' No one laughed. It was a very old joke.

'The deceased in me card index cabinet he's…' Brenda said.

'He's what?' Madge said.

'RC. They won't have burnt 'im on account of the Resurrection. It's a thing they believe in ye knaa.'

'I'm sure his immortal soul is safe so long as he stays buried in your system,' Madge said.

'I'll leave 'im down as buried then,' Brenda said.

Half an hour later Mitchell breezed in and announced, 'Sorry I'm late but I've been on fire. Whoosh!'

When he grinned at this Madge shook her head and thought that perhaps he should be entered on a client referral form and added to the team's caseload. Perhaps Brenda was right, perhaps he was mad. Or was he just an overgrown schoolboy? Did this man take nothing seriously?

'Word reached us that you had been cremated. Obviously not. Are you hurt?'

'Cremated? Whoooosh! Only my pride. Fortunately my camera is undamaged.'

'And your car?'

'A write-off, burnt out, I'll have to buy another one.'

'What caused your car to go on fire?'

'Marcus.'

'Surely not Marcus?'

'I cannot be sure but I think that indirectly it was due to Marcus.'

'Marcus set fire to your car?' Surely the man was going mad.

'No, not directly but he told me that one of his student friends knew a lot about cars and could do with some extra cash so I gave the go-ahead and the friend worked on the car over the weekend. It needed a service and this seemed a cheap option. A nice chap too, a school chum from Winchester, Marcus said. So a financial win for the student and for me.'

'Until you caught fire?'

'Yes, I suppose you could say that.'

'I just did.'

Any thought she might have had of recommending Mitchell to the local garage she used evaporated with those words. Clearly the car and perhaps the man were beyond repair. Billy at her garage might take it off Mitchell's hands, bodge it together again, sell it to some mug but no, that was not a good way to go. Fortunately it was the car rather than the man that had been cremated in the poignant scene enacted beside the A167, and that for the moment was that.

To get him out of everybody's way she found him an empty office where he could spend the morning burrowing into further files in the sample of cases identified for his research.

When he was still around at lunchtime she could see no alternative but to ask him to join her in sharing the social and culinary joys of the canteen. As they joined the queue at the serving hatch she handed him a plastic tray from the heap on a trolley. A powerful lungful of air enriched with the steam from overcooked vegetables made her even hungrier. She said she would pay and he accepted gladly. She had no idea how much professors at the university earned. His scruffy working attire in no way pointed to opulence. That was the thing about men: they expected to be waited upon, their underpants washed, socks darned and shirts ironed whereas women were generally capable of taking better care of themselves. There were exceptions of course, Melanie Farrant being but one.

They settled at an empty table where Lorraine and Simon joined them as did a circle of curious men from the council's housing department who formed a group standing next to their table. They were staring suspiciously at Mitchell as if he were newly arrived from the Hebrides.

Mitchell turned to them and grinned. 'Lucky you flagged me down when you did. Frightfully grateful and all that. I didn't realise I was on fire. I can't thank you enough.'

The council men stared back at him. Someone at the back could be heard muttering, 'Whyaye, mebbes a few notes in me back pocket would help.'

Then another voice asked, 'Whyaye man, yer mean to say yer didn't knaa yer was on fire?'

'No, had no idea.' The growing circle of men stared at him in disbelief.

A man to one side asked, 'What set the fire away?'

'A student, a friend of my research assistant, disconnected the fuel line from the petrol tank to the carburettor while he worked on the engine. When he was finished he forgot to reconnect it properly. Petrol leaked from the carburettor hose on to the hot metal of the cylinder block and caught fire. Then whoosh! Of course with the engine in the back I didn't see a thing, just wondered why so many cars were shooting past me with the drivers waving in my direction. Just being friendly I assumed so I waved back. Only when one of you chaps forced me over did I finally suspect a problem. As soon as I turned off the engine the carb stopped pumping petrol on to the cylinder block and things took a turn for the better.'

'Yer mean after we disconnected the battery?'

'Yes, that too.'

'What's your employment then?' asked a voice from the back of the throng.

'I work at the university. I'm a professor at the university.'

'Is that, like, paid employment, or more like voluntary, unpaid?'

'Paid.'

'Whyaye man, that must be a cushy number.'

'Yebuggermar, sounds canny that,' came another voice. 'Yer'll be needing a new motor then?'

'Yes, it's a write-off I'm afraid. I shall have to buy another one.'

'Yer knaa, A might be able to help yer there yer knaa, me brother-in-law sells good motors from a yard just off the High Street. Aback o' the Golden Slipper. Yer'll knaa that place. A'm sure he could fix yer up, nee bother at aal.'

'That's very decent of you but I think I would prefer to go back to the little man I bought the deceased car from. He sells souped-up cars in a field on the edge of Rudham, a chap called Divine, in fact Divine of Divine Motors. Believe it or not I only paid £100 for that Hillman Imp. I'm sure he'll have another of the same for much the same price. You see for me cars are only a means of getting from A to B.'

Madge knew that for the men gathered around them cars bought with council loans over five years were a perk of the job, their one hope of owning a status symbol. A £100 Hillman Imp would never be on their shopping lists. They would not understand this 'A to B' nonsense.

'Whyaye man, yer was daft, yer was robbed there man.'

Mitchell laughed. 'Maybe, but I'm unlikely to be so unlucky a second time. Before I go I wonder if you would mind if I took a photograph of you all? Local interest. I've got my camera with me.'

Madge was finding this scene so embarrassing but knew by now that this was Mitchell as was. But as what? A man who carried a camera in a case around his neck in case he happened on a moment when he wanted to take a local interest snap?

Like examples of primitive peoples posing for a photograph for an anthropologist the Housing men stood before Mitchell with much running banter and then, after a promise from Mitchell to let them have copies, they set off back to their offices laughing though not before Mitchell explained to them how a special device in his camera bag enabled him to take photos at right angles to the subject.

'That way,' he said, 'I can take pictures of people without them knowing I'm doing it.'

'Yebuggermar, you mean tits an stuff like that?'

'Good Lord no, nothing like that.'

Seeing Mitchell relaxed and at ease with the council men suggested he was even less how she imagined a typical academic. Allowing for an accent or two, north versus south, here he was playing along in his own way as one of the lads, not that they would see him as that. But what was a typical academic? She had to admit that she had no idea whatsoever. Rudham University remained a foreign land whose natives belonged to an unknown tribe. It must be such a sane, well-ordered world compared to the world of the social services.

She was starting to quite like Mitchell, his quaint idiosyncrasies, but he was as if from a distant land, a man in need of a lot of mothering and she certainly wasn't going down that road. Before that line of thought went any further she chided herself for taking even a single step along that path.

Walking back down the corridor she overheard two of the council workers still chewing the fat over Mitchell. 'Yer knaa he's a canny enough lad for a professor at the university like.'

'Whyaye, taalks fancy, must be a clivvor bogger an all.'

'Howway man a job like that and getting paid, that's what ah caall clivvor. A cushy number mind. Ah wish ah'd got Coonsellor Brown behind us and gone in for that job.'

***

Mitchell phoned the following morning. 'I'm rushing off to the darkroom to print up some negatives – the dark arts eh – just wanted you to know the faculty meeting is a week on Wednesday 4 May at 2.15. I don't think the Dean altogether liked the idea – "an outsider, not one of us" sort of thing – but I explained about the research project and though he hates the idea of sociology he warms to the Home Office research grants and publications I bring in for the university. In any event we have his blessing, sort of.'

'How kind,' she said. How patronising, she thought.

She did not know whether to be pleased or curious or just anxious and when she thought about it decided it must be some of all of these things. But what about County Hall, how might they react? There were policies and rules that covered almost every possible contact between staff at various levels and outside bodies. Only the Director could speak to the press but this was not the media. Should she inform the Director? Did she require his permission to accept the invitation? Would she have to be accompanied by the Director? Would the Director take over the invitation and attend without her? Would he send one of his beehive of underlings in his stead? Puttock perhaps? It simply did not bear thinking about. Sometimes it was just too difficult trying to remember all the rules of the game, what was policy, what down to local discretion and what sanction followed which misdemeanour. There might be repercussions if she went to the meeting on her own and without the Director's prior knowledge. She decided in the end that she was just past caring.

And then there was 'What shall I wear?' Nothing fitted, nothing suited her, no outfits that were even slightly smart awaited in her wardrobe. She had to nag Mitchell repeatedly before he proffered advice. His eventual response was unhelpful if unequivocal: 'Dress sedately and conduct yourself with decorum.' This came as a general relief to her as it best suited her own instincts in the matter. But after experiencing initial feelings of relief she was left with some anxiety as to the particular. She could easily slip into 'decorum' mode, for after all that was the code of everyday dress and behaviour she demanded of herself. On the other hand, a Saturday trawl round the clothes shops in Rudham City only served to confirm that nothing on sale nowadays was to her liking, almost all of it targeted at young women with pencil-slim figures. In the old days women wore dresses or a skirt and blouse; now it was not uncommon to see a woman in trousers and not just in leisure time. If this went any further women would end up looking like men, behaving like men and feeling like men.

She thought back to the days when she had been a teenager preparing for an important date. That was no help at all. Lipstick, brightly coloured lipstick plus her glad rags. Not much else. It was all so different then. She seldom thought back to her teenage years, for after those magical dates there had been years of emptiness. Till now? A date? Was that what Mitchell had done, dated her? No, that was ridiculous. Yet nothing about his research on her patch of the social services department stood to be advanced in any way by her attending this meeting. And if it was a date was this what she had come down to: listening to a room full of old fossils talking about subjects foreign to her? Why, why, had she agreed?

Chapter 7

Dan was suspicious when she told him about the faculty meeting.

'Why did he ask you? What's the purpose of it?'

'I don't really know,' Madge said, which was true.

Dan came back at her: 'About Mitchell's research project. You have not briefed me fully on that.'

'I'll know more about it after the faculty meeting this afternoon.'

'Hmmm,' Dan said, and when he said 'Hmmm' it usually signalled his displeasure. 'Does the Director know about this? You will let me know how it goes, won't you?'

Cheek. She nodded anyway and then Dan continued, 'Tomorrow morning the Director has invited me to attend another briefing meeting with the local MP. I'll ask the Director what Mitchell is up to.'

She left it at that. How could she possibly hope to explain to him that the business of social work was people, not meetings of bureaucrats? Then, quite suddenly, it came to her: Mr Barkle had asked her to give another talk on her work to his Thursday Club. She would accept but what if, yes, what if she invited Dan to come along too, perhaps even give the talk? He would meet a cross-section of local people, admittedly the more affluent and better-ordered section of Moortown society, but the retired professionals amongst them, the one or two town councillors, were of some local significance, the sort of people that Area 13 must keep on side in support of the work that statute demanded of them. Dan, if he was to progress as he hoped to a more senior position, must learn the skills of diplomacy needed to keep the department displayed in a positive light. With a smidgeon of luck he might even come away with a better understanding of the people they served.

Next time she spoke to Dan she must suggest this to him; surely some part of him buried at whatever depth must be capable of change?

***

Come the day of the faculty meeting Madge was all a fluster. Had she chosen the right clothes? Would she be able to park? Rudham, the city, she knew hardly at all apart from the shopping area around the Market Place. Would she find the university? To someone like her who worked in and lived near dreary little Moortown a visit to the capital city was a rarity, beyond the shops in the city centre its university an unknown world, perhaps unknowable.

So she consulted the *Tourist Guide to the North of England*:

The ancient city of Rudham, capital of Rudham County, stands astride a hill from which it surveys large tracts of the county, its city status resulting from the decision of an eleventh-century property developer to build a massive stone pile above a bend in the river. When the developer, Lord & Co, used a full page spread in an early edition of the Northern Times to advertise his willingness to 'buy up your old hovel if you buy one of my new homes' (translated from the original Latin), people on the way up in the world rushed to put down their deposits on even a draughty corner in the new build housing estate. Keen to emphasise the appeal Mr Lord, who knew a unique selling point when he saw one, called his development 'The Cathedral' and established within its walls a Gifte Shoppe and Tea Roome. Cream Teas had come to Rudham.

So also came to Rudham the unelected Prince Bishops who ruled large swathes of the north of England. Being gentlemen of the cloth they knew a bargain when they saw one. In the passage of time much that is worthy came to be written about such structures and Pevsner is the obvious starting point for anyone wishing to delve deeper into the history of 'The Cathedral'. By 1983 it attracted coach parties coming from far and wide to tour the ancient building.

In 1983 the city boasted four other structures of note: Rudham Prison, Rudham Castle, the scattered campus premises of the University of Rudham, and Rudham County Hall.

A prison is a prison is a prison. Castles being thick on the ground in this part of the world no *more need be said of this particular motte and bailey example, apart from the fact that this is one of the few examples remaining largely intact, perhaps because renovation work is financially feasible now that it accommodates the better class of undergraduate attending the University of Rudham, the sort who feel at home in castles and can take their turn to say a Latin grace before meals in Hall, those who can be relied on not to steal the silver at Judges' Dinners.*

In the university, motto Veritas vos Liberabit, *'the truth shall set you free', staff and students labour tirelessly in the pursuit of knowledge for its own sake, in the quest for right and wrong, for what is beautiful and, above all, for what 'is'. Teaching and research are noble callings and at Rudham inspiration is drawn from roots reaching deep into the enriching manure of European culture.*

In the Easter Term student thoughts begin to turn to the upcoming end of year examinations while staff thoughts turn to a respite from the students during the summer vacation in their gites in France or villas in Spain. In spite of separate men's and women's colleges it is not unknown for sex to break out, sometimes even between students from different social classes. These occurrences are not always restricted to the students alone; there have in the past been episodes involving members of staff or, more exceptionally, perhaps better concealed, liaisons between male staff and female students.

Thus armed she headed for the metropolis.

***

She had decided on a neatly ironed white blouse with a long navy skirt. As a concession to the occasion she had bought a new pair of shoes and in case of rain she remembered to put her umbrella in the car as well as a cardigan in case it turned colder.

Mitchell was waiting in the entrance and greeted her warmly. With a good fifteen minutes to go before the start he planted her firmly on a bench at the rear of the hall in the area formerly reserved for the press in the days when this had been the chamber where the council met.

'You look good, just the right end of smart for an occasion of this monumental insignificance,' Mitchell said as he greeted her.

'A compliment I'm sure,' she said. But she wasn't sure. Was it a compliment or a put-down?

'No smoking, and no eating crisps,' Mitchell admonished her as he hitched his black gown on to his shoulder and left to take his place among the other gowned academics who were chattering like caged budgerigars while shuffling voluminous piles of paper. She noticed they were mostly men, the older specimens in suits as, so she noticed to her surprise, was Mitchell. A few among the younger generation wore jeans and open-necked shirts. The few women seemed to be about her own age and certainly no smarter than herself. One in particular was growing a quite extraordinary crop of straggling grey hair which seemed to reach for the ceiling where it did not trail in search of the floor.

The hard wooden seats formed a semi-circle facing a large table behind which sat an important-looking little man she took to be the Dean of Arts. He was stocky as a beer barrel and had a very red face.

When he winked and half smiled at her, perhaps remembering that he had permitted Mitchell to invite her to attend, she avoided returning eye contact thinking the man might simply be exhibiting a nervous tic. But when he winked at her again her reflexes returned a coy wink she never intended. She leaned her head over to the right to avoid his gaze only to find him leaning his head in sympathy. Lean to the left and he mirrored her movement. In desperation she stared up at the ceiling.

Then she heard the Dean say, 'May I call the meeting to order.' No one took the slightest notice. He spoke with a slight stammer. He cleared his throat, raised his voice and said it again.

The meeting had not been in progress for very long before her silent observer status led to the yawns she knew to be inevitable; it had been a tiring week and worrying about this meeting had kept her awake most of the previous night. Now falling asleep could not be ruled out. And so it came to pass.

When she shuddered back to wakefulness the Dean was wrinkling his shiny red nose and staring at her. What a wonderful Santa Claus he would make. Perhaps she might invite him to do just that at the Area 13 Christmas party for children. She hoped she hadn't yawned loudly, or exhibited flatulence while asleep. Had she snored? Embarrassed Mitchell? Disgraced Area 13? It was too bad. I must look away quickly, she thought, in case the Dean starts winking at me again. She looked over to where Mitchell was sitting; his head drooped forward; surely he had not dozed off?

The first item she was conscious of concerned the syllabus for modern English as published in the university calendar of courses. It quickly became apparent that almost everybody present had views on modern English quite regardless of their own subject specialism. After half an hour of nit-picking a scrawled note was passed back to her through the ranks of social scientists: '*The Eng. Lit. prof has apparently decided that "modern" begins and ends with the publication of* Pamela – *no room for Hemingway, Joyce etc. in the syllabus! Ciaran Mitchell.*'

What was the man on about? Who was Pamela? She knew about Hemingway and had once read one of his books. Something about hunting in Africa. Or was it boxing? Or a murder? Was she confusing it with things she had once read about the author in a magazine? Then it came to her: it was a short story, a murder. She remembered men talking in clipped snatches of speech; she had even imagined their American accents. My, what a long time it had been since she had last read a proper book rather than a succession of social services reports.

The champion of real Eng. Lit. won the day: at Rudham there would be nothing in the English syllabus that had been published in the last hundred years. Or was it two hundred?

Mitchell's note: so he was Ciaran. She had up till now only known him as Mitchell, Professor Mitchell. Rolling the name 'Ciaran' around in her mind made him seem for the first time a little more human, something beyond the fact that he was a man researching service delivery for the people industry. Ciaran Mitchell. Perhaps there was an Irish connection? Not once had he used his first name till now. For some reason it would be difficult to think of him as a 'Ciaran'.

Irishness might be a problem if she were to see more of him, for taken to extremes, according to her father, it usually meant that the slightest encouragement would lead on to a good deal of stuff and nonsense about the potato famine, mass emigration and it all being the fault of the English. Her father had disapproved of the Irish, all the Irish, any hint of Irishness, for high amongst their vices was the tendency to thieve and rebel against the British Crown. Her father held views about peoples who rebelled against the Crown. But Ciaran was a nice name even if he did not look or sound like a Ciaran. No, she would continue to see him more as 'Mitchell'. Mitchell was better suited to an academic researcher. It somehow endowed him with more bottom, a man who did not look or sound like a thief, a man unlikely to plant a bomb. And when she paused to think about it, and remembered him unencumbered by his academic gown, she had noticed a bottom she rather liked. Liked? Yes, fancied was too big a word.

When the English Literature syllabus discussion was finally put to rest the next item on the agenda involved arguments over changes to the Divinity syllabus. Half an hour was devoted to the planned substitution of *Romans IV* for *Romans V* in the calendar of courses with the Professor of Theology and the Professor of Divinity going hammer and tongs as one argued the need for change as the other pressed the case for constancy. The Dean smiled amiably throughout, apparently unable or unwilling to guide or limit the discourse.

Cometh the hour, cometh the sociologist. As the afternoon wore on the agenda reached Mitchell's turn to introduce his research proposal but even as he got to his feet to speak the Dean suddenly came to life, shuffling his papers ever more urgently.

'Five minutes, five minutes maximum, Professor Mitchell, it is the very end of the afternoon. I am sure we are all in urgent need of a cup of tea and, well, you know what! Ha! Ha!'

She listened carefully as Mitchell introduced his proposal in calm, measured tones. She was impressed by the clarity of his thought, at the articulate way he laid out his arguments like landscaped gardens, his voice firm. He said he hoped his proposal was no more than a formality, informing faculty of his work with the county council, how he had looked to this meeting to confirm his way forward. He lacked the near hysteria exhibited by the previous speakers. Clearly there was more to this man than she had realised.

She was therefore all the more surprised when, Mitchell hardly having sat down, the Professor of Divinity, allowed free rein by the Dean, launched into an attack on the proposal.

'Through the Chair, Dean, do they do it in Oxford?'

'I will ask for you. Professor Mitchell, can you help the Professor of Divinity with this one?'

'Yes, they do,' Mitchell said confidently.

'Ah, no need to do it here then, Dean,' said the Professor of Divinity, very slowly as if signifying great authority. The Dean glanced at his watch and nodded assent.

In an instant Mitchell was back on his feet, his tone and demeanour conciliatory. 'No, Dean, my mistake, my reply lacked clarity, they assuredly do not do it at Oxford University, not quite in the way that we intend. I apologise for misleading faculty.'

The Dean was starting to close up his folder of papers.

'But, but faculty is missing my point,' insisted Mitchell, 'they do it in Oxford – but not at *the* university.'

'Well then,' asked the Dean with no attempt to hide his exasperation, 'where do they do it, man? In the public lavatories, in the public houses, in the schools, as a so-called vocational qualification, or at one of those frightful things called technical colleges? I believe that's what they're called?' As he said 'technical' his face crunched into a grimace.

'No, at a university, but not at *the* university, at the polytechnic which as you know is very like a university.'

Shock horror, she thought, is anything, anywhere like a university! The very idea of it! Cymbals would crash and the world would end at the sound of these words. But how different all of this was from life in Area 13.

The Dean had obviously exhausted his patience. 'Enough, enough, gentlemen, this item is of necessity postponed to our next meeting. Now, next item. Ah! Tea of course,' he snapped, having clearly listened to enough of what he seemed to regard as this sociology nonsense. He rose to his feet and announced, 'Of course there are no other items so unless there is anything else we need to discuss I declare the meeting closed.'

Afterwards as she caught up with Mitchell leaving the building she offered commiserations.

'You work in a madhouse,' she said.

He smiled and said, 'Sometimes I wonder how much longer I can stand it. Have you time for a quick drink?'

'It might just save my life.'

They walked past the prison to the hotel around the corner. In the Ladies' bar she asked, 'What's yours?' not knowing why but trying to be Hemingway by affecting an American accent ridiculous in its inaccuracy.

'Are you getting?' he said.

'Yes, the age of equality.'

'A beer please, McEwans. But the accent?'

'Hemingway, short story, *The Killers*, if I remember right. Not suitable for Rudham obviously.'

'Much too modern I'm afraid. So you're a bit of a reader then?'

'Not enough, not recent. Funny that. I was thinking when modern English was being discussed how I read some Hemingway when I was young and hence the attempt at a drawl.' She laughed. 'That was how I imagined the Hemingway characters speaking.'

Now they both laughed. Mitchell said, 'They all sound the same do they? Perhaps practice makes perfect. But I am interested to find another Hemingway fan.'

'In my dreams perhaps, in my fantasies though I see myself more as Ingrid Bergman in *Casablanca*. But I must catch up with some more Hemingway. I have to say that although I hated his subject matter I did admire his writing. Not a word wasted. It was all so different from the dreary reports I have to write at work.'

He laughed. 'I have to write those too.'

When she returned from the bar with their drinks and joined him at a table near the window she blurted out, 'May I call you Ciaran?'

'Of course.'

It was a nice name, it suited him, she might get used to saying it, and the sound of it could become familiar if only she said it more often but no, Mitchell did suit him better.

He had agreed but she was sure that it didn't feel right so she said, 'Do you mind if I don't, if I stick to Mitchell?'

'As you wish,' he said, sipping his beer, looking puzzled.

Madge felt silly so she changed the subject. 'Who is this Pamela woman in your note to me?'

'Ah,' he replied, laughing again, 'so you aren't up to date with the Rudham modern Eng. Lit. syllabus! It's an early novel.'

She smiled but said nothing more. She was almost ready to concede that Mitchell was interesting and beginning to be fun. She would have to hunt down *Pamela*; time must be found for a visit to the Moortown public library.

So far there had been no mention of the potato famine, a good sign. Then she reined in these wild thoughts, drew back into her shell. She must not even think along those lines, she who had vowed years ago that there would be no further disappointments in her life.

'Are your faculty meetings always like that?'

'Always, mad, mad,' he replied.

'How dreadful for you. And I thought I worked in an asylum cunningly disguised as a county council.' Before her floated a vision of that institution, the nerve centre in the concrete building that from a distance looked like a beached ocean liner surrounded by acres of car parks, and beyond that a scrubland of semi-attached 'villas'.

'Perhaps it is the world that's mad,' Mitchell said, the froth from his beer lining his lips, 'but my fellow inmates capitulate in the end, or lose interest, find another mouthful of gristle to chew on. Change is what unsettles them. In another ten or twenty years they won't exist, professors of moral philosophy, logic and metaphysics, Latin, Greek and divinity, and most modern foreign languages – they will be gone in all but a handful of universities. The Professor of Divinity and the Professor of Theology only survive because this is a cathedral city. Before them the Professor of Logic and Metaphysics will bite the dust. Anyway, in the absence of a better alternative, it suits me for now.'

'And your sociology?'

'Mrs T will see to that and she controls the purse strings. She doesn't believe in society. No such thing apparently. Besides, we are all seen as raving Trotskyists.'

'But in our society, our clients, their communities, Moortown, Brownlow, what are they part of?'

'I would say "society" but there are those who see us as no more than unconnected motes of dust, freewheeling around in a breeze, just hanging around waiting to be flicked away with a feather duster.'

He lifted his glass, drank deeply, then eyed her through the distorting lens of his half-empty glass.

'All that sounds sad in a way,' she said. He leaned towards her and she caught a sniff of the beer as he took a deep breath. It was such a long time since she had been that close to a man smelling of beer: first her father and then the man who went away. She edged back in her chair.

Now he was well into a speech: 'Perhaps. Not just poor old English Prof, in ten years' time he will be lucky if he's still in a job even if it is a different job turning out teachers of English as a foreign language or a new breed of so-called creative writers. Left to himself he would pull the shutters down at *Beowulf* or, on a good day, Chaucer. In no time at all they will be drowned out by the men in charge of the new vocational subjects they so despise. Pasternak said it all when he wrote something like, "We do not need their PhDs to tell us Pushkin was a writer when all the time we knew he was poor blighter". At times I feel sorry for them all. University education is changing and somewhere deep down they must know that.'

'Pasternak?' she asked.

'Boris, Russian, *Dr Zhivago.*'

'Of course, I saw the film, seems such a long time ago now, I remember Omar Sharif as the doctor. Yum! Lots of snow. I must look for a copy of the book. But as for change I just wish I could point to the impending demise of the bureaucrats in County Hall, the men in suits, given the way the social services are going.'

'Who knows where the wind may blow, what leaves it may scatter to the gutters?' he said. 'At least your crowd all suffer from apparent sanity. Some of my university colleagues are mad as hatters. Take Divinity. He was well today but there are times when he flips completely, totally, and has to be locked up in the local bin for a few weeks and fed with a concoction of drugs which eventually bring him back to what passes for normal in his case.'

'Under the Mental Health Act? A compulsory admission?

'Oh I don't know the detail except that sometimes when he refuses to go of his own volition first a mental welfare officer and then a doctor and an ambulance come to take him away with the police in support.'

'Extraordinary! And the university stands for all that?'

'Yes, he is well liked by the students who line up on the college steps and raise three hearty cheers as the ambulance drives off from the college forecourt. He has a list of learned publications as long as your arm.'

'Extraordinary. Will the new people you describe be mostly men?'

'I would bet money on it. With very few exceptions I'm afraid.'

'Some things never change.'

'No, slowly if at all. But not all things move slowly, take the coal industry, just look at the slag heaps grassed over around Moortown, jobs have been obliterated, communities have died. There's worse to come if this strike goes ahead.'

'It won't, will it?'

'Don't know. Scargill and Thatcher seem hell bent on a fight.'

'But your academics, the divines and their kind, surely they ought to be able to think more flexibly, more logically than Mrs T and Arthur S?'

'Did you see evidence for that this afternoon? The Professor of Logic and Metaphysics was silent this afternoon, probably asleep, but you ought to behold him in full flow. Flexible, logical? Quite the contrary I'm afraid.'

'Some of it sounds more sad than bad.'

'We all find ways of getting by. I take my brain out,' he said, miming the action of opening a flap at the front of his head and removing the contents. 'Yes, I take my brain out and leave it in the lockers in the entrance hall every time I go to a faculty meeting.'

'Do you actually enjoy your work?' she asked.

'Yes, if it's the research side but even then some of my left-wing colleagues hate me for taking Home Office research grants. Most of their time is taken up arguing the finer points of Marxist ideology or extolling the virtues of Mao's China or Castro's Cuba or Nyerere's Tanzania. They see those as promised lands a future Britain ought to embrace. Cloud-cuckoo land. Over on the right most of the snobby academics regard sociology as a joke, intellectually sloppy and the work of devils – Marx, Lenin and their kind. The admin, the bureaucracy which is part of the job is a bore. But I enjoy teaching; the students come to us with such open minds, such energy. Sadly some of my colleagues soon iron that sort of nonsense out of them.'

'Would you miss it?'

'The research, the students, yes, I think so. Most of the things the university stands for not at all. Trouble is the two go together, no university, no research and teaching. But what about you?'

'Increasingly I feel like I work in a welfare system that cares less and less – not what brought me into social work in the beginning. Like you I find good things: the people we serve, some colleagues.'

'Not your Dan, I suspect,' he said.

'No, not Dan. Recently the silly early retirement memo made me think about a few things, my future I suppose. Suddenly I am less sure about where I am now, where I want to be in future. But I suppose for me there is, well, how to put it, no other world I know. Change seems impossible. And there I was assuming your world would be different and better ordered than mine, full of clever people doing good things and making a difference. After what I saw this afternoon I'm far from sure of that.'

'Perhaps all institutions are madhouses of a kind, differentiated only by the signs at the gate.'

'Now we are getting serious! Perhaps we should both escape.'

'But, escape to what, that is the question. *Ne plus ultra.*'

'Mitchell, whenever you talk sense you always go and spoil it all by talking clever.' There it was, she was back to calling him 'Mitchell' not 'Ciaran'. She felt more comfortable that way.

'Except it's not very clever, just means no more beyond, for both of us perhaps.'

She laughed and felt happy.

'Another drink?' he asked. 'My turn. What's yours?' His American accent didn't work very well either.

'Same again I think.'

'Another G and T?'

When he came back with their drinks she broached the delicate subject of her imagined view of his secretary. As he listened to her fumbled question he smiled gently. 'No, to be frank she's a bit dreary really, in her fifties, well turned out, the cut-glass accent a bit forced, probably had elocution lessons, working-class Sheffield originally I think, let herself go a bit, off the pace fashion wise, a dowdy dresser, I'm always surprised when she doesn't turn up in a moth-eaten twinset and chipped pearls and with soup stains down her front. Sometimes I think she fancies me a little, ridiculous really, certainly not mutual.'

'And your wife?' He sat upright at this and looked down at his feet. 'No, no wife… there was once but she became fed up with the poverty – her word – of the academic life and married a successful writer or something, moved to Oxford, haven't seen her for years. She was beautiful, could be fun. Part of her plan was for me to take on the discarded wife of the successful writer but I said "no". We had no children. I would have liked children.'

They sat silently for a while, Madge surveying the students and academics conversing urgently, joking loudly, and frequently calling for more beer. No shortage of money among these motes of dust. Mitchell was now ill at ease, downing his drink in apparent haste. He looked restless and he confirmed this, saying, 'I must head off to the university photographic society meeting. We're working in the darkroom this evening.'

'You're a serious snapper then?'

He nodded and said, 'See you again in Moortown,' before threading his way through the throng of students in the bar area, heading for the door. Madge swallowed what was left of her drink then followed down the corridor towards the sign saying 'Ladies'. Reaching it she joined a queue with no equivalent queue beside the sign saying 'Gents'. The age of equality, she reflected, is not yet upon us. There was a time when she accepted these things as part of the natural order; not now, she made a mental note to write to the head of the company that owned the hotel complaining that the facilities for women were inadequate.

If this faculty meeting she had witnessed bore any resemblance to what went on in the rest of the university then clearly a proportion of the inmates were as mad as mad can be. Alongside them the officers of Rudham County Council were relatively sane. Even Puttock.

And Mitchell? Yes, she did like him but clearly this was not mutual. What had she done that caused him to rush off like that? The mention of his wife? Why use photography as a silly excuse? But 'Mitchell' the name? Yes, she would stick to 'Mitchell'. And yes, she had enjoyed spending time in the company of someone who was neither a colleague nor a client. She was curious to know more of this other world. Perhaps if she had met the right man at the right time more might have been possible. But there had been a right man in the once upon a time before he went away. Now it was too late.

It might be good to get back to reading proper books.

If only there was time enough. Driving home slightly tiddly and not wanting to look ignorant in front of the professor another time she determined to look into this Pamela woman and the man called Pasternak. But for the moment all she could think of were the new shoes and how they were hurting. They were new so there could not be pebbles lodged towards her toes but that was what it felt like. In spite of that she felt happier than she had been for as many years as she could remember. The funny thing was, not once had they discussed his research proposal; there was time enough tomorrow for all of that, time enough tomorrow, just like Lorraine always said.

And Mitchell the man? She would not give up without knowing more. Companionship, something outside work, that might be nice; certainly she would not want nor could she expect any more than that. She knew by now not to aspire or hope any further.

A week later Mitchell phoned to say he was off to France on holiday. Marcus would also be away, he knew not where. They would resume the research on their return.

MICHAELMAS TERM
1983

Chapter 8

For Madge the summer flitted by with work and spare time gardening round the cottage. The grand designs she had for the garden – a herbaceous border, a rose bed, a water feature – never came close to fruition but at least she was clear of most of the weeds come September.

But there was more than that to her summer. In every free moment it was the incident with Puttock, and the part Dan may have played in it, which left her anxious by day and tossing restlessly at night. Puttock had not replied to her memo and this lapse into silence increased her unease. At times it seemed to her that Dan or Puttock, perhaps both, were out to get her. When time passed without a reply to her grovelling memo her anxiety increased: what was going on up at County Hall? Why was Dan spending so much time there in the company of Puttock and the Director? Why did Dan never report back after his visits there? What did he know about the early retirement issue? How should she interpret his hints about an impending reorganisation of the department? The questions just multiplied but answers came there none. Something was brewing, but what?

And added to these gnawing worries was Mitchell. Why on earth, she wondered, was she worrying about

Mitchell? After the university term ended Mitchell and his camera bags had disappeared to France. Marcus and Lorraine went to Spain for a fortnight and when she returned Lorraine said it was just like Cape Town. Madge decided not to bother going away. If the weather was nice, she would put her car's fitness to the test with a run up the dales to Barnard Castle one Saturday or Sunday. She had always liked the silver swan in the museum there and no matter how often she watched its mechanical movements she always felt the same childlike excitement.

Meanwhile the work of the office went on remorselessly, her staff coming back in turn from their annual leave with endless snaps she felt bound to admire. Lorraine was wonderfully tanned, Brenda looking at her legs and wondering aloud how high up her thighs the golden tan would turn to pale white skin that had not seen the sun. Alan was of the view that it was most likely that it was gold all the way. And while he was at it he would like to check out her buttocks. No one thought to ask Marcus and he wasn't saying.

***

In October every year the academic machine cranks back into action. As autumn takes hold of the weather professors, lecturers, researchers and administrators troop back to the watery sun of Rudham. Parent cars loaded with music systems, guitars, clothes freshly laundered and ironed by mums convey excited freshers to their residential colleges segregated by social class and gender. A few days later the old hands troop in and make it abundantly plain that seniority rules. Fresh sightings of Mitchell and Marcus began to be seen in Moortown and Brownlow.

Mitchell drifted back to his project tanned from his French exposure and excited by his snaps – photographs he preferred to call them or, better still images.

Asked about his holiday all he said was, 'Glad to be back. I was lonely, can't think why, usually enjoy my own company.'

Madge found him distant, preoccupied and no longer much interested in chatting to her. Where once he had encouraged a friendship which she thought to be mutual and capable of growth he now seemed only able to give his attention to his number crunching. Perhaps he had found a friendship among the university women? Might he be in love? What had she done to dowse their friendship?

***

Mitchell returned just as the office was facing up to the incident of the horse. Like so many things over in Brownlow it was the Farrants who held centre stage.

It was early in October when Lorraine came into Madge's office and announced, 'The Farrants have acquired a horse.' This came as no surprise to Madge for without doubt the Farrants could boast horse thieves going back in the family for several generations.

The arrival of the horse caused her no immediate concern. Even the Farrants would hesitate to apply to the DHSS for allowances for riding lessons, saddle, reins, jodhpurs, boots, a riding crop, helmet, bridle and bit, let alone Pony Club membership. Clearly stabling was not an expense about to impact on the public purse. They might in time have the brass neck to ask for help with hay and veterinary bills but not today, their actions were seldom planned in advance. If food for the horse became a crisis then a demand for instant help would most likely land on her desk just as the office was closing for the weekend late one Friday afternoon. She would of course reject payment for such a claim knowing full well that it would benefit the pub trade rather than the horse.

It was only when Lorraine added that they were 'keeping it in an upstairs bedroom' that Madge straightened her back ready to address the enormity of the task before them.

The Farrants might argue that as the legal tenants they had the right to live as they chose with a horse which they would no doubt insist was legally theirs. In the unlikely event that the council housing department had a clause in the lease stipulating 'no horses in upstairs bedrooms' it might take months to secure an enforcement notice. As so often happened occurrences that fell between the cracks in the wider welfare services ended up on her desk. Her instinctive feeling was that this was not the last she would hear of the horse.

'You should be telling this to Dan not to me,' she said in exasperation.

'Dan's not in today.'

Typical, Miss Perfect thought but did not say, absolutely typical.

'Is the horse causing an immediate problem?' she asked.

'Ja, man, you see, it's upstairs in the front bedroom with its head out of the window. The cops are demanding we do something as there have been several near-miss car accidents with drivers glancing up at the horse's head staring back at them from the bedroom window.'

To emphasise her point Lorraine made a loud horse noise, or what Madge took to be an attempt at a horse noise, sufficient in any event to bring Brenda running down the corridor.

'Is everything all reet?' she asked.

'Yes, if it wasn't for the horse.'

'What horse?'

'I'm just trying to find an answer to the very same question,' Madge said before asking Lorraine, 'Please tell me more?'

'Ach, it's laughing at the poor bloody motorists and the housing department want us to do something.'

'Why us?'

'Because the Farrants have applied to the council for a larger house on the grounds that they now have a horse.'

Do what exactly? Miss Perfect wondered. Like, why oh why is Dan never here at these times?

'Have you tried the RSPCA?' she asked.

Lorraine nodded. 'They say they're short-staffed and anyway it's nothing to do with them if the animal is not being ill-treated. The woman I spoke to just laughed, said it was a pity more people didn't treat their horses as well as that. Even asked if I had checked the bed was comfortable enough and was there a dressing table with a supply of make-up. I am due to make a routine visit in an hour with Marcus. What shall I do?'

'Am I right in thinking Marcus is a hunting, shooting, fishing man?'

'Ja.'

'Excellent, that means he knows about horses, the man is custom-made for the job. I hereby appoint him volunteer officer-in-charge of Operation Horse. Brief him accordingly. Report back to base after your visit.'

Dan appeared in the doorway. 'What horse?'

'I thought you were not in today,' Madge said. 'In any event it's sorted. The Farrants have acquired a horse. They're keeping it upstairs in a bedroom. Lorraine and Marcus are tasked to sort it out.'

Brenda asked, 'Do you think that's wise leaving it to those two?' Lorraine scowled.

'Probably not,' Madge said, 'but I have no better ideas where our new client, the horse, is concerned.'

Dan said, 'A bit dodgy, Marcus is not employed by the council so we aren't covered by the insurance if anything goes wrong.'

'Fiddlesticks,' said Madge. 'Marcus is a hunting, shooting, fishing man. Horses are in his breeding. Nothing is going to go wrong.'

'Should I enter a card for the horse as a client in the filing system?' Brenda asked.

'No, just put it in under Farrant.'

'Is that council policy?' Brenda said before seeing the expression on Madge's face. She scurried off down the corridor just as the phone rang. It was PC Pyott from the Moortown police station. 'It's about a horse, Miss P, not normally your line of business ah know but…'

'Jim, not to worry, I've got my best man, a volunteer actually, on the case. We can all sleep soundly in our beds tonight.'

'Do ah know him?'

'Unlikely.'

'His name?'

'Marcus something or other.'

'Foreign?' Jim asked.

'No, just sounds it but red, white and blue runs through him from head to toe.'

'Thanks anyway, Miss P.'

Having reassured Jim she did not like to mention that Marcus was from London. Jim distrusted anyone who belonged south of Darlington. In truth he also had misgivings about people from Darlington, every one of whom he believed to be a Quaker. Though normally a peaceable man, for some reason he regarded Quakers with great distrust.

'That's the horse sorted,' Madge said to Brenda.

At that moment Mitchell appeared in the doorway and said, 'What horse?'

Madge and Brenda laughed. 'Too difficult to explain right now,' Madge said, 'but I've borrowed your operative by the name of Marcus to sort it all out with Lorraine.'

Days like these she would sorely miss were she to be booted down the road to early retirement. But that was a big if. No way, if necessary up and at 'em it would have to be. She was determined to remain at what people, for reasons that eluded her, liked to call the coal face in spite of the fact that there were no longer pits in the area.

***

Mitchell, chirpy once again, phoned later in October one morning at ten. 'Not too early for you I hope?'

Silly question, she had been at work for almost two hours. This man could be irritating. Meetings with him might be better spaced out like cats eyes on a road, useful and reliable, safety aids with welcome gaps.

'No, fine,' she said.

'I just wondered – following our conversation after the faculty meeting earlier in the year – if you would like to see a little more of my world. The thing is our Michaelmas Term Founder's Day dinner at Green College, my college, is a week on Wednesday, short notice I know but I just wondered' – she sensed the tension in his voice – 'if you would care to join me as my guest for the evening? Might that interest you? I owe you a meal after the feast I enjoyed with your colleagues in the canteen which reminds me I never did give them copies of the photos I took then. I must bring them next time.'

'That's kind of you, Mitchell,' she said. 'Of course I shall have to consult my social diary.'

'Please do then get back to me.'

She laughed. 'No need as it happens. My non-existent social diary would show me as free that evening. Yes, of course I'd love to.'

Did he find communication by telephone safer than a rejection in person? Surely he could have broached the subject on one of his many visits to the office? Surely he could have given her more notice? Why had he become friendlier once again? If she really intended to expand her interests outside her work could there ever be room for Mitchell? Perhaps, strange man that he was, she should look on him as no more than a hobby, an alternative to basket weaving or Scrabble or, perish the thought, the Women's Institute.

From that moment all the usual anxieties began to flow. Why had she said 'yes' so impulsively, without giving the implications a moment's thought? What could she wear? Would all the other guests be younger, cleverer, and more attractive than her? Would she be out of her depth? Would…? The world she had glimpsed at the faculty meeting was foreign, topsy-turvy, and perhaps even mad. Her world was safer, familiar, peopled by characters, clients and colleagues, not without faults but possessing the virtue of things known. She was fond of most of her clients, liked to think of them as her adopted family. Colleagues, most colleagues, were people for whom she felt a certain affection. Over time she had served all of them in their hours of crisis. Even Mitchell, who did not have the benefit of her training, had pointed out that it seemed to meet some need deep down in her psyche.

Chapter 9

Her car was once again making extraordinarily vulgar noises, hiccoughing and belching her to and from work and around the district. It was time to nurse the juddering monster back to Billy's garage.

A strangulated hernia might be the problem. Her knowledge of medical conditions was slightly ahead of her grasp of matters mechanical but by combining the two she could usually arrive at an approximation to what might be ailing her car. For one who failed to fully understand the workings of the internal combustion engine her belief that similar phenomena occurred in people helped, even if the terminology might vary.

Social work salvation as taught to her lay in the words of Florence Hollis who had laid down the ground rules from across the Atlantic: study problems from all angles, reach a diagnosis, develop a treatment plan, and assess the outcomes. Force-fed *Casework: a psychosocial therapy* as the Bible, the staple diet of her training courses, she had found this approach to all and any human problems could not be bettered. When time permitted she would process her feelings for Mitchell through just such an assessment grid before coming up with his treatment plan. For the moment, having completed her diagnosis and finding her car to be in urgent need of a treatment plan, she headed for Billy's garage.

Reaching Billy's shed she saw at a glance that an instant cure for her engine was not to be, for a handwritten notice on the door announced 'The propitore has moved'. But moved where to? Then she corrected herself: 'moved to where' or would 'to where has he moved' sound better? County council English was gradually eroding her concern for the correct use of the English language. More importantly, if Billy had moved, was it to regular paid employment or, more likely, unemployment and a leisurely life on the dole, or was he banged up in Rudham Prison and staring through the bars of his cell window at the surrounding city roofs while down at ground level the carefree university students hurried to and from lectures?

Her next stop was at his home where the man who answered the door was certainly not the Billy of old. This was Billy transformed in appearance into an almost regular citizen. She found herself staring at him for a few moments, a little unsure as to his identity. He was now closer to neatness and cleanliness than his Maker had previously seemed to intend. 'Sartorial elegance' would be straying too far into the world of clichés and miracles but there was no doubt that this Billy was a changed man. His jeans looked new and were clean. Expensive trainers and a snazzy blue shirt, neatly ironed no doubt by Mrs Billy, all added to Madge's sense of disbelief. A glimpse into the front room revealed proper furniture, cheap-looking but none of it second-hand. A newish car, shiny clean, stood at the kerb. Well-groomed children frolicked behind him.

''Ello miss.' For a moment he looked a bit defensive as though his short life had long since witnessed too many visits by those set in authority over him.

Could all those early years of local authority care have produced this result? Of course it was not only the social services for there had been contributions from his brutal father, his inadequate gin-soaked mother, the police, the courts, the schools, the educational psychology department at County Hall, not forgetting various custodial establishments and foster parents. Adding it all together Billy had not come cheap.

'You look well, Billy. I called about my car but I found your garage closed.'

'That's reet, miss. Ah divvent dee cars nee mair yer knaa. Ah work mostly neets – things are busy neets.'

'Working as?

'The Golden Slipper down Stephenson Street yer knaa? The massage parlour. Ah telt yers aboot it afore. When the owld geezer who bought it went and deed Mrs Hill, me owld foster mam, took it over. Mr Hill was her deputy at first but then when he went and deed Mrs Hill asked me to be deputy manager and bouncer.'

'Mrs Hill is the manager?'

'Whyaye, Coonsellor Brown owns it. And like ah said afore, one of your lads comes in sometimes, mostly in his dinner hours, a right lad he is. Sometimes he comes with the MP, not that he caalls his-sel that but we aall knaa it's him from his pictures in the paper.'

Madge was incredulous. 'The MP? One of my lads? You're making this up, Billy… which lad would that be?'

'Him, yer knaa the one ah mean, they never say their names, their real names, caalls his-sel summat like "add a noise", summat like that anyhow.'

Surely he could not mean adenoids so she asked, 'Adonis perhaps?'

'Aye, summat like that. That's what our girls and the other gents caall him. They laugh at him. Fancies his-sel. The MP is crazy, says he gets his biggest kicks when he thinks of bein caned by Thatcher, says it's his big ambition in life. Yebuggermar, says she's the sexiest bloody bitch he ever seen and that's just seeing her on TV like.'

It was inconceivable, a Labour MP being disloyal to the party, dreaming of being caned by Mrs Thatcher! No, Shirley Williams perhaps. Wrong, hadn't she abandoned the Labour Party? Barbara Castle then. But no, the whole idea was simply ridiculous.

But all she said was, 'Himself, Billy, not his-sel. Can you try again to describe the one you refer to as "my" lad? Is he young? Old?'

'Owld.'

It was occurring to her that it must be Alan, her only 'old' social worker. And him a respectable married man. Or Mitchell, would he count as 'one of her lads'?

'But how old?' she demanded.

Billy paused to think. 'Say thirty, forty, fifty mebbes,' he said. Unless Billy had made a mistake it could not be Dan or Simon. Or could it?

But which? She saw them both as young but to Billy they probably seemed old. She did so hope it was not Simon. Stephenson Street and the Golden Slipper! Surely

Dan's pizza parlour, the place he said he visited every lunchtime, was close by? Perhaps the truth of the matter was that it was the Golden Slipper he called in at? And perhaps in working time! She had known all along it could not be Mitchell. It was bound to be a younger man. In time she would unearth the truth, unmask the offender. In the circumstances 'unmask' might not be the right word. She chuckled.

All Billy could add was, 'He likes the bondage stuff, yer knaa, handcuffs, chains, and the discipline stuff, yer knaa whips and canes and all that stuff. Yer'll knaa him for sure.'

And that was as far as she got. From now on though she must keep a close eye on the men in the office; anyone sitting down gingerly on the hard office chairs would be an immediate suspect with some explaining to do. The scandal, should the sordid secret leak out, would fill the *Northern Times* for days and might even destroy what was left of her career. The Director at County Hall would hold her responsible. Locally, Mr Barkle, frozen pillar of the community that he was, would certainly not approve.

She smiled to herself: at least Billy's gent from her staff could rely on the deputy manager's discretion. Ha! Ha! It could only be a matter of time before the truth emerged.

Billy joining the semi-respectable end of the spectrum of the human race gave her pause for thought. It would take some getting used to. For the moment though her loss of a mechanic to mend her car was uppermost in her mind. Billy half-heartedly recommended a mate who would look after her car for the same cheap rates he offered in the past, allowing of course for inflation. Later she spoke to Mitchell who recommended a student friend of Marcus but she remembered that this 'economical' solution had been responsible for Mitchell's car turning into a pyrotechnic display. In the end she headed for the main dealer and was pleasantly surprised to find it a whole lot cheaper and more effective than any of the supposedly cut-price alternatives.

***

Dan, when Madge next tracked him down, was sitting at his desk deep in concentration staring at one of his management books.

He looked up when she entered his office, pulled a cross face, said, 'Sorry, Madge, a bit busy right now.'

'Reading a book.'

'Yes, wonderful, the future is going to be so different, systems analysis is the way forward, and social work will become so much more efficient, more cost-effective.'

'We seem to manage somehow with the tried and tested methods that have stood the test of time.'

'The world is changing, Madge, and we have to change with it, change or perish, there is no alternative. It's all in this book.'

'That's as may be but I came to talk to you about something altogether different. Mr Barkle, the old chap who is always sniffing around here complaining about this and that, has asked me to give a talk to his Thursday Club early next year, a monthly meeting of pensioners, with guest speakers, tea and biscuits. I've accepted but I thought you might like to go along with me?'

'Sorry, Madge, far too busy.'

'You may find it useful to find the time; these are the people we need to keep on side, the people in the community whose support we need. They are more than conscious of the fact that our pay depends on their taxes. It's a chance for you to get to know them and them to meet you. It's important to make these links as you progress in your career.'

Dan closed his book, looked thoughtful. 'I see what you mean, Madge, yes, my career, I must think about how things will benefit me when I'm in a senior post.'

'Good, we'll go together then. I'll let you have the date. Just a thought but perhaps you might even like to give a talk instead of me? They've heard me before and of course as you so often point out I am a little off the pace where modern methods are concerned.'

Dan smiled. 'I see what you mean. Yes, I could find time to do that, get their thinking up to speed, explain how different things will all be when people like me are in charge.'

'Thanks, Dan, I'll tell Barkle we will both attend but you will be their speaker so he can plan next year's programme. Who knows, I might learn something too? Oh, by the way, they usually put a notice in the local rag so there may be a journalist present.'

Dan gave her one of his rare smiles. 'The press, great, a chance to make my mark.'

Madge was wondering if her plan for humanising Dan was going to work after all. Or was it a hope that he might fall head first into a woopsie at the Thursday Club? Either way he just didn't get the caring thing. And if this was the way of the future did she really want to stay aboard for the ride?

***

'See you tonight,' Lorraine shouted as she rushed down the corridor and out into the staff car park.

'Tonight?' asked Madge.

'At Green College, the Founder's Day dinner. Marcus invited me. He said the prof invited you.'

Madge hadn't expected to share the evening with the love birds and yet she might have seen it coming. Marcus was a member of Mitchell's college. Lorraine, flattered and naive, would enjoy the status of the occasion in that setting. Marcus, predatory and living for the moment, would feed her this crumb at no social or financial cost to himself. Perhaps the staff and students would see Lorraine as his bit of rough? For now they would have lots of fun. But would it last? Madge doubted it. At any time Marcus could walk away unscarred but what about Lorraine? How vulnerable was she beneath the skin of the wild colonial girl? And what about Simon who had seemed to be getting very close to Lorraine just at the moment when Marcus appeared on the scene? She hated seeing Simon hurt. He was still so vulnerable. Now he seemed depressed.

Neither was she sure she welcomed appearing at a social event with Lorraine. How ordinary she would seem by comparison. If only she had tried one of those new-fangled diets with their fancy names that always reminded her of something else, F Plan morphing into G Plan furniture or F1 fighter aircraft, and Cambridge becoming sedate saloon cars or treacherous homosexuals in high places. At these moments she resented her body; she had always felt less attractive than other women; now as she grew older this body of hers was getting in the way of her life. 'Look at that bum,' her father used to taunt, or 'stick it in, gal. It's like something out of the Land Army.' Or, on other occasions, 'like the back of a bus'. Those were the days when she had been young and as slim as she ever would be.

After calling at the cottage to change for the evening she headed on to Green, a proud if embarrassingly modern constituent yellow brick college of the ancient University of Rudham. She parked and walked to the main entrance where a shambling man wearing a plum-red waistcoat looked her up and down as her shoes squeaked towards him on the parquet floor.

'I've come to meet Professor Mitchell from Sociology for dinner.'

As she mentioned Mitchell's name followed by the word sociology there was a slight curl of the man's lips, the beginnings of a sneer. It was difficult to be sure which word provoked the greatest distaste. He looked a trifle old to be employed but perhaps old retainers in Rudham colleges had a longer job expectancy under their loyal masters than social services staff like her under the Director at County Hall.

'It's a formal dinner tonight,' he said, barring her progress.

'Yes, I know.'

'If you're sure you've got the right night you'd better follow me. I'll take you to the Senior Common Room. I don't think he has arrived as yet.'

As they approached a door marked 'SCR Private' she caught drizzles of conversation coming from the room beyond. There was a curious smell from the cork floor, perhaps a disinfectant in the polish.

'Where's Sock Prof tonight, Master?' It was a man's gravelly voice, a voice she had heard somewhere before. But where? Then she remembered; surely it was the Dean from the faculty meeting.

The reply was to the point. 'Sociology Professor has gone to a working chaps' club or something of that ilk to meet some retired miners and drink pints of beer with them. You know what Mitchell's like. He cares not a jot for the reputation of the college.'

'Oh, come now, Master, what miners? You know full well that miners in this benighted county died out years ago. Extinct species.' It was a new voice, too loud, the speaker laughing at his own joke.

'Their jobs may have died out years ago but they cling to the memories, all that nostalgia, all that nonsense about community life in the pit villages, the annual Miners' Gala with all those Labour politicians coming to Rudham and making firebrand speeches recalling mining disasters and coal owner profits. I ask you, where would they have been without the coal owners?'

'The Sock Prof is always banging on in support of the miners.'

'And now the few remaining miners are playing around with this strike threat.'

'Mrs T will sort them out.'

'Even Scargill?'

'Even Scargill.'

There was a pause before the Dean rejoined the conversation. 'I thought Mitchell was bringing some floozy to dinner tonight.'

With these words in her ears the college serf opened the door and ushered her through into the room where a man she took to be the Master advanced, saying, 'You must be Miss Perfect, Professor Mitchell's guest. He has told me all about you. Wonderful voluntary work you girls do amongst our less fortunate brethren. What is it, socialist work or something? Very Christian I'm sure. How nice to meet you. Charmed I'm sure,' and then as an afterthought, 'I am the Master, but then you probably guessed as much.'

At these concluding words he puffed out his cheeks and beamed down on her. She tried to beam back but found instead she had to stifle a giggle at the sight of his black bushy eyebrows. They must be false, she thought. Or was it just that the hair which once upon a time adorned his head had slipped down his forehead and come to rest over his eyes?

Mostly maturing men stood around in clumps, some wearing black academic gowns. They reminded her of pictures of colonies of penguins. A few women talking amongst themselves, wives no doubt, added touches of Laura Ashley floral colour. A second college servant, a young man dressed like his older colleague apart from a white napkin over his shoulder, appeared at her side with a silver tray bearing glasses of sherry.

'Sweet-ish or dry-ish?' boomed the Master. 'We have a decentish Amontillado – dry of course, the amber one – and a pale cream-ish you ladies seem to like – not sure if this is Croft Original or Harvey's.'

'Colour coded what-o,' the booming voice emanated from the man who laughed at his own jokes. The men around them seemed intent only on scoring debating points over their conversational adversaries. She now realised they were more hyena than penguin. Who would want to be an academic wife? Come to that who would want to be an academic? Noticing the Dean winking at her as he had done at the faculty meeting she turned away from his line of sight.

Just as she wondered where Mitchell fitted into this world, and on the verge of scurrying from the room, finding her car and heading home, Mitchell burst in.

'I'm so very sorry, Madge,' he spluttered. 'Held up in traffic coming in from a Rudham Miners' Association meeting in a village near the coast. Terribly, terribly sorry.'

'Do take off your raincoat, Mitchell,' the Master said disapprovingly.

'Yes, yes, of course, Master.'

Hard on the heels of Mitchell came a woman dressed in a shabby grey skirt and white blouse that was a stranger to ironing. All eyes turned in her direction as she bore down on the Master. It could only be the Master's wife, this statuesque lady smiling at Madge. 'You must be Perfect, Richard's guest,' she said, 'how nice to meet you. I'm the

Master's pet filly.' But who was Richard? She didn't like to ask.

A quick glance established that this woman bore more than a slight resemblance to a horse, especially her equine teeth and flaring nostrils. Fit her with a bridle and bit and she would be good for a gallop across the fields, the Master aboard with whip in hand. Madge pitied the fox. Tally-ho! Oh my God, the woman was coming even closer to her, she felt trapped like a fox, knew the feeling from the fox's view.

All she managed to squeak was, 'Thank you', knowing this to be an inadequate response.

Fortunately the filly raced off to greet other members of the Senior Common Room and Mitchell found seats in a quiet alcove near a window looking out on the cathedral.

'Who,' she asked, 'is Richard? Is it your middle name?'

Mitchell laughed. 'Good Lord no. She calls all the men Richard. When challenged she just laughs and says most men are called Richard so most times she must be right.' She was struggling to remember any men in Moortown or Brownlow called Richard.

'But they aren't,' she said.

'Try telling that to the old bat. It saves her trying to remember.'

'Don't the students mind?'

'No, they laugh behind her back of course but most of them just love it. They see her as an eccentric, a character, like the mother, the nanny or the governess or the dame that ruled over them in their public schools. She may even be the mother they wish they once had. Of course some of them did. Poor sods.'

'Do your colleagues mind?'

'They keep very quiet at least to her face. She's powerful not only in the college but in wider academic politics as well. She can make or break careers, you cross her at your peril. Her power comes from her dalliances with the Vice-Chancellor.'

'She sleeps with the Vice-Chancellor?'

'They don't get much sleep from what I hear. And then there's the Dean.'

'That creep from your faculty meeting? Put our puritanical Director in charge here and he'd soon sort out that sort of behaviour.'

'No, that's the Dean of the Faculty of Arts. Madam is said to be a close 'friend' of the Dean at the cathedral, on the face of it a dry old stick with not much libido, but if faith can move mountains... Oh, by the way, apropos of nothing much, the man talking to the Master now is our distinguished visitor from the International Monetary Fund in Washington, the American Washington not the one up the road on the way to Newcastle. He's giving a seminar for the economists in the morning.'

Was this the same planet as Moortown, the place of that name just a few miles down the road? Were these people members of the same human race or perhaps a distant offshoot, a similar species, victims of generations of inbreeding? Did they share any of the sentiments known to the Farrants?

The Master's wife person circled back and pounced from her left. 'Must just show you where we ladies powder our noses – should the need arise of course,' she said.

Madge stared at the unnaturally large protuberances on the woman's chest before deciding 'falsies'. Not since her aunt died had Madge heard anyone talking about 'ladies powdering their noses'.

'Thank you but no need,' Madge said. Perhaps unwise, it would no doubt be a long and tense evening before she was able to scuttle home.

The chatter died on the clanging of a distant gong. With Mitchell at her side they walked through to the dining room which immediately struck her with its ordinariness. After the attempt to make something special of the SCR with its portraits of former Masters, reproduction tables and chairs, and the ornate curtains, the dining room was stark and in need of a coat of paint. Dreary metal windows were curtainless. Long tables occupied the floor space with parade ground formality. It was not at all what she had expected. As she lined up at High Table next to Mitchell she caught sight of Lorraine and Marcus happily laughing and talking till the room fell silent and one of the students walked to the end of High Table, turned to face his fellow students and said, '*Benedictus Benedicat*'.

With a scraping of chairs and benches everyone sat down and Mitchell whispered, 'The Senior Man, a friend of Marcus. The grace wasn't quite right, that form is only meant for less auspicious meals than Founder's Day.'

More urgently though she could see that Lorraine had reverted to type. Her dress was a shiny collision of colours. Was it at all appropriate to this occasion? As usual she was showing too much bosom. She must mention it to Dan in the morning. What might pass muster in Cape Town was hardly appropriate in Green College in Rudham.

Lorraine, catching sight of Madge, waved. The Master leaned over and whispered in her ear, 'Splendid young pup sitting next to that young lady. Father's in the government don't you know, an Oxford Blue in his day don't you know. We must invite the young man and his lady friend to the SCR for liqueur and a cigar after dinner.'

Picking up her soup spoon she heard the man from the IMF ask Mitchell, 'Founder's Day, why Founder's Day?'

'The founder was Earl Green, a father figure of the British Empire no less. The college is named after him and Founder's Day celebrates his birthday.'

'How interesting,' said the IMF. The IMF did not sound greatly interested.

'Your subject for the seminar in the morning?' asked Mitchell.

'I shall be talking about the Hansen-Samuelson multiplier accelerator interaction model, nothing much to do with the IMF but a pet hobby of mine. Lots of second order difference equations.'

'Fascinating,' said Mitchell who looked far from fascinated.

Undaunted though, IMF man was keen to share his enthusiasm. 'Think Tacoma Bridge disaster. Waves. To me foreign trade is the problem you see. The model can accommodate consumption, investment and the government but foreign trade introduces one or two tricky problems.'

Their conversation lapsed and Mitchell turned to Madge instead.

'Fascinating,' he said.

'Of great practical value no doubt,' she replied in a quiet voice. Why did these clever people need to speak in riddles? What she wanted to hear was the practical application of the ideas of these no doubt brilliant men and women. She wanted new insights into human behaviour that she could take back to Moortown, new ways of responding to aberrations occurring in the community.

What happened next took her completely by surprise. At first she thought she was imagining it but no, something was nibbling her knees, left then right in turn.

'Mitchell,' she hissed, 'I don't want to alarm you but I think a mouse or something is nibbling my knees.'

'Oh dear no, not in Green College, no, no, it's only the Divinity professor. You must remember him from the faculty meeting.' Mitchell laughed. 'Nutty as a fruitcake. He's having one of his turns. He occasionally crawls along under the table and nibbles the knees of the ladies at High Table. Quite harmless really. Some even admit to enjoying it.'

Perhaps seeing Madge's disapproving expression Mitchell ducked his head under the table cloth and said, 'Back into your cave, old chap.' A cackling laugh came from under the table and the nibbling ceased. Knocking his head on the table as he came up from below, a salivating figure appeared in what had been a vacant chair at the end of the table. There, grinning before her, sat the Professor of Divinity, a man who caused confusion in faculty meetings and nibbled women's knees during formal dinners.

But when she looked around the table she saw that all eyes were upon her and people were laughing, the Master's pet filly throwing back her head and braying loudest of all. This place, she thought, should be reconstituted as a psychiatric institution. Moortown had never seemed so far away. This was quite simply another St Clement's Hospital, a madhouse operating under another name.

Just then there was a sudden buzz of excitement among the students and Brussels sprouts started raining through the air as if between two warring armies. Volley after volley of Brussels sprouts flew from left to right followed by a rapid response from right to left.

'What is going on?' she hissed to Mitchell.

'A Brussels sprouts fight.'

'Is this normal?'

'Yes, it's tradition.'

'But why does the Master not put a stop to it.'

'It's tradition. Besides, masters don't have much power, they're not seen as proper academics, more superior hoteliers, yet they are paid professorial salaries. Some people resent that.'

Then she noticed that the Master was laughing, he too was enjoying it and so too was Lorraine, standing on a bench and lobbing sprouts across the room till they bounced off the pictures of local scenes lining the walls.

'Ach sus, lekker,' she was shouting, 'we never did this in Cape Town.'

Marcus beside her was shouting 'Tally-ho' over and over again.

'Jolly good sport that young pup, learning to fly don't you know,' the Master shouted above the din.

Trying not to see any more of the battle Madge tried Mitchell again. 'But, but, what will the man from the International Monetary thing make of it?'

'He'll just think it's tradition. Americans love tradition.'

Madge wondered why, if that was the case, the man was looking quite so bemused.

'And all this top table stuff, us and them, staff and students?'

Mitchell frowned. 'Not the way I would like it to be but… I did try eating with the students for ordinary meals but they didn't like it. Took me a while to work out why. Truth is once they have served their time as undergraduates they want to inhabit a world which demarcates them and the others, the also-rans.'

'Depressing,' Madge said, 'but in a way like us social workers, we too are us and them, in some ways we even perpetuate the divide.'

'Until the revolution,' Mitchell said.

The meal itself was less than memorable though it far exceeded the finest lunch provided by the canteen at the office. Sitting in a dimly lit alcove back in the Senior Common Room they drank coffee and she enjoyed the sweetness of Benedictine while Mitchell sipped a malt whisky. Sitting beside him she noticed he was nudging closer beside her as she looked out on the floodlit cathedral standing proud in the surrounding darkness. Perhaps, she thought, I am enjoying an occasional window on half-grasped things eternal? Or was it the wine? It was easy to see why people might settle for a way of life as cosy as this.

Or was it like her father believing there was a crock of gold at the end of rainbows? Well, almost believing. Sometimes when he was in one of his rare good moods they had scoured the countryside to find that elusive crock of gold. After Clive, the man she loved in her young life, went away, she had given up hoping to find crocks of gold and turned instead to the consolation she found in caring for others.

And now, just perhaps, now there was Mitchell who knew about so many things. Or was it again just the wine affecting her judgement?

Gazing out on the cathedral she said, 'It's beautiful, isn't it? Sometimes I glimpse things that may be more important than my work.'

Mitchell nodded then said, 'I would get out my camera but the artificial light on the cathedral is always too bright. All my best shots are taken in low light.'

Beyond the floodlit stones the night was as dark as an unlit coal mine. For Mitchell perfection seemed to lie between extremes. Strange man, she thought, married to his camera and bad light. 'Do you mind if I ask you something?'

'Anything,' he said.

'How do you cope in this strange world of the university?'

He considered the question for a moment. 'Sometimes I don't,' he said, 'some days I could walk away with my camera and travel the world taking pictures.'

'I see,' she said, but she didn't.

Then he said, 'What drives you on in your work? You seem so committed to the disadvantaged, especially to the welfare of children who are cruelly treated.'

'Perhaps it's just a duty to me.'

'I don't believe that. It must come from somewhere. Was your own childhood happy, secure?'

'Yes and no.' She clenched her teeth, looked away from Mitchell. Stay noncommittal, she said to herself; some things she would not, could not share, certainly not with Mitchell, not now, perhaps never.

'Sorry I asked,' he said.

Turning sideways she noticed Lorraine and Marcus scuttling up the path alongside a notice announcing 'Staff Flats' no doubt intending to do something they also did in Cape Town. She tugged at Mitchell's sleeve and nodded towards them.

'As a postgraduate Marcus qualified for a staff flat,' Mitchell said.

'How nice for him,' Madge said.

'Of course daddy being an important person does him no harm when it comes to things like that.'

The end result in this particular instance was that Lorraine would almost certainly be late and yawning till coffee time in the morning.

'Young love,' she said. There had been no sign of them in the Senior Common Room. Perhaps the Master had forgotten to invite them or perhaps they had just gone to the student bar which would be more fun.

'Surely love is not necessarily restricted to the young?' Mitchell said.

'I read in the *Northern Times* that some Italian psychiatrist has discovered that love is a kind of madness,' she said.

'In that case I doubt if Marcus is in love unless with himself.'

'How goes it with his flying lessons?' she asked.

'He's pretty committed, goes down to Teesside at least once a week. Says daddy has promised him a plane when he is twenty-five if he passes his private pilot's licence. Would you like coffee in my flat?'

She thought for a moment. 'No, thank you but no. It's been a lovely – well – illuminating evening and now I must get home. Work in the morning.'

'A book at bedtime then?'

She just smiled. Perhaps for all these years she had misjudged men as a species. Mitchell was eccentric but he was fun and he was kindly. She thought she might even be able to come to regard him as an almost suitable man. After all, not all men were bad, not all men were like her father. Not all men went away and stayed away as Clive had done.

***

Lying awake she wondered if Mitchell was the only sane academic and she the only sane local government employee. Yet how could anyone be sane in a madhouse? It was perfectly clear; they were both detained in sanatoriums. Hadn't some study or other shown that it was often impossible to distinguish the staff from the patients in such institutions? Was insanity a bond that could bind them? But perhaps he was sane, his sanity highlighted by the insanity around him? There was the evidence of the faculty meeting and now the college dinner. Perhaps, all things considered, he was just eccentric, a man who did not smoke or drink to excess. He was relaxed, humorous and kind, not a perfect man but then when she had a perfect man all those years ago he had gone off and left her, taking with him the special magic dust he had sprinkled over her.

Still sleepless, she wondered once again how long it was since she had read a 'proper' book. She had meant to tackle this after the faculty meeting all that time gone by. Of course she did read a lot but mostly dull social service committee reports or the occasional updating article or textbook, but it was ages since she had read anything that could be called 'serious literature'. She must make another effort to track down Pasternak. And that Pamela woman. If she was to spend more time in Mitchell's company, and she was forming a clear opinion she wanted that, she would have to make an effort to overcome her ignoramus side so as not to appear a complete dunce in his company. Perhaps she should go back to her first love, Georgette Heyer, but no, that was not highbrow enough. Perhaps Hemingway?

Failing that there was always good old Florence Hollis, or Florrie as the students nicknamed the unseen woman. Perhaps she could make that sound as clever and as important as – what was it – something about the nipples and accelerants of the IMF man?

Until now she had seen Mitchell as a strange mixture of eccentric and dull but measured against his college colleagues he appeared positively normal. Magic was not everything. He was in need of some care and attention. But washing his socks and underpants? Only a strong woman could hope to take him in hand, knock him into shape. But the needs of Area 13 were as much as she could possibly manage. Besides, Mitchell came from a mad, mad world. They should all be sectioned under the Mental Health Act. If he went off round the world taking pictures would she volunteer to carry his camera bag?

Suddenly County Hall seemed incredibly sane in comparison. Sane but dull, dull, dull. She fell asleep.

Chapter 10

For once Dan was lunching in the canteen showing his 'I am a man of the people' face to his team. They sat together at a table by the window and nodded and beamed at whatever it was he was saying. Only Lorraine was missing. Waiting in the food queue Madge caught occasional words: 'change' and 'Director' and 'the future' and 'computer'. When Dan saw Madge looking for a table he waved her over and everyone shunted along to make room for her.

'Just talking about Christmas, Madge,' Dan said.

'So soon when we're still only in October? Making plans for the office party already?'

'Yes, of course, forward planning is key.' Dan smiled and his coterie looked awkward.

'I see,' Madge said.

Dan got up to go. 'Pizza again tomorrow – the finest in the north-east, Tosca's Pizza Parlour off Stephenson Street. Oh, by the way, Madge, before I go, just one little thing, I forgot to mention that Lorraine has heard of a homeless family arriving in our area with what little they could carry. They seem to be relatives of the Farrants. They're in the Homeless Unit but plan to move in with the Farrants on a temporary basis till they get a place of their own.'

'Yes, I remember Simon mentioning something like that a while back. We were too busy then to look into it. What more do we know of them?'

'Nothing. Oh, mum, dad and a little lad I think.'

'Where did they arrive from?'

'Don't know that. Can't see it matters. None of our business surely? Our resources must be targeted at things that come within our statutory obligations.'

Irritated by Dan's attitude Madge found anxieties creeping up on her.

'We need to make sure they don't have form. Their name?'

'Lorraine didn't say.'

'How old is the lad?'

'Don't know. I'll ask Lorraine to speak to the Farrants. We can't stop the Farrants taking in their relations.'

'Lorraine must enquire without delay,' Madge said. 'I may be wrong about this but it sounds ominous. First a horse and then relations from we know not where. Let's see what Lorraine comes up with. Can I leave it to you?'

'Sure, sure,' Dan said.

But Madge was thinking, Funny that, Dan spending almost every lunchtime in the area of the Golden Slipper.

***

The following morning the *Northern Times* conveyed the baleful news: 'MP DEAD'.

Madge's grief was muted and she read the article with increasing displeasure: the MP had died suddenly and it seemed he was a great loss for here was a son of Rudham County who had devoted his life to the welfare of his constituents from all walks of life. He had left school and gone down the pit at the earliest possible age to eke out the family income after the death of his father in a mining disaster, he had volunteered for the merchant navy in the Second World War, risen in the ranks of the union when he went back into the pit after the war ended, and then studied at home in the evenings before going to Fircroft College in Oxford which existed to enable working men and women to extend their basic education. In short he was a working-class hero, a man who had taken every opportunity to better himself before devoting his life to Rudham County and, or so it seemed, the world beyond. It failed to mention that, on the evidence of Billy, he had been a celebrant at the Golden Slipper in Moortown.

Madge sat at her kitchen table with the paper spread out before her as she crunched her cornflakes increasingly loudly. The man was admirable in so many ways, more so if all of this account of his life were true. It seemed there were no doubts on this point. The leader of the Labour Party had sent condolences from London. The Rudham City Chamber of Commerce was grieved to hear the news for here was a man who, regardless of his Labour politics, was widely respected across the business community. The Rudham Labour Party praised his achievement in helping to ensure that unemployment in the area never went much above twice the national average. The Rudham Miners' Association, the Co-op and each and every trade union scrambled to outdo one another in their praise. The funeral would be a lavish affair; mourners would converge from far and wide.

Later that morning she sat at her desk in the office with the paper crunched up in her waste bin. Mitchell arrived, saw what was in the bin, smiled and said, 'I see you have been reading about a most melancholy occurrence.'

'Bollocks, if you'll pardon my Geordie,' Madge said. 'Far from melancholy, a blessing in disguise. But what is it with this melancholy occurrence thing?'

'The Victorian papers were full of it. You only had to drown at sea or in a river or be run over by a coach and horses to become a melancholy occurrence.'

'I see this occurrence as opening the door for a more able candidate with greater integrity,' Madge said.

'And do you seriously think that will happen in Rudham?'

'No, I suppose not, but cynic that I am I can dream of something better.'

To herself she thought: Poor bugger, died before he could be caned by Mrs Thatcher. Would he be missed at the Golden Slipper? This was not an observation she chose to share with Mitchell.

***

A week later, and after another morning when Mitchell had been in and out of her office like an irritating horse fly, nattering to her about nothing in particular, he phoned from the university in the afternoon to ask, 'What would you say to the idea of spending a weekend in the Lakes?' Like the phone call inviting her to dinner in Green College it seemed a way of safeguarding himself from the possibility of face-to-face rejection.

'Winter is so cold in the Lakes,' she said, taken aback not so much at the weather prospect as at the thought of going away with Mitchell. It was so sudden, unexpected and yet, and yet, might it make a nice break?

Mitchell persisted. 'We're just into November. The weather should be OK. Why not? We could find a cosy little lakeside hotel with welcoming hosts, friendly other guests and roaring log fires.'

It was tempting. She laughed. 'Before I decide I must sort out some newcomers on the patch, a family from where we seem to know not. I have a bad feeling about them.'

'When you have sorted your newcomers out let me know what you decide about the Lakes,' Mitchell said.

'Do you think your car would get over the Pennines? I know mine could not,' Madge said.

'It's not the Pyrenees,' he said, sounding hurt.

She knew she should be firm with him, say no, nicely; letting the idea run was almost like agreeing to it and against all her instincts. But her father was no longer around to say, 'not good enough'. Now she had lobbed a decision on the matter into the future it seemed safe because the planned event was not now this minute. In time, if she said 'yes', she might have to think about what to wear and what they might talk about for a whole weekend. It would mean shopping for an outfit in Rudham and giving thought to enough items of conversation to fill their time together. In future she must learn to say 'no' to this man decisively.

Meanwhile things at work were beginning to slip. It was so unlike her to feel that the office and the clients were getting away from her: she said to herself over and over again, 'I am not now in a good place.'

**

Each weekday was punctuated by work highs and lows amongst which more often than not the ultimate high was the clanking mid-morning arrival of Doris with the tea trolley. Finding herself next to Lorraine in the queue Madge asked, 'What news of the Farrant relatives?'

'No news, I only know that when I last saw Melanie she mentioned they had some relatives new to the area who might be staying with them for a while.'

'Surely Dan asked you to find out who they are and where they come from? I asked him to make sure that happened.'

'He never said anything.'

'I will speak to him again but as a matter of urgency I want you to put in a visit to the Homeless Unit, find out where they come from, who's who in the family, and how they think they plan to manage all cooped up in the Farrant house.'

'Sus, I see what you mean, Madge.'

'And the horse?' Madge asked.

Lorraine looked down at the floor. 'Marcus and I are working on it,' she said.

Madge persisted. 'Oh, and by the way, how goes your treatment plan with Mrs Farrant?'

'What's that got to do with the horse? Anyway, I'm working on Mrs Farrant but I'm taking it easy at first, giving her more time to get to know me before I tackle the underlying problem. Marcus is helping with the Farrants as well as the horse. He says there are ideas coming out of Chicago that could solve the Farrant problem.'

As if on cue Dan came into her office and said, 'That bloody horse still knocking around?'

Madge said, 'Dan, your worker Lorraine is supposed to be sorting out the horse with Marcus.'

'I didn't know Lorraine now has a horse,' Alan said as his head came briefly round the door.

'Not funny. Never mind the horse for now,' Madge said, 'we urgently need to follow up on the arrival of this new family on our patch – the family I asked you to make sure Lorraine checked out.'

'Sorry, Madge, I've been too busy,' Dan said.

Trying not to sound angry Madge said, 'Just do it. I want Lorraine and Simon to tackle it together, Lorraine at the Farrant end and Simon finding out where the family are coming from.'

'But that's two workers to one case, a case that may have no legs anyway. Our productivity ratio will be straight out of the window if we go on like that.'

'Just do it,' Madge said, 'just do it.'

'Great,' Lorraine said, 'two workers to one family, conjoint family therapy, I studied it in Cape Town. It's a chance to transfer my learning from Cape Town to Brownlow.'

***

Should she decline the weekend away with Mitchell? She was increasingly anxious about the whole idea. But he deserved an answer one way or the other. It might be enjoyable. Might, might. She did not like leaving the checks on the new family in town to Dan's oversight but Lorraine and Simon between them would establish the facts. There would then be time enough to take whatever action proved necessary. The chances were the new family on the patch would prove unproblematic. But her gut reaction of concern persisted, her anxiety perhaps symptomatic of a deeper unease within her.

An hour later word reached the office from multiple sources recounting how Mr Timms, silly hat and hand stuffed in makeshift waistcoat, was at it once again. The neighbours were not buying his story that as Napoleon he had the right, nay a duty, to shout abuse at them while throwing the furniture supplied to him by her department out of the window of his upstairs flat, the flat negotiated with Housing for him by her staff. Gratitude indeed.

Although no one had been underneath when the furniture came clattering down, local residents were getting upset being not at all relieved to be in on the foundation of the new empire being forged with its capital Moortown or, as Timms saw it, Moortown-Paris with its Boulevard High Street. Worse still, an item of furniture might even land on a councillor.

Once again 'something ought to be done'. Once again her life seemed populated entirely by people who thought something ought to be done, and done by her. But remembering she had a deputy she went in search of Dan.

Before she even began to explain the Timms problem he said, 'Sorry, Madge, no time, I'm just off to an urgent meeting with the Director.'

Why all these meetings with the Director? Why did the Director choose Dan to attend when he was her deputy and vastly less experienced than she was herself?

'You will report back on all those meetings won't you?' she said.

'Of course, Madge, of course,' Dan said. Why didn't she believe him? But at least the MP would not be present today.

Chapter 11

In the office next day Simon was waiting to see her. 'I've traced the Farrant relatives, the Oldfields, back to Cumbria. It's not good news. Little Alistair was in care there after a non-accidental injury case conference. Then, out of the blue they did a runner.'

'Your source?'

'Ms Page, a social worker in Workington. I rang the social services HQ in Carlisle and they checked their county case records and passed me on to the relevant district office. They've been pretty worried about their Oldfield family.'

'Have you discussed it with Dan?' Why did so many people come to her when Dan was their line manager?

'Dan's not around,' Simon said. 'Anyway he seemed to think it was sorted now that we have traced the background, done all that you asked.'

'Sorted my R-spectus...' Madge snorted.

It was not Simon's fault that Dan was not around; it was her fault for not knowing why or where.

'Simon, if you talk to the Clerk's department at County Hall about the legal position I will ask Dan to arrange a case conference as soon as I track him down.'

Simon nodded and went through to the social workers' room.

Dan was completely beyond her control nowadays; it had happened quite gradually but she had clearly failed to line manage him, allowing him to spend too much time at County Hall ingratiating himself with the Director and Puttock. With allies at the top at County Hall he was by now untouchable. That part of her which seethed with anger at his attitude sat side by side with her managerial self-reproach. Whichever way she looked at it she had let Area 13 down.

***

She was sufficiently concerned about young Alistair Oldfield to chair the case conference herself. She did not feel confident leaving it in Dan's hands. Sometimes the sadness of other lives touched her own, sometimes the pain witnessed in her work was almost unbearable. Where clients were concerned there was always 'What if I had intervened sooner, or later, or in a different way, or spent more time with that family…?' Dan was always guarding his back but this had never been her first concern.

Her office was just about large enough to accommodate those attending the meeting: Dan, Lorraine and Simon from the office, a solicitor from the Clerk's department at County Hall to give legal advice, Ms Page who had driven over from Cumbria, the Farrants' GP Dr Sangakkara who seemed far from overjoyed to be adding Farrant relations to his workload, the Head Teacher from the school Alistair had recently joined, and PC Pyott representing the local forces of law and order.

Simon began by presenting his well-informed, carefully structured report combining recent developments since the arrival of the family in Moortown with the now known history provided from Cumbria by Ms Page from Workington, a short, chubby young woman, young in the way that thirty plus or minus young people seemed to Madge who guessed she was somewhere in between Lorraine and Simon in age. In her sensible skirt, neat blouse and pretty blue cardigan she managed to represent the exact opposite from Lorraine who then read her report on the role of the Farrants in the shenanigans.

When Lorraine finished Madge said, 'Thank you for that,' before turning to Ms Page, asking, 'Anything to add from your end?'

'No, nothing new, Alistair's welfare gave us grave cause for concern while they were in Workington, their doing a moonlight only added to this.'

Madge asked PC Pyott, 'Any offences by dad or mum in Cumbria?'

'Not good news, nothing major but frequent callouts on account of domestic violence. Allegations only really. Mrs Oldfield always retracted her statement before anything got to court.'

Madge and Jim Pyott had worked together on a number of cases over the years. A good man, someone who had a feel for things being just about right or seriously wrong, he could always be relied on to tell the difference. She too had a nose for things, a sense she often trusted even when the hard evidence was lacking. Call it instinct or call it experience. Underneath the gruff exterior Jim actually cared about people.

As the ensuing discussion drew to a close Simon said, 'Holly has been ever so helpful.'

So, thought Madge, Miss Page was now 'Holly', a promising development for Simon perhaps. But all she said was, 'It seemed as though the Oldfields came from nowhere and yet I just knew all along that they would be in somebody's system, that they must have form, I knew it in my bones.' Jim nodded enthusiastically in support.

In summing up Madge concluded that they were looking at a child who had been at risk in Cumbria and was now at risk in Rudham. For as long as the Oldfields were living with the Farrants the concern was bound to be greater. The housing department though had promised to re-house the Oldfields early in the New Year. In the end the county solicitor agreed with the written recommendation from his opposite number in Carlisle that the care order should remain with Cumbria but be supervised by a social worker in Rudham for as long as the Oldfields remained domiciled there. Alistair would be placed with specialist foster parents locally. Simon would be the Oldfields' social worker and liaise with Ms Page while Lorraine would continue working with the Farrants. Madge was content with this outcome; in truth she trusted no one's handling of these case conferences as she did her own. Dan was simply a long way off the scale of those she could trust.

'We'll go ahead like that,' Madge said, nodding to the solicitor and making a mental note to keep an eye on Dan to make sure there was no back-sliding in his supervision of the case.

After the meeting broke up Madge heard Lorraine saying, 'I would be happier all round if the Farrants and the Oldfields had a proper doctor and not old Sangakkara.'

'Proper' still meant 'white' to Lorraine. This was one battle Madge decided not to fight today. It would only end in Lorraine's 'You people who never lived there just don't understand' speech. But for all of that tomorrow was another day.

Instead she said, 'Miss Page, I do hope you can join us for lunch in the canteen before you set off back across the Pennines?'

At which point Simon, looking awkward, said, 'I've already asked Holly for a pub lunch and she said "yes" which is nice.'

Holly smiled and said, 'But thank you for inviting me to join you, Miss Perfect. I'm not looking forward to the return journey across Bowes Moor; the weather was pretty wild coming over.'

'Travel safely,' Madge said. What she left unsaid was her own fear of travelling over the spine of the country to the Lakes with Mitchell in his rattling little car on wintry roads. But her mind was made up. In for a penny, in for a pound, she exhorted herself.

She phoned Mitchell and said, 'The Lakes is on if we get a break in the weather.'

'Good! I'll book something,' Mitchell said.

Now easy in her mind about the Oldfields, confident in her ability to apply her skills and knowledge to difficult cases, she felt ready to relax away from work; now all she was worrying about was the weekend away with Mitchell.

***

Madge called at the Moortown public library and announced to the young woman behind the desk, 'I've come to find *Pamela* and Pasternak.'

A blank look. 'No one with either of those names works here.'

'*Pamela* is a book.'

'Never heard of it.'

'Pasternak, the writer?'

'Never heard of him.'

'No, I guessed as much. I'm after a book of his. Can you look him up please?'

'I suppose I could. What's it about?'

'Love among other things. But that's not why I want to read it – to find out what it's about . . . the book I mean, not love.'

'What's it called?'

'*Doctor Zhivago*. It was made into a film.'

A look of relief followed by, 'Sorry, we don't do medicine except for slimming, fitness, middle age, ageing, care of the elderly, that sort of thing. You might find something on those shelves. Otherwise you'll have to try the main library at County Hall.'

The cheek of it. Madge responded with one of her best withering looks but this seemed to bypass the intended recipient. How dare the young woman, this whipper-snapper slip of a girl even think that slimming, fitness and ageing would be of interest to her? Clearly neither *Pamela* nor Pasternak would be found lurking in the Moortown library catalogue. No way would she risk a repeat experience at County Hall. If she could find the time she would order them from the bookshop in Rudham.

***

With the November weather beginning badly she relaxed, thinking the trip to the Lakes would never happen. Then Mitchell announced that he had booked two nights in a hotel. Two days later he contacted her with the bad news: 'My new second-hand car has been impounded by the police. I'm not sure if or when I'll get it back. We may have to use your car.' This was only three days before their planned departure.

'My car not sensible I'm afraid, things have taken a turn for the worse, the condition of the beast is fast deteriorating, I may have to have it put down by the car vet.'

'OK. I'll let you know as soon as I hear anything. It seems we may have to cancel our weekend away.'

But, half relieved at the abandonment of the project, half regretting the weather and Mitchell's car letting them down, she realised she had grown accustomed to the idea and didn't want it to be snatched away from her.

As an afterthought she posed the obvious question: 'The reason for the police seizing your car?'

'Old Divine of Divine's Motors who I bought it off seems to be a dodgy character known to the police. They think it might be stolen. They have him in custody.'

'If it was stolen you will not get it back.'

'That's what they said.'

'You may be prosecuted for receiving.'

'That's what they said.'

She had no intention of consorting with a criminal; how foolish to ever think otherwise.

***

Although Christmas was still weeks away Lorraine was becoming ever more excited.

'I spent all day on Saturday shopping in Newcastle trying to find some special clothes to wear at Christmas. But the clothes are all so dull. I wish I could shop in Cape Town.'

Books and brochures on Yorkshire country houses and flying magazines were slowly replacing social work files on her desk.

'You're spending Christmas with Marcus?' Madge asked. She was beginning to worry about the amount of time Lorraine was devoting to her life with Marcus.

'That's my plan.'

'Is that his plan too?'

'Ach sus, bloody better be. He always goes home to the family at Christmas and I am so looking forward to meeting them all. I just hope they like me as much as Marcus does. He says he just can't get enough of me. I can't think what to get them all for presents.'

At least, Madge thought, there is no apparent danger of Marcus leaving Lorraine and going abroad as my Clive did. Lorraine would not be disappointed in the way that she had been all those years ago.

***

On Thursday Mitchell phoned again. 'Our trip can go ahead. The weather forecast is good and I've heard from the police. The car is kosher. It was one of their cars written off after it collided with an emergency ambulance. Apparently the Rudham police write off cars at an astronomic rate. They sold it for scrap and Divine bought it and put it together again using cannibalised parts from another police car of the same make wrecked in another collision. So we're all right for the weekend.'

'Sounds a bit like Humpty Dumpty. Is it safe?'

'Heavens yes! Nothing like Humpty Dumpty. All put together again and safe as a nun. Good as new. I phoned Divine. His very words, good as new.'

Up to now she had only hosted doubts about what might be expected of her during the weekend away with Mitchell. A new anxiety now cast a shadow over the enterprise. Could she risk becoming any closer to a man who bought stolen or wrecked police cars from dodgy dealers? Perhaps all academics were a tad eccentric? But no, these doubts aside, she was looking forward to the weekend away from the office and the machinations of the Director, Puttock and not least Dan. With the Oldfield case conference behind her she would be able to relax, enjoy herself, even in November in the Lakes with Mitchell.

These thoughts were interrupted by Dan bouncing into her office with the smug expression he habitually wore when he was savouring a juicy piece of County Hall gossip.

'Great news,' he said in the way he had of announcing things which he deemed to be of importance, 'I almost forgot to tell you how busy the Director is canvassing support for his nomination as Labour candidate in the forthcoming by-election,' adding through a smirk, 'and what an excellent choice he would be. We heard all about his plans for the constituency over a drink in the council members' bar at the end of the course. He's asked me to help with his campaign.'

Dan was away so much of the time now that she was never sure whether he was up at County Hall on whatever staff development happened to be called at the moment, or a meeting with the Director, or just on leave.

It was difficult to think of the Director as their MP until she remembered with a shudder the handsome tributes in the *Northern Times* trumpeting the selfless service rendered by the previous incumbent. The Director would no doubt sell his own personal attributes in the same way. He would be just another Labour stalwart devoting all his working life to the service of the downtrodden in Rudham County. Oh please, yuck, pass me the sick bag.

In Rudham Labour votes were weighed not counted, a well-known fact. It was never necessary to canvas for votes during election campaigns. If the Director gained the nomination the result come the election would be a foregone conclusion. He might as well go to the Bahamas for the duration of the campaign; his plans for the constituency would be of no relevance whatever.

Madge smiled. At times Dan was like a yelping puppy handed a bone to gnaw on or a ball to chase round the room. Seeing himself as a member of the Director's inner circle was doing him no good at all. Seeing himself as a confidant of the future MP was worse still. At these moments he often said or did the most idiotic things.

'I almost forgot to tell you,' Dan said, 'the Director has put the restructuring plan on hold while he seeks the Labour nomination. He's had it in mind for a while but now he's asked me to pass it on down the line.'

Madge smiled at the news. 'Good, good, in fact I still haven't had a memo from Mr Puttock in reply to mine but if the restructuring is on hold I know where I stand.' How nice it was to know she was safe from the threatened compulsory early retirement on derisory terms.

'Everything tickety-boo then,' she said.

Dan pulled a face. 'Tickety what?'

'Boo.'

'You've got me there. Oh, some more news, Mr Puttock has been promoted to a new post of Assistant Director of Human Resources in a much expanded department. I have sent him a congratulations card.'

'I suppose that means he gets paid more.'

'Of course, extra responsibilities, a larger budget, more staff.'

There's a surprise, Madge thought. She asked, 'Did the Director know any more than we read in the papers about the death of the sitting MP?' Rumours had been flowing from mouth to mouth around Moortown.

'Indeed, the Director was a close personal friend. A shocking business when he died. He was in the queue in the Trawlerman fish and chip shop in Moortown when he collapsed. They went on serving with people having to step over his body to collect their orders. One of the girls from the Golden Slipper was in and she tried giving him the kiss of life. Some people are saying they should have closed the shop until the ambulance men removed the body – out of respect for their MP.'

How did Dan know about the woman from the Golden Slipper? The mystery of Billy's 'one of your lads' remained unsolved. Dan? Surely not. But he was after all 'one of her lads'. Ignoring that line of thought she said, 'Priorities I suppose, business is business, after all we are in Thatcher's Britain. On the other hand at least the gravediggers aren't on strike now as they were a few years ago.' She remembered how difficult it had been under Heath finding space for the bodies queuing for burial from the aged persons' homes in the district. That was when the Director ordered no more admissions to the homes so it was not the county's problem when it came to burials.

Dan said, 'Yes, progress at last, efficiency, economy, these are the words that signal the way forward.'

But Madge was still thinking of the MP. 'They may not have known he was dead when they went on serving,' she said.

Dan looked puzzled but said nothing.

'Had he been drinking?' she asked.

'No, they say he had his best suit on.'

'Was he in female company?'

Dan looked at her blankly and shook his head.

'Natural causes then, no suggestion of foul play?' she asked.

'Certainly not, who could possibly want to see him dead?'

'Who indeed?' she said. Who indeed, apart from anyone hoping to succeed him on the Westminster gravy train, and she knew who that might be.

***

As the week wound down the gales eased. At lunchtime on Friday the pale blue Hillman Imp arrived at her cottage and Mitchell clambered out and said, 'Grand weather for the Lakes,' before pointing to the car and adding, 'A beauty isn't she?'

'Perhaps in the eye of the beholder,' Madge said as she pulled a face at the smell of the exhaust fumes. 'Can you turn the engine off while we load up?'

'Better not to. Can be a problem starting again.'

She attempted to put her holdall in the boot only to discover that she had happened on the engine compartment at the rear. Another of Divine's design changes? Mitchell laughed, opened the bonnet at the front and dropped her bag into the space next to his small suitcase and the flat spare tyre. 'The boot,' he said.

As they headed west Mitchell launched into a short history of the Hillman Imp. 'One half of a Coventry Climax racing engine, Divine told me. Goes like a bomb.'

Listening to the noise of the engine she grasped Divine's point.

'Shall we nickname it the Human Imp?' she asked.

He thought for a moment. 'No, let's call it the Hillycopter. Then we can imagine we're flying.' They both laughed and the tension between them leached out from the car as they crossed Bowes Moor talking about the hills coming closer, the clouds now threatening rain and what they might eat in the pub that evening. If we get there, Madge thought, as the engine spluttered and struggled up a slight hill.

Along the way there was a wave from the driver of an oncoming blue Hillman Imp with a flashing emergency light on the roof and POLICE on the side.

'A nice touch that,' Mitchell said, 'he most probably mistook our Hillycopter for an unmarked car with a policeman and woman acting undercover.'

'How romantic,' Madge said.

**

Does it always rain in the Lakes? When she was fifteen she had camped with her father for a weekend of wind and rain. When they met other guests on the campsite he was jovial and friendly to all, giving a perfect performance as the loving father. It was her rite of passage into the world of adult hypocrisy.

She remembered him spreading an ordnance survey map on the wet grass as the wind tugged at an edge till the paper tore straight through Dove Cottage. He shouted at her as though the wind was her fault. Although she had never known him turn to poetry he had in recent weeks come over all Wordsworth. Perhaps it was a memory from his schooldays, most likely concerning daffodils. Then when they descended the hill, skirted the lake and arrived at Dove Cottage a notice announced that it was 'Closed'. It felt like her fault. It was too late in the season for daffodils so in his despair her father drove them silently back home to Staines a day early, the sun starting to break through the clouds as they headed south.

It was the only holiday she spent with her father. Now she remembered so very little of her father and nothing with affection. He had died while she was at college. At his funeral she came closer to celebrating his death than his life. Had he loved her scarcely remembered mother, had he mourned her? In her childhood she had never been aware of other women in his life. The lavish praise from the few fellow mourners only showed how little they knew the man. Mrs Dobbs from next door said, 'I'm so sorry, Madge, try not to upset yourself, your father was a good man. He only ever wanted what was best for you.'

As a teenager she had been part of a camping trip in the Lakes arranged by the school in the summer holidays. Miss Bairstow her class teacher had been fun, letting the girls cavort over the fells causing mainly harmless mischief. The rain which came with the storm clouds over the Pennines had been but a temporary blight on youthful spirits. Miss Bairstow's specialism, her passion even, had been wild flowers and to this day Madge could name most of the common species. She remembered 'Miss' with some affection: a spinster living a lonely private life while devoting her energies to her work, her girls. Not so very different from little old me, she reflected.

Towards the end of her schooldays Clive entered her life. She was so young, too young. They promised themselves a week under canvas near Windermere when the war was over. Had that week come to pass she was certain the winds would have been gentle, the sun always shining, and the moon a silver disc bold in the sky as they lay locked together on the grassy knoll outside their solitary tent. Dove Cottage would have been open. They would lie on the grass all night on warm summer evenings, Clive eager inside her. There would have been fields of daffodils. After the cream teas and before long there would have been a child, then children.

But then, back in the long ago, in spite of everything there might have been a child, for one afternoon lying in the field beyond their homes she said to Clive, 'Shall we make a baby?'

Perhaps it was a moment of madness. Clive looked downcast, thought a long while then said, 'War is a savage beast, let's wait till it's all over, something to look forward to.'

He took the usual precautions before they made love and then when he was done he said, 'I'm going down the pub.'

And when the war was over so was Clive.

***

Would Mitchell be able to hold back wind and rain? For once he was not actually wearing his disreputable raincoat but glancing to the back seat she could see it in a heap at the ready. Looking across at him concentrating on driving, she admitted to herself that this was no superman, certainly not a man to control the elements.

'A penny for your thoughts,' he asked.

'Nothing in particular. Somebody I once knew. Just a memory here, a memory there.'

'Good memories?'

'Mixed I suppose.'

'You mentioned your mother dying when you were young. What about your father?'

'Died when I was still at college.'

'He brought you up?'

'Him and a couple of maiden aunts. He never remarried.'

'Was he nice?'

'No, didn't do nice, not with me, other people perhaps. Always said I wasn't good enough.'

'I'm sorry, can't have been easy for him, single parent and all that,' Mitchell said.

They crossed Bowes Moor and descended into the valleys with the road now running downhill. Was that Helvellyn she glimpsed showing through a break in the clouds?

Arriving at the Ploughshares Inn the receptionist asked, 'Although you are booked in as singles – perhaps we had no doubles at the time – we do have a double now if you would prefer it?'

'Perhaps not,' Madge said, 'singles will be just fine.'

Mitchell looked disappointed.

They met up in the bar where a mix of locals and visitors occupied separate ends of the room. The locals were arguing about the miners and their threatened strike.

'String 'em up if they go ahead with it,' said one red-jowelled man. No one disagreed.

'Aye,' contributed another, 'pits o'er West Cumbria are long gone, people 'ave to move with times. Take nuclear plant at Sellafield. That's way of future.'

One of the visitors, a woman sounding from the stockbroker south, joined in to agree that the strike should be put down. 'Holding the country to ransom,' she said, 'but our Margaret will see us through.'

Mitchell winced but looking down into his beer mug said nothing. When they were seated in the tiny restaurant area and out of earshot of the bar he said, 'Funny isn't it? The difference geography makes. In Moortown and Brownlow folk are mostly in support of the strike. In my university just a few miles down the road most are against it. And here… perhaps it is something to do with landscape?'

He looked despondent as his voice trailed away.

The meal they agreed was mostly so-so, not nasty but not especially nice. After another beer for Mitchell and Benedictine for her they went off upstairs to their separate rooms.

'Night-night,' she called after him. He looked back but did not stop. Part of her wished she had said 'yes' to the double room. But it had been so long since… since she had done anything like that… and then only with Clive in a meaningful way. It only ever really meant anything doing it with Clive. She wished now she had been true only to him. But it was his silly fault for going off and dying. Now she had let it go too long, overweight, her skin beginning to wrinkle; the one sight she liked least in the entire world was seeing herself naked in a full-length mirror. How could he possibly want to spend a night with her naked beside him?

She had a tepid shower and went sleepless to bed. Tossing and turning till the sheets wrapped around her like a shroud, all her worries about Mitchell, the office, and memories of Clive whom she had loved and so wanted his child all churned in her brain. Was Clive to blame for everything that followed, her work becoming her life? Why had she turned her back on so many things in life and devoted all her energies to caring for others, especially children who were badly treated? That would be forgetting her father. And how could she forget her father? If only that were possible.

***

Sometimes it seemed like a dream but it was a memory that came to haunt her when her mind was empty of other things. At the weekend her father had his bowls club and beer with his friends down at the Duke of Wellington. She remembered the first time he came home from the pub and announced sternly that she was 'very naughty, simply not good enough' and had to be 'taken in hand.' That first time he fetched her mother's hairbrush from the dressing table in his bedroom, the room that had once been her mother's as well, the hairbrush that in her mother's hand had once been a source of such comfort.

'Young lady, this can't go on, enough is enough, I require you to kneel on your bed with your bare bottom showing,' he said. But what 'this' was he never said. Then he told her not to cry or it would go worse for her before he spanked her hard with the hairbrush. Sometimes she dreaded him coming home from the pub with his beery breath because that was most often when he found most fault. As time went by the spankings increased in severity, the hairbrush now too small and light for his purpose so it was replaced by his thick, heavy slipper and the loud slap on her bottom became louder, the pain harder to bear. She never did cry. When he was finished he lay down beside her and cuddled into her body. She always lay quite still, hating the smell of the beer on his breath, frightened of making him angry again.

'There, there,' he said, 'if you behave from now on I won't have to beat you again. You only need to be good enough.'

But no matter how hard she tried it was never good enough. In time she came to hate him and the injustice of it seared a part of her for life, left her hating unfairness and cruelty, wanting to do something, anything, about it.

Mrs Dobbs said, 'Your father is a hard man but he only wants what's best for you, dearie. He's only doing a father's job. It's difficult for him bringing up an only daughter on his own. He only wants to set you off on the right path. You'll be glad of it one day. Just be careful not to give him any more cheek.' But when she made every effort to be respectful, work harder in the house or at school, it made no difference.

Birthdays and Christmases brought a card and a ten bob note from the aunts until one died and then the other.

Looking back she could only remember that through all those years she had simply not been good enough. When she left home, went to college to train as a child care worker, she thought of him as a very sick man the way he had treated her. It was not something she ever mentioned to the other girls. Only during her social work training did she realise there must be reasons, coming from somewhere deep in his past, why he treated her as he did, the pleasure it might bring him, his perversion and abuse of power. Then he died and it was too late to explain to him how the use of psychodynamic casework, in which she was becoming well versed, might help to cure his problem, their problem. And yet, with understanding came an even greater hatred of his memory, channelled then into a hatred of unseen cruelty to children, a hatred which drove her life's work. Try explaining that to Dan or Lorraine.

Would any man find her wanting? What if her father had been right, what if she was just not good enough? Could she ever explain to Mitchell these things almost too painful to remember which flitted around her brain?

***

Towards morning she heard raindrops hitting the window panes. A wind had come up in the night. Soothed by the sound of the rain she fell asleep and only woke when Mitchell knocked gently on the door. 'Coo-ee, breakfast, we need to be down pretty quickly or we'll be too late.'

Mitchell was impatient over breakfast and hurried her along. 'No time for a second coffee, this weather is perfect for my photography.' At first she thought he was just impatient with her, disappointed at her distance. But no, it was his photography. 'Must get out on the hills before the light is too bright,' he said.

Wrapped in raincoats they trudged along the path lining the valley floor and then up to a ridge from where they could look back through the gloom onto Ullswater. She was fast coming to the conclusion that it did always rain in the Lakes. Mitchell though was ecstatic at the conditions. 'Perfect,' he said, 'just drink in that light through the clouds, the shadows, the mist over the lake. As good as it gets if we can't have snow as well.' Then he set to work snapping away, reading his light meter, changing lenses, fiddling with filters, asking her to hold things. She had never seen him as happy as he was that morning.

After an hour the sun came thrusting through a gap in the clouds and gradually the clouds themselves dispersed and Mitchell said, 'Damn, damn, damn, the sun has come up. That's gone and ruined it. Let's find somewhere we can get a cup of coffee.'

'Somewhere' meant a long walk back along the shore till they joined a road beside which they found a little tea room with a notice saying 'Closed' but when they peered through the steamed-up windows it was obviously open. A plump and uncommunicative woman served them with apparent regret at their presence. 'We really are in "do you ken John Peel" land,' Mitchell said quietly when she disappeared through a jangling chain curtain into the kitchen.

'We must be grateful for small mercies,' she said.

He smiled. 'Sounds a bit religious. Are you that way inclined?'

'Not really, not since…'

When they were back on the lakeside and paused for breath Mitchell looked at her while pausing as if to collect his thoughts before asking, 'You once mentioned a chap called Clive. The fellow in the black and white picture on your mantelpiece. A moustache. Handsome. Laughing. He must be very special to you.'

'Yes, Clive was, very special.'

'I'm sorry. It didn't work out?'

'No, he went and died.'

'I'm so sorry.'

'It's all a long time ago. You see it was the war.'

Mitchell took her hand in his. 'I'm terribly sorry.'

Was it the wind blowing on her cheeks, was it tears, even Madge was not sure.

'Thanks,' she said, 'thanks.'

As the hours dragged by she wanted only to be back home and by herself again. When they once again spent the evening in the bar and then the dining room the conversation was laboured before they retired for the night.

Next morning bright sunlight streamed through her threadbare curtains and she was up early in time to take a short walk on her own before breakfast. The surface of the lake glistened, the early morning sun low in the sky. So, she concluded, it does not always rain in the Lakes, and that was enough to turn her mood so that when she found Mitchell in the dining room tucking in to kippers she was smiling and on the verge of happiness.

'Morning,' he said, 'no need to hurry breakfast this morning now it's a sunny day. On the other hand I just can't wait to get back to process the photographs from yesterday.'

'You do your own?'

'Of course, of course, in the university photographic society's darkroom.'

'Sounds clever. I used to take snaps – haven't taken any for a lot of years now. I had a Box Brownie and used to take the negatives to Boots and then collect the prints a week later.'

'No, no, I'm nothing like that,' he said. 'I'll have the film developed, dried, prints made, perhaps some enlargements, all ready by this evening.' He stopped short and pulled a face. 'Oh God, I just hope the darkroom hasn't run out of chemicals.'

And because he was in a hurry they packed up in haste and headed back over the Pennines. As the Hillycopter roared east with Mitchell beside her and smelling of kippers he said, 'It's Clive isn't it. Clive is between us.'

'Yes, Clive and me, I just can't see how you can want me in that way.'

Mitchell said, 'Do you think you might ever be able to allow me into your life, fully I mean, be something more than just good friends?'

She didn't answer because she didn't know. He was bound to lose interest after the way she had treated him this weekend. She had not attended to his pleasure and surely that was a woman's duty? Given the chance would he have attended to her pleasure? Probably not. After all that was not a man's duty.

'I've been thinking,' she said.

Mitchell smiled. 'Good thoughts or bad thoughts?'

'Good I think. I know it is still some weeks away but I just wondered if you would like to come to the cottage for lunch on Christmas Day. It would only be the two of us I'm afraid.'

'I would say yes, I would love to but – you see the Master of Green College and his wife always ask me round for Christmas. I think they feel a bit sorry for me all on my own. I don't like to let them down.'

'You must do what's best for you.'

She was disappointed and wished she had not asked and yet as her father used to say, 'If you don't ask you don't get.' But Madge had learned long ago that very often even if you did ask you did not get. Mitchell would share Christmas with the Master of Green and his filly; Madge would Christmas alone, she was used to that. She could not hope to compete with the more convivial prospect of Christmas with college folk.

Was this as good as it got?

***

For the rest of the day thoughts of Mitchell jostled around in her mind. What exactly did he mean about allowing him into her life?

Back at work on Monday morning first on the phone was Jim Pyott from the cop shop. 'There's a horse running free on the road out of Moortown. So far no motorists or pedestrians have been injured but cars are swerving te avoid it.'

Madge paused to digest this fresh intelligence. It was not difficult to guess which way Jim's mind was going.

'That does not sound like a social services problem, Jim.'

'The PC attending the scene tells me it looks like the same horse as was causing chaos with its head out of the Farrants' bedroom window. Seems it has some sort of colouring on its coat, varnish or paint or summat.'

'Can you be sure, Jim, and even if – I mean, even if it is, we do not deal in runaway horses. We have any number of statutory obligations but that is not one of them.'

'Ah thowt...' said Jim, pausing to deliver his killer blow. 'Ah thowtt ye had an expert in this line of work, a volunteer, name of Marx.'

'Marcus actually. Tell you what,' Madge said, 'I'll go to the top.'

'Ye mean your Director?'

'No, the father of Marcus is in the government, in the Cabinet. Perhaps we should go to the father?

'Yebuggermar, ye haven't half got a sense of humour, Miss Porfect. One of yer volunteers has a fatha what's in the bloody Tory government! Ye nivvor used te make jokes… you all right?' There was loud laughter down the phone.

'Never been better, Jim, but you've called my bluff, the animal has been ill-treated if it's been painted over so I'll give the RSPCA a call. Time I received some payback on all the donations I make.'

Chapter 12

Lorraine arrived back in the office after home visits in Brownlow. 'I need to speak to you urgently, Madge, about the Farrants, about my treatment plan... I may have to revise it.'

'Problems?'

'Yis, problems, you see... when I asked Melanie how it was for her in bed she asked me which man I was talking about. That surprised me for a start. So I said I was talking about her husband and how they only had one child, young Gary. She laughed, spat in my face, asked had I never noticed how many kids in Gary's class at school looked like Gary, seems they may all have the same father.'

'I see,' said Madge, not in the least surprised that erectile dysfunction was not a factor in this case. Perhaps diagnoses honed in Cape Town did not work when imported as treatment plans to Brownlow?

'Besides,' Lorraine continued, 'it seems it suits her best because other women have the cost and aggravation of bringing up his kids. She likes the way it is, says it's what suits her best.'

'And sharing the blows from his fists,' Madge said before Lorraine went on.

'So then I asked her about her own guilt feelings and she said "What you mean?" I said "Masturbation" and she just laughed, said I was a sad case and she had never known a social worker like me and why don't I fuck off and go fuck myself. Then she opened the door and shouted, "Bugger off, ya foreigner".'

'I see,' said Madge, 'and how do you intend to proceed now? You seem to have broken the ice. It feels like progress. You've got through to her.'

'You think so? Well, if you don't think the case should be transferred to another worker I could go down the road Marcus recommends.'

'Which is?'

'Well, something to do with Chicago, you know, it's in America, but I don't understand that bit. Marcus says it all comes down to economics; people need monetary incentives rather than my psychodynamic shit. He thinks that I should concentrate on getting them a new house, a bigger house, get it decorated and some new furniture. He says material progress is everything, provides all the incentives people need.'

'Marcus thinks that?'

'Yis. He says all human problems, including marital problems, crime, everything, can be solved by economic incentives in free markets.'

'I see, and you believe that?' Madge said.

'There's more, his father in the government has told him that everything that's wrong with the country can be solved by controlling the money supply using the interest rate, whatever that is.'

'You believe all that?'

'Yis.' On the whole she preferred Lorraine saying 'yis' rather than 'ja'.

***

Madge's life settled down to the relentless routine of client demands and mostly overworked staff, relieved by an occasional evening drink with Mitchell in the village pub. He and Marcus were in and out of the office like water boatmen flitting on the surface of a pond. Thoughts about her future retirement rarely troubled her and if her mind strayed in that direction Lorraine's Afrikaans dictum about tomorrow being another day allowed her to put it on a high shelf labelled 'nae bother' as PC Pyott might say.

It was almost the season of glad tidings when the man himself phoned. 'Ah've good news for once, Miss P, ah've just heard that the horse has gone and crossed over the boundary into Darlington, poor bloody beast. Serves Darlington right, wouldn't be surprised if them Quakers go and eat it!'

'Act of God then, not our problem, Jim. By the way they're not French in Darlington, it's the French who eat horses.'

'Bloody hell, them Quakers must be bloody Frenchies, ah might have known it. Well anyway let them bloody Quakers sort it out, and you can tell yer contact in te government to leave off messin with missin horses in Rudham! Should give them more time to spend mekkin peace with the miners.'

Mitchell dropped into the office on his way to Brownlow with Marcus. While Marcus went to have a word with Lorraine, Mitchell said, 'I had a word with the Master and his wife. They were frightfully understanding when I explained my predicament – a competing Christmas invitation that is work-related. So, yes please, if the offer still stands I would love to join you.'

So that's what I am, she thought, a work-related predicament, but she said, 'The offer still stands. I look forward to it.'

'Wonderful. I'll put it in my diary and remember to bring wine.'

And she was looking forward to it though she failed to see why a seemingly intelligent man needed to write down his plan for Christmas Day. Fear he might forget? Yes, that was it, no doubt his mind was forever on higher things or, failing that, his camera and his snaps.

Seeing Lorraine and Marcus chatting and laughing in the corridor, Madge concluded that she was not alone in looking forward to Christmas.

How Moortown was moving with the times, the new Moortown Garden Centre off the roundabout one sign of this. On her way home in the evening she was admiring the Christmas tree with its brightly coloured lights and decorations outside the garden centre gates when she caught sight of Billy striding purposefully towards the town pushing an old pram with a selection of garden canes sticking out at the front. The seasonal spirit was reaching into the most unlikely corners. It was good to see Billy taking an interest in winter gardening, or perhaps thinking ahead and preparing for the spring? Or was it just that items of essential equipment were running low in the massage parlour?

It was a moment to reflect once again that Billy was one of the greatest successes of child care provision in Area 13. Others before and after him had liked to set fire to schools, lacerated their arms, attempted suicide, thieved, attacked policemen, murdered a parent, but few like Billy had graduated from minor crimes to sober citizenship. If Dan were to see Billy in this light perhaps he might flog the therapeutic treatment plan to the other twelve districts: a chain of massage parlours the length and breadth of the county? She chuckled at the thought.

Relaxing in the cottage that evening, sipping a glass of Benedictine, she weighed her life's current hopes and fears. Mitchell would spend Christmas with her rather than at Green College. A number of families seemed to have benefited from her life's work. Billy was but one, there were others, not as many as she might have hoped at the outset of her career, but then it was never easy with people who stepped out in life on the wrong foot. Her job was secure, the latest memo from Puttock had confirmed Dan's story that the restructuring was on hold so that there was now no fear of redundancies. She had sorted out the Oldfield-Farrant situation. Today there was much to be thankful for.

In early to work the next day she ran into Simon in the corridor and asked, 'How is young Alistair Oldfield settling in with the foster parents?'

'It's looking good,' Simon said.

'Dan is keeping his eye on the ball supervising the case?' Madge asked.

'I think so,' Simon replied. Nothing about the way Simon said this was convincing. She must check from time to time.

Then suddenly Lorraine was the victim of a disappointment. Madge going to the ladies' loo heard someone sobbing in one of the cubicles. She waited for the distressed party to emerge and Lorraine said, 'I'm sorry, Madge, I shouldn't cry, it's just that Marcus has told me he is going to spend Christmas with his family without me.'

'I'm so sorry, Lorraine.'

'Ja, my ma always said men are brutes. He says it is in my best interest, he says his family are ghastly, especially at Christmas.'

In mid-afternoon Mitchell, back at the university, came on the phone sounding very agitated.

'Christmas all right?' she asked.

'No, not exactly, I've a problem at work, the Vice-Chancellor has asked me to lie low while he investigates. He's worried about any adverse publicity harming the university.'

'Oh my God, investigates what?' she snapped. 'Have you been suspended?'

'No, the VC said he is stopping short of that at the moment.'

In spite of her previous conviction that he would be the one person who was definitely not a customer of the Golden Slipper she was now no longer sure. All the time she had told herself it must be Dan, could not be Mitchell. She knew now that she had been anything but dispassionate in the matter because she always wanted it to be Dan and never wanted it to be Mitchell.

'Does it involve women?'

'Yes and no,' Mitchell said.

'The massage parlour?'

'What massage parlour?' he snapped.

'The Golden Slipper in Moortown.'

'Never heard of it. Never been near a massage parlour in Moortown or anywhere else. No, no it's something quite different, well almost.' His voice trailed away, he was clearly upset. She immediately regretted her suspicions. Connecting him with a massage parlour could not have helped but it did still look as though he was being far from frank with her.

'We must talk,' she said, 'but not on the phone. Can you come round to the cottage tonight?'

For the rest of that day Madge was not minded to go anywhere, do anything other than stare out of the window watching the clouds swirling snow over the hills across the valley. She had one of her bad feelings and this time it was about Mitchell. What was this thing which was different but not different from the massage parlour? How had she been so stupid getting involved with a man from a different world? Why had she allowed him to enter her life? Why let herself entertain hopes for a shared future? Had she really gone that far? Yes, yes, she knew she had. Fool, fool. Now all she could do was re-inter herself in work, forsaking all else.

But she could not see out the day feeling sorry for herself. The strident demands for help from the Matron at Moortown's old people's home, recently rebranded by the Director as one of his 'Part 3 Happy Days Aged Persons' Homes (APH)', could be ignored no longer.

Arriving at the home she found Matron awaiting her at the entrance, grim-faced, disapproving, but then Matron took a dim view of most things in life, not least area controllers and people in any way associated with County Hall. She had views on dying including her oft repeated assertion that she would never end up in a home like this but would choose instead to shuffle off by her own means long before she became confused, incontinent, dribbly, toothless, hairless, or unable to feed herself. She conceded that people had to die, if only because it was in line with county policy, but would much prefer them to get on with it and do it before entering her home. If she had been idealistic when she took the job that was now a distance away in the once upon a time.

As soon as Madge arrived, Matron harangued her with the latest bad news. Mr Smith, aged eighty-five, had been found naked in bed with Mrs Hair aged eighty-two, also naked. Mrs Hair suffered from dementia. Apparently Mr Smith's problem was unrelieved lust, disgusting in a man his age, perhaps in a man of any age, certainly in a man enjoying the hospitality of her home. If the county had a policy to cover such eventualities, and it almost certainly did, Madge neither knew the policy nor where to find a copy of it. She would have to use her common sense.

The incident might have been glossed over were it not for the fact that Mrs Hair had a husband living alone in a nearby warden-controlled bungalow. He visited his confused wife regularly which was how he came upon the incident in question.

'Hello my darling, my you are restless,' Mr Hair was reported to have said, reaching under the bucking bedclothes and finding a handful of scrotum belonging to Mr Smith who gave angry voice to his sudden switch from pleasure to pain.

Being a jealous man Mr Hair had then threatened to kill Mr Smith by setting him on fire using his fag lighter. Following the dictates of county policy Matron pointed out that smoking was forbidden on the premises. The arson attempt had failed but Matron, seemingly more concerned that the fabric of the home might have burned down, and with it her employment, than the likely death of the residents, demanded to be reassured that 'County' was supportive of her position.

Madge faced a stark demand. 'Miss Perfect, I need you to speak to Mr Smith and Mrs Hair, I need you to tell them it must never happen again. Lust cannot be allowed to infect my corridors.'

'I'll do what I can,' Madge said.

'Oh, and by the way, perhaps you would call round and talk to Mr Hair, calm him down.'

Yes, she would have to do what she could. Whatever that is, she wondered, until she remembered that the self-styled office authority on sex, both theory and practice, was Lorraine. Smiling at the thought, she wondered whether this was the best way forward in this particular instance. Masturbation, even if free from masturbatory guilt, was unlikely to be approved of by Matron. After all you could never be sure where in the building – the smokers' lounge, the dining hall perhaps – Mr Smith might let off steam by pleasuring himself.

But that would be Matron's problem. Why shouldn't Smith and Hair enjoy a tumble before their lights went out? Succumbing to this thought she said, 'I have a member of staff who is ideal for just such a situation, name of Lorraine Burgher, very sensitive in these matters, very experienced where sex is a problem. I'll ask her to be in touch and arrange to visit.'

Matron gave grudging thanks. 'As soon as possible, Miss Perfect. I'm sure that, being like me a mature single lady, your instincts are to leave such things in the hands of the younger folk.'

'Tee-hee!' Madge thought. 'Just so,' she said, almost believing that the case of Hair v Smith would be safe in Lorraine's hands.

***

She was late leaving the office that evening and following an accident there was more traffic than usual on the road to her village. Mitchell was waiting in his car beside the cottage. He joined her as she opened the door. He looked more dishevelled than usual, his hair all over the place, his expression strained. She led him indoors, sat him down, turned on the electric fire and poured two glasses of wine.

'I'm so sorry, Madge,' he said, 'so very sorry.'

'What has happened? It's not the Golden Slipper?'

'No, no, I've never even heard of anywhere with that name.'

'What then?'

He hesitated for a while before launching into the story. 'Do you remember the wife of the Master at Green?'

She nodded and said, 'The Master's filly. Puts herself about a bit, you said. Not with you too?'

He shook his head. 'It all started when I went to the photographic society darkroom after we got back from the Lakes. There were some students larking about drinking cans of Carlsberg. They may have been high on pot; I noticed an unusual smell in the room. I don't know who let them in, who had a key. Anyway they had a nude model in for the evening and were larking about photographing her. I'd never seen them before, I'm sure they weren't members of the photo soc. When one of the students, a girl, stripped off and posed, I put an end to it, explained that the university photographic society darkroom wasn't intended for that purpose.'

'Seems you did no wrong.'

'No, but a day or two later one of the students, the girl who stripped off, took a print she claimed to have found on the enlarger to the Master at Green and said I had been cavorting in the darkroom and taking nude pictures of female students. The Master passed it to his wife and she told her friend the Vice-Chancellor and he called me in to say that there had been a complaint from a student which he must take seriously so that it would be helpful if I stepped down while he investigated. In the meantime he would stop short of suspension.'

'Why might the student have it in for you? No doubt the powers that be were pleased to have a chance to do down Sociology.'

'Who knows? When I asked the students how they came by a key they said it was from someone I knew but when I asked who they just smirked.'

'Marcus?'

'I doubt it. He's not a member. I'll never know for sure.'

She poured him another drink then lit the coal fire. 'What happens next?' she asked, resting her arm around his shoulder.

He drank some wine before answering. 'The VC will organise some kind of investigation, everyone involved including yours truly will have to be interviewed, and then there will be a hearing at which I must be present.'

'And until it is resolved?'

'Rumours are flying around. Those who despise Sociology are fanning the flames. I can't bear to stand around and watch it all, try to overhear whispered conversations. No, I'll come back if and when I'm needed.'

'Till then?'

'I'm heading off to London on the morning train. I won't be coming in to your office; Marcus can carry on for now so the research project is not compromised.'

'And Christmas lunch?'

'Sorry, Madge, but I will be in London. I have friends there. I might go on to Ireland which I love. Besides I can't involve you in this, you must be free to carry on your life untainted by scandal.'

He stood up to go. 'Mitchell, Mitchell,' she said, 'I am involved with you in all sorts of ways. Surely we can face it together.'

'No, no,' he said, 'it would not be right.'

Then she kissed him on his cheek and he was gone into the night.

She drew the curtains, sat down staring into the fading glow of the coals on the fire she had lit for him. Why am I weeping? she wondered, then realised she knew why. Mitchell would leave such a gap in her life. If he did not return she could concentrate instead on becoming what she had started to dread: a celibate old maid wedded only to her job, retirement at the normal age not so far down the line. Why had she said 'no' to a double room in the Lakes?

Before going to bed she laid the book she had bought him for Christmas on the hall table. She had not even wrapped it yet. Tomorrow would be soon enough to decide how to dispose of it. Tonight she could only think of the pain of it all. Just when she had become used to finding the toilet seat in the upright position the perpetrator had migrated out of her life.

As Matron had said, it was probably better for single ladies, no doubt an abbreviation of 'single old has-beens', to leave such things to younger folk.

***

For the very first time Madge was dreading the office Christmas party. Worrying about Mitchell, missing him like hell, she was finding it difficult to sleep, to concentrate on work issues now that she was back to 'normal', her work her life. Had she never needed to love or be loved? With Mitchell gone should she no longer worry about his feelings for her or hers for him? Looking back on her life she could see that apart from Clive she had never been loved since her mother died, certainly not by her father. And had Clive really loved her? Then, late in the day, there was Mitchell, a tease, his feelings hidden beneath a protective carapace. She had loved Clive and begun to feel similar things for Mitchell. Beginning to love someone, being loved herself, had floated before her. Even if no more than a possibility it had served to remind her that there might after all be more to life than work. Now Mitchell, disgraced, had disappeared to London.

The cases she normally worried about had slipped to the back of her mind. Even her irritation in the presence of Dan had largely evaporated. Where before he had been a succession of mosquito bites he was now but a fly, alighting hardly noticed on her skin. What else was there to fear after losing Mitchell? Why didn't he phone or write? Not even a Christmas card. Was he all right? Where was he? London? Ireland?

Reaching the office she realised that never since Clive's death had her feet dragged as reluctantly as when she walked the short distance from the car park into the office party.

Brenda, standing behind a desk covered with red and green crepe paper and host to a collection of booze, greeted her with, 'Red or white, hinny?' Now only Brenda normally retained her preferred more formal mode of address except at moments like this when she relaxed her guard. With a glass of red wine Madge headed towards Lorraine who looked miserable sitting on her own in a corner.

'Oh, hello Madge,' she said. Her speech was already slightly slurred; she had made an early start on the wine. From the corner by the filing cabinets came the tinny sound of a cassette churning out Christmas carols. 'Jingle bells, jingle bells, jingle…' went on and on till it reached the next tired carol.

'Enjoying the party?' Madge asked. She was surprised to see Lorraine in jeans and a scruffy blouse, not what she expected of the fun girl of the office at a party.

'Not really. Like I told you my ma always says men are brutes.'

'I'm truly sorry.'

Madge found herself missing Mitchell as much as Lorraine seemed to be missing Marcus. Men, they lead you on only to head off in a different direction when it suits them.

'Ja, thanks, Madge. He thought I would find his family awfully stuffy, better I have some fun over Christmas, that sort of shit… even when I said I wanted to send him and his family a Christmas card all he would tell me was to send it to him care of Yorkshire. He said that would find him for sure.'

Unlikely, Madge thought. She would have been willing to bet a sizeable sum of money that Marcus had always entertained other plans for Christmas. She guessed

Lorraine now thought much the same. She could not help feeling sorry for Lorraine and, had things been different, would have given her a motherly hug. Motherly? They were just two women abandoned by their men. Lorraine had ceased to irritate her as much as she once had.

'What are you doing over Christmas, Lorraine?'

'Just dossing around in my flat I suppose. I'm not taking any leave days. I want to keep them for when Marcus is back.'

'I could offer you lunch on Christmas Day if you don't get any better offers.'

Lorraine looked astonished. 'Ag sus, baie dankie, Madge, that's very kind, mooi, thank you so much. I could cook some bobotie and bring it with me.'

'Well then,' Madge said, silently worrying that she might be going soft in her old age, 'we shall have a feast.' Feeding two people would mean less of the turkey going to waste.

She moved on around the room stopping to chat here and there, dodging the Christmas cards flapping on the wall or falling to the floor where they lay scuffed by passing feet. When she passed Dan she scarcely noticed him and only meant to stop briefly to wish him a happy Christmas with his family. He mentioned he would not be in again until after the New Year. She no longer cared where the hell he was. He hadn't consulted her about leave but so what. She would have planned leave herself but now that Mitchell was gone what was the point? What was the point of the whole bloody thing?

A Christmas card with a large coloured print of County Hall edged with an adornment of holly caught her eye. Someone, Dan she suspected, had cut out a large cardboard arrow which pointed to the card in its solitary isolation on an otherwise empty space on the wall. Below it no doubt the same someone had printed the words 'FROM OUR DIRECTOR'. Yes, it could only be Dan, for he was standing before it as if on guard at a sacred site.

She went over to him and said, 'You're carrying the flag for the Director then?'

Dan grinned. 'The nomination meeting is in the middle of January. No time at all till we know the outcome. They're bound to choose our Director, best man and all that.'

'I think there is a woman candidate,' Madge said.

'A no-hoper,' Dan said, 'make-weight.'

She knew of course that Dan was right; the Director would no doubt win the Labour nomination, win the by-election and begin his new life as an MP at Westminster. Fat little difference it would make to her all the same.

Then Dan said, 'I don't know if you remember the horse business? The Farrants had a horse and Marcus helped the Farrants to dispose of it. When I told the Director he just laughed, said it was a wonderful use of a volunteer resource. The use of volunteers impacts positively on our cost structure, outputs with zero costs, increased efficiency. The Director was delighted, praised me for my initiative.'

'Your initiative?'

'Yes, Lorraine, my worker. Sorry, must dash.'

When she next glanced round the room he had gone home to his family Christmas, not back till the New Year.

She still hoped that he might in time become human, yet was uncertain he would make it. Give him twenty years, ten perhaps, and he would be near or on the top of the County Hall pyramid.

Simon came up to her and said, 'Dan had to rush home to the family. He asked me to wish you a merry Christmas. Seems he forgot to say.'

And what, she wondered, sipping her wine, had happened to Marcus' intervention seeking a larger house for the Farrants? Just when it looked as if Lorraine might be deflected from masturbatory guilt and erectile dysfunction it seemed as if the economic model of human behaviour, imported by Marcus to Moortown and Brownlow from Chicago, had lost in a shoot-out with the psycho-babble approach, Cape Town style. At the moment it was one surprise after another, and greatest among these was Dan's newly found 'initiative'.

There was nothing whatsoever about this throng of her chattering staff to lighten her mood. Once she had loved the north, her job, liked most of her colleagues. So many things had changed. It sickened her to see the cronyism and corruption, the opportunism catapulting the Director to higher office.

'What are you doing over Christmas, Simon?'

'Not a lot but I'm happy with that. I've signed up for some slots on the emergency duty rota.'

'Would you like to come to my cottage for Christmas lunch? Lorraine is coming round.'

At first she thought he was about to accept but perhaps it was Lorraine's name that decided it. 'Thanks but I'm happy the way it is. You're very kind. Frankly I'm worrying a little about young Alistair Oldfield.'

'Why so? He's surely safe with the foster parents.'

'That's it though. I just hope he has a good Christmas now he's home on trial. I just hope it goes all right.'

'He's what?!'

'Home on trial. Dan decided he could go home for a family Christmas. On trial. He's due back with the foster parents in the New Year.'

'Dan didn't consult me first.'

'I'm sorry.'

'Not your fault, Simon.'

'Dan said we must always balance the risk against the cost of keeping a child in our expensive care. He was quoting some economics book or other. Or perhaps it was the Director.'

'I doubt if Cumbria social services on whose behalf we are supervising Alistair would see it quite like that. Have you spoken to Miss Page over there recently?'

'Not yet. Better had.'

Madge raised her gaze to the paper decorations running round the top of the walls, zigzagging in green, red and yellow loops.

'Are the Oldfield parents still staying with the Farrants?'

'Yes, till the end of January.'

'As you are on duty over Christmas, Simon, keep an eye on the Oldfield situation. I'm not happy about that.' Even in his absence and in her present mood Dan did have the power to annoy her. So unprofessional. At least she had something to worry about that wasn't Mitchell.

Simon nodded and said, 'You know the worst thing?'

My God, she wondered, what could possibly be worse? Simon said, 'The Oldfields bought a second-hand electric Scalextric car race set for Alistair for Christmas.'

'But even if Alistair should have been with his foster parents over Christmas he will at least enjoy the Scalextric.'

'That's not what saddens me – you see the Farrants' electricity was disconnected a week ago so he won't be able to play with it. He was so looking forward to it, poor kid.'

Brenda came up and nudged Madge's elbow. 'It's a phone call for Simon, some woman from Cumbria, Holly something wanting to say Happy Christmas.'

Brenda grinned as Simon blushed and Madge said, 'How nice, pass on seasonal greetings to our colleagues in the west, Simon, perhaps keep back the Alistair news till the New Year.'

As Simon hurried off Brenda asked, 'Is that the canny lass that came over for the Oldfield case con?'

Madge nodded.

'Well I never,' Brenda said, 'well I never.'

Walking around the room Madge noticed how often talk now turned to a likely strike by the miners next year. The miners would stand behind Scargill and face up to Thatcher. Brenda, as ever anticipating events, was going round the room rattling a bucket of coins and as Madge drifted towards the door she said, 'Just collectin for the strike fund, it's for the miners and their families.'

'They're not on strike,' Madge said.

Brenda pulled a face and said, 'They soon will be.'

Madge scrabbled around in her purse and put in a fiver. 'God help us all,' she said.

Brenda said, 'Amen', and moved on, shaking her bucket. Madge heard one of the men saying, 'Time we swung them Tory bastards from the lampposts.'

The cassette player which had changed from carols to dance music growled to a halt and Brenda put down her bucket and went over to the machine and dragged out the mangled tape. Simon came back from the phone and Madge thought she saw the beginnings of a smile on his face. Well done, Miss Page.

Brenda picked another cassette and said, 'I like this one, it's more seasonal.'

It was even more mawkish. 'Away in a manger, no crib for a bed...' Madge threaded her way through the throng. To her surprise she saw that Brenda was now kissing Alan, or was Alan kissing Brenda? Neither was objecting. It must be the effect of the alcohol.

As soon as she felt she decently could she waved from the doorway and headed out into the darkness of the car park. No one seemed to notice her going. Standing still for a moment she felt alone and insignificant. She moved on as the chatter from the party faded and all that was left as she reached her car was the saccharine sweetness of the distant... 'the little Lord Jesus lays down his sweet head...'

Until she switched on the headlights it was as dark as she imagined it to be down a pit, a place where no woman could ever go just as no woman could ever aspire to reach the top at County Hall. It used to disappoint her that even in this day and age, in ways large and small, the dice were stacked against her kind. Now she no longer cared. In the sudden cold after the warmth of the office she realised that a speedy return home was essential for she now had an urgent need to trickle down. At least some things could be relied upon for their regularity. The same could no longer be said of her job in social work; since the Mitchell business her heart had gone out of it.

Snow was just starting to fall. Back in the security of her cottage and with another glass of wine to hand her thoughts strayed into a melancholy review of the season. Each year, month after month, families erupted, the elderly suffered crises, and mental health produced urgent referrals, yet every Christmas Area 13 went ominously quiet. 1983 had begun uneventfully, produced a surprise in the form of the early retirement memo, picked up with the arrival of Mitchell, wobbled over her difficulties with Dan, and sunk lower with the departure of Mitchell.

The prospects of an upturn in 1984 looked far from promising even without a strike by the miners. If she had believed in star signs she would have laid a bet that it was shaping up to be a year of melancholy occurrences which would begin when the local population swung back on the pendulum of crises as soon as the New Year began.

And the Oldfields with little Alistair enjoying Christmas in the Farrant home? Perhaps no harm would come of it, perhaps Dan was right after all.

Chapter 13

On Christmas Eve Madge put up a few relics of the decorations from the box she kept in the cupboard under the stairs. She would have got around to it sooner, made more of an effort, if Mitchell had been coming. It was only right though to go to a little trouble with her impulsive invitation to Lorraine to come round for lunch.

The few Christmas cards she received were mostly tawdry and sentimental, a robin or two and several snow-covered scenes in picturesque villages mostly in the south. One or two were from the neighbours she seldom bumped into. Then there were the unexpected; these required reciprocals in return. The only card she looked forward to was from a college girlfriend; they had been close as students but never met since. When her friend married and raised a family they kept in touch, her Christmas cards always including an account of the near perfect behaviour and scholastic, sporting and musical accomplishments of her children, as well as a husband rising steadily through the ranks at work. As the years went by she found this account of a perfect family increasingly tedious but in a strange way it was a reminder of normal family lives, not like hers, not at all like the Farrants. From Mitchell there was still not even a card let alone a phone call.

Choosing what to wear posed the usual problem. She and her wardrobe had aged together. She fancied a dress but after much headshaking at what was on offer on the rack in the wardrobe she settled on a rather dull dark green and navy tartan skirt going back to the year dot. A cream blouse that did not need ironing would be good enough. She laid them out ready for the morning.

She slept little that night, all the while worrying about Mitchell, missing him, cross with him for not being with her, envying the friends in London or Ireland who would share his Christmas.

She was up early the next morning bustling about in the tiny kitchen and stuffing the turkey. The raucous shrieks of children in the next house were already annoying her. A packet of sage and onion stuffing bought from the grocer wasn't ideal but it would do. Potatoes, Brussels sprouts, carrots all had to be prepared then parked in pans of cold water ready on the hob. Where had she put the chipolatas and bacon? Not in the tiny fridge but outside the front door in the shed in which she stored gardening tools, as cold as any fridge in this weather. She must not forget the add-ons: gravy, bread sauce, cranberry sauce. Why did it all seem such an effort?

Just after midday Lorraine arrived in an outfit that looked pure Diana, perhaps even a copy of something worn by the princess, the dress a flowery print with padded shoulders and a full skirt with a flounce round the bottom, the sleeves puffed. It signalled good, expensive taste but Madge was not altogether sure it looked good on Lorraine, nor sure that it would have gone down well in the baronial hall of Marcus and family in their castle in Yorkshire. There could be no doubt it was the outfit carefully planned for her anticipated Christmas with the toffs. Madge reckoned it must have cost more than Lorraine earned in a month.

How pretty, Madge thought, well almost, a proper young lady in her Christmas dress, all the bluster drained out from her.

'I've brought you a card,' Lorraine said. Madge opened the envelope, it was another robin in a holly tree. She mumbled thanks, tried to remember if she had a reciprocal left, perhaps there might just be the odd one in the shoebox with cards collected down the years with missing envelopes. She would choose a discreet moment, scribble a message when Lorraine went to the bathroom.

They sat in front of the fire sipping mulled wine, Lorraine's carefully styled big head of hair circling above her face.

Lorraine said, 'I didn't even get a card from Marcus. Bastard. Nix.'

'I'm sorry,' Madge said.

'I sent him one with his name and care of Yorkshire, like he said, just for bad, I know it can't possibly find him.'

'No, not possible,' Madge agreed.

What else was there to say? Work was a safe place so Madge said, 'I haven't heard any more from Matron so I assume you managed to stamp out sex in the Happy Days Aged Persons' Home?'

Lorraine laughed. 'Ach no, wasn't me; old Mr Smith went and died. Matron said best thing, problem solved.

Apparently Mr Hair told her it was God's will, vengeance of the Lord and all that shit.'

'Poor bugger,' Madge said, 'but perhaps he died happy.'

'Perhaps not after Mr Hair squeezed his balls,' Lorraine said, her clunky bright red earrings bobbing up and down as she spoke.

'Is Mrs Hair missing Mr Smith's company in bed?

'Nix, she's telling everyone she's taken Clark Gable as her new lover. To conceal his identity from the other residents she calls him Mr Butler.'

'That's dementia for you. There you go, good old Rhett, gone with the wind but alive and well in Moortown,' Madge said. 'The good Lord works in mysterious ways his wonders to perform.'

Lorraine asked, 'Do you believe all that bullshit?'

'Sometimes.' She didn't say that she would have been closer to believing had Mitchell been with her for Christmas. Or Clive.

Lorraine said, 'I'm writing an article for *Social Work Tomorrow* on sex in the north of England. The editor seems keen on the idea. I'm basing it on the Farrants.'

'My God,' said Madge, 'you won't name them.'

'No worries, Madge, I've called them the van Rensburgs, makes it sort of anonymous.'

A small mercy albeit an unusual name in Brownlow, Madge thought, for if masturbatory guilt in Brownlow was to hit the newsstands there was no way of knowing where it might end.

Before serving lunch she turned on the record player and put on the first LP that came to hand. She did not have very many and this one was a collection of Christmas carols so she rapidly replaced it with Dvorak's *New World Symphony*, pleasant enough as an analgesic in the background. It had been her first ever LP and the scratches that from time to time distorted the sound were evidence of age.

As they picked their way through the prawn cocktail Lorraine said it was just the same as they got in Cape Town. Then they had a small portion of the bobotie that Lorraine had brought, a Cape Malay dish she said: minced lamb, eggs, chopped almonds, dried apricots, sultanas, curry powder and lots more of this and that. Nice, Madge thought, but a meal in itself.

When they reached the roast turkey Lorraine said it was the same as they got in Cape Town. When they finished off the meal with Christmas pudding set alight by Madge she knew she would not want another meal for a week. And said so. Lorraine said it was just the same in Cape Town. All the while the wine flowed, rather more so than Madge had intended.

Searching around for something more to say she asked Lorraine, 'Your first Christmas in England? How do you find it here?'

'It's so cold. My flat is so cold. But it's not just the weather. Some of the clients got to me before Christmas. The Robinsons are all registered mentally handicapped yet someone gave them a tank of fish with a notice on the side saying "Piranhas – Dangerous fish". But not one of them can read.'

'Probably a cruel joke,' Madge said. 'Perhaps they're any old fish.'

'Would anyone do that?'

'I'm afraid they would in Moortown,' and then after another slurp of wine, 'By the way, how are you getting along with Dan?' She regretted asking the moment it was too late not to ask. It must be the wine. She must be more careful, more discreet.

'OK I think, he's fussy, worries about the paperwork, worries about what County Hall might think, finds me disrespectful of the suits at County Hall, doesn't like what I wear.'

Madge coughed. 'I know what you mean.' She did not mention her own concern about Lorraine's office clothes and certainly had no intention of admitting that it was she who had spurred Dan into action on this matter. She was not altogether comfortable sharing Christmas with this young woman from abroad, the layers of blue eye shadow, the cheeks enhanced with bright blush shades. Perhaps it was as well Lorraine had been stood down from Yorkshire.

After helping herself to another glass of wine Lorraine went on, 'You know he is disloyal to you I'm sure. He often says you are too old for the job, too slow, not adapting to new ways, too focused on the clients. Ach sus but I don't think he should say that to us monkeys lower down the tree. It's disloyal. I mean he can think it but not say it to us. It's not right.'

'I know what you mean.' Clearly the wine was also getting to Lorraine who trampled on asking, 'What is a frump? Dan sometimes uses that word when he mentions you and I don't like to let on I don't know what it means. Is it like a compliment?'

'A frump is… I'm not sure myself.' Madge knew she had let the Dan conversation run too far already. The wine…

She changed the subject. 'Do you listen to the Queen's Christmas broadcast to the Commonwealth when you're in Cape Town?'

'We're not in the Commonwealth any more. Some of the older English-speaking people pick it up and get all sentimental. But you have to move on, times change.'

'Will times ever change in South Africa?'

'Ja, once we defeat the terrorists. But sus man they went and let that Mandela off the death penalty.'

Madge could think of nothing fruitful down that road so she said, 'What would you be doing in Cape Town at Christmas?'

'I'd be jumping in the back of a bakkie and heading down to the beach at Muizenberg. I'd be playing around with the boys near Surfers' Corner. There'd be beach volleyball. Then a braai and a few cans of Castle.'

'Braai?'

'Barbecue.'

'And in the evening?'

'In the evening we have roast turkey with all the trimmings, just like here.'

Madge found herself staring at the phone willing it to ring. If he phoned she could say how much she was missing him. If only she hadn't been silly about the double room in the Lakes they might have been close enough now to stand together in his hour of need. If only she hadn't suspected he had been to the Golden Slipper. The unwrapped present she had planned to give Mitchell, a book about his hero the photojournalist Robert Capa which she had found in the posh university bookshop in Rudham, lay beside the phone. It hadn't come cheap. Come the New Year she must drop it in at a charity shop in Moortown.

She asked, 'Are you very fond of Marcus?'

'Ja, I know he's a right shit but all the same I'll be pleased to see him back after New Year. He said he wasn't sure Prof Mitchell would be back ever. Wouldn't tell me what that is all about though I'm sure he's somehow involved in it. You quite like the prof, don't you?'

Measuring her words carefully Madge said, 'Yes, I do quite like him.'

All the while though in her private inner world she knew she would be more than glad to see Mitchell back in 1984; what scared her most was that she might have seen the last of him. What if Marcus knew more than she did? What if Marcus was right? What if Mitchell never came back? She knew the answer; she would go on working till she dropped. Perhaps, with or without Mitchell, it had always been thus?

They moved back to the chairs by the fire where Madge fell asleep. When she woke Lorraine had gone, leaving a scribbled note: 'Dankie, Madge.'

So many things had changed since the first memo from Puttock, even her feelings for Lorraine. She still noticed the accent, scowled at the sight of some of her outfits, hated her racism, but now she saw some good qualities as well. Lorraine was hard-working in a slapdash way and under a decent manager, anyone but Dan, she might have grown in the job.

On Boxing Day she did the washing-up left after the Christmas lunch. She had drunk far too much wine. Dan was right, she was a frump. Her head throbbed. Cooking smells still hung in the air. Lorraine had offered to help but Madge knew that in the morning she would be glad of anything that distracted her from the emptiness of the holiday weekend. Was work all that was left to her now that Mitchell was disgraced and gone? She moped around looking for things to do, did some washing, walked shivering round the misty garden with spider webs stretching like aerial ropeways from plant to plant, tried to read a book but became bored, drank some of the leftover wine, dozed in front of the fire.

On Tuesday, a bank holiday, she leafed through the Robert Capa book that she had been ready to give to Mitchell. All those black and white images of war. The Normandy landing beaches: could Clive be one of those dots of men struggling ashore? Should she add it in memory of him to her little bookshelf? Ridiculous! Sentimental tosh. Give it to a charity shop? Would there be much demand for it in Moortown? No, none. Perhaps in Rudham, after all it was a university town, a city, a place where people might read books like that. She left it lying on the hall table. What would her father be thinking of her were he to be looking down on her now? 'Stupid girl,' he would have said. His voice still echoed down the years.

In the evening Simon, who was covering an out-of-hours emergency duty slot, phoned sounding agitated.

'It's the Oldfields,' he said, 'they seem to have done a runner taking young Alistair with them. The foster parents phoned to say Alistair had not been returned by the promised time today. I visited the Farrants but found no one at home. I talked to a neighbour and she said the Oldfields had left after loading heaped cardboard boxes with their stuff into a banger on Christmas Eve. She knew nothing about the Farrants.'

'You must speak to Dan asap when the office reopens in the morning. It's his responsibility. There isn't much we can do tonight. Have a word with the police and reassure the foster parents that we will be searching for Alistair.'

'Only one problem, Dan isn't back till the day after tomorrow. He phoned me to say one of the children is ill and with his wife due back at work he has to stay at home and look after the kiddie.'

'I see.'

The next morning Simon was waiting outside her office when she arrived for work.

'Any news?' she asked.

'No news,' he said, 'anyway Dan always said it would be good riddance if they left the district.'

'Surely not. We know differently. Alistair is in the care of the local authority in Cumbria and we supervise on their behalf. It's our responsibility. He's clearly at risk.' She knew Simon was upset, probably blaming himself and not Dan who authorised the home leave, yet even Simon was still grasping at Dan's straws.

He said, 'Dan always says their departure back to where they came from will help our statistics, improve our success rate.'

Biting back the sarcasm she felt, she said, 'Depends what he means by success. In any event you must follow up with the police, check with Cumbria.'

'But they may not have gone to Cumbria. The family could be anywhere by now.'

'So we must try everywhere. Most likely they've headed back to Cumbria, they must have family or friends there. And ask Lorraine to try the Farrants' house again, they may be back, may know where the Oldfields have gone.'

'Will they tell us if they do?'

'Probably not but we must at least try. After all they are relatives. If anyone can get sense out of them Lorraine will. She's flavour of the month since she told them Marcus will use his influence with Housing to make sure they will soon be rehoused into a bigger council house.'

When Simon rushed off Madge pulled a face. She would not put it past Dan to have given them the train fares just to get them off his patch, improve his statistics.

Dan and his bloody statistics. Statistics! But wasn't that also the world of Mitchell? Where was Mitchell? Doing what?

The day passed without news of the Oldfields. Lorraine called in to the office at five-fifteen.

'I asked the Farrants if they knew anything but Melanie told me to go lose myself down the bog – none of our business where they've gone.'

'Helpful as ever,' Madge said.

'I shouted at them, "Go crap yourselves, you pathetic losers".'

'You didn't?' Madge said. 'They'll make a formal complaint, they'll go to the *Northern Times*.'

'Sus man, I did it,' said Lorraine, 'but in Afrikaans. For once I managed to silence them. I think Melanie thought it was a compliment.'

Thanks to Dan the Oldfields had exploded her belief that nothing much happened over Christmas. They had done a runner with little Alistair, who knew where? How long before Puttock at County Hall got wind of all of this. And when he reported it to the Child Care Manager, who would report it to the Director, they would unleash the hounds baying for her blood once again.

EPIPHANY TERM
1984

Chapter 14

Arriving at work the next morning she was more than a little surprised to find Billy, deputy manager of Mrs Hill's Golden Slipper, lurking suspiciously and quite obviously waiting for her as she pulled into the office car park. It was not high on the list of surprises she might have hoped for.

'Well, Billy, what brings you here?'

Billy shuffled his feet. After taking a good look into the sky as if he had acquired a sudden interest in clouds he muttered, 'Ah'm in court next month, miss, and ah needs a character witness. I thowt yer would do.'

'Billy, although I might "do" it would be quite improper for me to act in that capacity. After all the bad times we went through when you were younger I cannot make things up, I cannot lie for you.'

Perhaps this was a little harsh given Billy's transformation from naughty boy to family man with a regular job but somewhere a doubt lurked. Time would be the arbiter as to the permanence of change.

'Ah divven't need yer to lie this time, miss.'

'I never lie, Billy.'

'But miss, yer knaa them court reports yer used to write?'

'Yes, Billy.'

'Yer knaa the ways the magistrates always said yer'd done a great job on them reports.'

'I do.'

'Yer knaa some of it was crap! I was kidding yer along yer knaa.'

'I never doubted that, Billy. Anyway, what are you accused of now?'

'Some stuff's gone missing from the cooker factory on the industrial estate and they're saying ah had some part in it.'

'That's not good, Billy.'

'But ah didn't do nothink. It's aall circumstantial.'

When Billy used the word 'circumstantial' it meant only one thing: he knew the case would be difficult for the prosecution. It didn't necessarily follow that he hadn't done it. How many times had she heard Billy swear blind he wasn't there, or someone else had done it, or the police had fitted him up? The excuses were as long as a winding cable lowering a cage full of men down a pit.

'That may be true,' she said, 'but proving in court that you weren't involved will depend on the evidence.'

'Yer knaa, ah'm older now, ah'm reformed.' From his earnest expression she could tell he really meant it. Then she remembered he had always been very good at sincere expressions of innocence. She tried not to smile while remembering his earlier problems with school attendance, appearances before the juvenile court, custodial sentences, the dodgy deals when he ran the local garage, his role in the massage parlour, and not forgetting the rumours that swirled around the town about some of his other activities.

To speak up for Billy as a model citizen might put her own reputation at risk and require powers of persuasion well beyond anything she could in conscience offer to the bench.

'I'm sorry, Billy, it's just not on.'

Billy surveyed the clouds once again. 'But, howway, miss, ah've summat yer want, summat in exchange.'

Almost against her better judgement she asked, 'What?'

'Well, knaa yer boss man?'

'Which boss man?'

'One of yer top men, yer knaa him. Often comes to the massage parlour. Ah telt yer afore. Dresses flash. The girls aall laugh when he is gone. Sometimes caalls his-sel the bishop, other times it's like add-ons.'

'Billy, you're having me on.'

'Whyaye yebuggermar, it's true, miss, true, it's him. He used to come with that dodgy MP before he went and croaked soon after visiting us. They were close those two. Mrs Hill even gave yer top man some free sessions out of sympathy after the MP deed. The girls themselves are very kind to him since his friend deed.'

'And all this in working time?'

He pulled his 'don't be daft' face and said, 'Naa, he deed in the fish and chip shop in the evening.'

She managed not to say 'don't be stupid' but just said, 'I know where the MP died. I want to know who it is the girls are kind to, Billy.'

'Why man, it's like ah said. Yer will be my character witness, miss?'

She was tempted to pursue the matter but she had her own standards of behaviour to consider. Nonetheless she thought long and hard before saying, 'I couldn't possibly speak for you, Billy, I am sure you must be mistaken.'

Billy shook his head and said, 'Yer'll be sorry, miss.' It sounded like a threat. Then he shambled off looking disappointed. Madge wondered if she had missed a trick, for what if Billy was right? No, impossible. Principles, right or wrong, were things you lived or died by. Her father was sitting on her shoulder, watching for any sign of weakness, his slipper at the ready.

Back in the office she hunted down Dan, now returned to work and wanting to sound off to a sympathetic audience after enduring sleepless nights with his sick child. Madge found sympathy hard to come by and quickly turned to updating him on the Oldfield situation. One thing seemed increasingly certain: Dan was no longer a possible candidate for the mystery caller at the Golden Slipper.

To her surprise and annoyance he seemed unconcerned when she said, 'You allowed Alistair home for Christmas knowing he was in our care. You did not consult me. And now the family has disappeared with the lad.'

Dan laughed and said, 'One less family on the patch for us to worry about.'

Madge only just managed not to launch into a tirade.

'What are you going to do about finding the family?' she asked.

Dan looked at her and smiled. 'They went walkabout on your watch. As you know I was on leave. Not my responsibility.'

She swung round and strode to her office. Bastard! Staring out of her steamed-up window at the hills across the road she muttered expletives. Could she tackle Dan's performance? Too late, too late. He had already secured his defensive positions. Safe in his secret bunker in County Hall he had become untouchable. Shit.

Finding Simon in the social workers' room she was shaken to find his normally carefully combed hair in a wayward state, no doubt a man who had slept little and tried every possible key that might unlock the door to the Oldfields' hiding place.

'Can I have a word?' she said. He followed her through to the privacy of her office.

'You look rough,' she said.

'My fault, you see, I've tried everything, I just can't forgive myself for letting it happen.'

'Not your responsibility,' Madge said, 'it was Dan's idea and his responsibility.'

'But it doesn't feel like that,' Simon said.

'Have you tried the social worker from Cumbria, Miss Page, there must be a good chance they went to friends or family for Christmas, she could check that out for us don't you think?'

'I'll phone Holly now.'

Madge said, 'Meanwhile I'll ask Lorraine to put pressure on the Farrants who must know where the Oldfields went. What about the police? Have they picked up any clues on their radar?'

'Not a dicky-bird.'

An hour later Simon reported back on his phone call

to Holly Page in Workington: she would send someone round to check any known addresses. She was concerned that her manager would be unimpressed at Alistair being allowed home from the foster parents while Rudham was supervising the care order on their behalf.

***

When she thought about Dan's virtues, a rare and far from favourite occurrence, she realised that he was one of the few young people she trusted behind the wheel of a car in which she was a passenger. He always accelerated gently, drove slowly, braked gently, left a large gap before the car in front, stopped at traffic lights, even seeming to anticipate the orange light. In his driving she had complete confidence.

'You're a very safe driver,' she said as they headed for Dan's talk to the Thursday Club.

'I take care of my car,' Dan said, 'I don't want any scratches on my paintwork. When I eventually come to sell it I want the top price for its age and condition.'

The front seats were covered with a loose bed sheet to keep them pristine, all part of a pattern Madge thought. Perhaps he was an obsessional hand-washer? There was no way of knowing.

As if part of a funeral procession they crawled to the Moortown Cricket Club on the edge of town. With the season now long past, no young men in white flannels graced the field beside the paint-peeling, weather-beaten cricket pavilion with its recently amended sign:

M.C.C.
THE W G GRACE – Arthur SCARGILL
MEMORIAL PAVILION

Madge smiled at the ambiguity for it was common knowledge that Mr Scargill was still very much alive and a hate figure in the south, even if some, not least Thatcher, lamented his survival.

Waiting to greet them at the door was Mr Barkle, the retired bank manager and veteran complainant about the nest of 'politicos' in the social services office spending his taxpayers' money and generally buzzing around making trouble for decent people like him.

He stretched out an arm. 'So glad you could make it today, Miss Perfect. I know how busy you are with that gang of scoundrels you try to manage. Radicals!'

He then turned to Dan. 'Hello Aubrey, good of you to offer a talk. We've got a reporter to cover your speech, young chap from the *Northern Times*.'

Barkle waved to the 'young chap' sitting at the back beside a mound of greying, seen-better-days batting pads and jock straps with their tracery of broken straps. The musty smell of unwashed men's cricketing apparel hung in the air, catching in Madge's nose, rasping down her throat.

'Not Aubrey,' Dan said, 'he's a colleague name of Simon. I'm Bagley, Dan Bagley'.

'I see, I see, funny name that,' said Barkle, harrumphing. 'Not what Miss Perfect told me but I suppose you may know best.' Madge noticed Dan looking disdainfully at the tired, elderly man before him: check jacket, discreet tie, and trousers with razor-sharp creases. Most of the other men were similarly dressed and with hardly a wisp of hair amongst them, soldiers in the neat and tidy brigade. What was Dan thinking? He was certainly a stranger to sympathy. Fellow feeling was something he just did not do.

'Just one thing I ought to mention,' Barkle said, drawing Dan closer and taking hold of his sleeve, 'I want you to look into my disabled person's parking badge.'

'Is there a problem?'

Barkle snorted. 'Some young chaps are parking in the disabled parking bays without a badge. I want you to sort it out.'

'Not for me I'm afraid, you must speak to the district council or the police. I'm county council.'

'But your department issued the badge. It must be your responsibility.'

'Afraid not.'

'Fiddlesticks, young man! I'll have a word with Miss Perfect later. She always sees me right.' More harrumph. 'Be that as it may, young Aubrey, our members are looking forward to meeting you and seeing your demonstration which comes so highly recommended by Miss Perfect.'

'Seeing what demonstration?'

'Ahhh… Shooting. *My Life with a Twelve Bore in the Kenya of Yesteryear* is our topic for today. Hope you've brought your guns. In the car still? I'll have one of the girls fetch them for you. I say, look sharp, Flo! Flo! Run and get this chap's armaments would you.'

'I'm sorry, Mr Barkle, social services is my line of country.'

'Ah, yes, but you couldn't give a talk on that. People wouldn't want to know. Ah yes, I suppose somebody has to do that sort of thing but we would never have asked for a talk on social services. Socialist nonsense, eh! I made that plain didn't I, Miss Perfect? How strange, I would have sworn you said our speaker was a shooting man, growing up in Africa, that sort of thing what? Shoots a good line you said, ha-ha-ha. And something about the elephants in Africa. Kenya I think, yes, yes, I could swear it was Kenya, must be. Your father fought the Mau Mau I believe?'

'Not mine.'

Dan was by now scowling at Madge who put on her most regal 'this is me beaming at my people' smile.

'You fought the Mau Mau?! Surely you were far too young to have a crack at the black chappies.'

'I'm social services, I'm talking about social services.'

'Oh dear, never mind, it can't be helped, the members will be disappointed but never mind. Just do your best, give it your best shot what!'

'Jack, over here a minute, I want you to meet our speaker, changed his name from Aubrey for some reason, now Bagley Biggles or something, Biggles like the pilot chap, you remember him and his chums Algy and Ginger, surely you remember them?'

'Of course,' said Jack, 'my favourite books to this day.'

'Funny that should be this fellow's name,' Barkle continued, 'and by the way it's not shooting, he's social something or other, nothing to do with the elephants in Africa though he's been a socialist worker there.'

Jack had been searching somewhere in his memory. 'Remember *Biggles and the Black Menace*, Mr B? I do! Bit of a disappointment.'

'I know,' said Barkle, 'the black menace turned out to be a dog and not a native. Pity that, a dog getting shot instead of a black chap. Ha! Ha!'

'Oh damn,' said Jack, now looking hard at Dan, 'I wouldn't have come if I'd known that our talk was on socialist nonsense. But… hello young fellow – why, I know you.' He turned to Barkle and went on, 'I've met this fellow before, it's Mr Fife, a friend of my daughter. I've already told him how I used to share my crops with the pigs in Africa. That's what attracted me about your talk on pig-sticking in Africa. Anyway – ha! ha! – nice to meet you again, Fife.'

'Well actually I'm Dan, Dan Bagley, and I've never been to Africa.'

'What's the fellow say, Barkle?' bellowed Jack. 'Seems he says he's never been to Africa. Funny thing to conceal. No need to be ashamed of a furlough in the tropics I would have thought.' Then he added, 'Even if it is full of black chaps.'

Mr Barkle cut through this confusion by ignoring it and announcing, 'Time to make a start. Pad up now, you chaps, and bring your coffee with you to the wicket. Can't be helped.'

Madge found a chair near the back of the hall as Dan followed Barkle to a baize-covered table facing three lines of hard wooden chairs. In his eagerness to keep up with Mr Barkle, Dan spilt his coffee, crunched a polystyrene cup underfoot and heard Jack whispering loudly, 'Damn bad show, he's invited one of those chaps who mutter. Can't make out a word he says. And the fellow says he doesn't shoot.'

Before introducing him to the audience Barkle announced that he had invited a journalist chappie from the *Northern Times*, a 'Mr… I forget the name but welcome, my dear sir.' There was brief applause as all heads turned to the back of the room where a smartly dressed young man sat notebook in hand. Dan looked pleased; it would no doubt be good for him to have publicity for the sweeping changes that would soon transform the social services.

Barkle then continued his lengthy introduction by apologising for the fact that 'Miss Perfect would not be speaking today, for out of a spirit of generosity she had stood down to make way for a young chap, her junior in age and status, who was hoping to make a career with the council. The change from the advertised subject was in no way her fault…' Here he glanced at Dan and went on, 'It was the fault of today's speaker who has come to our meeting without preparing a talk on his experiences in Africa'. The talk would not cover *My Life with a Twelve Bore in the Kenya of Yesteryear*. There were cries of 'shame!'

Madge looked around the room. All of the audience looked well into retirement, perhaps small businessmen, or middle-ranking men in the armed services, as well as a huddle of mature ladies with blue rinsed hair and suede coats, no doubt the 'girls' to serve tea and coffee for the 'men'.

No sooner did he begin his talk on *Production Functions in the Social Services* than Madge had cause to congratulate herself on the little woopsie she had landed Dan in; after all she had found a book on *The Art of Public Speaking* in the library, added it to Dan's heap of books, wished him well. Now it was up to him. Originally she had meant well by introducing him to the real world. Not now. The deeper the hole he now dug for himself the more pleased she would feel. Naughty, she knew.

Dan though had given little thought to the content or his delivery. He was confident with his subject matter – managerial efficiency – but as he sketched in the background to the way he intended to match service delivery with resource constraints in Area 13 she noticed glazed looks, foot-shuffling and the occasional snore from the audience. It was unfair because he clearly knew what he wanted to say and firmly believed in his ability to say it well. To him it must have seemed irresponsible that those present seemed far from eager to take advantage of the opportunity to listen to him. At least someone was wide awake and attentive: the journalist scribbling away at the back while nodding vigorously and smiling encouragement.

Undeterred, Dan marched on, leading his audience down the road he knew best, travelling in the vehicle he found most comfortable. Population was the inevitable starting point and after beginning with the total number in Area 13 he broke it down into percentages of clients using the various social services: of children, elderly, mentally ill, mentally handicapped and physically handicapped. Hoping to reassure his listeners he went on to quote the number of aged care homes and the average age of residents, the number of family group homes for children in care and the number of foster parents, at which point he threw out a plea for more members of the public to come forward to make a contribution by looking after socially and emotionally damaged teenagers, some of whom might be handicapped, or black, or known to the Moortown police.

He was warming to his theme and was probably planning to move on to the role of County Hall policy and the Director's plans for the future when Mr Barkle bounded to his feet showing little sign of his physical disability and said, 'Jolly good show, old chap, but I think we'll stop there. Time perhaps for one or two questions.'

Dan looked cross as a hand went up in the front row.

'What about the wee laddie you lost before Christmas when you were supposed to be looking after him?' It was a kindly looking lady with thinning grey hair. Madge had noticed her asleep till Barkle interrupted his talk. The journalist started scribbling.

So word had leaked out into the community; was it her staff, the police or someone in the know up at County Hall?

'Indeed,' Dan said, 'regrettable, unfortunately I was on leave at the time and… well, let's just say lessons will be learned, changes are afoot.'

The journalist stopped writing and raised a hand. 'Are you talking about Miss Perfect?' he asked.

'Shame, shame,' said Barkle to a background murmur of agreement.

'Not for me to mention names,' Dan said.

'And,' the journalist persisted, 'is your department committed to preventing further incidents of this nature?'

'Ninety-nine per cent, statistically speaking, of children in our care are safe with us, safer than with their parents,' Dan replied, always happiest when he could quote a number and adding, 'These things can never be one hundred per cent, the resource costs would be far too high. Somewhere, sometime a child will disappear, die even.'

The journalist, head down, wrote furiously.

The audience growled disapproval. The journalist asked, 'Do you expect to find the missing child?'

'We can never be sure,' Dan said.

'Alive or dead?'

'One or the other,' Dan said.

Next a surly-looking man in the front row piped up, 'Have the police dealt with the family yet?'

'I'm afraid you'd have to ask the police that question.'

'I'm asking you, young man.'

'I'm sure they will,' Dan said, seemingly not liking the turn things were taking.

There was a further murmur of discontent from the audience till the questioner asked, 'Well, what's the answer to it all? I'm Basham, a retired copper myself, and in my day famous for murder cases.'

'Solving them I hope,' Dan said, hoping to lighten the mood. It didn't work. The man scowled in what could only be taken to be a threatening manner. Nobody smiled or laughed.

'The answer,' continued Dan, perhaps hoping to regain the initiative, 'is efficiency, economy, responsibility. As I was trying to explain, production functions...'

Barkle was on his feet again: 'Next question please.'

Madge noted that there were more answers than questions, all present having views, to them the correct views, all culled from the university of life. Jack thought that only someone who had shot elephants, who understood the mind of the native and had shared his crops with the pigs in Africa ('Ha! Ha!') should be involved in 'molly coddling' other people, the work-shy scroungers.

The more liberal, thoughtful element was at times hard to identify in the emotional pleas for the birch or the cane, preferably both (for almost everything), hanging (for almost everything else) and sterilisation ('for those kind of people'). Those kind of people were apparently not people like these kind of people. And at times it was not altogether clear whether social workers in general, and Dan in particular, might not themselves benefit from a dose of these favoured regimes.

And then at the very end, one of the ladies who had taken no part in the discussion asked very gently, 'What I want to know is what about the book you are writing?'

'What book?'

Barkle snapped, 'Oh get on with it, young man, Miss Perfect said you were writing a book.'

'Did she? Am I? Of course it's an excellent idea.'

Mr Barkle rose to his feet. 'It is of course a matter for great regret that Miss Perfect did not speak today. We know from her previous visits to our little band of brothers that the talk she would have given, based on her real experiences growing up in Africa, would have been first rate.'

A voice interrupted from the front row: 'I used to share my crops with the pigs in Africa, wild pigs of course. Ha! Ha!' It was of course Jack once again.

Mr Barkle scowled at the speaker and continued: 'Miss Perfect even promised that she would have discharged her father's elephant gun on the pavilion steps... in the direction of the council estate.'

Madge smiled her sweet-as-apple-pie smile and mouthed, 'A joke of course, just a joke.'

At which Jack repeated, 'Ha! Ha!' as the rest of the audience laughed and applauded as they turned towards Madge.

'Just my little joke, all that,' Madge said.

'But, alas, it was not to be,' Mr Barkle continued.

'I think though,' Mr Barkle went on, 'that we ought to thank young, um, um, Aubrey I think, nice young chap here, for a jolly good first try at giving a talk. A first attempt what? Not his fault Miss Perfect did not speak today.'

Once again there were cries of 'shame' from around the room.

'Well, um, in spite of everything shall we do as we usually do?' With this Mr Barkle led the brief and half-hearted applause.

'Good show,' he went on, 'jolly good show. But now, Aubrey, back to your wish-washy, softly soapy, lazy liberal job?' Mr Barkle said as he saw Dan to the door, the journalist heading hurriedly on ahead to his car. Madge followed behind.

Dan said to Barkle, 'Well, actually, no, not quite that, you see I no longer work with people as I am now the Deputy Area Controller beneath Miss Perfect. In fact, perhaps I shouldn't say this but one day I hope to be...'

He got no further as Barkle looked at him blankly then interrupted, 'Jolly good show anyway working under Miss Perfect what, with you like a District Officer in the Africa of old, one down from District Commissioner, all before the black chaps took over.' Then Barkle slapped him heartily on the back. 'Discipline. Discipline is what they need, that's how to control 'em. The birch and the sight of a gun is the only thing they understand don't you know. Jolly good show what. Remember that in your job as arrears controller what-o!'

'You set me up, Madge,' he snarled as they drove back to the office at speed. She could see he was angry and understood why. Perhaps he would seek revenge but then, be that as it may, tomorrow was another day.

'I didn't set out to, but tit for tat perhaps?'

'What do you mean?'

'Just think about it... how did word reach the town about the missing boy?'

'Nothing to do with me.' That was always Dan's excuse. Nothing that went wrong did ever seem to be to do with him and if she hoped meeting the Thursday Club and giving a talk would help to humanise him she could see how foolish that hope had been.

Suddenly Dan calmed down and said, 'That was a good idea of yours, me writing a book about the modern methods in the social services. It might sell well to managers up and down the land. Lorraine is talking of writing a book about northern men and if Lorraine can write a book then for sure I can write a fucking book.'

'Yes, I think that's Lorraine's subject,' Madge said.

'What do you mean?' Dan snarled.

'Fucking.'

She knew that from now on the gloves were off. For the moment she was just relieved that the car had slowed to a more sedate pace. Her well-meaning attempt to introduce Dan to the local community had failed but she knew then that his woopsie would live in her memory.

I really am a very naughty girl, she said to herself.

Chapter 15

Marcus was back from Yorkshire. Apparently it had been an opportunity to get in some flying hours. He had received the Christmas card addressed to him care of Yorkshire and Lorraine was 'bloody amazed because it would never have happened in Cape Town'. She was smiling again, a shade more warily than before Christmas. Although Lorraine never said as much, Madge had the feeling that a degree of doubt still hung over Marcus' claim that standing her down from the family gathering had been in her own best interests: she had overheard him reeking with insincerity telling Lorraine that Christmas with the family had been 'simply frightful, ghastly, darling'.

Madge was not smiling. Where had the Oldfields gone with Alistair? Before setting off for work she stood at the window looking out on what in the summer would be the prettiest part of the garden. Now all she noticed was a lone seagull sitting on the fence. She had always wondered about seagulls: do some seagulls live so far inland that they never see the sea? That would be sad, to live in Moortown or Brownlow and never fly away to the sea. And how do they manage in the winter? Do they find somewhere warm? And where was Mitchell? My how she could do with him by her side now.

Later she remembered it as the week the telephone never stopped ringing. It had begun with young Alistair Oldfield and his parents still missing and all lines of enquiry leading nowhere. If anyone knew anything they sure as hell were keeping it to themselves. The Farrants who may have known of other relatives or other places where the Oldfields might have lived in the past simply distanced themselves from any help they might have given. PC Pyott reported to Madge that he had warned them that it could be an offence to withhold information in respect of a missing child.

'Just laughed in me face,' he said, adding that he was certain they knew more than they were willing to say. Madge felt sure that Jim Pyott was right.

She had slept very little that night and went in early to work but sitting at her desk staring out of the window achieved nothing; she felt helpless and afraid. An hour later Dan arrived in the office looking furtive.

'Great news,' he said. 'The Director was nominated as the Labour candidate at the party meeting last night. I was there. He's asked me to help with his campaign.'

Before she could think what to say in response he bustled out. She relaxed at the thought that now she could not be blamed as she surely would have been had the Director lost out with the nomination.

Brenda came in and said, 'You all right, pet?'

'Not really.' Brenda calling her 'pet'; what was Moortown coming to? What had she come to?

'Dan just says not to worry; they'll turn up with the boy. Storm in a beer mug, he says. I'll make you a cuppa. You mustn't let the buggers get you down, you know.'

That was all she needed, Brenda trying to be kind, acting as a mouthpiece for Dan. Brenda was right of course. Up and at 'em it ought to be but where would she find the strength?

Her addled thoughts were interrupted when the phone rang. Relief, it must be news of the Oldfields. She willed it to be news of young Alistair. But instead it was Mitchell's voice. Just when she thought it would never happen it was Mitchell on the other end. Why did he choose this moment of all moments?

'My God,' she said, 'where are you? Are you all right?'

'I'm fine. I'm back in Rudham. I've news…'

'I want to hear your news, of course I do, but not now. We're operating in crisis mode.'

'Can I come round this evening?'

'Of course.'

She had been waiting for this phone call ever since Mitchell went away but now she was too worried about the Oldfields to feel either relief or joy. When it came to time for lunch in the canteen she closed her office door and sat staring out of the window. Grey clouds implanting patches of clog-shaped shadows on the ground scudded above the line of hills between Moortown and Brownlow. For so many years Area 13 had been almost all of her world and now it felt as though it was slipping away beneath her, the achievements of her years of service shattering before her, the broken shards of her life. Then there was Mitchell, back at Rudham, bearing news, his dismissal perhaps, but no, surely he had sounded too perky for that. Snow began to fall.

Later, as her troops came down the corridor from lunch she intercepted Lorraine. 'I think we ought to try the Farrants one more time. They must know something. I know you tried but let's go together and give it one more shot.'

After driving across to Brownlow through gently falling snow one knock on the Farrants' door brought Melanie snarling like a cornered animal. 'Fuck bloody off, yer bags of shite,' she shouted, and behind her down the hall Gary repeated, 'Fuck bloody off'.

Mrs Farrant said, 'That's reet, Gary, ye tell em.'

As they returned to the car the normally invisible Mr Farrant appeared at the door and shouted, 'Nowt te do with us,' before slamming it hard.

'I'm sorry, Madge,' Lorraine said, 'it's not your fault, I know that.' Things must be getting serious with Lorraine feeling sorry for her. Or, perhaps she had misjudged Lorraine?

On the return journey Lorraine said, 'It's my fault for not getting to grips with the Farrants' sex life. If I'd succeeded they would have been more cooperative, they would have seen the sense in helping us find the Oldfields.'

'Perhaps,' Madge said, silently disbelieving it. Then she noticed that for the very first time she had not for a single moment worried about Lorraine's driving.

'I blame Marcus,' Lorraine said. 'All that crap about concentrating on material things for the Farrants, a bigger house, more benefit money, economic incentives, something to do with Chicago, money and markets solving everything.'

Madge mulled over the reactions of those around her. Here was Lorraine blaming herself for not getting to grips with the Farrants' sex life, still believing that the family was dysfunctional because Mr Farrant was a typical northern male and hence an inadequate lover, this condition somehow leaving Melanie emotionally frozen by her masturbatory guilt. Was it not enough to know, as Lorraine now did, that Mr Farrant had fathered a fair proportion of the children in Brownlow? The cost of the existence of Mr Farrant to taxpayers like Mr Barkle would show up in the costs of school places, demands on the health services as well as the work of her own office. Goodness me, Madge thought, I'm rapidly becoming a right-winger.

Lorraine had softened in some ways while she had been with them. Now that she and Marcus were an item once more, lower key maybe, the disappointment of Christmas left behind, her mood was back to loud-cheerful. If there was a cooling in Lorraine's excitement at every sighting of Marcus that was only to be expected, for nothing in life ever stayed the same.

All the players in the little drama strutted through her thoughts: Simon blaming himself for letting it happen, Dan who had set it away and now distanced himself from the bonfire as soon as the flames were lit. Brenda who had nothing to lose or gain was both concerned and comforting.

***

Arriving home she was so tired that she had almost forgotten Mitchell was coming round when there was a knock on the door and there he was with the old lopsided bounce in his step as he entered. She helped him to extricate himself from his raincoat. Mitchell hadn't changed. She felt pleasure and relief at the sight of him. After she had settled him in the easy chair by the fire she poured two glasses of wine.

'Just the remains of a bottle from Christmas I'm afraid,' she said, 'but tell me, what happened?' It had been easy to forget that Mitchell too was back from a dark place.

'Where to begin?' he said.

'I've been worried about you. I missed you,' she said.

He smiled as if to say 'thank you', took another gulp and started. 'It all got resolved. Marcus went to the Master's wife who went to the Vice-Chancellor.'

'That tells me nothing. Saying what?'

'That it wasn't me. Marcus found out it was a put-up job between the nude girl – the student not the model – and a student from Green, a chap not in the Marcus circle.'

'Marcus stood up for you?'

'Seems so. He said he could not stand by and see me brought down by some oik from a comprehensive school. Possible though that he did not want to lose me as his research supervisor at the vital stage of his dissertation.'

'Oik?'

'Lowlife I suppose to Marcus.'

'So you're back at work?'

'Sure am. It's left a mark though. People are backing off from me, even those who were friendly before. But we shall see. I'll be down to your office again on Friday. I don't know if word of my problems reached your colleagues or indeed your clients.'

'Probably nothing. People are generally cocooned in their own little world until something untoward creeps up and bites them. They probably just assumed you were away down a pit somewhere taking photographs of miners. Meantime we've had one or two things on our minds.'

Now it was Mitchell's turn to probe. 'How's your work been while I was away? Has Dan been behaving himself?'

'No, but not just Dan. It's been a worrying time. Don't ask, not now. Something has happened with one of our cases and if it turns out badly I'm likely to get the blame. At the moment I'm a frightened rabbit sitting in their gunsights hoping things will turn out OK.'

'Do you want to talk about it?'

'Not now.'

'It might be better if you shared it with me. I've been worried about you,' he said.

So she told him the whole sorry story of the events surrounding the disappearance of young Alistair who was in her care, and her fears for the security of her continuing employment.

'Rough, Madge,' he said when she had finished. 'That's terrible. And you are so sweet, they surely don't deserve you.'

'Just don't call me sweet, don't you dare call me sweet,' Madge said. Then they both laughed.

Madge was left hoping she meant more to Mitchell than a walk-on part in a rational process.

She thought for a moment then said, 'Would you like to stay the night?'

When he said 'You bet' she fetched the Christmas present still languishing on the hall table and handed it to him.

'What's this?' he asked.

'It's your Christmas present and it's not a pair of socks or handkerchiefs with your initials. Why not look at it and see?'

He opened the book she had bought him, and his face sprung to life.

'Capa,' he said, 'Robert Capa. You remembered my interest in photography. And my hero. It's a book I've always wanted, photographs by Robert Capa.'

'How could I forget? And if you had been here for Christmas I would have wrapped it.' She kissed him gently on the cheek.

Going to bed with Mitchell raised a number of issues. To begin with there was the matter of a bed fit for purpose: both the narrowest of singles in her tiny bedroom and the sofa in the lounge were clearly inadequate. Her size was against it; where lightweight Lorraine might have managed with ease, Madge knew that although she might manage with difficulty there would be the constant fear that as she lay on her back with Mitchell on top the structure beneath them might fail at any moment. She considered organising an eiderdown and a blanket on the carpet in front of the fire. Romantic though it seemed the eiderdown was torn and there were coffee stains on the blanket. What would Mitchell think?

Taking all in all spontaneous, impulsive sex was out of the question but she had made up her mind after Mitchell departed before Christmas that if ever the chance arose again she would take it. Now that the moment had come she felt almost too exhausted to want anything more than the warmth of his body beside her, the feeling that someone cared for her. Giving up her bed for him and sleeping on the sofa herself was not a solution.

Hope returned when she remembered that the sofa folded down into something approximating a double bed. Mitchell helped as they yanked it into submission till it lay helpless and fully extended in front of the dying embers of the fire. She threw on more coal while Mitchell went in search of a bandage for the hand he had cut on the jagged metal opening mechanism of the sofa bed. That gave her long enough to put on her pink floral nightie, flannelette for its winter warmth, then lie down in readiness, a pagan sacrifice waiting for Mitchell to strike like a cobra. Would he like what he saw?

As she waited for the bandaged Mitchell to reappear she wondered if she was offering herself out of duty or desire. She was not sure which, perhaps both. It was not his fault he was not Clive. Mitchell's absence in London had fanned desire; great was her relief at his return from the city. She must not let him out of her sight again even if it did mean letting him have his way with her. Oh come to me now, my Greek god, she mused, then remembered that Mitchell was not Marcus, certainly not Clive.

But if the choice of a bed and Mitchell's injuries were issues now resolved a further problem emerged when Mitchell returned to the living room. The additional issue was Mitchell himself.

'I've got this problem,' he said, looking uneasy and nothing like a Greek god, standing before her in his underpants and waving his bandaged hand.

'I'm sorry about your hand.'

'It's not that.'

My God, she thought, erectile dysfunction, he can't get it up. What a fool she had been just assuming, assuming he was up to it, up for it, rampant like the red-hot poker of the long gone but now cold and decomposed Clive. How cruel of her to embarrass him in this way.

'Can I help?' she asked.

He hesitated, pulled a face. 'I doubt it. My problem is Hegel.'

'I haven't heard of that,' she said, fearing the confession of some physical abnormality or sexual disease must surely follow.

But before he could say a word yet another issue emerged when he suddenly let fly with a loud, explosive sneeze. She pulled a face in response to the sneeze and said 'tut-tut'.

'You don't approve of sneezing,' he said.

She laughed and said, 'Certainly not.'

Mitchell was not one to give in that easily. 'It's a health and safety issue. I remember a boy at school being reprimanded for sneezing. Next time he felt a sneeze coming on he held it back. Fatal! Next moment his brains exploded straight out of his ears, splattered the walls, buckets of blood, dead as coal mining in the north-east of England.'

She couldn't help but laugh. She liked the fantastic tales he told. But what if it were true? She never could tell with Mitchell.

But when he added, 'A good sneeze is the next best thing to sex – the sneeze between the knees they say,' she did not know quite what to say by way of a riposte so she just said, 'Is it?' She hoped it sounded as doubtful as she felt.

But who were 'they', she wondered, who said these things about sneezing, the weather, the miners' strike, foreigners, the economy, the England cricket team, or according to Mitchell – sex? Throughout the country there must be a legion of people with views on matters large and small who said things. These were the unseen 'they' people. And now she knew that Mitchell was among their number.

As it was the first time he had mentioned sex she saw in it the possibility of a forward step. Or had she reconstructed her living room for no more than a whiff of pepper and a communal sneeze with Mitchell? And all the while the broken springs under the mattress of the sofa bed were stabbing her in the back. So much for the importance of loving feelings and the delicate foreplay she had read about under 'marital problems' as part of her training course.

At least he had at last mentioned sex. It was so long since Clive that the feelings of sex were dulled in her memory, that place where passion and pain had slowly eroded over time. Now here was Mitchell worrying about a malady called Hegel and enjoying sneezing while ignoring her proffered body.

'Mitchell, what is your Hegel problem?' She was impatient now.

The word was distantly familiar yet she could not locate it. Who had she known who had suffered from Hegel? Who might have mentioned it?

She went on, 'What is Hegel?'

'Not what but whom,' he said. He looked surprised as though he expected everyone to know the answer.

Now she seemed to be getting somewhere she pressed home the advantage. 'Is he someone I should know? A client?'

'Nope, German, born in the eighteenth century, died in the nineteenth. You see he had the idea that history is part of a rational process, not just random and meaningless.'

Madge began swimming in a vast lake of incomprehension and fading desire. 'Where does your crisis come into it?' she asked.

'Hegel surveys history from Greece and Rome, moves on to the Middle Ages and then on to what was for him the present day.'

'I see,' she said, but she didn't. Mitchell was marching up and down the room, oblivious to his dangly bits, a loose floorboard creaking every time he stepped on it, as he explained what was on his mind. He seemed to struggle for the right words.

'For Hegel it came down to the spirit of freedom. When I came to your patch in Moortown I started wondering if I could apply Hegel's philosophy and his interpretation of history to this place and time. And I soon found it didn't work. Take the Farrants for example: their lives appear to be random and meaningless and they are not striving for freedom but... striving for what?'

'More money from the benefits people? Perhaps they have found a sort of freedom?' she said.

'Ah, but not in the Hegelian sense. As a sociologist Hegel is of central importance to me. If he is wrong in this where does that leave me? Surely I must be wrong? If I can only reconcile Hegel and his theory of history with what I observe at Moortown I will get an article on it in a leading journal, perhaps even the *British Journal of Sociology*.'

'And that is important to you?'

'Absolutely! Publish or perish. My career may depend on it.' He was vehement on this point.

'You intend to plough on working then?'

'Of course, what else is there?'

She didn't like to say the word 'sex' or the word 'retirement'. And mercifully the Farrants would never know how much was riding on their behaviour. But enough of that line of enquiry.

'Mitchell, stop prancing around the room and if you don't mind just come to bed. Please.'

Which he did. 'Lie back and think of England' people in the know used to say but now there was scarce time for thought as their brief intimacy of push and shove ended with Mitchell saying, 'Whoosh'. Just as suddenly he was snortling gently asleep beside her. To ease the pain in her back from the springs she turned on her side and put her arm around him. Funny, incomprehensible man she thought, funny without meaning to be, always kind, annoying in ways. But she did almost love him, didn't know why. His squishy-squooshy juices running down her thighs were becoming sticky and by the time she drifted into sleep they were drying and clinging to her nightie. So that's it, she thought. The earth had not moved but at least the sofa bed had not collapsed. Even allowing for the bedsprings sticking into her back it had been pleasant enough to leave her hoping for more another time, Hegel permitting. Clearly she would have to work hard at it if he was ever to love her more than Hegel – or his Hillycopter.

When they awoke in the morning he sat up and looked across the room at the grey ashes in the grate and the pictures on the mantelpiece above. She looked at his grey, receding hair and stroked his neck. Nice skin.

'You're out of practice too,' she said.

He looked surprised. 'Guess so. Just the occasional fling here and there a few years ago. Nothing that meant anything.'

'It must be tempting with all those young women around, your students I mean.'

'I never go there. It seems an abuse of power. We have so much power when it comes to exams and references.'

So he was a principled man. She liked that.

Then he said, 'That's your Clive staring at us.'

'I'm sorry,' she said, 'I'll put him away in a drawer.'

'I'm not sure you can,' Mitchell said. He raised both hands to emphasise the point.

'I'm not sure either,' Madge said.

Mitchell said, 'As I was saying about Hegel…'

'Don't go back to Hegel. Let's move on,' she said.

'And, talking of moving on, try to stop worrying about the missing child. The family will return at some point and it will all blow over.'

When the phone on her desk rang as she arrived in to work in the morning it was Jim Pyott. From the first sound of his voice she knew something was wrong. 'Ah thowt ye ought te knaa, Miss Perfect, we've had someone phone in reporting a child's body in a field on the edge of the new estate.'

'A child? Is it Alistair?'

'Not identified yet. The man who found it said he recognised it from the photo in the *Northern Times*. Seems he's been on to the paper about it and the radio and TV people have picked it up from there. They knew afore we did.'

'You mean the press knew about it before the police?'

'Afraid so. Ah reckon the informant hopes for a few notes from the paper for giving it to them first. It's a scoop for them.'

'And money for him by the sound of it. Who found the body?'

'Divvent knaa that yet either, a member of the public as we say at these times. Aall we knaa at the moment is what the journalists are telling us. Me lads are out investigating.'

She caught her breath, answered, 'Thanks, Jim, I'll contact the Director at County Hall right away.'

'Ah think you should. It won't be long till the radio and TV people in Newcassel are ower here.'

'Holy shit,' Madge said.

'Ah thowt ye might think that, Madge,' Jim said.

Lorraine chose that moment to pop her head around the door. 'I just heard, please say if I can help, Madge, just say.'

So word was getting around already. Madge smiled and said, 'Thank you so much, Lorraine, those are the nicest words I have heard today. Is Dan around?'

'Afraid not.'

'County Hall?'

'Afraid so.'

No surprise there. Madge thought a moment then said, 'If you run across Simon say I'm in my office if he needs me. He will take this very badly. If it is young Alistair in the absence of the Oldfields he may have to identify the body when it gets to the morgue. He won't ever have done one of those.'

'I'll be nice to him.'

When Lorraine was gone Madge found a tissue in her desk drawer and wiped her eyes. She stared at the phone just begging it not to ring again, not ever, knowing all the while it would ring and ring and then ring again. Perhaps it would be quiet long enough for her to phone the Director's office and write a report on what little she knew about the circumstances surrounding the finding of a body, making the as yet unconfirmed link to the disappearance of the Oldfield family while Alistair was placed with foster parents while supervised by the county council.

The message she left with Mrs Busted, the Director's secretary, provoked an immediate response from the Director himself. This was a man like Puttock who famously never talked in person to his area offices. Now here he was shouting at her down the phone.

'The press,' he snarled, 'you are not authorised to say a word to the press, simply refer them to me at County Hall. I don't care whether they are radio, TV or the *Northern Times*; they are to be referred to me. And I will require a report on the case on my desk within two hours. Remember I've a by-election coming up.'

'I shall of course refuse to speak to the press, Director, and I am working on my report.'

'Do it, Perfect, just do it. It was bad enough when you let young Dan Bagley tell a journalist some children in our care are bound to die.'

So that was her fault too. No matter what he did, or didn't do, no blame ever attached to Dan.

She organised Simon to hook up his latest report on the Oldfield case and put it in a folder with her update. She drove it at speed up to County Hall. As she walked in the main entrance the staff on reception stared at her as though she were a murderess. Was that what they thought? She handed the latest report to Mrs Busted, the Director's secretary, who snatched it from her angrily, saying, 'The Director has been nominated as the Labour candidate and then you go and do this to him. He's furious because it will affect his vote in the by-election.'

Back in her office calls were raining in from journalists, all eager to work up a good story, all knowing their jobs depended on the stories they filed selling papers. Enhanced career prospects were riding on events like the death of Alistair. Why oh why had she become so cynical? Things were changing though. Gone was the time when she respected most journalists for exposing crimes and corrupt governments even if they never turned their attention to County Hall and the Labour mafia in Rudham. This was different. Or perhaps she had never experienced it before. Her role now was straightforward: in line with county policy she simply referred the hungry journalists up the line to the Director in County Hall.

When an outside broadcast crew arrived from one of the TV stations in Newcastle she went out into the car park and told them she was not authorised to say anything. Disgruntled, they packed up and went off to County Hall.

When she arrived home that evening she was surprised to see an unfamiliar car parked outside her cottage. As she pulled on to the drive a familiar young man got out of the car and walked towards her. It was the journalist from Dan's Thursday Club talk.

'Miss Perfect, I think,' he said.

She nodded and he went on, 'Can I have an interview for the *Northern Times*?'

'Certainly not,' she snapped.

'It might be better if you agreed to talk to me first,' he said, 'it's going national, the London papers and television and radio are on to the story.'

'It's not a story,' she said, 'it's a little boy's death.'

'That is a story and just when your Director is standing as the Labour candidate in the by-election,' he said. He held up a camera almost in her face and she was momentarily startled by the flash.

'Thank you, Miss Perfect,' he said.

'I've nothing to say,' she said and went in to the cottage, sat down on the sofa and quietly wept. Her father had been right all along: she was rubbish, no more nor less than could be expected of any woman. Now the weight of the years joined with the Oldfield crisis to roll her near the edge. Down the years new ways of doing things had nibbled away at the job she once loved, a new breed of staff were now hardly tolerable, and when she surveyed her present predicament she was by no means sure that she either wanted to or felt able to continue.

She switched on the local BBC television news at six. Even the calm presence of George House, her favourite presenter on the screen, did nothing to reassure her. The tragedy at Moortown was the first item. Inevitably it made much of the discovery of a body of a child. The fact that the Director of Social Services was the Labour candidate in the forthcoming by-election in Rudham was noted by the reporter speaking from outside the ramshackle offices of Area 13 in Moortown. He said that no one from County Hall had been prepared to appear on camera. He then read a statement prepared by the chair of the social services committee in Rudham County. The statement agreed that it was indeed an unfortunate occurrence but every effort was being made to rectify the situation. The council took this incident very seriously and a full enquiry would urgently seek to establish the facts. If a member of staff had acted without due care and diligence the council's disciplinary procedures would be invoked. In addition further resources would be allocated to child care in

Rudham. The training section would be updating all social workers on non-accidental injuries and the supervision of children in care. A greater proportion of the budget would be allocated to training. Such an incident would never occur again. The Director was personally overseeing such action as might be required. Staring at the screen Madge thought, 'Bla, bla, bla.'

Next item: a singer she had not seen before sang a witty song about Tyneside. It may have lifted the mood for some but for her the effect was quite the opposite. She used to so enjoy the songs of Alex Glasgow but then he had gone off to Australia leaving his beloved Gateshead behind. Why did everything have to change? Perhaps she could change, go to Australia?

She could see whose head was about to roll and it was certainly not the Director's. She phoned Mitchell but his photography club met that evening; no, he hadn't heard anything, no he couldn't come over tonight, yes, he would make contact in the morning.

Chapter 16

Next morning she hurried to the paper shop. There she was splattered over the first page of the *Northern Times*. The shopkeeper looked at her guardedly. 'A spot of bother?' he asked. She was now a local pariah, her life's work devalued, her employment at risk. Why go on? she wondered. Why fight such a hopeless battle? Even up and at 'em was not going to win this day.

She arrived in the office and found everyone in the social workers' room staring at her photograph. 'Never mind, luv, it'll soon pass over,' Brenda said. No one else seemed to know what to say apart from Dan who put on his preacher voice to intone, 'It's now a problem of news management. It couldn't have come at a worse time for our Director.'

On an inside page there was a picture of a vengeful Melanie Farrant under the headline *SOCIAL WORKERS BLAMED FOR DEAD CHILD*. Beneath it was a photograph of the Director and an interview in which he apologised for the lack of cooperation shown to the TV crew who called at Moortown. He expressed profound regret at the discovery of a body. A comprehensive investigation was underway. Lessons would be learned so that such a death could never happen again. And yes, those responsible would feel the full force of the council's disciplinary policies and procedures.

Someone had to be saddled with the blame with the by-election coming up, someone had to leave the Director looking squeaky clean, and she could see now with total clarity that she had been chosen to be the sacrifice. She felt defiled.

She heard the phone ringing down the corridor. She moved quickly. It was Mitchell, bloody Mitchell, the same Mitchell who had been too busy to come over when she needed him last night.

'I've been thinking,' he said, and from his hesitant voice down the phone line she knew he had been thinking about something he found too taxing to say to her face. He always phoned when that happened. That he had been thinking struck Madge as truly unremarkable for wasn't this what academics spent a good part of each day doing? In Mitchell's case this most often involved his friend Hegel. But it was nice that he was thinking about her, perhaps showing real concern. Action Man he might not be, any more than she was Sindy doll. Think on!

'France,' he went on, 'I've been thinking we might hop over to France in the Hillycopter, perhaps in April or May. I spent the evening looking into what might be possible. What do you think?'

'Mitchell, I've been thinking of nothing other than the crisis here at work. But why France?'

There was a pause before he answered. 'Clive, you said once you had not even visited his grave. Might it help?'

'How? With what?'

'I just thought…'

'Mitchell, the only help I need right now is handling the Oldfield case and Brenda, I see, is gesticulating in the doorway signalling an important call on another line.'

'Sorry, Madge,' he said, 'I was just thinking.'

'Not now, Mitchell, you obviously haven't seen this morning's paper. Your timing is just awful.'

'Can I help?'

'Can we talk tomorrow? Right now I'm beyond help.'

With Brenda now waving frantically she cut Mitchell off and took the waiting call. She was surprised to hear the normally welcome northern sound of Jim Pyott's voice, not University of Rudham, certainly not cut diamond, more broken beer bottle, warm and somehow reassuring.

'It's a mystery, Madge, but we cannit find the body. There's nothin at aall in the area where it was reported to have been seen. We're followin it up wi' the man who reported seeing it.'

'You think it's been moved?'

'No way of knowing.'

'Have you found out yet who reported it?'

'A certain Mr Timms.'

'Bloody hell,' said Madge.

'Ye knaa the gentleman in question?'

'Bloody do. I've sectioned him often enough. I thought he was still in St Clement's.'

This time it was Jim who said, 'Bloody hell.'

'And by the way, Jim, is there anything you can do about journalists harassing me at home?'

'Not a thing Ah'm afraid. It's caalled press freedom. We suffer from it an aal. But they'll soon lose interest and leave yer alone. A story like the Oldfield boy only ever lasts in the headlines for a day or two.'

Madge was not so sure and the next time the phone rang it was not the *Northern Times* nor the local radio or even one of the two Newcastle TV stations. Instead it was Puttock or, in Puttock speak, 'HR speaking'.

It was a surprise, if far from welcome, for this was a man who did not speak to people, so a phone call from Puttock could only mean one thing: bad news. Somehow he had managed to climb the County Hall ladder by not speaking to people. Or did he only speak to the people who mattered? Or people who needed a good kicking?

'Area 13 speaking,' she said in reply and immediately regretted it. In the lengthy catalogue of qualities lacking in Puttock, humour came high on the list.

'I need to speak to you urgently, Miss Perfect. I have made space to see you at County Hall at two-fifteen this afternoon.'

'That's not awfully convenient. As you can imagine we're frightfully busy here.'

'Two-fifteen.' The phone went dead. Silly me, she thought, Puttock doesn't do imagination.

When the tea trolley came around mid-morning she realised that by the time she got to the head of the queue all of the scones would be taken. Dan was one ahead of her in the queue.

'I'm up at the Hall this afternoon,' she said to Dan who smiled. Was it because he knew why she was up at HQ or just because he was in time to grab the last scone? Failing in the scone race was probably for the better, she thought, resenting it like hell while grateful that temptation had been taken from her. Having embarked on a degree of intimacy with Mitchell she must, must, try harder to watch her weight.

Driving to County Hall she wondered what had happened to her up and at 'em spirit of barely a few months ago. A child's body had been found then lost. Where was it now? Who else could it be other than Alistair? She cared about Alistair but the weight of County Hall bearing down on her had drained her energy.

Puttock's desk was devoid of papers. On the wall behind him hung a poster of a girl on a tennis court hitching up her short skirt and scratching her bare bum. Contained like a sausage within its skin Puttock sat in his ill-fitting dark suit, grim-faced, oblivious to any niceties.

'The Director has instructed me to proceed with a disciplinary investigation in your case,' he said. The young woman in the poster seemed happy to ignore Puttock. Perhaps a mosquito had bitten her bum? The poster was ridiculous, Puttock was ridiculous, County Hall was ridiculous, yet here she was playing their game. To Puttock she was now a case.

'On what grounds?' she asked.

'You allowed the Oldfield boy home for Christmas when he was in our care. Someone, probably someone in your office, leaked the story to the press landing the department with a load of adverse publicity at a very bad moment for the Director. The by-election is only weeks away and bad publicity could harm the turnout for Labour. And now the Director has a body, a missing body, on his hands.'

'His sole concern then is that he might now not win the seat?'

Puttock snapped back, 'That's outrageous! His concern is for the child.'

'Outrageous? So is your treatment of me. If you go ahead with your disciplinary nonsense what are the consequences for me?' She was getting angrier, up and at 'em was resurfacing.

'There is a chance you may be dismissed. What do you expect? First a child in our care goes missing, then we have a body only for the body to disappear.'

'And my pension?'

Puttock could not hide his irritation at her attitude. 'Under the pension scheme rules you will be free to draw your pension when you are sixty.'

'And enhancement of my pension?'

'None, not a penny.'

'I won't go quietly on those terms. This job has been my life. I'm proud of my contribution to the council and to the people in my area. I've noticed how all of the senior men who leave early go out with their pockets bursting with unearned silver whereas I would have no income till I reach sixty.'

'Stuff and nonsense,' said Puttock.

'I am so disgusted by what has become of a once great social service profession that I might be willing to cooperate with early retirement given an offer of my pension now plus a modest enhancement.'

'Out of the question. You're in no position to tell my Director what you would or would not do, your terms, you could resign, your choice, and in that event we could simply say it was for health reasons, or personal reasons, whatever you like,' Puttock said. When he 'harrumphed' she left his office in haste.

Leaving County Hall she was surprised, then after a moment's reflection not surprised, to see Dan heading for the entrance. He brushed past her, ignored her, as though his reputation might suffer if he was seen to associate with her in any way. No, the fallout would be hers alone. On the road back to Moortown Puttock's words tumbled around in her brain like clothes in a washing-machine at the launderette. She could consult a lawyer but what good would that do and anyway how much might it cost? The trade union was in cahoots with the management; as a mere woman they would certainly not support her.

She arrived back in Moortown angry and depressed. Feeling so hopeless certainly did not help. The forces of evil ranged against her meant she did not have even a woodworm-ridden wooden leg to stand on. It seemed no time since her job meant everything to her. The people she served still meant a great deal to her. They had given what meaning there was to most of her adult life. But being shoved out of the door without an immediate pension was one thing she would not easily accept. But was there an alternative? There were moments when her resolve returned. She might go gracefully leaving them all in the clear but not on any terms. She would be their scapegoat, Dan would probably fill the space she left behind and Simon, who she was determined to protect from his own good nature, would be safe, sheltered from any blame that might attach to him over Alistair. In time he would make good in a career founded on her kind of values.

Was it up and at 'em or down and out?

The story was once again the first item on the evening television news.

'In the absence of a spokesperson from County Hall in Rudham, or the social services office in Moortown, we sent a television crew to Brownlow to interview an important witness.' Madge watched as onto her screen came a shot establishing the location, a familiar street with its jumble of discarded furniture and innards of cars, and then a familiar shabby council house, unmistakably the Farrants' house. And yes, as the shot moved in to close-up it was Melanie Farrant on the step gabbling away to the sharp-suited reporter.

'It's them social workers what done it,' she said, 'them that come from Moortown. They've ruined me marriage and me family and drove me relatives and their bairn away. Now the bairn is deed and they cannit find the body. It's them social workers what done it. Mr and Mrs Oldfield, they nivvor did nothing wrong yer knaa and look what them twats from Moortown did... drove them away. By, those social workers should be shot... just my opinion, mind.'

Madge wanted to cry but couldn't. She was tired, too tired to cry, all she wanted to do was sleep, sleep, sleep. But she was too tired to sleep.

Oh, Mitchell, why can't you come to me, be here by my side when I need you most? She found enough strength to turn off the television and pour a stiff gin and tonic.

It could all wait till morning and then, one way or another, if she could find the energy, up and at 'em it would have to be. But somehow she knew her energy was fast running out. The Director was concerned only for his chances in the by-election. Dan, sensing a vacancy in the post he so obviously desired, was on the brink of victory. Poor, hapless Melanie Farrant would go on dancing in the media limelight.

There was a knock at the door. It was Mitchell. She hugged him till he said, 'Enough, my dear, let's have a drink and give thought to what might be done. I'm so sorry, this Oldfield business has been beastly for you.'

'They want me out,' Madge said, 'I'm sure of it. That's nothing new but now they have a pretext. Puttock is one of the men who've risen by sucking up to the Director, councillors and the trade union. I know in my bones that I do not fit into their proposed new structure.'

'That's so unfair,' Mitchell said. 'From what you say they must see that the stupidity and laziness of Dan set the whole thing away?'

Madge smiled. 'They don't know about that and even if they did he always comes out squeaky clean. No matter, what comes will come. The Director has been nominated as the Labour Party candidate for the by-election. He is determined to get elected and then leave his mark on 'his' department before he departs for fresh coalfields and spoil heaps new. I am sure he and Puttock think the department would be more efficient without me. It's not said openly but it's obvious they are particularly keen to promote younger people and needless to say I'm too old. And, of course, I'm a woman.'

'So what next?'

'I'll have to see when the dust settles. When I feel strong I am resolved never to give in. But I don't always feel strong these days. I could resign and just walk away.'

'That's rotten,' Mitchell said, 'and you really care about the people on your patch. Dan doesn't. Sounds as though neither your Director nor Puttock do either.'

'I know, but so be it. I don't want to go in disgrace. I don't want to walk away on bad terms financially either. But enough of my woes, what's next for you?'

'Fortunately my research project is almost complete. What next? I know not at the moment. Research money is tight. The university seems unwholesome since the photographic society debacle.'

Chapter 17

Once again the phone was already ringing when she arrived in the office next morning: drang-pause, drang-pause, drang-pause... Why answer it when it was almost certain to be news of Alistair's body? Reluctantly she lifted the receiver.

'It's Jim here, Madge, ye won't believe it but the "body" has been found, down by the river, and – guess what? – it's a doll, one of those Sindy or Barbie things, seems the local kids have been kicking it around the toon.'

'But, but,' she said, 'how can a doll have been mistaken for a child's body?'

'Aye, seems it can that with your Mr Timms. Swears blind he saw it near the housing estate, swears blind it looked just like the photo in the paper of young Alistair at the time he went missing. Says he thowt it would be at peace by the river, water of life or some such, so he moved it without telling us. Seems he carried out some kind of religious service over the body afore he shifted it.'

'The old devil.'

Jim laughed. 'No point in charging him with wasting police time but you might get one of your mental welfare officers te call on him.'

'I'll do that,' Madge said, 'and he may also need a community psychiatric nurse to poison his arse.'

'Aye,' said Jim, 'ah'd quite like to shove something up ees arse meself.'

Madge laughed. 'Thanks, Jim, you're a good man. I'll give County Hall the good news.'

She phoned County Hall and left a message for Puttock. For the first time in days she began to relax, feelings of relief washing over her. Now, surely there would be no disciplinary hearing? The Oldfields were still missing with Alistair but he was not dead. At some point their heads would pop up above water like frogs in the stagnant pond that was Brownlow.

The media storm blew over as suddenly as it had arrived. County Hall went silent. It was once again as if Area 13 did not exist. The glare of publicity had switched to the prospect of a strike in the coal industry.

She phoned Mitchell. 'I've been thinking,' she said, 'your France idea, can we talk about it?'

'Great,' he said, 'a chance for me to have some quiet time to ponder Hegel.'

The following day he appeared in the office. Much of her free thinking time was given over to worrying whether she was the right woman for him. It was easy to convince herself he must have regretted their intimacy given her obvious shortcomings: her age, her short legs, her obesity and no doubt many other imperfections. She was no good at sex, inexperienced, of that there could be no doubt. What was there to like about her, what to desire, what could compete with his passion for Hegel?

After he bumbled around in the office annoying the admin girls most of the morning he poked his head around her door and wearing his quizzical expression said, 'About France.'

She left him to struggle with whatever was on his mind till he continued, 'I think we should hop across the Channel to visit your Clive's grave. I do think it might help.'

If it was kindness he intended the immediate effect was pain. Clive was locked away in a private place, somewhere only she was admitted. She should never have mentioned him. Clive was sacred. She did not answer, just stared at Mitchell.

'I think it might help,' he repeated.

'I don't even know where the grave is,' she said.

'You told me once that he took part in the Normandy landings. His name might only be on a memorial but there is a good chance he has a grave. Either way I can find out details.'

None of the reasons why it might be a good idea came to her. How it would help, with what it might help, she had no idea.

'I know you mean well,' she said finally, 'and I think you are the kindest, daftest man I ever knew but...'

'It might help,' he emphasised, wearing his hangdog expression.

How? What? After all this time? It was impossible to find her way round the jumble of feelings he had stirred up.

Finally she said again, 'Can I think about it?' She was learning not to say 'yes' without thinking things through.

He took her hand in his and kissed her on the cheek. 'Of course you can,' he said.

She did not add that she had never been to France, never been abroad; nowadays when everyone went by coach or flew to the sun, who would believe that a woman in her fifties had never been to France, never been anywhere abroad? What little schoolgirl French she remembered would be wholly inadequate. What did one wear to go to France? Nor did she ask what he thought it might help with. What later lodged in her memory of that conversation was the kindly intent in his voice as he anxiously blurted out the invitation. It was beyond doubt that he was a kindly man who meant well, something of a mixed blessing perhaps?

Clive, whom she had loved all her life, was a simple soul in comparison, beer froth in his moustache, sharing blokish jokes with the chaps around the bar, always hungry for another tumble in the grass. He had left school at the first opportunity, taken a job delivering mineral waters from the back of a van. She liked it when he said rude things about her father behind his back, liked it less when he went all smiley faces with her father face to face. And yet, as the years wore down he had somehow become Saint Clive, without fault except that he was the man who let her down, stole what would have been their perfect life together.

How different from Mitchell. Yes, all men were imperfect, fault-ridden. But was one such better than none such?

Around the office talk kept returning to what Thatcher and Ian MacGregor, head of the National Coal Board, might do next. It had not gone unnoticed that as head of the British Steel Corporation MacGregor had turned the company around by halving the workforce in only two years. During coffee breaks in the social workers' room opinions were unanimous apart from Lorraine's insistence on the need to crack down on rebellious workers, almost as though British miners were a variety of black South African worker whose right to strike she firmly denounced.

'They're simple people,' she said, 'they don't know what is best for them so we treat them like children, our people we call them, onse mense, and like children they need firm discipline.' Alan was incensed by this; she saw him struggling to contain the slow-burn inside him that Lorraine caused. She worried it might even come to blows.

Mitchell liked to join in these discussions and though he had never worked with his hands the men in the office seemed to welcome his contribution because he was sympathetic to the miners' cause. When miners at the Manvers complex in Yorkshire walked out Mitchell pointed out that things would get worse before they got better. In March it was announced that five pits were to be subjected to accelerated closure. It could only be a matter of days before Arthur Scargill declared a national strike.

Madge was saddened at the way things were going. Although the pits around Moortown were long gone, landscaped into folksy hillocks of grass, surrounded by 'nature parks', many of the families in the area remembered the 'old days' through what seemed to her at times rose-tinted spectacles. Yes, there had been the camaraderie of the pit villages, the slogans, 'All for one and one for all', and 'Not a penny off the pay, not a second on the day', the banners and marching bands and speeches on Miners' Gala Day. But there had also been strikes, hardship, accidents and harsh working conditions. With their easy profits it was only the coal owners who had enjoyed complete satisfaction.

All Lorraine said was, 'We've got gold mines that are miles deep and the workers never complain.'

'I wonder why?' said Simon.

'It's obvious,' said Lorraine, 'they know what's good for them. They are like children, we treat them as our own children.'

The office fell silent at these outbursts and Madge wished Lorraine would at least stay silent.

***

The Oldfields' return to Brownlow went unannounced; the radio, television and the *Northern Times* were all silent on the matter which had so recently seemed of consummate interest to them and their publics. The Oldfields signed the tenancy agreement for their newly allocated council house and left the Farrant home and moved in to their nice newly built house. Madge asked Simon to help them get some furniture together from the council store and negotiate with the DHSS for a grant to meet any shortfall in their requirements. Soon a cooker, washing machine and fridge came knocking at their door. Lorraine, visiting the Farrants, had happened upon the news that with the electricity back on in the Farrant house Alistair had been able to play with his cars on the Scalextric race track for an hour before going back to live with the foster parents. Where had the family been? Somewhere south... How far south? Beyond Darlington... mebbes... Nobody's business but theirs. Was this a police state or something?

Once back at school the school had reported that Alistair was causing no undue problems apart from a playground fight to the death with Gary Farrant. In accordance with county policy both boys had been caned to make the point that violence would never be tolerated, was always wrong and never right. The headteacher declared the matter closed, the problem resolved. After school the two boys finished the fight in the street and after receiving a report that both boys had bruising around their eyes, Madge had to send Simon to investigate the facial injuries which were, in county council terms, potentially non-accidental. The following day Mr Farrant and Mr Oldfield arrived at the school and threatened the Head Teacher for unjustifiably punishing the boys who they said had done no wrong. When the Head Teacher threatened to call the police the fathers, swearing volubly, moved out into the girls' playground before resorting to fisticuffs as they blamed one another for their sons' misfortunes.

As Simon placed his non-accidental injury report on Madge's desk he said, 'There can be no doubt the bruising resulted from the fight so I recommend no further action but perhaps we should investigate the physical pain caused by the Head Teacher.'

'No point,' Madge said, 'it's council policy.'

The phone rang and it was the Head Teacher. 'I've done all I can, something must be done.'

Madge said, 'We will keep an eye on both families and hopefully things will calm down from now on.'

'In that case the boys can remain in the school for as long as they mend their ways.'

Next she must inform County Hall that Alistair was safely back with the foster parents. She spoke to Puttock who this time did take her call. He did not seem over-excited at hearing from her.

She took the opportunity to ask, 'Will the disciplinary be dropped now the Oldfields are back with Alistair safe and sound?'

'I'll speak to the Director,' Puttock said.

Once again the Director and Puttock went into silent mode.

Two days later she phoned again. 'Yes,' Puttock said, 'the Director has agreed to drop the disciplinary.' Big deal, she thought.

'And the conditions on offer if I opt now for early retirement?'

'I can only repeat what I said on an earlier occasion: you can resign, and you would get your pension at sixty.'

'No enhancement even at sixty?'

'Certainly not, the budget is tight already with all these government cutbacks.'

That is just plain wrong, she thought, but what can I do about it?

She phoned Mitchell. 'They won't do a deal on retirement,' she said, 'I shall have to struggle on till I'm sixty or resign and go quietly with no pension till then.'

'Bastards,' Mitchell said. 'Solidarity though, I'll stay on

a bit longer as well, keep you company, keep an eye on you.'

Till that moment she hadn't realised Mitchell had also edged so near the end of the gangplank. She had noticed he seemed depressed about his job in the wake of the scandal but clearly the wounds had cut deeper than she had seen; preoccupied with her own difficulties she had been oblivious to his. Wrapped in her own anger and misery she had forgotten to care for him; perhaps she had forgotten how to care. Had years of soaking up client pain deadened her sensibilities? The dreadful word 'burnout' which was much in vogue came to mind.

As she explained it to Mitchell that evening, it was all so unfair: Dan was to blame; if she had been born a man it would have all turned out differently, instead her years of service counted for nothing. And all the Director was concerned about was his vote in the by-election.

Once again she forgot to ask Mitchell how he was bearing up when his concern seemed for her rather than himself.

He said, 'Some time in France would give you time and space to decide whether to fight on or concede defeat.'

She had thought of little else but an escape to France and now none of the reasons why it might not be a good idea came to her as she answered, 'I'd like that, thank you.'

Mitchell had been thinking of her future. She knew he saw Clive as being very significant to her, and hence his Normandy idea, but he was also concerned for her future at work. A few days away from the office might give her the space she needed to sort out which way she should go:

resign or stay? As for Clive, when she allowed him house room in her head she could almost see ways in which a trip to France might help. It was unreasonable of him to keep her under lock and key for a single day longer. The trouble was finding the key.

Mitchell smiled and kissed her on her cheek again. 'That's wonderful news, I'll see what I can find out before we go,' he said, adding, 'Time for me to think about my future as well. Since the uproar over the nude photographs my job has never been the same. There is a smear still hanging over me. We photographers sometimes put a trace of Vaseline on the lens to creatively distort the image. I feel my colleagues now see me through just such a lens.'

She hugged him, relieved it was not just about her and Clive who, having got himself killed, could hardly hold her to ransom forever. The balance of her life was changing, the scales tipping away from work and towards Mitchell. Yet how could she explain to herself, let alone put into words to Mitchell, how unsure of everything she suddenly felt? Worrying about work, uncertain about her future with Mitchell, these were anxieties that now nagged away as she lay awake at night. At least getting away from Moortown for a few days would give her a chance to sort out her head, perhaps even her heart.

With the by-election now only weeks away Dan was seldom in the office, 'working for the Director while on special leave,' he said, and she knew that meant canvassing across the county, claiming wads of car mileage money though it was on the Director's election campaign not county council business. Rudham, she thought, corruption is thy name. Word reached her that the Director was still bitter about the effect the Oldfield saga would have on his chances in the election, for which he still blamed 'that bitch Perfect'. Clearly he would not relent.

After several days when these uncertainties swirled around in her head Mitchell came round to the cottage one evening and said, 'I've located the grave. It's at Bayeux. We could visit the grave, call in at the museum there and see how his unit fitted into the battles in that area, and of course visit the beach where he would have gone ashore.'

Now a trip to France did not seem such a daft idea after all.

So she said, 'I'm ready for a break and yes I would like to do those things you suggest.'

She meant it. The noose being dangled by County Hall was always there somewhere. Dan plotting was always close at hand. She must decide something before they pounced. And she would be proud to visit the grave of Clive, the man who gave his life for his country and ended their hopes of happiness. She could not go on blaming him for that forever.

Mitchell said, 'A break will do you good. And me too. I need to think too. As I mentioned to you the university is getting me down after the scandal. Nobody looks at me the same way anymore, each day brings some new niggling slight. It has even been suggested that I might prefer to move on from Green College to one of the newer colleges.'

'We're almost in the same place,' Madge said. 'I'll make sure there is cover in the office. With me away I only wish it could be Dan who carries the can if things go wrong.

Except he would find a way of absolving himself. It will be a chance to think things through… my job I mean.' She meant about Mitchell as well but she wasn't going to say that. Could there be a future for them? Did she want that? Did she want Mitchell accompanied by his chum Hegel as lifetime companions? Then she remembered to wonder what Mitchell might want and realised that she had little or no idea.

On 12 March Arthur Scargill declared a national strike without waiting for a ballot. Lorraine said that with communists running the country things could only get worse. Alan told her to 'shut it'. South Africa it seemed to Lorraine was the only country capable of keeping the world safe from communism. Brenda came round with her plastic bucket collecting for the miners' families.

Madge liked the prospect of living out her days in the north of England less and less. So many things had changed, so few for the better.

EASTER TERM
1984

Chapter 18

Easter fell late that year and wishing to travel when the roads would be quieter they set off for France early one morning at the end of April.

Mitchell, who had put work to one side for a week, was childlike in his enthusiasm. 'We are going to sea in a beautiful pea green boat. We have packed some honey and plenty of money wrapped up in a five-pound note.'

'Plenty of money? What if I decide to resign before I'm sixty?'

'Oh Madge, dear Madge, you are so unromantic. I've raided my piggy bank for our trip.'

That's as may be, Madge thought, perhaps I am short-changed in the romance department, but keeping my feet on the ground is what kept me going all these years.

All she said was, 'I only hope I don't disappoint you, Mitchell.'

Quite apart from the ghost of Puttock marching in step with them for every mile of their journey, going abroad for the first time was an anxiety in itself; travelling that distance in the Hillman Imp came into a category labelled 'grave cause for concern'. Like Madge the Hillycopter had never been to France. Leaving the country in such a vehicle, leaving the office at a moment of industrial crisis with her own future working life uncertain seemed unwise. But hell, the Hillycopter might make it there and back, it had after all crossed the Pennines to the Lakes and back, and surely there was not much more that could go wrong in the office over the next few days.

But then there would be her return. What would she say to Puttock? She could resign, go quietly, but at what cost? No pension till she was sixty. How different it would be if only she was a man. She remembered Lorraine echoing her mother: 'Men are brutes'. Yes, at County Hall it was men who held all the power.

She had tackled Mitchell over his cruelty to the Hillycopter, doubting that it was able to bear the burden of their combined luggage. In addition to the suitcases there were Mitchell's camera bags; at times it was difficult to tell whether the camera bags or the suitcases were greater in weight. It was almost more than the little Hillycopter could be expected to bear. The extra burden made the engine noisier and more fitful than ever.

Supposing she would be interested in such things he spent much of the journey south explaining the ins and outs of the minimum photographic necessities: apparently any photographer's essential resources included three cameras (two 35mm, 1 two-and-a-quarter inches square – the numbers referred to film sizes apparently), a range of lenses offering varying lengths and diameters of phallic suggestiveness, lens caps to keep out dust, lens-cleaning cloths to remove dust that had not been kept out, lens-cleaning brushes to reach into awkward nooks and crannies where dust that had been dusted and brushed had accumulated, a range-finder, light meters (two, one in case the other got lost or stopped working), a large tripod and a 'pocket' tripod, filters, films (black and white and colour with a range of film speeds), and his device enabling the photographer to take pictures at right angles to the subject which he said were ideal for 'those candid shots'. Given the near disaster of the university darkroom incident Madge felt slightly nervous at the thought of anything candid. She certainly had no intention of posing naked by a rock pool in the interests of Mitchell's art.

When he had finished explaining all of this she did wonder if he would have been just as happy leaving her behind and going alone on holiday in his Hillycopter with Hegel and the cameras. Perhaps some men even went to bed with their cameras.

When they were well down the A1, still about fifty miles north of London, she noticed columns of police vans heading north ready to confront the striking miners in Yorkshire on Monday. Would the strike never end? Would Thatcher not relent until she had her heel pressed down hard on the throat of the NUM?

'A nice slab of overtime for some. Regardless of cost, that woman is determined to break the miners,' Mitchell said.

Madge had never heard tell of such a powerful woman. Perhaps in future more women could become powerful, perhaps one day a woman might rule County Hall. Perhaps Mrs Thatcher would use her power to improve the lot of women.

Closer to London they passed signs for a diversion to Watford as they joined temporary roads where construction work on a huge ring road to encircle the capital was now causing traffic chaos. They dodged slow earthmoving equipment and huge lorries. Men working in their yellow jackets and hard hats served only to further slow their progress.

'We could go straight through the centre of London,' Mitchell said, 'but I think we will be wiser to go round the edge.'

After skirting around London they headed on to the ferry port at Newhaven, pausing for an overnight stop. Next morning the Hillycopter groaned at the demands the steep ramps on board made on its tired engine. As they left the harbour Madge looked back on the coast of England till it was a smudge on the horizon. What was the last view of England that Clive looked back on forty years ago? How long ago and far away it all seemed now. When she joined Mitchell in the on-board café they settled for the gastronomic delight of pie and chips.

'The food will be different once we reach France,' Mitchell said. 'The little hotel I have booked at Auffay serves wonderful rich Normandy dishes, mostly meat with cream sauce and gallons of Calvados or cider. The apples are a regional speciality, you never saw so many different apples: colours, petite, large, wiry, and smooth, you name it. You'll love it.'

Approaching the French coast, the light leaking through the clouds gave the choppy sea the texture of an oil painting; the sky with its grey clouds and glimpses of blue was a watercolour. As Dieppe came closer she was back on deck watching the families on the beach, the sailing boats tacking back and forth heading into the harbour while beyond stretched the skeletal architecture of a busy working town.

The ferry entered the harbour as she stared down on the groups of people staring up at the boat from the breakwater. She was surprised when they continued down the channel and into the town till they juddered to a stop opposite a line of shops and restaurants.

The Hillycopter said little but seemed pleased the voyage was over, relieved to be back on dry land. Mitchell let it have its head going south along straight roads lined with trees towards their next overnight stop.

Auffay was a small village set in a landscape of rolling agricultural land. France looked so different from England but when she thought about it at all she found it difficult to say what the differences were. All along the verges of the road stretched a profusion of some of the wild flowers she loved: buttercups, meadow daisies, sorrel, ragged robin, Queen Anne's lace, broom, colt's foot and much, much more. As the signs for Auffay came up on the road Mitchell became excited at what lay ahead.

'Came here with my parents years ago,' he said. 'It was around Christmas and there was snow on the ground. The Maurices, husband and wife, ran the place. They worked ever so hard, the younger generation in a hotel which had been in the family since the year dot. Monsieur's parents were a very old couple, a silent presence in the background.'

'Sounds a good memory. I never asked about your parents.'

'Not much to say. Dad was a teacher, Mum just a bored housewife. No, not "just" for she ran the show until they died in short order ten years ago.'

They pulled up outside the Aigle d'Or and as they carried their bags into the hotel the Hillycopter gurgled with relief at the prospect of a chance to rest. Mitchell bounded in ahead of her and introduced himself, saying, 'Vous devez surement rappeler la famille anglaise qui a séjourné chez vous dans les années cinquante?'

Monsieur and Madame looked at him blankly. Madame was in pink slippers. Her hair had gone wild and her clothes were food-stained and worn. Monsieur was gap-toothed and balding, a shrunken little old man. They both looked tired of life.

'Non, Monsieur, je ne me rappelle pas,' Madame replied. She stared at Mitchell, her eyes vacant as if to say, 'Who is this strange man?'

Mitchell turned to Madge. 'They don't remember me or my parents. I am surprised.'

He looked back at Madame. 'Nous pouvons manger?'

'Oui, bien sûr,' she replied.

'We can eat here,' Mitchell said. Then he asked, 'Notre chambre?'

'Suivez-moi,' Madame replied.

'We're to follow her to our room,' Mitchell said.

The old lady led them up a creaky wooden staircase which they accessed through a door in the corner of the bar. Their footfalls on the stairs set off explosions of dust. There was a musty smell hanging over everything. Peeling wallpaper hung down on to the worn carpet, a tracery of spider webs criss-crossed from the ceiling to peeling paint below. They passed open doors into what must once have been bedrooms but were now junk rooms full of rolled carpets and broken furniture. Their bedroom which came at the end of the corridor was little better: a huge double bed with dusty bedding, a cracked mirror in front of the window where once there must have been curtains, and everywhere dust.

'I am so sorry,' Mitchell said to Madge, 'this is nothing like I remember it. The people we just met were young then, probably in their forties. They were "the young couple" when I was here before. Monsieur worked hard behind the zinc counter of his bar, laughing and joking with the customers, lively as a cricket. From the bar you could see beyond the tables with check tablecloths to the cooking area where Madame slaved away. There was even a function room at the rear where they had a ballroom for weddings. How time changes things. I remember them so clearly yet they don't remember me at all.'

'Perhaps things change time? They must have met endless English families, for you it was probably the first of the few French families you ever met.'

Had she meant time changes things?

'I suppose you're right.' With his shoulders hunched he looked completely dejected. Then he said, 'I almost forgot, I've a small present for you.' He went to his suitcase and pulled out a paper bag labelled Rudham University Bookshop. Puzzled, excited, surprised, perhaps all of those things, she opened the bag. Inside was a paperback book by someone called Susie Orbach, someone she had never heard of. The book was called *Fat is a Feminist Issue*.

She must have looked puzzled for he said, 'I thought it might help, it's a new edition of a book well respected in feminist circles, sociology I suppose.'

'Help with what?'

'Well, you know how you worry about your weight. You shouldn't, no need, research evidence shows that most people are less obese than they think they are.'

Mitchell was digging himself in to an ever deeper hole.

'I see,' she said. She didn't. 'Thank you,' she said.

'I missed out by not giving you a Christmas present when you gave me that lovely book on my hero Robert Capa.'

'Shall we go down for dinner?' she asked. Here was the kindest, most well-meaning man in the world trying to do good, not seeing how his gift might feel to the recipient. She was overweight, fact, that was that. She had no time for all this feminist nonsense but she said nothing for fear of hurting his feelings.

Dinner was no more than nettle soup and chunks of rather dry bread. Afterwards they walked around the village as the light faded. She was constantly reminded, as she had been all day, how different France was from England; why exactly she couldn't say. She noticed a café by the church called 'Les Jacquemarts'.

'What does that mean?' she asked.

'I'll show you,' said Mitchell, glancing at his watch and then pointing up to the church clock, above which there were two figures holding bells and smoking pipes. 'I remember being told they were Huguenots who refused to accept the Catholic faith and for their punishment had to ring the church bells for every service for the rest of their lives. When they died they were replaced with these automatons, as we say in English'.

Was it like her father's legacy, she wondered, her having to slave till the end of her days caring for children, driven from the start by her need to save others from the abuse she had suffered at his hands?

Just then the figures suddenly moved and the bells clanked. 'There you are, Les Jacquemarts,' said Mitchell.

There was certainly nothing about Auffay to remind her of Moortown.

'Let's have a good cup of café crème,' said Mitchell, guiding her to a table by the door.

They sat for an hour quietly watching the cheerful banter between the proprietor and his customers, most of whom were drinking beer, not coffee. 'This is more as I expected it,' she said.

When they returned to their bedroom in the hotel the water in the bathroom down the other end of the corridor was cold, the toilet bowl was stained. With nothing much else to do they threaded a route through the jumble of miscellaneous broken furniture to bed.

'You sure know how to show a girl a good time,' Madge said. They made love gently so as not to disturb more dust or perhaps break the bed. She clung to him seeking reassurance from the insecurity she felt about the hotel. Then, tired from the journey and the disappointment of the hotel, she slept till the noise from the market in the square woke her.

'O Madge my love! O Madge my love, what a beautiful pussy you are, you are, and what a beautiful pussy you are!' It was Mitchell whispering in her ear with light pouring in through the dirty windows. She for a while lay watching the motes of dust floating in the sunlight.

Then he made one of his announcements. 'Every time I start with a new razor blade I know that by the second shave the blade will not be as sharp as the first, and the third as sharp as the second and so on.'

She didn't like to say 'So what'. Was he profound or ridiculous? Was he talking about sex? Their sex? Or Hegel? What was he talking about? Funny man, must be a victim of his intelligence and the academic lifestyle. She said nothing. Why did he never express any feelings he might have for her? Did he have feelings? Could he possibly love her? Or was it Hegel he was in love with? Frightened now of losing him again she was carefully guarding herself from the love she was feeling for him. Love? At her age? Ridiculous.

Today they would carry on to the cemetery at Bayeux. Was it a mistake to come at all? She just wasn't sure.

Trickle down time. She clambered out of bed causing a flurry of feathers to surround her and the bed. When she found her way to the bathroom the water was now slightly warm, the basin coated with the grime of ages, the residue of long gone visitors. A jumble of sounds floated up from the street which had been so silent when they arrived the previous day.

Once back in the bedroom she saw the cause of all the noise. Mitchell was leaning out of the window watching the bustling market below, with lines of stalls selling fruit and vegetables, flowers and plants. Vibrant colours bounced back at her wherever she glanced, everything looked clean. A woman in a Citroen van open with a counter on one side was selling an amazing array of cheeses. The smell of chickens cooking on a rotisserie reached the window from further down the square. At the far end of the market place a grey, severe-looking church seemed to ooze disapproval of so much laughter, so many raucous voices, all disrespectful under the eyes of an all-seeing God.

'Auffay itself hasn't changed,' he said, 'but the past can disappoint.'

She crossed to the window and, out of sight of the people below, hugged him from behind.

'I'm sorry about your hotel,' she said.

'I'll take some photographs anyway, such a wonderful subject, so much vitality amongst so much dereliction,' he said.

After a long drive with the Hillycopter protesting at the workload they reached Bayeux and found a side road off the bypass where they could park within sight of the cemetery. 'You OK about this?' Mitchell asked. She bit her lip, nodded.

The graves were laid out in rigid rows and columns like chocolates in a box, serried ranks of gravestones radiating out from a rectangular centre piece, a building containing the list of servicemen buried there. Mitchell searched the list and wrote down the reference number and then together they walked till they found the right row and gravestone within it. Below the regimental crest she read:

313

14416416
PRIVATE
C. ALDRIDGE
THE MIDDLESEX REGIMENT
7 TH AUGUST 1944 AGE 19

Mitchell walked on while she sat silently at the foot of the grave. If Clive was here it was some consolation. The parcel of feelings she had kept in a secret place must have gradually spilled open over the years, the feelings scattering to who knew where. Clive, who had always been a part of her, always would be, or so she thought, had faded; the once unbearably painful ache for him now dulled. She wanted to feel moved, to be able to acknowledge her love for Clive but no feelings came.

Feeling guilty at these thoughts she turned to admire the well-tended plants growing in the dark brown soil between the graves. Rosebuds were swelling ready for the summer and in between them grew helianthemums, the rock roses in vibrant colours. Heleniums, for which she liked the common name 'sneeze weed', were sprouting from the base ready to share their summer glory as the months went by. A Helenium next to Clive's grave looked as if it might be her favourite, Moerheim Beauty, of which she had two in her neglected long bed by the fence at home. Little sedums crawled into gaps between the gravestones, their sometimes grey, sometimes red stems trailing bunches of many-coloured little flowers. An oak tree lay in her line of vision past Clive's gravestone and on beyond the well-drilled lines of graves.

Like clips from old films, black and white images of her past caught on thorns of memories. There was Clive in his long, baggy trousers, his open-necked shirt, hair flowing in the wind. Funny how he always wore a vest even in summer. Clive laughing, saying 'See you soon' and 'Love you forever' after making love for the last time. The day she heard the news that he would not be coming back to her. All these images begged the same questions: what happened next, why did it happen, what if…? The questions went on and on and on.

Now there was Mitchell who was fun and immensely kind, caring for and about her in a way that no one else did. Was that enough? Where was the magic? Could he fit into her life alongside her job? If she decided to resign she would be hard up till she could draw her pension. She would never live with Mitchell if she had to depend on him financially, become a burden to him. No, he must remain a free spirit, able to roam with his camera down coal mines and other places in search of bad light which was good.

Why wasn't Mitchell in the war? Because he was too young at the time. Silly question. That was it. Time changes things. Her feelings for Clive proved that. She could see it all now, how each passing year rust grew on the iron of memory. Now she could be honest with herself: Clive had withered to no more than a memory trace.

She noticed trees in the distance, heard the rumble of traffic on the bypass road passing the cemetery. In the farm field over the cemetery fence young stalks of sweetcorn were starting to gain height.

When she rejoined Mitchell he said, 'OK?'

'OK.' He took her arm. 'Let's cross the road to the museum. We might find more about the action Clive fought in there. Perhaps I should have tried for his war record.'

'No need,' she said, 'I only wanted to visit his grave. But let's take a quick look-see in the museum.'

In the museum, bristling with self-important ex-army types and their memsahibs, Mitchell went from cabinets to wall displays making notes as he went. She stared helplessly at the displays of military hardware, pictures, maps, photographs all explaining more than she could begin to grasp. She had come to find Clive but where was Clive in this jumble of things from the past?

He summed up his findings. 'The D-Day landings began on 6 June 1944. That was the big day. But Clive didn't die till 7 August. So either he landed after the initial push, or he was wounded on or after the sixth but didn't die immediately.'

'I hope he didn't suffer all that time,' Madge said.

'Or,' Mitchell went on, 'and I think this is most likely, looking at the battle plans here in the museum, I think he may well have died in the fierce fighting in the push inland around the Falaise pocket. It rather looks as though Montgomery made a pig's ear of that operation.'

'It really doesn't matter exactly where it happened,' she said.

What was his underlying motive for the visit? Another camera trip? An act of great kindness? He was like a schoolboy with his enthusiasm, his heroes not footballers or cricketers but photographers like Capa or writers like Hegel. It was difficult not to see him as something of an oddball. Trouble was she quite liked the oddball in him. He did not collect stamps and neither did he do jigsaw puzzles. He was not a trainspotter. There were worse men out there. He would never be boring. Would he?

Mitchell meanwhile was chatting to a visitor who was recalling how he had been the first man into Brussels on his motorbike when the war ended.

'What did you do before the war?' Mitchell asked.

'I was a miner.'

'What did you do after the war?'

'I was a miner.'

'And now?'

'I'm unemployed.'

'Thatcher?'

'No, not the bitch Thatcher. I had an accident at pit. I make a few bob trundling round Doncaster selling ice creams.'

Mitchell came over to her, took her hand. 'Let's find a bed for the night and a good restaurant for a proper French meal.'

Tired from travelling, Madge weary at finding Clive's grave after all these years, they achieved a good meal and a comfortable bed in which they slept undisturbed till the traffic noise woke them in the morning.

After coffee and croissants in the town Mitchell said, 'Let's take a look at one or two of the landing beaches before we head home.'

They drove two or three miles along the coast before settling down on the terrace of a café overlooking the sea at Arromanches. It was by now midday and the high-in-the-sky sun was warm on her skin. Mitchell ordered a Croque-Monsieur and a glass of cider for them both. Below them on the sandy beach the damaged hulks of what remained of the Mulberry Harbour lay unyielding against wind and tide. Waiting for the food to arrive she tried to marry this summer scene with the black and white images of the Allied landings they had seen in the museum.

Mitchell said, 'Robert Capa was here, you know, he was present at the D-day landings. You remember the book you kindly gave me for Christmas?'

'I do indeed and were it not for that I would have assumed your friend Mr Capa was a significant general.'

'No, no, a war photographer. Co-founder of Magnum. Died in Vietnam.'

'When he came ashore in the Normandy landing how did he cope with all the kit you snapper types find necessary?'

Mitchell looked annoyed at this. 'Not snappers, photo journalists. Capa was working at a different time, in different circumstances, he was travelling light.'

Madge decided not to pursue the matter. They had come to find Clive not some dead snapper. Fortunately Mitchell never seemed to mind when she did not know what he was talking about and showed no interest in finding out. Sometimes she wondered if he quite liked being the brains of the operation. Or was he just relieved to escape the academic world he seemed to like less and less.

She could not imagine war on this beach where dogs raced up and down scattering the sand, their owners screeching instructions that were ignored. It was much the same with children except for the younger ones working industriously with buckets and spades in the pools left by the outgoing tide. All the while there was the sniff of the sea, salty enough to catch in your nostrils, and seagulls scavenging for scraps of food fallen from the tables.

She munched through and enjoyed the strong cheese and salty ham of the Croque-Monsieur. The sweetness of the cider was a perfect complement. Why did thoughts of Puttock have to intrude and spoil it? She must decide before they returned to Rudham yet she had hardly given it a thought since the first day. What she must do was coming to her though, like sunlight breaking through a dense bank of clouds. It was obvious really, had been all along.

Her thoughts were interrupted by the two loud military types who were sitting at the next table talking about a memorial plaque to a French-American.

'Can't be right,' the older man said, 'he couldn't have died in Indo-China, the Americans were never in Indo-China.'

'No, only Vietnam,' his companion confirmed.

As they walked back to the Hillycopter Mitchell said, 'Time to go home.' She nodded assent. He had this strange gift, she thought, of stating the obvious one minute and something totally arcane the next.

'Yes, tis indeed,' she said. 'I am glad we came, sorry to go but also worried about Area 13, Moortown Area Office, how they are managing without me.'

'Have you decided what to do next?'

'Yes, I think so, I would like to fight them and get a good deal but I can't see any way in which I could win when they hold all the big cards, have all the power. I'm going to resign, somehow manage till my pension comes in when I'm sixty, forget about the suitcase full of enhancement money given to the blokes who retire.'

'I'm sorry, Madge. No more up and at 'em?'

'No, I'm fresh out of up and at 'em. But don't be sorry, it's not of your making, and the time away from the office let me come to terms with what is and can't be changed. And visiting Clive's grave meant a lot to me. Without you I would never have done that. I feel now that I can put him away in a safe place belonging to the past.'

'How will you manage financially?'

'I've thought about that.' So she explained to him how in a battle between Madge and Goliath she had no chance of winning when she was a mere Area Controller ranged against Goliath who was Puttock, and Puttock was Assistant Director, Human Resources with the Director behind him. Why fight a contest if victory was impossible? She would resign, draw on her savings, live very simply, manage without a car, and cut out all unnecessary expenditures, with minor indulgences the first to suffer. Chocolates were not good for her anyway, nor all but the occasional glass of wine.

Mitchell slipped an arm around her waist. 'I do sort of love you, Madge,' he said. She squeezed his hand. 'And me you, sort of,' she said.

'You know,' he said, 'I never could do casual sex, one-night stands, that sort of thing, only when I've had feelings for a woman. There have been precious few as a result, laughable in this day and age. I know I'm not very good at it.'

She smiled. 'I like you just the way you are.'

The Hillycopter headed east leaving Clive behind. Just when she thought she would never fall in love again she had. Sort of. No, not sort of, perhaps she had, really had or, as Lorraine would say, really, really had. Home was a long way away and she was asleep for much of the journey to the port while the undulating farm fields, the tree-lined roads and the wide open vistas all showed off their attractions to Mitchell at the wheel.

***

When the Hillycopter pulled up outside her cottage she patted the bonnet and said, 'Well done, Hillycopter', then kissed Mitchell chastely on the cheek and said, 'Well done, Mitchell'.

'It did help?' he asked.

'Yes, and in ways I did not expect.' Then as he revved up the Hillycopter she waved and shouted, 'Thanks for the book.' A strange man, but nice, and she refused to see her regard for him as a feminist issue.

Lying awake that first night back in the cottage she remembered the deaths of her mother, father and Clive;

she had not been allowed to see her dead mother or attend the funeral, she had felt nothing at her father's funeral and Clive, well Clive had gone away to die and apart perhaps from some fellow soldiers he had died and been buried alone. Only now did she feel able to unravel the layers of grieving. Surely, as a trained social worker, she had waited an unnecessarily long time before doing this?

***

Arriving back in the office next morning she found Lorraine waiting for her with a knowing smile. 'Had a good time, Madge?' she said. 'Was it good for you?'

'Very nice thank you, lovely food. French food is so different.'

Lorraine winked. 'And that too! Watch yourself, Madge, you know what men are like.' Just for once Lorraine had forgotten to add that it was just the same in Cape Town.

So Lorraine had guessed. Perhaps everyone knew by now what she had been up to. Or thought they did. What the hell!

'Oh, one other thing,' Lorraine said, 'I almost forgot, Billy was looking for you yesterday, Madge. He seemed a bit anxious. Said he'd call again today.'

Well, she wondered, what does Billy want now?

Chapter 19

There was no sign of Billy the next day. The town was contaminated with by-election posters and cars blaring inaudible exhortations to vote for the best man. Madge thought it likely the best man might not win but such was the price of democracy. Photos of the candidates, mostly the smiling Director representing Labour, stared from house and shop windows. She was almost certain one Labour-supporting car was driven by Dan.

In the evening Mitchell came round clutching an overnight bag. Why not? she thought. Let us embrace routine, in for a sterling penny in for a decimal pound. They sat together grumpily watching the local TV coverage of the count. The Tory and the Independent candidates looked glum as the piles of voting slips in the Labour heap grew ever larger. Prancing in front of the cameras the Director looked ever more confident. Madge now hated him more than ever. They all looked rather ridiculous with their giant brightly coloured rosettes and servile followers clustered in their wake like bees round a hive.

'A fine subject for some latter day Rembrandt,' Mitchell said.

There he goes again, Madge thought, off into his own imagined world. Suddenly she started forward, stared at the screen. 'Could that be Dan at the Director's side?' she asked.

Mitchell did not answer. He had slumped against her fast asleep on the sofa. She stared hard at the screen and yes it was Dan looking even more pleased with himself than usual.

Close to midnight Mitchell rolled over without waking just as the declaration of the result came through on the radio. It was no surprise: the Director was the duly elected Member of Parliament for the Rudham constituency. In spite of all the adverse publicity resulting from the Oldfield story the Labour majority had increased.

'There is no such thing as bad publicity. They'd vote for a monkey up here,' Mitchell said, waking suddenly.

'They once did,' Madge said. 'I think we need another drink.'

Was her voice ever so slightly slurred? Was that what they had driven her to, a boozy old floozy? How it all hurt. How could she be anything but bitter as she remembered all the senior male staff who took it in turns to be Director, upping their final salary and pension before retiring early with a lavish enhancement package? Had she just let it all happen to her? What more could she have done? Whatever happened to up and at 'em? What would her father say were he to see her now as she prepared to hoist the flag of surrender rather than fight them to the death? Tomorrow was another day, as Lorraine still announced at every available opportunity. Madge didn't like the look of tomorrow, the knowledge that they would turf her out one way or another. The fight had gone out of her; choosing between fighting on or going now waiting for her pension at sixty and with no golden goodbye had come to seem a no-brainer. What was the point? They would win in the end. They had been willing to drop the disciplinary hearing but perhaps they had worked out they might not win. Now she must sleep, she would worry about the future in the morning.

'Let's get ourselves to bed,' she said.

It was becoming a habit. Bed was sometimes comforting, occasionally fun and yet, in ways she could not comprehend, it still did not feel quite right.

***

A week later Billy was back waiting for her in the car park. 'Ah've got more, miss.'

'Billy, I did tell you I can't do it, won't do it.'

Billy then played his trump card. 'That's not aall. Ah've got more, miss. We found some letters he left behind. Mrs Hill had a look in his briefcase while he was fucking one of the girls. She found 'em. Wait till yer see these, miss.'

He looked at her triumphantly then pulled out a sheaf of neatly rolled pages held in place with a rubber band. 'Aalreet, read 'em,' he said, 'just read 'em.'

Madge knew she should send him on his way but reluctantly decided to combine virtue and necessity. If something improper involved someone important then surely this should become widely known? The idea appealed to her. The powers that be had shafted her. Yes, looking into it in case it mattered in the public interest was the least she should do. Surely necessity now outranked virtue?

Unrolling the letters she guiltily began reading the first page.

And what should emerge from the pages before her but the very private correspondence between Pixie Languid Leaves, a naughty pupil at Miss Polkinghorne's Academy, and the headmistress and mistress of discipline, Elf Sleepy Petals. As she read on the amorous language bordered on the obscene.

'Thank you, Billy, but how disgusting, I do hope you did not read it,' she said. 'Of course we cannot be sure who wrote all this.'

'Ah can, miss,' said Billy, 'and Mrs Hill can an aall. And she kept copies.'

'But there are no names.'

'Yous not looked. There's a name on last page.'

And there it was, faintly in pencil, the words 'Busted – Private'.

'That's only one name, Billy, though I do know a lady with that name. But who is the other person?'

'It's him, miss, one of yer lads, like I said reet at start.'

A grave suspicion requiring only confirmation had entered her mind.

'Well, Billy, I'll take care of these papers and ensure they get back to the right person, the person they belong to. It would be awful if they fell into the wrong hands.'

Billy laughed. 'Mrs Hill thinks we cud tek some big money off the geezer if we telt him we had em.'

Madge put on her stern face, reserved for rebuking the young. 'That would be blackmail, Billy. I will take care of the letters and ensure they are handled in the best possible way.'

'Is that aall, miss?'

'Yes, Billy.'

'But yer will speak up for us in court?'

Then she remembered and paused a moment. 'Yes, Billy, of course I'll be your character witness in court. With pleasure.' Seldom had she found the simple word 'pleasure' quite as pleasing.

Billy smiled and said, 'Ah divvent understand yer, Miss Porfect, ah nivvor did but Mrs Hill said yer would come roond if ah put it to yer right. She said ye would see there's money in them letters.' Then he swaggered out into the road as Madge headed for the office door, down the corridor and into her office smiling all the way. Principles, she was thinking, can only take a girl some of the way in life.

She went straight to the phone. 'Remember your friend Robert Capa? The photojournalist we almost met at Bayeux?'

'Not my friend,' Mitchell answered.

'Your hero then. I do know he's dead.' Why, when she tried to be witty did it fall so flat?

'So?'

'Combining his photojournalism, his bravery under fire and your right-angle lens for candid shots – I have an idea. I need the Robert Capa in you. The truth is I find I need some leverage in the social services department.'

'Intriguing,' he said.

'Come round this evening.'

Now she needed to plan her forthcoming up and at 'em campaign. It required a plan of action or, as Dan often said, an action plan is a plan of action.

***

When Mitchell saw the letters that evening he whistled softly. 'Poor sod and him now the MP,' he said. 'What are you going to do? Return them? Burn them?'

'I wouldn't want to embarrass the poor man so I won't return them straightaway. I'll keep them safe for now. Till I decide. But in the meantime I want to build a watertight case. At the moment I only have Billy's word for it that these are the Director's letters stolen by Mrs Hill.'

'Meaning what exactly?'

'Meaning that you, Mitchell, are about to go undercover in the public interest to confirm a man's identity and hobby in black and white. You are my photojournalist, my very own Robert Capa, my own dear member of the paparazzi. According to Billy our new MP likes to call in for a quickie on his way to work.'

'Gosh, gee whizz,' he said, 'if you think he might be in tomorrow I'll do it before I head off down the coast to catch some shots of the Red Arrows at the airshow. I'll do some quick contact prints and get them to you before I go. By the way, would you like to come with me to the coast?'

'No, not this time, I have other business to attend to, but enjoy. A girl has to wash her hair, bake some cakes, you know what we're like. Take care. Try not to get arrested and tortured as a spy in search of military secrets.'

Mitchell looked down at his feet. '... by the way, when I get back...'

'Yes?'

'Remind me to ask you to marry me.'

'Oh, Mitchell, that's ridiculous, what an oddball you are. You want to marry me but I have to remind you to ask me. And you don't even say why.'

'That's right. Geniuses always have more important things on their minds.' Like Hegel, she thought. He went on, 'If you must have the real reason, I need a camera bag carrier. Will that do?'

'That will do for now. Can I give you my answer now?'

'No, not till I get back and then, if I am arrested for spying at the airshow, and locked away for years and years, you will remain a free woman in search of another toy boy.'

'Is that what you are – my toy boy?'

'Something like that.'

She gave him a kiss on the cheek and said, 'I love you. I shall of course visit you in prison with a hacksaw hidden in one of my lemon drizzle cakes but in the meantime I'll start thinking about what I might wear on our big day – if I decide to say "yes".'

'You will remember to smuggle a camera into the prison? Research purposes of course.'

When he had gone she wondered: I do love him but am I in love with him? Is there a difference? Does it matter? Perhaps that Italian psychiatrist had been right: that love is a kind of madness. Would her feelings for him survive even if he spent years and years in prison for spying? Or if they were married for years and years would that be like being in prison? Could she survive his jokes as his favourites kept coming round, the ones he laughed at most loudly but no one else saw the funny side of?

While he was away over the weekend she would grapple with the 'shall I, shan't I' dilemma over marrying Mitchell. Marrying him would be the easy part but what about living the life of an academic wife? If she did retire now without a pension would coming on to his payroll be fair on Mitchell? And what about her lost job? How much would she miss it, would the clients miss her? But she would no longer have to silently witness Dan's machinations and the men in suits cutting down on staffing costs mainly at the expense of women? Now up and at 'em was suddenly back on the agenda.

***

No sooner had she arrived for work the next morning than the phone rang and it was the usually reassuring voice of Jim from the cop shop; except that this time it was not altogether comforting.

'Ah wonder if you can help, Madge, ah'm short-staffed today so ah'm charge sergeant, custody sergeant, clerical officer, tea lady and general muggins.'

'Sorry, Jim. Don't think it's a quiet life here.'

'Ah'm sorry te trouble ye, Madge, but ah'm ringing as custody sergeant, temporary ye understand. Probably nowt to do with you but ah've a gentleman in custody who claims he is known te you. We arrested him an hour ago. Seems a right nutter. Unshaven, scruffy clothes, drink on his breath, homeless mebbes. Sez you are his controller. Odd lookin fellow. Sez he is some kind of professor at Rudham University. Socialist something or other. Pull the other one, ah said to him. He just laughed. Sez his name is Mitchell.'

Madge took a deep breath. 'Yes, Jim, he is known to me. What's he done?' Behind the stentorian tones in his voice, she knew Jim as a good copper of the old school. He was not like some of the younger intake fresh from the training college, some of them graduates. Her path had crossed with Jim down the years in the juvenile court, child abuse enquiries and sometimes in mental health crises. Jim was down to earth, understood people, had a way of calming things down. But he was not a man to value humour; she must maintain a serious tone.

'Followin a complaint from a member of the public we found im hidin behind some bushes in the park takin photographs of – well, that's it, we're not sure of what except that the local primary school is next to the park.'

'Ah, I think I may be able to help… he is working with us on a research project… as part of that project he is… recording scenes of street life in Moortown… for posterity.'

'That's not quite what he said. In his statement he claims he was capturing urban landscapes early on a cloudy day. Some load a shit that is, ah told him. Then he said the light was great, as bad as it could be for the time of day for taking pictures without the sun, bollocks ah thowt.'

331

'Much as I expected,' she said. 'These university people always make things sound more complicated than they really are.'

'Is he dangerous? It's just that with the primary school close by we cannit be too careful. He's not under a section of the Mental Health Act then?'

She wanted to say, 'Not yet', or, 'I can't think why not,' but settled for, 'No'. Jim might not appreciate her humour. Nor Mitchell.

'We'd better release him then if ye think he's no danger to anyone. Ah cannit find an offence to hold him unless it's wasting police time.'

Only a danger to me, and not physically, Madge thought. 'Thanks for that, Jim, perhaps rough him up a bit first, then I promise to keep an eye on him.'

'Why man ah'll do more than that,' Jim said, 'ah'll explain it to him that he'll never take a good snap if he doesn't wait for a sunny day and mek sure the sun is behind his left shoulder.'

'You're a generous man, Jim, I'm sure he will appreciate your expert advice.'

An hour later Mitchell arrived in her office. Did he look shamefaced? Did he hell.

'Oh Mitchell,' she said, 'as my agent, my spy working undercover, as the new Robert Capa, you are a total failure. Next time I send you on a mission you must wear something a little more respectable than that scruffy tweed coat and that silly moth-eaten black woollen hat you found in a drain on the road.'

'That's my disguise.'

'Oh Mitchell, Mitchell, you are but a child let loose in an adult world. How have you survived this long?'

'By working in a university of course!'

And yet he seemed the sanest of all she had glimpsed in that zoo. She was cross. 'But you've missed our one opportunity.'

'Nay gadzooks, my good woman, suspend your judgement till you see the photographs.'

'You got him?'

'I think so. Banged to rights – sorry, I'm falling into the lingo of the place where I was so recently incarcerated. I'll get back to the darkroom as promised and have contacts back to you in an hour or so before I set off for the coast. I think it is the man you're after. Short, podgy, dark suit, shifty-looking, went in for about half an hour. Came out looking even shiftier.'

'But who is it?' she asked.

'Not one hundred per cent sure but it looked like our new MP as plastered all over the television on election night.'

When he came back with the prints there was no mistaking the identity of the man entering the Golden Slipper. It was the outgoing Director, now the MP elect, and Madge gave Mitchell a kiss and said, 'You're a genius.'

'Trouble is,' said Mitchell, 'geniuses are two a penny at the university whereas clever men who can do things, make things happen, ascend the greasy pole while remaining members of the human race are much rarer.'

'Women too,' said Madge.

***

Madge signed out in the new book kept in the office for that purpose and headed for Rudham. As she approached the city the concrete mass of County Hall appeared proud on the horizon.

Her occasional visits to County Hall following rare summonses to attend meetings of the top management team, or queuing around the outside of the building once each year to renew her vehicle licence, did nothing to fill her with any affection for the place.

It was widely believed that the Director and Mrs Busted, his personal secretary, enjoyed extra-marital sex. More than that it was widely believed, or perhaps only believed by Mrs Busted, that the Director planned to leave his wife so they could put their coupling on a more circumspect and more frequent footing. But would his election as MP put an end to that plan? Madge knew the rumours but no one seemed to know about the Golden Slipper. My, how tongues would wag should the truth emerge.

She rarely saw the Director; his rise from whipper-snapper admin clerk to the top job had been almost overnight, the speed of his rise deceiving her eye. From the start he had worked on those councillors who could make or break careers. And now he was the duly elected member for Rudham. She wondered who it was that once said, 'You can't keep a good man down'. The flipside was obvious: like a risen cake at the wrong temperature a bad man could sometimes collapse. Mitchell's pictures and the correspondence between Elf Sleepy Petals and Pixie Languid Leaves might yet collapse the cake.

As she entered the building the two girls on the reception desk were too busy to raise their eyes as she approached. One was polishing her nails, the other leafing through a magazine.

'I've come to see the Director,' Madge said.

The blonde filing her nails did not look up but said, 'He doesn't see people.'

'I think you'll find he makes exceptions,' Madge said.

The girl looked up and viewed her suspiciously. 'Very well, I'll see if his Mr Puttock in Human Resources can see ya.'

'Ah yes, Human Resources, I knew him when he was Head of Staffing.'

'It's called Human Resources now, the people's the same.'

'I see, no need to trouble Mr Puttock,' Madge said, 'I'll see the Director.'

'He's out for lunch.' Surprised, Madge glanced at her watch. It was almost three o'clock.

'I'll wait,' she said.

No doubt Puttock would have been awarded legs up on the salary scale when Staffing became Personnel and then again when that became Human Resources. It made her cross just thinking about it.

Sitting patiently beneath a plastic palm tree just inside the main entrance she noticed an agitated man enter the reception area and hurry to the desk.

'Red Bandit Leader,' he shouted, 'we have bandits at two o'clock. We must scramble the squadron. Get word through to the war room at once. At once!'

It was none other than the sometimes mad, if always intellectually brilliant, Professor of Divinity, he who had tried to tie Mitchell up in knots at the faculty meeting, he who nibbled ladies' knees under the High Table at the Founder's Day dinner at Green College, the man who 'went in' for treatment cheered on his way by the students.

'Take a seat, will ya,' the reception desk said, 'someone will be down to see ya.'

'But time,' he shouted, 'there's no time.'

'Take a seat please,' the receptionist repeated. At this he gave up and came over to the waiting area. Madge hid her face behind a large leaf and made as though she was actually reading the magazine she grabbed from the table in front of her. Now the second young woman stood up behind the reception desk.

'Yours are bigger than mine,' she said to her colleague.

'I know,' came the reply, 'it's just like scrambling.'

What is that all about, Madge wondered? Was it a secret language spoken only in County Hall?

'Scrambling now are they?' shouted the Professor of Divinity bounding to his feet. 'By all that the good Lord holds dear, we've got them on the run now, whiz bang, give 'em hell, give 'em socks!'

The seated receptionist stopped polishing her nails and looked up. 'Are you all right, sir? Someone will be down to see ya.'

It was immediately apparent to Madge that the poor man was tossing about in the storm of a florid psychotic episode. Perhaps he hadn't been taking his medication? He would have to go to hospital. It was only to be regretted that the

Green students were not present to applaud the ambulance as it departed. Yes, it would have to be a compulsory admission – there was no way he would agree to go in as a voluntary patient. But, hooray, it was not her problem, for as Area Controller she had not been required to retrain in order to become an approved mental health professional under the 1983 Act. She breathed a gust of relief.

'Do you think he's all right?' the still standing receptionist asked.

'Naa.'

The professor was by now windmilling his arms around in a sudden frenzy. 'I know, it'll be the Air Vice-Marshal, I teach his son don't you know. Splendid young pup.' He came over to Madge, eyed her knees, then sat down beside her. 'Don't I know you? I'll bivouac here till the Ministry respond.'

'The polis?' said the receptionist, busy again with her nails.

'What aboot a social worker? That woman from the Moortown office is waiting over there, waiting to see the Director. Miss… something or other… ye must know who ah mean? The old girl who's leaving the council soon…'

But then she spotted Madge behind the leaf and changed tack to, 'Ah mean, don't you think he's a bit – well you know what ah mean?'

'Daft?'

'Oh, ah see what yer mean. I do now. But…'

'What?'

'Them upstairs are all away on a nuclear war disaster training day so the lady from Moortown is the only social worker here asides from the Director. I don't suppose he'd be best pleased if we called him for this one.'

The professor leapt to his feet at the sound of the words 'nuclear war'.

'What did I tell you?' he shouted.

Then, just as Madge reached full seethe at the irreverent reference to her as 'the old girl who's leaving the council soon', the entrance doors installed in memory of those who had suffered at the hands of unscrupulous mine owners swung open and in, fresh from a very late 'lunch', walked Pixie Languid Leaves and Elf Sleepy Petals, both somewhat flushed about the face. Elf Sleepy Petals, aka Mrs Busted, the Director's secretary, had a figure like a wedge of cheese, clothes dowdy but expensive and overlooked by a face set in granite. The youngish man in the shiny suit was the Director, the new MP.

'Ah'm sorry, Director,' said the receptionist, 'but this gentleman here has asked to see you – someone – about his problem.'

'Not my problem, you must know I don't see people,' snapped the great man.

'There's no one else in this afternoon, Director, they're all away on disaster training.'

Madge would have sworn in court that she saw the Director silently mouth the word 'fuck'.

'My dear good man,' said the Professor of Divinity, stumbling over and embracing the Director in a crushing bear hug, 'it is a matter of the utmost urgency – we must put the forces of evil to flight. They are trying to destroy pure knowledge, they are trying to allow women to reside in the men's colleges, they are trying to admit pupils from comprehensive schools, they have even installed wash basins in the bedrooms, but hearing their siren voices in my head I knew they could not win in the end. Victory is ours, you see – we, we, with God on our side, we will destroy them.' He waved his hand expansively towards the patch of sky visible through the recently installed Arthur Scargill Window. As if on cue the Red Arrows flew over in diamond formation on their way to the airshow on the Yorkshire coast. Madge wondered if Mitchell was awaiting their arrival with his long lens pointing up into the sky.

When no one spoke the professor continued, 'You see, it's a sign. They're going to bomb the Senate House. We stand on the edge of a nuclear abyss.'

'Who are you?' the Director asked.

'I'm Divinity, a Rudham divine don't you know. I'm sure you must have heard of me, you must know of my credentials.'

In her corner, under the plastic palm, behind the magazine she was no longer even flicking through, Miss Perfect sunk lower in the chair. She smiled.

The Director rattled out orders. 'Phone the police, phone the Area Controller for Area 1, Rudham City, immediately. Tell him to send an approved mental health officer to HQ without delay. The officer will need to set up an assessment, contact the medics, the nearest relatives, the police, and the Rudham brass band – whatever is necessary.'

Then he headed for the lift with the Professor of Divinity jabbering away as he clung to his arm. Mrs

Busted, still slightly flushed, followed in their wake. Madge grinned at the thought of their sex in the lunch hour, sex in work time, sex with a man whom even Billy's young girls in the Golden Slipper were unable to drain dry. So much for the reputation of his department. Was this a man well equipped to be Member of Parliament for Rudham?

Now the receptionist was saying to her colleague, 'For meself ah don't mind how many she's had but…'

'Naa, they say she was thinking of leaving her husband if the Director left his wife but now he's an MP…'

'You mean he's going down to Darlington?'

'Why no man, London, London's the capital of England not Darlington.'

'That's not right man, should be Darlington.'

'Who says?'

'Me dad.'

It seemed a perfect moment for Madge to scuttle to the exit. But first she scribbled a note and handed it to the receptionist to pass to the Director via Mrs Busted. It read, 'Re. PLL and ESP – just to say that either or both will always be welcomed with open arms by Miss Perfect and the other ladies in Moortown. PLEASE DISCUSS. Perhaps the Director would care to be in touch…?'

Where was the harm in that?

'Yer what?' said the girl.

'He will understand, I'm sure,' Madge said. 'Yes, please just pass on the message. I would have waited to see him but a new emergency means I must get back to my Moortown office.'

'Yer what?'

'Just that, if you please, if you wouldn't mind.'

'Who shall ah say called?'

'Just say Perfect, Miss Perfect.'

Even if the Director was as limited in the upstairs department as he was active between his loins she was in no doubt that he would understand her message. And act accordingly? She would have to wait and see.

Eternal thanks be to thee, young Billy. And of course to the power of well-known facts.

***

No phone call came but arriving home at the cottage she was more than a little surprised to see a large green car parked across her drive. A badge proclaimed it to be a VW Scirocco, clearly the mode of transport of a very important person. What would the neighbours say? As she pulled up behind it a dark-suited, sober-tied man leapt from the car and advanced down the pavement. It was the Director, now the MP. As she opened her car door and eased herself crab-wise on to the pavement the great man smiled, held out a hand and said, 'Miss Perfect, we must talk.'

'Indeed,' she said in her most starchy voice as she led the way into the cottage.

As he settled in her best chair, the only good chair, he said, 'All this is very embarrassing, I must explain this unfortunate occurrence.'

'Indeed,' she said.

'You see,' he said, 'some private papers of a friend of mine seem to have come into your possession, how I know not, but I am anxious to recover these papers on behalf of my friend.'

'Indeed,' she said, 'your friend is fortunate having such a good friend as yourself. I am sure we can come to some arrangement which will solve your friend's little problem.'

Which is what they did. Madge laid out her terms: early retirement with immediate pension plus enhancement and – it would be so nice if he could see his way to saying a few words at her leaving do, nothing too extravagant just noting her years of devoted service. Through clenched teeth he agreed and then after she wished his friend well he was gone, the green VW purring down the street and away.

All the while he had looked equally embarrassed and angry. Of course she had promised that the letters, negatives and prints she would hand him were the only copies; no need to mention that Mitchell had kept copies of the photographs just in case a need should arise. No doubt Billy and Mrs Hill had done the same with the letters. The great man had seemed content with her reassurance, judging perhaps that she was so unlike himself that her word would be her bond, the word of an honourable woman. It was the sort of situation Alex Glasgow might have written one of his funny songs about, deflating the balloons of the rich and powerful.

And when he was gone she chuckled loudly, poured a G and T and said 'Good girl, good old Dad, up and at 'em won the day.' Had it not been for Puttock's original memo she would have had to face more years in the company of the likes of Dan.

Chapter 20

Friday was her last day in the office. Good Luck cards signed by the staff were lined up on her desk. There was one from Matron at the Aged Persons' Home saying she hoped Miss Perfect was doing the right thing at her age. Cheek. The one she valued most was from PC Pyott, with no more added below the picture of Rudham Cathedral than his scribbled name. Then one from Mr Barkle, a British Legion card, strangely inappropriate but no doubt well intentioned. A few from clients she had known down the years. Nothing of course from the Farrants or Mr Timms. Now that she was so close to walking out of the door for the last time she felt both sad and relieved at the same time. She would learn to cope without work, she would find new interests and friends, she would, yes she would. But then doubts crept in: what if, am I doing the right thing, is Mitchell the right thing?

For most of the week Dan had strutted along the corridor looking important with a large book under his arm: *Operational Analysis in the Social Services, a mathematical treatise for senior managers.* 'It's the way of the future,' he said to Madge, 'the outgoing Director who is now our MP was impressed when I quoted it in my interview for your job.'

'Can it be applied in Moortown?' she asked, noticing again the strong waft of scented aftershave which now announced his every presence. Since his interview he had appeared daily in a new dark suit, often remarking on the need to tighten the office dress code.

'Not only in Moortown but throughout the county. They're already using it in Darlington.'

She smiled at this, sometimes it was easier just to indulge him as she would a fractious child. 'How interesting,' she said, meaning the opposite.

'Yes,' he said, 'the chapter on stochastic elements in service delivery is particularly relevant here. The only trouble is that it's a little complicated so even I am going to have to spend time getting my head inside it.'

'Perhaps you mean getting it inside your head? Or your head around it?'

'That's what I said.'

She smiled. 'Stochastic?' she queried. It was one of Mitchell's words. She blamed him for bringing it into the office like dog dirt on a shoe.

'Uncertainty. But yes, I mustn't assume that everyone understands these things. Mitchell does, I know, because he introduced me to stochastic variables. The Director also does, I'm sure, but I think it was lost on the county councillors on the selection panel.'

Madge smiled again while at the same time silently cursing Mitchell for a fool for planting this seed in Dan's brain. Now Dan sounded more and more like the old Mitchell that arrived in her office a year ago. Time had changed both men, one for the better, one for the worse.

'I have no doubt both your head and eloquence were equal to the task,' she said. She wondered if his heart suited him for any job in a caring environment. No doubt he would get her job; he had done all the necessary spadework with the Director and key councillors, and only time would prove whether welfare would prosper with his new-fangled methods.

'Good luck,' she said, and in a way she meant it, someone had to take on the job. It wasn't only Dan who had taken a wrong turning; he was on an accelerating conveyor belt of change not of his making. He was merely trying to march in step with the new order, an unseeing victim of change rather than a perpetrator.

She was staring aimlessly out of the window when the phone rang. It was Jim Pyott, her partner in crime and caring for many years. 'Sorry you're going, Madge,' he said, 'we'll miss ye, won't be the same.'

'Thanks, Jim, I have always appreciated your help, well most of the time.'

Jim laughed. 'Times were better then, Ah won't be far behind ye.'

'How is the miners' strike affecting you?'

'It's difficult for some o' the lads, most of us round here have family connections wi' the pits. But that Thatcher, she's not daft, she's sending in busloads of coppers from down south. They've no feelings for wo lives here, cruel thugs some o' them, enjoying it, te them it's just buckets full of overtime.'

***

345

After lunch she wandered into the social workers' room. The ten desks were almost empty, the four phones silent as most of her staff – she still thought of them as her staff – were out scurrying around Moortown and Brownlow completing urgent home visits before the weekend. She sat down at an empty desk and leafed through some case files she needed to update and sign off before the leaving party at the end of the afternoon. She hated leaving parties. At least the staff would enjoy it, surely the point of these dos? And soon she would be free, forever free. Free! It felt like leaving school all over again. Then she remembered how that euphoria had been short-lived. This time it would surely be different. Wouldn't it? Yes, of course, she was older, wiser. Wasn't she?

Glancing up she noticed Simon and Lorraine enter the room. They were talking quietly but just within earshot, picking at files, drifting into desultory conversations that seemed to lead nowhere. Then she noticed Lorraine was sobbing quietly. Madge watched as Simon touched her gently on the shoulder.

'You OK?' he asked, his gentle voice so soft now that Madge could hardly hear him.

'No! That bastard only wanted to see how the other half screws.'

'You mean Marcus, he's finished with you?'

'Ja, klaar, finished. Given me the chuck. Given me the dull thud. Capput! Gone to join big daddy in London working as his parliamentary researcher, together with one of those fucking "ra" girls from St Catherine's College. And although I saw them talking and laughing together these last few weeks I didn't see it coming. It seems she was with him and the family at Christmas. Man, I just didn't put two and two together. I was so stupid. I only saw what I wanted to see. All he said to me was, "Thanks, kid, it's been fun". Now he's gone and passed his private pilot's licence and flown away free as a bird. I could kill him, shoot him down in flames, I hate him so. I hope he burns in hell.'

'I'm sorry,' Simon said. Noticing the genuine concern in his voice Madge wondered why he had not thought of becoming a vicar rather than a social worker; she could see him as a reverend. He moved closer, perhaps meaning to touch Lorraine again but, Madge guessed, unsure how she might react, stepped back instead.

'At least his excuse is more flattering than quoting your excess of age and experience.'

Wrong! Madge winced at the difference between meaning well and doing well. She had been wrong; Simon was not suited to the cloth. Faced with a parishioner *in extremis* might he say, 'You're dying? Well, every cloud has a silver lining.' On balance he was better suited to social work where he could reach words down from a shelf of ready-made phrases and simply offer the prospect of 'closure'.

Now Lorraine looked what she had always been, a young woman a long way from home, trying to fit in but sometimes falling flat on her no doubt suntanned buttocks.

'Thanks,' she said, looking up at Simon and wiping her eyes, 'social workers really are bloody marvellous, warm, caring, concerned, and sensitive at all times. Thanks a bundle.'

'Sorry. It was crass of me. But you did rather set yourself up as the office fun-lover. And I think we all wear out the warm, caring things in this job. I know I have.'

Ouch! Simon shut thee mouth. Madge pretended to be immersed in a file in front of her.

There were a quiet few moments until Dan breezed into the room, nodded to Lorraine then announced, 'I've got a new upgrade to my home computer on order. I'm pushing it up to 48 RAM...'

Lorraine stopped crying and wiped her eyes. 'Dan,' she said, 'go fuck yourself. Just get lost for a while.'

'Only trying to lighten the atmosphere,' Dan said. 'Sorry, I'm sure.' Madge watched as he scuttled from the room. He had been like a dog on heat since the interview and each day that passed since his trip up to County Hall for interview found him more agitated and irritating than the day before.

Lorraine half smiled and looking after the departing figure said, 'Prick!'

Simon nodded. 'Still thinking of going home to South Africa?'

She looked up at him. 'Yes, I've had enough; I'm going to register for a PhD in Cape Town. I'm done here. First Marcus and now Melanie Farrant's asked for a change of social worker. After I got them a new house and more in benefits as Marcus advised. The silly thing is I'd got quite fond of Melanie and Gary, especially Gary. But it's a culture I'm not used to though it's the same in a way, like the blacks always turn on those who try hardest to help them. There were those nuns who got murdered for trying to be kind.'

Madge knew that feeling of hurt at being rejected by clients though she knew it was unreasonable to expect gratitude from people who more often than not resented interference from 'the authorities'. She realised at the same time that there were times when she felt more affection for some of the people on the office's caseload than for some of her colleagues.

Simon said, 'I don't know about the nuns but I'm sorry the Farrants have hurt you, sorry you want to go back to SA. What you say about culture is true for most of us. It's also a class thing. Our clients are the dispossessed, hardly any of us have the faintest notion what life is like for them, where they are coming from, their lives when we are not there interfering. Our older colleagues who grew up around here, worked down the pits, fought in the war, worked for the union, belong in a way we never can. We often meddle to little purpose as we rush around meaning well but… Anyway I've had enough too, in a different way.'

'Where are you going?'

'Back to the tower.'

'Tower?'

'The only one I know. The ivory tower. University. What else is there? Where else is there for folk like me, fugitives from life?'

That is so like Mitchell, Madge thought, nesting in the university because he belonged nowhere else.

'But – what about them out there, the poor families at the base of your tower?' asked Lorraine.

349

Simon smiled. 'What about them, the huddled masses? Let them eat cake.'

'You don't believe that.'

'No, I'd like to think good could be done in the world by me but it can't, not by me. I've had to face up to that.'

'You're wrong, Simon, you are a good man.'

'I wish. Anyway I must get out on one more visit before the weekend. Then after Madge's leaving do I'm off to the Lakes for the weekend camping with Holly. Her grandfather left her a bell tent he bought as army surplus after World War One.'

He threw some papers into his briefcase as Lorraine said, 'Have fun with the tent but go easy on Miss Page, she looks so pure and sweet.' Madge hoped Miss Page might one day marry Simon and become Mrs Aubrey. I am, in my old age, becoming far too sentimental, she thought.

When he had gone Madge walked over to Lorraine.

'I couldn't help but overhear your conversation with Simon. I'm sorry.'

Lorraine looked surprised. 'Thanks, Madge. I know I've only got myself to blame. I was so fucking stupid, that's what makes me cross. But it's not all bad news.'

'How so?'

It seemed no time at all since she had resented Lorraine calling her by her first name but when it caught on and everyone in the office did the same she came to rather like the informality. Lorraine had thawed some of the ice, the barrier that once protected her. Now she did not even mind too much when some of the office girls called her Madge. Looking back she could see how it had served as isolation from the warmth of close human contact. She had given her life to caring for others; all along she had forgotten to care for herself. Till now.

'I heard yesterday that *Social Work Tomorrow* have accepted my article on sexual inadequacy in northern working-class males,' Lorraine explained.

'Well done you,' said Madge, reflecting that in the light of this development it might be just as well that Lorraine had chosen this moment to leave the country.

'Thanks. I've also heard from a literary agent tipped off by the magazine. It seems there is a market for books on the subject of my article. Even talk of a contract. Anything with sex sells.'

'I'm pleased for you,' Madge said. And to her surprise she actually meant it, adding, 'We have liked having you with us.'

Lorraine smiled. 'Thanks, Madge, but ach suss man, I did really love him. Pig!'

Then she too hurried out on a home visit leaving Madge thinking, Yes, you'll make it all right, you'll get into print, complete a doctorate at Cape Town, and forget all about Marcus once you're back on the beach at Muizenberg and cavorting with the boys at Surfers' Corner. But surely something from her time in Moortown and Brownlow would remain with her? Lorraine had all the makings of a woman who would do a good job and not spend childless years of disappointment brooding on a lost love.

Simon though was different. Madge felt sad that without crazy idealists like him there was little hope for the future of her kind of social work. He was like she had been at the beginning of her career yet a couple of years had burned him out. The likes of Dan were poised to inherit the earth.

She went back into her own office for the last time, cleared the desk and emptied the drawers in readiness for the next occupant.

***

By four o'clock most of her troops had returned and she went back into the social workers' room to find it transformed for the party with plates of sandwiches, crisps, nuts, cakes and biscuits laid out on two desks. In a corner near the door was a rickety table with bottles of wine and soft drinks.

It was now time for Chinese whispers. Alan asked Dan if he thought the Director might attend in view of Madge's long service in the department. 'No chance,' Dan said, swatting the idea as he would a troublesome fly on his face, 'no question of the Director visiting Moortown now he is the MP, far too busy, far too important to spend time anywhere as insignificant as Area 13. Of course he sends apologies.'

That voice and I-am-an-important-person manner never failed to irritate Madge. Dan knew about so many things but he was so often wrong in his judgements. He had simply constructed this version of events to show himself as the man who knew everything. Only she and Mitchell knew that part of her understanding with the Director was that he would attend and say a few kind words about her years of service.

Now Dan headed her way and shepherded her towards a corner by the filing cabinets where in a low, conspiratorial voice he said, 'Between you and I, in confidence of course, I happen to know that the Director has already been earmarked for high political office once Labour are back in government.'

'Between you and me,' she said.

'That's what I said.' He stared at her looking puzzled.

'No, you said between you and I which is grammatically incorrect. It should be between you and me.' He looked at her as if to say, 'I don't know what you're talking about' and she concluded that was exactly the position between them and always had been.

'He is the ideal man for Rudham and beyond. He may even find a future role for me in London,' Dan said.

She smiled again. 'How nice for you.' She was proud that she had managed to say this without even the trace of a murmur in her voice. You oleaginous creep, she thought, smiling at him. Two creeps, she reminded herself, the Director and Dan.

Then she sallied forth into the gaggle of staff drinking wine, eating crisps and making small talk, from where she heard Dan's voice continuing: 'A young finance chap from London is now the hot favourite for the adjoining constituency. He's been up north and hosted a dinner for our councillors. I've offered to help of course.'

Just so, she thought. It must be that sleek and slimy young man, a local Rudham boy, public school and Oxford educated, who had called in at the office briefly to proclaim his concern for 'those less fortunate' on his way to another lunch to host a gathering of all the local businessmen and bigwigs in the Labour Party. If anyone would make a worse MP than their esteemed Director of Social Services then this slimeball would fit the bill.

She kept an eye on the door. It would be the first time many of those present even sighted the great man. Most, like her, may never have seen an MP up close. Madge followed the buzz of conversation rippling through the congregation by making sure that she was always in a position to hear what she wanted to hear.

Down the years she had heard most of the rumours and smiled because from the snippets of conversations going on around her she realised that the Director was in fact well known to one and all. Although nicknamed The Invisible Man everybody talked about him, rushed around trying to do his bidding, yet all the while hardly anyone below the rank of Field Marshal even knew what he looked like. Distant sightings of the great man often proved as unconfirmed as many a kill in aerial combat. Nevertheless descriptions of The Invisible Man ballooned in the minds of his staff.

So it was that confidences crackled around the room. What did he look like, the man behind the mask? He was young, he was old, good-looking, far from good-looking, in fact no oil painting, he was bald, had a good head of hair, was fat, thin, tall, short, bad breath, had inherited his uncle's wooden teeth, wore spectacles, had dandruff, did not, dressed always in a suit, was always scruffy in a purple sweater with a tear on the right sleeve. No, the left sleeve, definitely the left sleeve, got pissed every weekend, never touched alcohol. He played golf every weekend; had not played golf since losing an arm in a car accident. Or was it a leg in a skiing accident? Which door did he use when entering or leaving HQ? How was it he was so rarely sighted by his staff? There were these things staff both knew and did not know.

For all that he was a man of many parts – was it not said. An outrageous belief, that in spite of an operation for cancer of the testicle he still had three testicles, now had no testicles, had one like Hitler or, according to Madge's unspoken belief, 'had always been a man without balls'.

And what was he like as a person? He was clever, thick, grasping, generous, loyal, out for number one, had a sense of humour, and was dry as dust. Did he have family? There was a wife, there had been a wife, there had been two wives, he was gay, bisexual, he worshipped his dog, was a cat man, loathed animals, had a son in the church and an unemployed daughter, he had no children – and all this depending on who you had spoken to last. Then there was his mother, deceased, packed off into a home in Bournemouth, mad as a hatter, living with a Maasai tribesman in Kenya. He was a distant relative of the Duke of Beaufort. He had athlete's foot. His mother reportedly sewed him into his cellular underwear at the start of each winter and only cut him out in the spring.

He was clearly a man much feared and talked about yet greatly admired to his face by a select few. They, thought Madge, were the fortunate ones who could always count on a beer at the members' bar in the County Hall or a pint of Federation in the Rudham Working Men's Club – and the ability to be able to recount to an eager audience what he was *really* like, his many achievements, his hopes for *his* department. And so down the years the word had spread, rippling out in waves until everyone knew all there was to know about the man now headed for Westminster, but a man whose secret pleasures were known only to Madge, Mitchell – and Billy.

Coming up from behind Madge Lorraine asked, 'What is the Director really like, I mean really, really like? You must know, you've met him. We're all wondering.'

'The Director, or should I say MP... Well, if you really want to know, and to put it at its simplest, he's a perfect little prick. Big car, five per cent over five years with a county council loan for the purchase of, big office, big desk, carpet, bookcase, leather briefcase, but little prick, nothing the council can do about that.'

'Oh.'

Before moving further into the room Madge chortled. 'They seek him here, they seek him there, those middle managers suck him everywhere.' Why didn't I leave this job sooner? she wondered.

'Truth is,' she said over her shoulder, 'he's a right arsehole but ask Dan of the brown nose – he knows more about the man than I ever will.' Then she laughed again. 'I am starting to enjoy leaving,' she said.

A few minutes later, Lorraine, now trapped by Dan, looked desperate and far from the dwindling supply of booze. If Marcus had been here the Red Sea would have parted and become alcohol. Madge sidled into a space behind Dan and Lorraine to earwig their conversation.

She began to wonder what people would talk about after she was gone when she heard Lorraine ask Dan, 'Do you think Madge's enjoying her party? I think she must have shifted a few drinks before she came here tonight. She's pickled. She told me, in response to a question about the Director, that she thought the middle managers had to fuck, or was it, suck him. Oh, and that he was a prick.'

For a moment words failed Dan. Good girl, Madge thought, spot on, now let Dan wriggle out of that.

Dan smirked. 'Still our Director for a little while longer and now our MP as well! I think you must have misheard. I don't think Madge drinks. Now, taking it one at a time, try "luck" in place of "fuck". The middle managers wish him luck.'

'And "prick"?'

'Try "brick" in place of "prick"! He's a brick. See, easy when you know how. In the old girl's language the Director is a brick and much sought after as a result, his staff wishing him good luck.'

Lorraine grimaced then shook her head slowly. Perhaps, surveying Dan, she was thinking 'Little Prick'? All she said was, 'Is dit a good thing to be a brick?'

'Of course she's wrong on a lot of things,' Dan went on, oozing pomposity as he dropped the self-satisfied smirk and moved into his grim-faced serious mode. 'She's just demob happy. Been in the job too long. It's all changing and she just isn't able to change with it. She's wise to downsize her life while she still can.'

Cheeky, Madge thought.

'From things he's said to me at times Simon appears to agree with her,' Lorraine said.

'He would. But the old girl has reached the end of the road. She's all Freud and Jung and stuff from the past. That's all gone. She's somewhat late in the day, off the pace. But then Simon's the same but for different reasons and he's on his way out too. I've tried to bring him on, get him up to speed but he hasn't got what it takes to succeed.

Lorraine tried to edge past Dan to reach the booze as she asked, 'What about you? Any news of your interview?'

Madge smiled as she reflected on the number of references she had written for Dan. She had long since lost count of the number of unsuccessful job applications he had made.

'Not yet,' Dan said, 'nothing definite but I've been given the nod, reason to hope... Puttock had a word in my ear after the interview... they were under pressure to appoint another woman which would be a mistake... but even if I do not get the Area Controller's job there may be other things on the horizon, perhaps even something up at County Hall... they want young men with my vision, my profile and ambition to advance rapidly... no, no, I mustn't say more.'

Madge had heard enough. She wriggled her way through the throng till she reached Simon who asked her, 'Are you looking forward to the wedding?'

'Can't wait. Ah there IT comes, at last.'

Mitchell entered the office and came towards them with his coat wet from the downpour she had noticed dripping in through the sides of the ill-fitting windows. He looked harassed and ill at ease. 'Marital bliss,' he said, nervous and awkward among comparative strangers, 'is like postmodernism or international liquidity – everyone talks about them but nobody knows what they are!' He laughed at his own joke. No one else did.

'Take off your raincoat, Mitchell, I know of no one who talks about postmodernism or international liquidity or marital bliss, and try not to laugh at your own jokes,' she said, still sometimes wondering just what it was she had let herself in for as he whispered, 'I've handed in my resignation, had enough of that madhouse.'

'My God, Mitchell, we'll be penniless. How will we manage?'

'Do you mind not becoming an academic's wife?'

'Not that but…'

'You mustn't worry, not on your big day, just remember how we once went to sea in a pea green boat with money wrapped up in a five-pound note. We can do it again.'

'Mitchell, you are insane.'

But all he said was, 'We have tarried too long and now must be married.'

'And live on fresh air?' she asked.

'Not air, my dear, but mince and slices of quince as we dance in the moonlight.'

'Insane,' she said firmly. No matter though, they would find a way and she had dreaded becoming a college wife.

Just then the door swung open again and an unremarkable little man, the new MP, making one of his farewell appearances as Director of Social Services for the county of Rudham, marched in wearing a dark grey suit and a county council tie. His entry, unannounced, was followed by the insignificance that was Puttock. The room fell silent except for Lorraine who whispered to Madge, 'Who the fuck are they?'

For a moment even Dan was silent but then, as if finding himself suddenly on a road-to-Damascus experience, he leapt towards the pair, hand outstretched. 'Welcome, Director, and welcome, Mr Puttock, thrice welcome.' Twice would have done, Madge thought.

'If that's the Director,' Lorraine said, 'why does he look so angry?'

'No idea,' Madge said.

'Thank you, Mr Bagley,' said the Director, grasping Dan's hand. 'My Puttock and I felt we had to make the effort to attend today and pay tribute to Miss Perfect, her contribution to my department down the years, and to express our anger at her hostile treatment in the press over the recent incident involving the little boy who went missing, so unfair.'

Dan seemed startled as Madge stepped forward and shook the outstretched hands of first the Director and then Puttock. 'Very kind of you to find the time,' she said winking, 'so very kind.' She tried not to giggle, tried not to conceal her total insincerity. There was pleasure in her feelings of revenge.

Brenda from Typing reached for a tray of drinks which she offered to the two men. Madge thought at first that Brenda had curtsied but decided it might have been no more than a stumble in the presence of such greatness.

'I am also able to announce,' the Director continued, 'that we have decided to offer the post of Area Controller,

Area 13, to Mr Bagley here and, from what he has told us about himself, this will be a very popular appointment.'

'Wonderful news,' cried Dan, 'I shall do all I can to carry forward your inspired vision of the social services of the future.'

'Together, I am sure,' said the Director cum MP, 'with the new Director who will shortly replace me here, a man of vision. But now my steps lead to London and a chance to improve things on a bigger scale.'

Dan clapped vigorously but apart from one or two of the junior staff who knew to be deferential in the face of authority the majority of those present just looked crestfallen.

'In the meantime,' the MP continued, 'the social services committee has promoted my Puttock here to be Deputy Director of Social Services with immediate effect.'

Dan shook Puttock's hand as Brenda tried to put another glass of wine into the hands of the visitors.

'What the hell was all that about?' Mitchell whispered to Madge.

'Only thee and me know, my love, oh Mitchell my love, oh wise one,' she said, tapping her nose with a finger before turning to the Director, raising her glass and saying, 'A toast to all our clients and all those of us who truly serve them, and of course our new MP who leaves his mark on the people of Rudham, men, and of course women, and who now heads to wider opportunities in London. May you find as much satisfaction in London as you did in Moortown.' She raised her glass. 'Bottoms up,' she said and everyone drank to that.

To which the Director, after spluttering as he sipped his wine added, 'And of course to Miss Perfect, a loyal servant of the department down many years. I am happy to say my secretary, Mrs Busted, has sent a bouquet of flowers for Miss Perfect; my Puttock will now fetch it from my car.'

Puttock went out scowling while Dan shouted, 'Hear! Hear!' perhaps for want of something else to say.

'Well, isn't all that a surprise,' Madge said to Mitchell before heading to her office with the ex-Director now MP and handing over a folder marked 'Private and Confidential'. When he snarled, 'Thank you, Miss Perfect,' she knew that such was the fury in him at that moment he would have been pleased to see her drop dead.

'You promised you would keep no copies.'

'I did indeed. My pleasure,' was all she said.

Back in the office Puttock just looked puzzled. There was a buzz around the room after the two men left. Madge, clutching the bouquet from Mrs Busted, went over to Dan and shook his hand. 'Congratulations.' Brenda, close to tears, stared after the great man. 'The Director, I mean our MP, he's not at all as I imagined him,' she said.

'No,' said Madge, 'he's not as anyone imagines him.'

Then Dan clapped his hands and turning to Madge shouted, 'Speech! Speech!' and the room fell silent.

'No speeches,' Madge said, 'except thank you to one and all for arranging this send-off... and my very best wishes to you *all* in your future careers...'

'She's going to cry,' Lorraine whispered to Dan.

'Oh no she's not!' Dan said.

362

And for once he was right. Instead she was whispering to Mitchell, 'I hear your Marcus has ditched Lorraine?'

'My Marcus! Well, you might say that but I can't stand the fellow. It was made plain to me – though unspoken – that my research grant for work on the social services in Rudham depended on me taking the son of a Cabinet minister into my team.'

Dan handed over two wrapped parcels to Madge. 'To remember us by,' he said. Madge thanked him and all the staff and said she would open them later.

Then Dan made a speech in which he mostly extolled his own virtues, of which he apparently had many. He thanked everyone present for the support which had enabled him to become Area Controller, Area 13. He promised change, but change that benefitted clients and staff alike. He was taking Area 13 down the road that led to the river of reform, a bridge to the runway leading to take-off in the sea of the future, the gateway to the modern world. Just when Madge thought they might still be here on Monday morning he said, 'And now last but not least', before waving to Lorraine who advanced bearing a large bouquet wrapped around the base with the *Northern Times*. Madge eyed the flowers, aware she might be blushing. A secret admirer? No, she thought, how sweet of Mitchell. But no, neither of those, for Dan went on, 'A parting "thank you" from one of Madge's long-standing clients: Billy who used to run the crap little repair garage up the road.'

As she carefully unpeeled the newspaper a large card fell from the flowers at her feet addressed to 'Miss Purfec from Billy'. When she turned it over she read the other side:

SPACKMAN
Hilda (1930-1984)
IN LOVING MEMORY OF OUR MUM
Close in our hearts forever
from
Darren, Julie, Gary, Mandy and Dave
and Mopsy the rabbit

She slipped the card into her pocket and said, 'How sweet of Billy to think of me'. Billy had made the effort to call in at the cemetery. Considering his start in life she patted herself on the back: job well done, Madge, well done, Billy.

Lorraine said, 'It's just like this in Cape Town.'

Brenda wiped her eyes and kissed Madge on both cheeks, looked as if she might kiss Mitchell but recoiled at the last moment. Instead she gathered up her clanking bucket and went round the room collecting for the miners and their families. Brenda never had quite come to terms with Mitchell.

Enough. She gathered up Mitchell and they went out into the car park on their way to marital bliss. It was warm for early May. Summer had started early.

After their simple registry office wedding in Leatherhead where Mitchell had lived as a child they scrambled into the Hillycopter and were gone, heading north no further than an overnight stop near Birmingham.

In bed that first marital night Mitchell returned to his favourite bedtime preoccupation: Hegel. So much for marital bliss.

Before he fell asleep he said, 'And Dan, are you glad to leave him behind?'

'Not only Dan,' she said, 'but in a different way Clive also.'

No sooner had she replied than Mitchell was snortling quietly beside her.

After breakfast they continued westward along the A5, through the lovely Welsh hills, across the flat and straight land of Anglesey, before finally arriving at Holyhead in time for the ferry.

'Is it wise to travel in the Hillycopter as far as Ireland on our honeymoon?' she asked Mitchell.

'Sound as a bell,' Mitchell said.

'I know, let me guess, ding-ding, boom-boom, it still goes like a bomb.'

'Exactly. Like a bomb,' he said.

'And your friend old Divine said so, I know. Guaranteed it all the way to Cork.'

He smiled. 'Ah, yes, guaranteed to Cork. By the way I meant to mention that we shall call on Bishop Berkeley nearby in Cloyne.'

'A friend or a car repair man?' she asked having long since learned to be suspicious whenever Mitchell began a sentence 'by the way.' It usually meant that he had taken a day or two before he could summon up the courage to mention something she might disapprove of.

'Well, yes and no, sort of in a literary way I suppose. Preoccupied with his bowels it seems.'

'How fascinating. You tease me so, Mitchell, when you talk in riddles but I do sort of love you and if you want to meet someone who may or may not be a friend so be it.'

They boarded the St Columba and were tossed about on the dark green Irish Sea with the lonely Hillycopter cohabiting with unfamiliar cars and fearsome lorries on the deck below them. To distract her attention from the pitch and toss motion of the vessel as it ploughed through the swell she began writing her 'thank you' letter to her former staff at Moortown. She was already missing some of them a lot and wondering how Lorraine would get on back in her tribal homeland. And Simon back in the university? But, naughty, naughty, it was nice to think she would never see Dan again.

As they approached Ireland she went on deck and watched as Dublin Bay came into view and then, gradually growing in size, the city itself.

Once ashore at Dun Laoghaire the Hillycopter invaded Ireland on a sunny afternoon with a succession of bangs which seemed to signal pleasure at being back on dry land.

'I'm not sure she sounds well,' she said, 'more like the arrival of the IRA.'

Mitchell smiled. 'What did you expect, the arrival of the Queen of Sheba? She'll be fine, just fine. Cork here we come. The Brits have landed and Ireland is at our feet leaving your Dan and my university behind. Will Dan cope without you?'

'After a fashion.'

Chapter 21

Back in Brownlow Dan was already 'getting a grip', 'taking things in hand', 'shaking things up' as he prepared to 'rattle the tree' to dislodge any 'low-hanging fruit'. He was in no doubt that he was starting to 'get a handle on things'. Area 13 was now 'customer-facing', constantly reacting to 'market forces'.

Excessive usage of paper clips had already been slashed by three per cent and wherever he looked – telephone message notepads, staff mileage claims, lighting, heating – the cost improvements were almost as significant. Biros were only issued from the locked stationery cupboard in exchange for a pen proven to be empty. Expectations of punctual attendance and a full day's paperwork were becoming the norm. All expenses claims were now checked three times. Staff who might resort to rounding up rather than down to the nearest miles travelled knew there was 'no hiding place'.

The new Director was introducing a computer system and before long the necessary hardware would be installed in the Moortown office in a space in the admin office cleared in readiness. Dan was excited at having all clients, reports, case notes instantly available at the press of a button. Once the system was up and running fewer admin staff would be needed. Perhaps Brenda, who he suspected of keeping in touch with Madge, should be the first to be made redundant. There would also be a reduced need for social workers, assistant social workers, home meals organisers, occupational therapists, youth workers and community liaison officers. These savings, marching in step with the consequential service improvements following the more efficient use of scarce resources, went on and on.

For the moment the principal economies were resulting from case closures. The Farrants had been archived: there was no point in devoting scarce resources to families unless there was a demonstrable pay-off. As Dan explained to his staff county policy was there to be implemented not interpreted. If staff did not quite understand the point they wisely said nothing.

Most gratifying of all were the one or two members of staff who complimented him on the new regime. 'How did we manage before?' they could be overheard asking when he was in earshot. Some no doubt had an eye on the vacancy on the rung of the ladder he had recently vacated. But they need not think they could win him over that easily, oh no, he would choose his own man, new blood, preferably a bloke from outside Area 13 who understood resource constraints and signed up to his smart dress code.

And when several of his staff approached him for references for jobs coming up in other districts he saw this as a sign that they were keen to spread his ideas across the county. Even those he judged to be out of step with the developments he proposed for Area 13 left with glowing references. He simply got rid of them. If they insisted on putting caring first then let them become someone else's problem.

***

In the course of time an envelope bearing an Irish postage stamp arrived in the office. It contained a postcard with a view of Cobh Harbour and a lengthy letter from Madge addressed to 'All staff'.

Written in her tiniest, most spidery writing it took Brenda an hour and a half and many 'bloody hells' before a readable version could be passed around former colleagues.

Dear friends,

I begin with sad news: After we visited the monastery at Glendalough Mitchell's much loved Hillycopter finally died in the beautiful Wicklow Mountains. She is buried in a scrapyard a few miles away in distant sight of Lugnaquilla, the highest peak. Though I could tell the end was near Mitchell was in denial and found the final stages very distressing. Like the loss of any close friend this has hit him hard. The funeral, even in this comforting setting, has hardly been the most propitious start to our married life. But Mitchell draws comfort from the fact that the dearly beloved did not suffer as the headlights faded and finally died. The end

369

was peaceful, silent in fact. Fortunately, thanks to my training and knowledge of the writings of Colin Murray Parkes I am able to counsel him through the stages in the grieving process.

As if echoing the mortality of the beloved Hillycopter our honeymoon touring Ireland in a hired car – it starts first time, has a radio and even a heater, both built in – means we are forever here today, gone tomorrow, as we move from place to place, B&B to B&B. I am enjoying the time that now mostly belongs to me which is how I find myself writing at some length to tell you about my new life.

Last night we reached Cobh, the port of Cork, which in the unforgiving light this morning is a teensy bit touristy but still a lively fishing harbour with predictably fishy smells. The guidebook is a mine of information. The very first steamer to cross the Atlantic sailed from here in 1838 and in 1912 the Titanic called here before setting off across the Atlantic on that fateful voyage with a loss of over 1500 lives. It was also the last port of call of the Lusitania before a German submarine did for her and almost 1200 souls in 1915. These tragedies help to set lesser losses in life in a light less harsh. Sobering omens nonetheless for anyone setting sail on the sea of matrimony.

Mitchell is as always on the lookout for bad light for his photography and Ireland ticks that box. Now we are here he has also turned to his family history when the light is too good for photography.

Genealogy is a subject I have always found tedious in the extreme, especially when people go on and on about how they can trace their descent back to Moses parting the Red Sea, William the Conqueror, Churchill, or something equally silly. But Mitchell has traced details of his great-great grandfather whom it seems was a curate from Cork who eloped with a nun. Sounds fun and not possessing a habit I feel quite dull in comparison.

At other times he has his head down in some book or other. He has temporarily put his friend Hegel to one side only to replace him with a chap called Berkeley, Bishop Berkeley in fact. Apparently we are so close to the home of the Bish at Cloyne that we are to visit tomorrow. In so far as I can understand it his ideas are big in philosophy and even quite fashionable. As Mitchell explained it to me things such as tables and chairs are no more than ideas in the mind of the observer – if we do not see them they do not exist. Make sense to you? No, nor me. Perhaps though if Dan reads this he may find it applicable to families like the Farrants? (I joke of course!) So much for the Bish who, I should add, like Mitchell's Mr Hegel and the Hillycopter, is sadly no longer above ground and amongst us. Mitchell tells me the good man was obsessed with his bowels, perhaps this was the cause of his demise.

When Mitchell disappears silently into his bookish academic mode I pick up a novel recommended by him and try to remain awake but silent. I am still looking out for a book called 'Pamela' and a novel by Pasternak, both of which he recommends. I think my lack of interest in Hegel and Berkeley is a disappointment to him. He thinks I should try to write about my time in the welfare services. But I know that nothing I could write would be of interest and after years of report writing it does not appeal. Anyway, what could I say that would do justice to you all and our work? Be warned though, I have had the opportunity to reflect on the events in my early life that made me want to make a difference for some young people in cruel circumstances, and I may have a bit of a dabble with pen and paper some day!

Thank you all so very much for the generous present and all your good wishes. The two sets of water glasses will certainly come in handy. We also appreciate the framed picture of the High Street in Moortown early in the century, with the telegram delivery boys posing with their bicycles, perhaps bearing news of sons or husbands killed at the front in WW1? Our wedding was a quiet affair in the registry office at Leatherhead which is close to where Mitchell lived as a child.

We had planned to head south on our return, perhaps to Eastbourne, probably at the genteel Beachy Head end. Though I love the north my roots are southern, 'born in a southern wild', Mitchell says – not sure what that is about. He would continue his research on a Home Office grant which would mean working at home a good deal as well as travelling up to London to attend occasional meetings. I would look around for some voluntary work.

But we have liked Ireland so much that our thoughts are turning in this direction. It is a different world, a fresh start for both of us. Perhaps Mitchell had this in mind when he suggested Ireland for our honeymoon. He has contacts among sociologists in the universities in Cork and Dublin so there may be opportunities for him to carry on researching. Of course not everything here is entirely perfect; from what I read in the papers corruption at the highest levels is not unknown, a reminder perhaps of Rudham; or is it just that people are the same the world over, some venal, some saintly, most of us somewhere in between in a life where almost everything involves compromise of one sort or another? At least here there is freedom from Thatcher.

Speaking as a beginner I find that on the whole marriage is a good thing though you may not be surprised if I tell you that I think certain aspects leave something to be desired. Mitchell is a kindly man and good fun. I owe him so much. He often quotes Hegel saying that the only thing men learn from history is that men learn nothing from history. Perhaps it is the same for women! And marriage? There was a time when work was my whole life, a time when I forgot there might be more to life than work. Fortunately, and thanks largely to Puttock,

and of course to Mitchell, I realised in time how
wrong I was. From thinking I would never cope
with retirement I now find myself embracing it
effortlessly.

Suffice it to say that thinking back to when
he once mentioned 'marital bliss' in the office –
followed if you recall by loud guffaws – I am not
sure the reality is altogether how I imagined it!
But the fondness I feel for Mitchell grows and goes
beyond that.

Sorry, must dash, it is raining which means
himself is agitating to get out with his cameras and
I am his 'bagman' (I am loathe to become a 'bag-
lady'!).

I wish you all well,
Madge Mitchell (previously Perfect)

Dan spilt his coffee over *Managerial Mathematics in*
the Welfare Services as he frowned reading the letter in
a break from his latest attempt to fully understand the
stochastic elements in his matrix of client needs and
departmental resources. He was still smarting from the
new Director's recent twin rebukes, the first for making
further ill-advised comments about the inevitability of
non-accidental injuries in children to a journalist from the
Northern Times; the second concerning the considerable
adverse publicity resulting from the Oldfields' most recent
disappearance with Alistair. Due to what he might have
called 'unintended consequences' he was now seldom seen
in County Hall.

Arriving at the end of Madge's letter he spat out through gritted teeth, 'The old girl is dementing; she's finally lost it,' adding, 'It's Mitchell I feel sorry for.'

Brenda listened and said, 'I'm sorry, Dan, can I get you a coffee?'

'Not Dan,' he shouted, 'Mr Bagley from now on. Standards are going up around here.'

'Sorry, I'm sure,' Brenda said, 'I understand, Mr Bagley.'

Meanwhile life in Rudham County, County Hall, Area 13, the cathedral, university, and prison all, like the river Rud itself, flowed on very much as before; it was still the sort of place where very little of note ever happened, nor had since the distant days of the purple-robed prince bishops.

***

And somewhere in Ireland, far out of sight of Rudham, Madge now smiled a lot. Letters from Brenda trickled news to her.

How many times had she written 'No Further Action'? Now she had written NFA for the last time. She was leaving behind Puttock and his silly little memos; the one announcing her non-acceptance of early retirement when she had not applied now seemed trivial in hindsight. But it had been one of the turning points, like a signal on a railway line shunting her life to a different destination.

Occasionally she would mockingly slap her wrist and, echoing her father, say sternly to herself, 'You are a very naughty old girl.'

Once upon a time there had been an old woman who lived in a shoe. Unlike Miss Perfect, she had so many children she knew not what to do. That old woman had given them some broth without any bread then whipped them all soundly and put them to bed.

But now one such woman no longer lived in a shoe, no longer strived to make the world a better place. Now she had a life.

It was time to finally write CASE CLOSED.

Hey diddle diddle,
The Cat and the Fiddle,
The Cow jump'd over the Moon,
The little dog laugh'd to see such Craft,
And the Dish ran away with the Spoon.

Mother Goose's Melody, London, around 1765

About the Author

Bernard Hall worked as an investment analyst in Edinburgh then taught economics at Glasgow and Durham universities before becoming a social worker. After failing to make the world a richer or happier place he now writes about growing up in apartheid South Africa, racism in sport, and the life and times of his great-great grandfather, born in Cork, who eloped with a nun.